HER SANCTUARY

HER SANCTUARY

A Novel
By
P.Q. Glisson

iUniverse, Inc.
New York Bloomington

Her Sanctuary

iUniverse books may be ordered through booksellers or by contacting:

iUniverse
1663 Liberty Drive
Bloomington, IN 47403
www.iuniverse.com
1-800-Authors (1-800-288-4677)

Because of the dynamic nature of the Internet, any Web addresses or links contained in this book may have changed since publication and may no longer be valid. The views expressed in this work are solely those of the author and do not necessarily reflect the views of the publisher, and the publisher hereby disclaims any responsibility for them.

ISBN: 978-1-4502-0226-8 (sc)
ISBN: 978-1-4502-0227-5 (ebk)

Printed in the United States of America

iUniverse rev. date: 1/06/2010

To my daughter Roxy, for having such great ideas.
To my husband Billy, who many nights went to bed alone. I love you.
To all my "special friends" who encouraged me to get published.

CHAPTER 1

Shannon pulled the motor home into the parking lot at the "Last Resort Café". *Funny name,* she thought as she looked around at the beautiful mountain vista. She made sure that she parked in the farthest corner since the last thing she wanted was to attract attention. She had been driving non-stop for over 18 hours and needed to refuel the "*Titanic*"......and herself. Except for a bag of chips and a couple of Mountain Dews, she hadn't eaten anything since early morning and it was getting close to dinner time.

She checked herself in the mirror. "Yuck!" she looked like she had been traveling for days. Grabbing the cloth sack, she went to work on her face. After a few minutes she checked herself again to make sure she was presentable. Her turquoise colored eyes were round under dark auburn eyebrows, the muted earth tone shadow complementing them perfectly. She couldn't help but smile sadly as she stared back at her reflection. She had her mother's eyes.

As she smiled, tiny lines formed around her kewpie doll mouth. *Laugh lines, yeah, right,* but she had to admit, she didn't look all that bad for 29. She was checking to make sure her lip gloss was straight when her eye caught the small thin scar that ran from the bottom of her earlobe down to the nape of her neck. Her eyes squeezed shut as she gave herself a mental shake and fluffed out her shoulder length strawberry blonde curls. She straightened the light green peasant blouse, retying the drawstring at the bodice.

Satisfied, Shannon took a deep breath, turned off the RV and walked across the parking lot to the café, the multi colored peasant skirt swishing to and fro as her bejeweled sandals made light tapping noises on the steamy black asphalt.

As she approached the front door she noticed a "Help Wanted" sign in the window. *It would give me something to do while I'm here. Besides, it could be fun and I might even make a friend or two.*

The café resembled a ranch-style home, white-washed with green and white striped awnings and flower boxes under the windows. She stepped in, making a mental sweep. There were no tables, but the front wall was lined with booths, five on one side, and five on the other. *Fairly clean,* she observed. *The furniture's not ratty and there's no sign of insects.* There was music coming from a juke box in the corner to the left of the entrance. At this particular moment you couldn't hear what was playing for the uproar. There seemed to be a party going on in the booths closest to the juke box. She thought it strange that all but one of the customers were sitting on just one side of the diner. *How odd.* She glanced over at the lone customer. She couldn't get a good look at him. He was looking down at his coffee cup, but his hair was shoulder length and black as night. Even without seeing his face, she could tell he was Native American. Shannon noticed a "Please Seat Yourself" sign, so she made her way to the bar that stretched the length of the café.

An older woman with flaming red hair and rhinestone encrusted black horn-rimmed glasses was behind the counter giving orders to a rotund older gentleman in the kitchen behind the pass-through. They both looked to be in their 60's. About the same age her parents would have been if they were still alive. Even though he looked pretty stressed out, the old man managed to keep the food coming out of the kitchen fairly quickly. Every once in a while the woman would reach out and lay her hand on the older man's sleeve. It was obviously a gesture of concern and affection. Shannon thought it was very sweet. She wondered if anyone else took notice.

The older woman looked up, surprised that Shannon had somehow slipped by her. She shuffled over, took a set of flatware wrapped in a paper napkin out of her apron pocket and set it in front of Shannon.

"Well Hi there stranger. Sorry I didn't notice you earlier. It's been a little crazy round here." Taking a pencil from behind her ear, she tapped it on the order pad. "Well now, what can I getcha"? She asked with a toothy grin. Shannon smiled back.

"What's the special?"

"Oh, but you are a brave one, you are. Well, we have meatloaf, mashed potatoes, green beans, and peach cobbler."

"Fine, I'll have that."

"Irene", she read from her nametag, gave Shannon an appreciative look, turned, and walked over to the pass-through to give the older man her order. Taking it, he winked at Irene playfully. Shannon guessed they were married from the comfortable way they were with each other. She couldn't help but smile. *It must be wonderful to have a love like that.* It was the only thing she ever wanted.

As she was waiting for her order, Shannon glanced around the café.

She looked over her left shoulder at the rowdy group. The men were in work uniforms. They were so loud she couldn't help but hear their crude humor and lewd comments.

One of the men noticed her looking and gave her a leering smile. He took his forefinger and middle finger, making a 'V' and put it up to his mouth. At first she wasn't sure what he was doing. Her eyes widened in shock as he stuck his tongue out and flicked it between his fingers. *Ewww.* Turning bright red, she jerked her head away, making a mental note not to look their way again. After regaining her composure she decided it might be safer to check out the lone diner on the other side of the room. She slowly inclined her head over her right shoulder and glanced around. In her wildest dreams she couldn't have prepared herself for what she saw. Two piercing blue eyes met hers. Shannon could feel her face flush, but was unable to look away. Her breath caught in her throat. Embarrassed at being caught he looked away quickly, returning his gaze to his coffee cup. His brow creased as he scowled into the cup. Flustered, she turned back around and took a deep breath. His eyes were extraordinary! Shannon had been so enthralled with his eyes that she didn't get a good look at the rest of his face.

She could tell by his stature that he was close to 6' 5" and from the width of his shoulders he was obviously well built. She wondered what his arms would feel like wrapped around her. Shannon was shocked as the thought jumped unbidden into her mind. It had never happened before. Sure, if the guy was good looking she looked, who didn't? But none had made her heart flutter in her chest. She thought again of his eyes. She had never seen blue eyes on a native before, not that she had seen a whole lot of Native Americans in her life. Still, she couldn't get them out of her mind. Their intensity burned into her soul. They were the color of a cloudless summer sky. Her hands began to tremble just a bit. It took all her willpower not to glance back over her shoulder.

Irene walked over and placed the "*special*" on the counter, snapping Shannon out of her thoughts.

"You sure you want to do this?" Irene asked with a playful glint in her eye.

"Sure, why not. I love living dangerously." Shannon grinned back at her.

"Well enjoy, sweetie." Irene turned and left Shannon to what she hoped would not be her last meal.

She unfolded the flatware and placed her napkin in her lap. She cut off a hunk of meat and tentatively placed it in her mouth. She was quite surprised to find that it tasted pretty good. More than pretty good, it was exceptional. She ate every last bite.

Irene came back to the counter to collect the empty dishes and smiled. "So you do like living dangerously."

"Actually", Shannon said, "it was probably the closest I've come to my mom's cooking in a very long time." Shannon decided this was as good a time as any to inquire about the job. "By the way, I see that you're looking for help", as she waved her hand toward the front window. "I'd really like the job if it's still open."

Irene looked at her as though she were an angel sent from Heaven. "Do you have any waitress experience? Cuz if you do, you're hired and even if you don't…lie. We're kinda hard up right now. Our last waitress didn't last a week. I guess it was too much for her. I thought she was gonna work out cuz her last job was at Denny's in the next town. Oh well. But thank God *you* came!" Shannon couldn't help but laugh at the kind woman.

"As a matter of fact I do have a little experience."

"Great. When can you start? By the way, when you work here all your meals are free so keep your money."

"Oh, no, I can't let you do that. I can pay."

"Put it away and if you don't want us to get off on the wrong foot you won't argue with me," Irene stated firmly.

Shannon raised both hands in the air and conceded. This woman was used to getting her way. "Okay, okay, I give up. Thank you so much. You won't regret it."

Irene appraised her. "No, I don't believe I will. I have a knack for judgin people and I can tell there's somethin different about you, though your eyes seem to hold an old hurt."

Irene was way too perceptive. Shannon was afraid that under Irene's scrutiny, her eyes might betray her.

Having an excuse to look away, she lowered her eyes to the table and removed the money she had placed there. She was afraid to look back into the old woman's eyes for fear of what she might read there. Shannon began to chew on her lower lip, a nervous habit she had developed whenever she felt uncertain or uncomfortable.

Sensing Shannon's unease, Irene thought introductions might lighten the mood. "I'm Irene. I own this place, along with my husband, Paddy. We've been here over thirty years and know just about every person in Sanctuary", she explained, a wide grin on her face. Shannon breathed a sigh of relief at Irene's strategic move.

"Hello, my name is Shannon Mallory and I'm very glad to meet you." Though Shannon had revealed next to nothing about herself, Irene could tell by her speech she must have come from a privileged upbringing. So what was she doing way out here, in Sanctuary? She decided not to pry......yet. She didn't want to take the chance that she might scare off her new waitress and Lord knew good waitresses were hard to come by.

"Can you start tomorrow morning? We're pretty busy with the miners. They get up at the crack of dawn and just about every one of them comes here for breakfast. I usually help Paddy in the back while the waitress takes care of the floor. Friday is our busiest day cuz that's when all the boys get paid. Do you have a place to stay? There's a boarding house in town but don't eat the food." Irene winked mischievously, "It'll kill you". She giggled at her private joke. Shannon didn't get it but she smiled anyway.

"Actually, I came here in an RV. It's parked way out in the back of the lot. Irene nodded her head as she examined Shannon across the bar, her red curls framing her round cherub face. They seemed to match her wide almost turquoise eyes perfectly. Her eye caught something under Shannon's hair. Before Shannon could catch her,

Irene quickly glanced away and looked back to her face. Shannon looked at Irene and smiled.

"Well Irene, I guess I'll see you in the morning. What time?"

"You'll need to be here no later than 5:30."

"5:30? Wow. Okay. I better go get some sleep so I can be bright eyed and bushy tailed."

Shannon started to gather her things when she noticed tall dark and blue eyed heading for the door. "Goodnight Irene." He said as he headed for the exit. Shannon watched him go, noticing his posture. She expected him to walk tall and proud as his heritage would dictate, not slumped over with his head down, trying to be invisible. Humph, *as if* that *were possible.* Even with his shoulders hunched over, his presence was formidable. Shannon's eyes slid down his back and rested briefly on his backside. *Yummy,* the thought was there before she could squelch it. She looked quickly away, her face flaming. What had gotten into her?

"Goodnight Seth! See you in the morning!" Irene hollered back over the noise.

Shannon couldn't stand it, her curiosity was killing her. She made her voice sound casual. "Who's he?"

Irene looked over and noticed the high color on Shannon's cheeks. "Oh, that's Seth Proudfoot. He grew up on the Rez. He's such a nice boy, just got dealt a bad hand if you ask me."

Normally she would discourage gossip. She always considered it an invasion of privacy, but her curiosity got the better of her. "Bad hand?" It didn't take much probing to get Irene to spill the beans.

"Yeah, his wife and son were killed a few years back and he hasn't been the same since. Keeps to himself. Some folks around here think he had somethin to do with their deaths but Paddy and me have known that boy since he was born, and I can tell you he worshiped his family." She let out a small sigh, "Ah, such a shame". Irene paused as a shadow crossed her face. Shaking her head she continued. "Now he comes in here everyday, breakfast, lunch, and supper. He still does some work out at the Rez but he won't step foot back into the town hospital."

"Wait, hospital? Was he a doctor?" Shannon asked, unable to link the painfully shy man she saw, with the superior self-assurance of a skilled physician. "Yeah, still is. Never lost his license… He just couldn't bring himself to go back there after……"

"After……?" Shannon asked as she gently prodded Irene to continue. What was it about this strange man that compelled her to know everything about him?

"After the day of the accident." The shadow was back on her face as she recalled the tragic event. "He had taken his family on a picnic up into the painted mountains. On the way back, he apparently lost control of the car, ran off the road and through the guard rail. The car careened over the mountain and Seth was thrown from the car. Naome' and his baby boy weren't so lucky. The car burst into flames as it hit the bottom of the cliff. He survived, but I guess he never forgave himself. He suffered a head injury and doesn't recall the moments before the crash. The fact that he can't remember haunts him to this day, but the town's people always thought that maybe he did it on purpose."

"Why would they think that?" Shannon couldn't understand and she really wanted to.

"Well, Seth is a nice boy but he's always had a bad temper. He was never the first one to throw a punch but he never backed down from a fight either. Did you notice his eyes?"

Shannon simply nodded her head. Boy did she ever!

"His mother was white and his Dad Native American. Because he grew up on the Rez, the other native boys couldn't accept his mixed blood. They made his life a livin hell. No matter how much trouble he got into trying to stand up for himself, he never gave up on his dream of becomin a doctor. As children, Naome' and Seth were inseparable. She and his best friend Joseph were the only ones who stood beside him when the other children ridiculed him and beat him down. They were their own little tribe. The fact that Seth was a half-breed didn't seem to bother his friends in the least. They were known at school as the two and a half little Indians. Naome's unconditional love was what made him strive to overcome all the hate. She had a way of calming him down, keeping him even. Joseph was more the "jump into the middle of the fight" kinda guy than the peacemaker. I think he actually enjoyed the scuffles. It seems kinda ironic that Joseph ended up the town's public defender with his own law firm. Joseph was the one who came to Seth's defense when the local prosecutor wanted to charge Seth with vehicular man slaughter. Joseph pushed, arguing that there wasn't sufficient evidence to prove it was Seth's fault. The judge had no choice but to drop all the charges. Funny thing is, when Seth was pronounced a free man he became belligerent and had an awful argument with Joseph. Ended up punchin him in the nose right there on the front steps of the courthouse. Everyone who was at the hearin saw it. Joseph didn't press charges, but as far as I know they haven't said a single word to each other since. Anyway, I'm gettin ahead of myself."

"Back in school all Seth wanted was to be accepted. When Seth and Naome' got married it was the happiest day of his life, until his son was born. He was living his dream of being a doctor and havin the perfect family. His life was blessed." Irene shook her head and sighed. "The day of the accident his world came crashin down. In a way, Seth died that day too."

"I often wondered what keeps him here but he won't talk about it, not with anyone. He stays in a cabin all by himself. He's always had talented hands whether he's doctorin or makin somethin outta wood. To help make ends meet, he makes hand carved furniture that he sells to the rich and shameless folks in the big cities. He does little carvings of animals that he sells in the shops round Sanctuary and the neighborin towns. Keeps busy enough but mostly just stays to himself."

Shannon hardly breathed as she leaned on the bar, listening intently. She was finding his story extremely fascinating. She was beginning to understand the reason for his anti-social behavior.

"So what you're saying is that because of his bad temper, people think he must have blown a fuse and purposely drove the car off the road? What could they possibly have been arguing about that would make him want to end all their lives?" Shannon couldn't believe it. Doctors took an oath to preserve life, not take it. But she didn't know him, so maybe he had snapped. *Happens all the time,* she thought, as an involuntary shiver ran down her spine. Part of her wanted to dig deeper but there was another part of her that was afraid. Unconsciously her hand stole up to the side of her neck as goose bumps broke out on her arms.

"Lots of folks seem to think that maybe she was havin an affair with one of the true bloods, though there was never any proof of it.

But like I said, me and Paddy, we don't buy it. We sorta think of him like our own son and we'll stand by him no matter what. This is the only place in town he can go and no one will mess with him. Paddy is a big guy. He might be old but he's a Veteran and can still hold his own. If anybody comes lookin for a fight with Seth, they'll have to go through us first."

Shannon was moved by her protectiveness. She found that she really liked this woman. She stood up to go, "Well thanks for the free meal. I'll see you in the morning then. Goodnight Irene."

"Night Shannon. Oh, by the way, we live upstairs so if there's ever anything you need, just holler." Irene patted the top of her hand and went to handle the rowdy crowd.

Shannon was having trouble going to sleep. Every time she closed her eyes, she saw a pair of electric blue eyes staring straight into her soul. She tossed and turned for what seemed like hours. Finally, giving up on sleep, she turned on the light above the bed and grabbed her sketch pad. It always seemed to help her get her thoughts together to just sit and doodle for awhile. Her mind concentrated on her work to keep from wandering back to Seth. When she was finished, she studied the drawings in her lap. There was a wolf in a thicket, a wolf standing on top of a mountain against a harvest moon, and a wolf standing by a stream. She realized with a start what she had done. Every one of the wolves had electric blue eyes. *Damn it! Stop thinking about him. You need to get some sleep.* Her mind went back to the conversation she had with Irene. "*He comes in here breakfast, lunch, and dinner.*" "*He'll be there tomorrow.*" her heart skipped a beat. Becoming irritated with herself, she tossed the pad to the bottom of the bed and jerked the chain to turn out the light. It was going to be a restless night.

CHAPTER 2

5:30 came way too early. Shannon took a quick shower and threw on a white button down men's shirt and her 501 Levi's. She applied her make-up and put on her Nike walking shoes. Grabbing her purse she flew out the door.

Irene and Paddy were already busy prepping the kitchen for the morning rush. "Good mornin Shannon! You're right on time! How bout givin Paddy a hand chopping the veggies and I'll get the tables ready."

"Okay." Shannon said as she grabbed an apron hanging on a coat rack near the kitchen entrance. She tied the apron around her waist in the fashion of a professional chef. Irene noticed the gesture and smiled to herself. *She really was telling the truth*'

As Shannon was chopping some onions, she heard the little bell above the door jingle, signaling the first customer of the day. She looked up, wondering who was coming in so early. It was Seth. She couldn't help but notice how tall he was. She also noticed how his muscular chest and abs rippled under his black tee shirt. His shoulders were so wide they almost filled the space in the doorway. Thinking there was no one around he walked with a smooth grace. The effect was mesmerizing. She couldn't take her eyes off him.

Shannon thought this odd at first and then realized that he must only feel comfortable around the older couple. She didn't realize she was staring until it was too late. His head turned toward the kitchen looking for Irene and Paddy, but his eyes found her. Surprise was clearly written on his face but it quickly turned to something else. Shannon wasn't quite sure what, but it looked to be, irritation, annoyance? Why would he look at her that way? *What did I ever do to him?* Considering she had first laid eyes on him last night, she felt it safe to say she hadn't done anything. Before she regained her composure, he cast his eyes to the floor as he made his way to the booth in the corner. *His usual table,* Shannon thought.

Irene walked over to where Seth was sitting and greeted him warmly. "Mornin Seth. I'll be right out with your order. Oh, by the way, let me introduce you to our new waitress." Raising her voice unnecessarily, she shouted, "Shannon, come here and meet Seth!" Shannon's heart skipped a beat. Needing to calm herself, she took her time washing her trembling hands as she prepared to meet the man whose eyes had haunted her dreams.

Stepping out from the kitchen area, it seemed like an eternity before she made it to where he was seated. "Girl, if you're gonna work here, you're gonna have to learn to get the lead out." Irene chided her good naturedly. Shannon blushed pink. Not wanting to seem like a silly school girl she met his gaze straight on. Her chin lifted a bit more than was necessary as she tried to project courage she didn't feel. She gave a slight nod of her head when Irene made the introductions. "Nice to meet you Seth", Shannon said curtly. "Yeah, you too." He grumbled back.

Irene sighed and turned to address Shannon. "Just make sure that his coffee cup is filled and you won't have any problems." They headed back to the counter and just as Shannon rounded the bar, all hell broke loose. Converging on the small parking lot were about ten vehicles honking horns and filled to the max with miners. Shannon guessed there to be about fifty men. Oh well, she loved a challenge. Smiling, she grabbed a pad and pencil from the bar and waited, her heart thumping in her chest.

Thirty minutes into service it was clear to Irene that this girl was a keeper. She had never seen anyone so efficient since, well, since herself. Not only did Shannon get the orders to the tables in record time but she managed to deflect the overly eager advances of the miners.

As Shannon walked past the booths, one of the miners reached out and pinched her round behind. The affront did not escape Seth. He growled low in his throat as he watched the scene unfold. He didn't know why, but something stirred deep inside him.

Shannon felt the offensive pinch and quickly grabbed his hand, twisting the man's little finger back painfully. He gave a startled yip. She just beamed at him, mentioning casually that he should learn to keep his hands to himself if he wanted to keep the use of his fingers. Seth laughed softly as she twisted and pulled the man's hand. She was definitely feisty. Shannon calmly explained to him how worker's comp probably wouldn't cover his full wages and she would hate to see his family have to go without because of his carelessness. The other guys just hooped and hollered, "Man, you just got burned!" They all laughed, enjoying the early morning show. It was going to be an interesting day in the mines. The man blubbered, his face all flustered. "Now, be a good boy and say you're sorry", Shannon grinned as she twisted the man's fingers a little harder. The man whimpered from the pain and managed to apologize through his clenched teeth. "Now, I believe we have all learned a valuable lesson today, which is…, "Keep our hands to ourselves," they all said in unison. "Very good, now, can I get you boys a refill?" Shannon smiled sweetly as she released the man's hand. He rubbed his sore fingers, shoving them between his legs.

Seth watched her every movement with a critical eye. She had a voluptuous body. He wondered how it would feel pressed against him. Her smile seemed to light up the room as she welcomed new customers. He found himself wishing she would turn that smile on him. He hung his head as the ache in his chest intensified. He had been rude to her earlier. It had been so long since he'd had a civil conversation with anyone. His social skills were rusty. Besides, it wouldn't be good for her to be seen talking to him, an outcast. His thoughts scattered as he saw her lean over to pour a customer a cup of coffee.

After making sure the men had what they needed, she headed over to Seth's booth. As she approached, she noticed a small smile playing across his lips…. His lips, well, they were gorgeous, full, and very kissable. When he looked up she made a point to really study his face. He had a high forehead, olive skin. His face was marred by a thin scar that ran from the corner of his left eye down his cheek to just above his ear lobe. It looked almost like a crescent moon. She thought it gave him character and a fierce ruggedness that combined to make him look dangerous and sexy. She had never seen anything like him in real life. He reminded her of a hero on the cover of a romance novel. His nose was straight and aquiline. His hair was so black that it reflected the colors of the sun as it rose over the Arizona Mountains. It took her breath away. All in all he was very delectable. Delectable? What had gotten into her?

"Would you like a refill?" Shannon croaked. God, did her voice just do that? Shannon cleared her throat as she felt the heat rising in her face.

Seth continued to look at her. What was wrong with him? He couldn't help himself. He wanted hours to look at her face, memorize it. *Stop staring at her you idiot!* He forced his eyes down and tapped his coffee cup. That was waitress sign for "yes". Shannon refilled his cup, her hand trembling slightly, the cup making a rattling sound as it came in contact with the carafe. He glanced up at her through his thick lashes. *Why is she shaking? Is she afraid of me?* He didn't know why the possibility upset him so. Normally, he was glad when people steered clear of him, but for some reason, Seth didn't want this woman to keep away. In fact, he found he wanted her closer... much closer.

Damn it! Why does he make me so nervous? Get a grip Shannon! Wanting to break the ice, she struggled for something to say. Why was it so hard? Her mouth opened and shut several times, but she couldn't think of a thing so she just stood there chewing on her bottom lip. Finally, feeling like a complete idiot, she turned on her heel with a grunt and left without another word.

Since Shannon had her back to him, Seth couldn't help but steal a glance at her retreating figure. He noticed how nicely she was built. She wasn't wafer thin like so many women strived to be these days. Seth guessed her height at about 5'6". Her hips were round, ample. They would have to be to support that bodacious behind. The rednecks in town would call it a badonkadonk. Her legs were shaped nicely. When she had leaned over a moment ago to refill his cup, he caught a glimpse of twin pale mounds as her breasts strained against the white shirt. It wasn't like him to be so sneaky but he found that he wanted to drink in everything about her. As much as he admired her body it was her eyes he couldn't seem to get out of his mind. They were so green they looked turquoise, almost an exact match to the small stone she wore around her neck. She had to be wearing colored contacts. *There's no way they could be real.* He quickly dismissed the thought. Though he didn't know her, she just didn't seem like a vain person. She would be happy with what God gave her.

His breath caught in his throat remembering the first time he saw her. *Don't even go there buddy.* Though it had been three years since his beloved Naome' had died, he still didn't think he had the right to think about Shannon. Not that he felt unfaithful. *There you go again. What is with you? Stop thinking about her,* he started rationalizing. *She's probably just passing through anyway. Besides, you're a hated man in this town. You don't have the right to think what you're thinking. The best way to avoid getting your heart crushed again is to nip this in the bud.* He made up his mind that it might be a good idea to skip lunch.

Seth stood, tossed some money on the table, and quietly left the café. Shannon was too busy cleaning up after the miners so she was unaware that he had left until she turned to see if he needed more coffee. His booth was empty. She shook her head totally disappointed. '*Shoot.*' Irene came over to her as she was bussing Seth's table. Shannon picked up the twenty dollar bill. Taking it to the register, she slipped it into the till.

"Shannon dear, there won't be very much traffic in here till around lunch so why don't you head into town and get familiar with the place". She held out her hand to reveal a brown paper bag. "Paddy packed you a Breakfast sandwich and a piece of fruit in case you're hungry. I know you didn't have anything to eat yet."

Shannon took the bag, grateful that they had thought of her. "Thank you so much for the food. It smells delicious. Thank Paddy for me. I actually thought it might be fun to ride into the mountains and do some drawings but I'll need to rent a car. I don't really want to maneuver Titanic on those bumpy back roads."

Irene burst out laughing at the referral to the motor home. "That's a very creative name."

Shannon chuckled, "Yeah, it just seemed to fit, especially since the first time I drove it I almost ended up in the ocean, but I'm a much better driver now".

Irene laughed again and then took a set of keys out of the pocket of her apron and tossed them to Shannon. "Take our truck. It's old but it runs great." Shannon caught the keys as a reflex action. "Irene, you don't have to do this. I'm okay to rent a car." "Child, just take the truck. Paddy only uses it durin huntin season, although he hasn't been huntin in three years." Irene leaned over the counter speaking in a hushed tone, "Between you and me, I don't think he enjoys it as much as he used to cuz of his health."

Shannon gave her a concerned look and Irene rushed to reassure her. "No, no, it's nothin like that. He's just gettin old and fat and can't act like a kid anymore. Least not all the time." She gave Shannon a sly wink that was fraught with double meaning. The look of shock was apparent on Shannon's face.

"Oh Irene, you're terrible." She grinned, "But thank you for the loaner and I promise I won't drive into the ocean". Irene laughed again at Shannon's joke. "Have a good time, dear."

CHAPTER 3

Shannon went to the back of the café and climbed into the front seat of the 1968 Chevy. She wasn't sure it would crank, but she turned the key and it immediately turned over with a deafening roar. She smiled to herself and thought, *this might be alright after all.* Pulling out from behind the building, she stopped off at her RV to collect some art supplies. After gathering the things she needed, she drove away from the café in the opposite direction of Sanctuary.

Shannon just figured she would follow the mountain road until she saw something that caught her eye. She turned off the main highway onto a dirt road that was flanked by forest. She thought the road would lead into the mountains. As she continued down the winding dirt road, she realized that she wasn't climbing in altitude but descending down into a valley. The road became bumpier and she did her best not to hit her head on the ceiling of the truck. Just about the time she decided she was probably lost and looked for a shoulder to turn around on, the tree line broke to reveal a beautiful meadow. It looked to be about ten acres of flat land with a stream running alongside. She caught sight of a family of deer. As she approached, they looked up from their grazing. Sensing danger, they ran off into the forest and disappeared. The scene was unbelievable! Shannon took a mental picture and stored it away in her mind for later reference.

About half a mile further down, she came across a log cabin with an unattached garage. Shannon could tell it was a log cabin because it was built with logs, but that was where the similarity ended. Unlike the average natural brown log cabin, this one was painted pale blue with white trim. It also had a wrap-around porch, a porch swing and two wood rockers. Dream catchers of all different colors and sizes were hanging from the eaves as well as crystal wind chimes. The suns' rays danced off the crystals and made a magical rainbow effect. As she drove closer, Shannon realized that even though the cabin was beautiful, it was definitely in need of some TLC. The paint was peeling and the front door, which had once been bright red, was now a faded pink. *Nothing a little paint couldn't fix.* She also noticed the garden that had originally been planted to house all types of flowers, was overrun with weeds. *Boy, someone needs a landscaper.*

Parking her truck about a hundred feet from the porch, she grabbed her sketch pad and started sketching the cabin. As she took in the surrounding area she noticed the garage which was on stilts, was obviously a much newer building. Instead of being built with logs, it was covered in pale blue vinyl siding. It looked like a smaller version of the house. Shannon decided that she liked the overall look of the place. There was a large black truck parked in the space under the small apartment. Shannon wondered if anyone was home. Having finished her rough draft of the cabin, she pulled on her jean jacket. Pulling the hood over her head to protect her from the cool wind coming off the mountains, she walked up the steps of the cabin and knocked on the faded door. Determining that no one was home, she decided to walk around to the back of the house.

The view literally took her breath away. Looking out, she saw a broad expanse of open space. Tilting her head upward, the mountains looked as though they towered over her. She had never seen anything like it… ever.

Feeling very small and insignificant, she stood with her mouth hanging open. Her sketch pad, forgotten, hung limply at her side. She was overwhelmed. Snapping out of her trance, she snatched up her sketch pad and raised her pencil….

"Who the Hell are you and what are you doing on my property?!" a rough male voice shouted. Shannon froze, startled. She regained her composure and turned to confront the owner of the voice. It was Seth… and he didn't look happy. No…. he looked pissed!

Remembering what she'd been told about his temper, Shannon ran for the truck. She was just about there when she felt a force knock her to the ground. Landing on her stomach, she felt the wind knocked out of her. He straddled her, pinning her hands over her head. Self preservation took over. She bucked and wiggled wildly. Managing to twist her body, she brought her knee up sharply against his crotch. "Shit!" Seth growled as he rolled over clutching himself. Suddenly free, Shannon sprang to her feet, sprinting toward the safety of the truck. The hood fell away, revealing her reddish gold curls.

Seth stared dumbfounded as her hair spilled out. *Oh God! I hope she's not hurt.* He struggled to his feet, raised his hand, the other was still clutching his crotch, and managed to croak, "Wait! Stop!" Sucking in more air, Seth managed to sound more forceful. "Shannon, stop!"

Shannon froze immediately. There was something in his voice. She stood there uncertain of what she should do. Her mind was yelling at her to run to the truck and drive away…. fast. Not wanting to be a coward, against her better judgment, she decided to confront him. Mustering all her courage, hands on hips, she spun, "What the hell are you trying to do, scare me to death?!" Her hair was disheveled and there were a few pieces of hay stuck in the tendrils. Her eyes flashed green fire, her breath shallow.

God she's beautiful. Seth couldn't help but be drawn to her. He remembered how soft she had felt under his weight. Slowly he limped over to where Shannon was standing, not wanting to frighten her again. Though she tried to put up a brave front, he could see she was debating whether or not to make a run for it. He held his hand up to stop her.

"I'm sorry I scared you, but you had on that hood and I thought you were a burglar." He raised one dark brow, "Are you alright?" It was the most she had heard him say. She found she liked the timber of his voice, low and smooth.

Shannon stared at him defiantly, "Oh, I think I'll live, thank you."

'*Sarcasm.*' He liked it. It seemed to fit her.

Seth wasn't sure what he should do but he knew he didn't want her to leave…. yet.

"Would you like to come inside and have a cup of coffee or a drink? You did have quite a scare." Shannon looked at him suspiciously. Seth watched her face, trying to read her expression. She was chewing on her lower lip. He found it oddly adorable. He crossed his arms over his muscular chest and raised an eyebrow. "Well, you coming or not?"

Making up her mind, Shannon nodded her head. "Yeah, okay. It is kinda nippy out here. Thanks." She started walking to the cabin. "No!" He growled and reached to jerk her back. An electric spark ran down her arm at his touch. Shannon stopped dead still. "Didn't you just invite me in for a drink? Are you bipolar or something?"

"No, I meant above the garage. That's where I stay." He sounded strangely apologetic. She could tell there was more behind that statement but, not wanting to make him anymore uncomfortable than he already was, Shannon responded genially enough. "Oh, okay then."

They walked toward the garage side by side. Suddenly Shannon stepped into a small hole. Losing her balance, she stumbled, falling against his side. Seth caught the scent of gardenia from her hair. His pulse raced as he caught her around the waist to steady her. His touch sent another electric shock through her body and she gasped. "Are you alright?" concern etched on his handsome face. Her heart beat faster as she met his eyes.

Pushing away from him, she regained her composure. "Uh, I'm fine." Seth let her go reluctantly, his arms feeling strangely empty. "You need to watch your footing out here. It's full of nature's booby traps." Taking in her peaches and cream complexion, Seth got the idea that she probably didn't go outside very much. "I take it you're more of an indoor kinda girl?"

Shannon couldn't help but giggle at the reference to her favorite movie. Though he was confused by her sudden outburst, the sound sent little shivers of delight down his spine. "What?"

"Oh nothing, I was just thinking of something funny, that's all." He noticed that when she giggled she scrunched up her nose. He also noticed that in the light you could see the sprinkle of freckles across her cheeks. It was adorable. *Okay Seth, get a grip. Oh, I'd like to get a grip…on her.* He chuckled to himself.

"What?" now it was her turn to look puzzled. Repeating what she had just said to him, Seth replied, "Oh nothing. I was just thinking of something funny." Shannon gave an exasperated sigh and followed him up the stairs.

The inside of the little apartment was nothing like Shannon had pictured. She expected it to be sparse and uninviting but when she stepped over the threshold she felt immediately warm and cozy. To the left a fire was roaring in a stone fireplace. Animal furs were scattered in front of the fire, flanked by a beautifully crafted rocking chair. On the wall, which faced the front, there was a large picture window with a comfy looking love seat nestled against it. Straight back from the entrance was a small economy kitchen with a beautifully hand crafted dining table and two chairs.

The right side of the apartment was what made Shannon gawk. The far wall on the right was lined with a table saw and a fully stocked workshop. Along the walls were shelves filled with intricately carved miniature animal statues. To her surprise and delight Shannon recognized the work. She had some just like them on a shelf in her RV. She had bought them from a vendor on the side of the road a few miles down from the café when she first arrived. She was shopping for fresh fruit and veggies when she spotted them. They were so beautiful that she impulsively bought all they had. Now here she was in the house of the talented artist who created them.

She walked over to the shelves to get a closer look. Seth watched silently as she examined his handiwork. He was never around when people looked at his work. He usually just dropped them off and picked up the money at the end of the month. He wondered what she thought of them. He cleared his throat. Shannon turned to look at him and he could swear he saw tears in her eyes. "Yeah, I did those", he said rather shyly. He didn't like attention so he never signed his name to any of his creations. Instead, he carved a wolf's paw with the initials S.P. in the middle. Shannon noticed a couple of small tables that could be used as end tables or entry tables. They were exquisite in detail. The wood was raw and she couldn't resist rubbing her fingers on the grain. It was like touching hard silk. There was an engraving of a wolf pack standing proudly on top of a mountain peak. Shannon had seen similar pieces in the penthouses where she used to attend charity events in New Orleans. Irene had mentioned that he sold his pieces to the rich and shameless. "These are beautiful Seth", Shannon's voice was barely above a whisper. Seth found he was very touched that she liked them. It seemed important to him somehow.

"Thanks", he murmured, making himself busy in the kitchen. "Would you like coffee or tea?"

"Coffee is fine thanks. Do you need help with anything?"

"Nah, I got it. Why don't you have a seat and let someone wait on you for a change."

How thoughtful of him. Shannon made her way over to the comfy looking love seat.

As she sat down she realized it was as comfortable as it looked. It was made of some kind of crushed suede. Shannon ran her hand over the cushions, luxuriating in its softness. Seth watched as her hands caressed the leather. The action struck him as incredibly sensual and his heart beat quickened. He brought over a tray with two cups. Setting the tray down on the hand-carved coffee table, he sat as far away from her as he could get. Their heads butted together as they reached for the coffee tray at the same time.

"Oh, sorry," Seth said as he jerked back rubbing his head. "Oh God I'm sooo sorry!" replied Shannon as she too rubbed her head. They looked at eachother and busted out laughing. Shannon loved the sound of his laughter and it made his face practically glow. *Well, I do believe we managed to break the ice,* Shannon thought as she fixed her coffee. They sat like that without talking for a while. Though the silence wasn't uncomfortable, Shannon wanted very much to hear the sound of his voice again. Though she knew he would probably feel embarrassed by flattery, Shannon just had to let him know how touched she was. Taking a deep breath, she blurted out, "Your work is amazing!" She saw Seth looking up at her through his thick eyelashes, but she forged on. "Now wait, I can tell you're modest, but I just felt like I had to tell you how your work moves me. If you got the right backing, you could be rich." She knew she was babbling but she couldn't seem to stop herself.

He scowled at her, "That's not what I care about. I do it because it helps to get my mind off...... things. The only reason I sell them at all is because I have bills to pay. I can't stand those uppity rich snobs. I have a broker who handles the money so I don't have to deal with their stupid asses."

Shannon realized she had just stuck her foot in her mouth. She didn't want him to be angry with her. "I'm sorry, of course you don't. You see, I have this defect. It's called Foot in Mouth Disease. There's no filter between my brain and my mouth. It's gotten me into a lot of trouble over the years so please don't be mad, Okay?"

Seth couldn't stay angry as he looked into those eyes. She was practically begging for forgiveness. Wanting to reassure her, he reached out and laid his hand on her shoulder. "It's okay, people have thought much worse of me."

The second his hand touched her, Shannon forgot how to breathe. Her skin sizzled from his touch. Seth noticed her stiffen so he jerked his hand back. The touch had its affect on him as well. He ground his teeth as he felt the aching in his heart. After his family was killed, he alienated himself from everyone around him, forming an iron shield around his heart. Now somehow, feelings for the woman sitting next to him were slowly chipping away at that barrier.

Shannon didn't know exactly what had happened to change the mood in the room, but she could see the warring emotions on Seth's face. *Man, this guy has more mood swings than Sybil.* She noticed the time on the clock. "Oh no, if I don't leave soon I'm going to be late for the lunch shift. I know Irene's a sweetie, but I don't think she'll tolerate tardiness, especially on my first day."

Placing her cup on the tray, she reached for her bag and sketch pad. It wasn't there. She realized at that moment that she didn't have it with her when she came upstairs. "Oh no, my stuff's not here!" Shannon looked around her frantically, "I must have dropped it when you tackled me."

"Your what?"

"My bag! I use it to get ideas for paintings. It's what I was doing when you scared the crap out of me."

So they were both into the creative arts. Seth found that he didn't want their time together to end, especially since this would probably be the last time she set foot on his property anyway. "I'll walk you outside and help you look for it", Seth offered. Besides, he needed to get some air. Being this close to her was unsettling. Not to mention her scent was driving him wild. "Oh, okay, thanks."

Shannon and Seth walked down the stairs together. There, right where they had wrestled earlier, were her things. Seth reached the spot before Shannon. He picked up her bag and sketch pad and unable to help himself, he started flipping through the pages. Shannon wanted desperately to snatch the pad from his hand, but she had looked at his work earlier so it wouldn't be polite to refuse him. Plus, she was curious to see what he thought. She stood perfectly still, chewing her bottom lip while trying to read his face. It was hopeless.

Seth kept his face blank as he flipped through the pages. *Wow, she's really good.* There were sketches of landscapes, beach scenes, cityscapes, animals, sunsets and people.... lots of people. As he was getting to the end of the book, he came across some color pencil drawings of wolves. It didn't escape his notice that the wolves' eyes bore a striking resemblance to his own. *Is it possible that she was thinking of me when she sketched these?* He refused to believe it but then something in the bottom right corner caught his eye. There it was, a tiny drawing of his face. Seth's heart felt like it would literally jump out of his chest. *Calm down. She probably just thinks you have an interesting face.*

As he flipped to the last page of the book, he saw the one she did of his cabin; correction, Naome's cabin. Closing his eyes he let his mind drift back to that day. He had built it for her before he even popped the question. He brought her here under false pretenses so he could surprise her. As soon as she saw the little cabin, she shrieked with joy and flung herself into his arms. As petite as she was, she nearly choked him to death. A tear fell from his eye, landing on the center of the page.

He wiped his face with the back of his hand, pulled himself together, and handed the pad to Shannon. "They're really good. How long have you been drawing?" "I just started a little over a year ago. I've always wanted to paint and draw but, well, *I was forbidden to have anything that brought pleasure to my life...*I just never had the time." She said instead.

"You really have a natural ability to capture the spirit of your subjects." That was probably the nicest compliment she had ever gotten. "Thank you," blushing, she made a move to climb into the truck but turned around at the last minute as a thought occurred to her, and met Seth's intense eyes just inches from her own. The close proximity was almost more than Seth could take. They stood there frozen, looking into each other's eyes. Time seemed to stand still. He found himself leaning in, getting closer until their noses were almost touching. Shannon's breath caught in her throat. His gaze was mesmerizing. She totally forgot what she was going to say.

They stayed that way for what seemed to her like an eternity. *Just move half an inch and you'll be kissing him.* She could feel her body wanting to move but uncertainty kept her still. Too late, Seth pulled away, clearing his throat. The spell was broken. Shannon sighed heavily. She wasn't sure whether she was relieved or disappointed. *I swear, with this guy, I don't know if I'm coming or going.* He made her uncomfortable in a most disturbing and exciting way. She realized it wasn't fear that kept her at a distance. She wanted to get closer to him and yet she couldn't trust her heart; the same heart that had betrayed her years ago and thrust her into a life of servitude in Hell.

"Here, you almost forgot this." Seth held out her drawing pad and she suddenly remembered what she wanted to ask. "Seth, do you think it would be alright if I came back on Sunday and painted the view from your back yard? It's really spectacular!" She held her breath, half expecting his rejection. "I'll understand if you say no." She added hastily.

Seth knew he should refuse, but the expectation on her face melted his resolve. He couldn't deny that he was attracted to her and wanted very much to spend more time with this woman but he was afraid of letting her get too close. He realized he was fighting a losing battle. What the Hell? "Sure, that's fine. If you like, I can cook something that day." He was shocked as the words left his mouth. What was he thinking?

Shannon was surprised, but beamed at his invitation. *Was this the same guy that Irene had said was anti-social?*

"Yeah, sure, okay. That sounds great!" Shannon grinned brightly. "Are you coming to the café today for lunch?" Her brilliant smile took his breath away. Seth had remembered thinking just this morning that he would skip lunch so he could avoid her, yet here he was inviting her for dinner. He looked into her eyes. He could tell her excitement was genuine. *She's hoping I'll say yes.* He was shocked at the thought. "Sure, I'll see you then", as he returned her open smile with a tentative one. "Let Irene know that I'll have my usual".

"What's your usual?"

"BLT on white toast with fries, extra crispy." Seth answered.

"I'll let her know. See you then." Shannon impulsively leaned over and kissed him on the cheek. His razor stubble was prickly and tickled, but his skin was soft. Just that brief contact sent shivers down her spine. It stunned her, but it stunned Seth more. Before she could consider what she had done, Shannon jumped in the truck and sped down the dirt road, leaving Seth standing in the dust with his mouth hanging open.

CHAPTER 4

Praying she wouldn't be late, Shannon sped down the rough road toward the diner. *Why did I do that?* She couldn't help but smile remembering Seth's reaction to her kiss. The look on his face was priceless. *Oh boy, it might get a little awkward come lunch time.* Her smile faltered and she began to chew on her lower lip. Even though he had been civil to her while they were alone, she had no idea how he would react to her in public. *Will he talk to me or will he be surly and noncommittal like before?* She just didn't know. The thought of him ignoring her made her feel sick to her stomach. It must have known she was thinking of it because her stomach rumbled loudly. Glancing over to the passenger seat, she reached for the paper bag from Irene and Paddy. The front left tire hit a mound of hard dirt causing the truck to lurch sideways, going into a spin. Shannon panicked, desperately jerking the wheel, trying to regain control. The truck lurched, landing the left rear tire in the ditch, at the same time, flinging her head violently against the drivers' side window. Shannon heard a crack then blackness washed over her.

Seth walked up the porch of the log cabin and sat in one of the wood rockers. It was as close as he would get to the house. He hadn't been in the cabin since the accident. He had started the renovations on his workshop immediately, turning it into a livable space.

As he sat rocking, he let his mind wander. A picture started forming in his head. Shannon, standing in his back yard with her golden red hair blowing in the wind, the vast mountain range rising up behind her, framing her angelic face as she looked at him with so much love in her eyes.

Seth's eyes flew open as he sucked in his breath. *What the hell was that about?* He shook his head to dispel the image. Although it receded to the back of his mind, it didn't go away completely. The voice of doubt that had been his constant companion, argued with him

You know there can never be anything between the two of you. Besides the fact that she's probably just passing through, she would never be able to stand against the hate everyone in town has for you. They may even turn that hate toward her or turn her against you. The thought was like a punch to his gut. *Would you really want to put her through that pain? That's no way for anyone to live.* His long silent heart spoke up. *Well, you've been doing it for the past three years.* His fist beat his chest, attempting to silence it. "No! I won't do that to her!" Seth growled. He bolted from the chair, his mind, and heart waging a silent war. He began to pace back and forth on the porch. Not even thinking what he was doing, he found himself striding down the dirt road toward the diner. It was a trek he made everyday…weather permitting.

His inner voices still arguing, Seth was distracted as he walked down the familiar road when suddenly, up ahead, he recognized the truck that Shannon had driven, lying sideways in the ditch. "Oh my God!" Seth exclaimed as he broke into a run. Reaching the truck, he ran to the driver's side. There was Shannon, slumped over, her head resting on the passenger seat, blood pouring from a gash on her temple.

Being a doctor, he knew that it was dangerous to move the victim of an accident but at that particular moment the knowledge did him no good. Sick with concern, he wrenched the door open and pulled Shannon's limp form into his arms. Her body was alarmingly still. "Shannon, Shannon, wake up! Can you hear me?! Wake up!" he yelled, shaking her. *Oh God, please don't let her die!* He took his hand and gently swept her blood soaked hair away from her face. When he firmly patted her cheek trying to revive her, Shannon's reaction was immediate. Her eyes flew open unseeing and she started struggling, feebly beating her fists against his chest. Then, just as suddenly, she went limp in his arms. He debated whether he should take her to the hospital or back to his place. Besides the fact that the hospital was miles away, he could just imagine how it would look if he walked into the emergency room carrying a bleeding, unconscious woman. The people of Sanctuary already had their suspicions. He didn't want Shannon to be a target for their gossip. Making up his mind, he hauled her out of the truck, gently cradling her in his arms as he made his way back.

Seth took Shannon and gently eased her down onto the love seat that they had shared just that morning. He went to the bathroom and grabbed his medical bag. Cleaning the wound, he realized it was going to need stitches. Afraid that Shannon would wake up in the middle of the procedure, he decided to give her a sedative.

Once he had completed the procedure, Seth sat back and took the opportunity to really study her at his leisure, something he wasn't able to do while she looked at him with those soul piercing eyes of hers. He took a lock of her hair, enjoying the soft texture, while he admired the golden red color. As the sun's rays shone through the window, he noticed it was several shades of red and gold. Her hair smelled of gardenias. He brought the strands up to his face and breathed in the intoxicating fragrance. He wanted to bury his hands in those curls. His eyes suddenly caught something he hadn't seen before. There, normally hidden by her hair was a smooth thin scar running down the nape of her neck.

Years of working in a hospital emergency room told him that it was made by a knife or razor of some sort. He reached out to run his finger down its length when Shannon spoke. Seth jumped back, startled, looking guilty until he realized that she was still under sedation. He leaned in close to hear. "No, please don't. I won't do it anymore, please. I promise, no, no, please, you're hurting me!" She cringed in her sleep.

What the hell happened to her? Seth felt a rage building up inside him. *Someone hurt her! I swear if I ever find out who it was, I'll make them sorry they were ever born!* Seth didn't know why he was reacting this way. Maybe because they had both been through something traumatic, or maybe it was because she looked so sweet and innocent that he felt a strong need to protect her. Whatever the reason, Seth made up his mind that he had to find out her secret.

Still waters definitely run deep with this woman. He looked closely at her face again. He gazed upon the freckles that seemed to dance across her nose and cheeks and he smiled as he traced a finger across them. There was something impish about them. His eyes traveled to her kewpie doll lips. Something stirred in him as he recalled those same lips pressed softly to his cheek. He remembered how she chewed her bottom lip when she was nervous. On impulse, Seth leaned closer to her mouth and breathed in. She smelled of honey and peppermint. The smell was intoxicating. Before he could stop himself, he gently touched her full bottom lip with his. "Umm", Shannon murmured. Suddenly she raised her arm and wrapped it around his neck, pulling him into a deep kiss. Seth's eyes flew open in surprise but he did not pull away for fear of waking her and causing both of them horrible embarrassment.

He allowed her to continue exploring his mouth, her tongue rolling around his as she tasted him. Seth could feel his body responding to her kiss, but he knew it would be wrong to allow this to go any further. He could never take advantage of anyone, let alone someone under sedation. That was just sick.

He stilled himself and reluctantly pulled away. "Seth," Shannon moaned and her face scrunched up as though she were pouting. Seth was rocked as she murmured his name. *Could she have been dreaming of me?*

Tucking her hands under her cheek she curled into a fetal position and promptly started snoring…. loudly. Seth pulled the blanket over her body with trembling hands. He was still reeling from that kiss. Knowing that she probably wouldn't wake up for a while, he grabbed his cell phone and stepped outside. He had some calls to make.

"Hey Irene, this is Seth. No, I'm fine, but listen. Shannon had an accident on her way back to the café."

"Oh no! Is she okay?!" Irene gasped, obviously worried. "What happened?"

"Well, I wasn't there but it looks like she lost control of the truck and landed sideways in a ditch."

"Where is she? Did you take her to the hospital? How did it happen?" Irene was firing the questions at him so fast that he didn't know which ones to answer first.

"She cracked her head on the side window and had to have stitches. I gave her a sedative and she's resting. No, I didn't take her to the hospital. I treated her at my place. I wanted to call and ask if you wouldn't mind having the truck towed to the garage. I don't know how much damage was done but whatever it costs, just send me the bill."

"Also, I wanted to let you know that she won't be making it back for the lunch shift and I very much doubt that she'll be taking the dinner shift either. She cracked her head pretty hard so I think she should stay here for a day…maybe two, so I can keep an eye on her. I just didn't want you and Paddy to worry".

Irene was relieved and a little intrigued. *What was Shannon doing at Seth's in the first place?* She decided she would get all the juicy details from Shannon once she was feeling better. She smiled to herself. It had been a long time since Seth had had anyone up at his place.

"Well, you just keep me posted and let me know if there's anything I can do, okay?" She would've headed right over there but it was about to be lunchtime and she couldn't leave Paddy to fend for himself.

Seth read the concern in her voice. "Shannon will be out of it for the rest of the night, so don't worry, nothing will happen. But if it does, you'll be the first one I call. I really think she just needs to sleep. I promise I won't take my eyes off her."

That will definitely not be a problem, he thought as he hung up the phone and walked back inside.

CHAPTER 5

Shannon was still snoring so he decided to make himself busy. He picked up a piece of wood and his carving knife and sat in his favorite rocker by the fire.

Seth lost all track of time until the darkening colors of the setting sun shone through the window, reflecting red off his carving knife. He looked up and caught his breath. Shannon was sleeping peacefully, the rays illuminating the colors of her reddish blonde hair and causing a halo around her head. She looked otherworldly. He had never seen anything so beautiful in his entire life. His chest felt tight. His desire for her was almost palpable. He sat quietly, watching the rise and fall of her chest as she slumbered. Suddenly her eyes fluttered as she struggled to wake.

He bolted out of the rocker and knelt by her side. Knowing how some people panic when they are coming out of anesthesia, Seth took her hand.

"Wha...where am I?" she whispered as she opened her eyes. She looked up to see the tortured look on Seth's face. Shaking her head, she tried to clear out the cobwebs that seemed to fog up her brain. Big mistake! Pain tore through her head making her nauseous. "Ohhhhh....my head...." She clapped her free hand to her forehead, a wave of dizziness almost making her pass out as she tried to sit up. Seth reached out, gripped her shoulders, and gently eased her back down onto the cushions.

"Shhhh, you need to rest. You hit your head pretty hard. Just relax, everything is fine but it's not a good idea for you to try to move", he whispered reassuringly. Shannon looked back at him and Seth gave her a reproving look, his voice hardening. "Do you know how bad you scared me? I don't know what I would've done if anything had happened to you. Where did you learn to drive anyway?"

Shannon cleared her throat, "I don't know what you're talking about. What do you mean I hit my head? How? The last thing I remember is driving down the road and reaching for the breakfast sandwich Paddy made me....Oh my God!" The memory came flooding back. She was reaching for the sandwich and something happened to the truck. It spun around as she jerked the wheel and then....nothing.

"How long have I been out?"

Seth looked into her strange eyes and said, "Pretty much since I carried you back here".

'He carried me?' she thought he was strong, but not that strong. She looked up at him awestruck, "That was quite a walk. After that, you may be the one who needs to see a doctor......a Chiropractor."

"I do it all the time. If the weather's good, I usually walk to the diner so carrying you back wasn't a big deal." *I would've carried her 100 miles if I had to,* he thought, his concern for her clearly displayed on his face.

Shannon didn't know what to think about his unusual behavior. It seemed to her like he was actually scared. "From the way you're gawking at me, it must be pretty bad. Why aren't I in the hospital?" Seth sighed, knowing that the truth would be the best thing.

"I'm a doctor, you were bleeding a lot. The hospital is miles away so I took care of you myself."

"I was bleeding, from where?" But somehow due to the excruciating pain, she guessed it was from her head. "Is it bad?" her voice flat as she reached up to feel the bandage.

Seth was concerned at her lack of emotion. *Maybe she's more seriously hurt than I thought.* "You had a pretty big gash from hitting your head, but the stitches should take care of it. You just need to take it easy for awhile."

She just looked at the floor and nodded her head. No tears, no hysteria. Seth wondered why she was so calm.

A memory slowly emerged from the back of his mind.

He had been working at the clinic on the reservation when one of the women came in with a busted nose, broken teeth, and a broken arm. As he was treating her injuries, the reservation authorities arrived and started asking her questions. With the same flat voice as Shannon, she had responded to their questioning, saying that she had fallen off a ladder retrieving a toy from the roof.

The police took down her statement, mumbled to each other, and left the room. Curious at their behavior, Seth stepped out with them and learned that she was the abused wife of one of the tribal leaders. She never pressed charges and always came up with some excuse. They told him that because the husband was revered by the tribe, if the wife didn't want to be kicked out into the street, she would have to endure the beatings. This angered Seth as he thought of how precious his wife was to him. He would never lay a hand on her...ever! As the officers turned to leave, he heard one say to the other; "Well, at least she's getting more creative with the lies". They both shook their heads helplessly in agreement and left.

His eyes went to the scar on her neck.

Though her head felt like it was going to fall off, Shannon had been in worse shape than this, remembering the numerous times she had been admitted for broken ribs, broken collarbone, broken wrists and several broken fingers, not to mention that last time, the razor...

"Listen Shannon, I think it would be a good idea for you to stay here tonight. I want to keep an eye on your progress in case something unforeseen should arise. If you'll allow me, I can go to your place and get some things for you. Just let me know what you need."

"Oh. Alright, I'll make a list."

"Wait, let me write it down for you." He grabbed a note pad and pen. "Okay, shoot."

"I'll need my toothbrush, toothpaste, a change of clothes, wait, how long do you think I need to be here?"

If Shannon had been taken to the hospital, they would have only kept her overnight for observation, but Seth found himself saying, "I would say a couple of days at least." He waited for her reaction.

She didn't even blink twice. "Okay. Then a couple of changes of clothes and my pajamas, they're in my panty drawer under the bed." Shannon felt the heat rush to her face at the thought of Seth going through her underwear drawer. "My clothes are hanging in the closet. Just pick something out. I trust you."

She stole a glance at him, his luxuriously silky hair falling across his cheeks as he bent over the paper.

"Right, okay. Give me your keys."

Shannon looked around her and looked back at Seth helplessly. "I don't know where my bag is. Did you bring it with you when you carried me back here?"

"No, I didn't. Shit! I better get down there before the tow truck takes off with it." He flew out the door and took the steps two at a time.

Jumping into his Black truck, he tore down the road to where Shannon's truck was stranded. It was still there. "Oh, thank God!" He breathed a sigh of relief and pulled her bag from the car. Because he knew that Shannon would want it, he also grabbed her drawing pad and stuffed it in her purse. He examined the cracked driver's side window. *That was where she hit her head.* He looked closer and saw there were several strands of golden red hair tangled in the spider web of glass, a small patch of blood in the center.

Man, she really cracked it good! It made his stomach drop to think that just a centimeter to the right and it would have been fatal. He left the key in the ignition for the tow truck operator and took off down the dirt road leaving a curtain of dust in his wake.

Upon arriving at the diner, Seth parked his truck next to the four wheel monstrosity and rummaged through Shannon's bag for the keys. Finally locating them way down in the bottom of the seemingly endless black hole, he pulled them out and noticed her key ring. He smirked, *so she has a thing for wolves.* He turned the figurine over in his hand. It had a small button on the side. He pushed it and the wolf's eyes lit up. *Cool.*

Turning the key ring over, he discovered what looked like a small canister of perfume. As he brought it up for a closer look, it suddenly went off in his face. "Owe, shit!" Seth cursed as he dropped the key ring and rubbed his eyes, tears flowing down his face. "Pepper spray? Great! Way to go, stupid ass!" He felt really dumb, but he had to commend Shannon for protecting herself. *She sure seems like a woman who can take care of herself.* He thought of how she handled the letch at the diner and the crotch in the knee trick she pulled on him earlier, wincing at the memory.

Regaining his composure, Seth went inside the motor home. He was completely taken aback by what he found. The place was very homey. *I bet everything she owns is in here,* he thought as he looked around the small space. The phrase "starving artist" fit perfectly.

The driver's seat had one of those covers made out of wooden balls. They were supposed to be good for your back when traveling long distances. He had seen many truck drivers use them for long hauling, but these balls had been painted pink. He chuckled to himself.

Stepping to the main living area he scanned the wall. It was filled with framed photographs. All of them were of Shannon participating in some type of extreme sport from skydiving to bungee jumping. There was a picture of her standing on a dock proudly holding up a giant marlin, one of her striking a pose on some tropical island in a conservative one piece, yet another of Shannon scuba diving and one of her mountain climbing. It looked as if she was bound and determined to milk every last drop out of life.

Something was out of kilter. He stood back and scanned the photos again, his brow creasing as he struggled for the answer. Then it hit him. They all had one thing in common. "She's alone in every single picture." He spoke out loud. It tugged at his heart. Why was she alone? It didn't make any sense. He had already come to the conclusion that she had been abused by someone in the past. *Could it have been a parent, a boyfriend….a husband?* The idea that Shannon could be married hadn't even crossed his mind until now. *Is she running away? No, those pictures don't look like someone on the run. Did she divorce his sorry ass and buy this thing with the settlement money?* Seth didn't know why but for some reason he didn't think she was the kind to turn tale and run. *What happened to you, Shannon?*

Seth went into the sleeping compartment. The small bed was made up with an old comfortable quilt and mismatched decorative pillows that were nestled at the head. On the wall were sketches of other people. They were alone in the pictures, but there were little hand written captions on the bottom of each picture identifying them: There was a man on a ski slope. The captioned read simply,

Jacque. The next picture was a man in scuba gear, Steve. Then there was a man hanging out of an airplane, David.

Seth didn't want to see anymore. He felt a wave of jealously hit him like a slap in the face. *How stupid of me!* He mentally kicked himself for what he'd thought earlier. *Of course she wasn't alone. She's a beautiful, vibrant woman, after all.*

He chided himself for being such a sentimental fool as he leaned down and forcefully yanked on the drawer beneath the bed...... obviously a little too forcefully. It shot out of its' runner, upending in his hand, spilling the contents onto the floor. "Great!" His face flushing, he leaned over to pick up the flimsy material. As he was shoving the lingerie back into the drawer, he noticed a small box that must have fallen out. He started to put it back but something stopped him. It wasn't one of those keepsake boxes where women kept sentimental trinkets and love letters. Instead, it was solid black with a small key latch. Curiosity got the better of him. He popped the latch and peered inside.

There were newspaper articles, photos of people at parties and expensive looking jewelry. He raised his eyebrow. *The style just doesn't suit Shannon at all.* He picked up the batch of photos. It looked to him to be just a bunch of snobby rich people, laughing, drinking, and having a good ole time. He wondered why Shannon would have pictures of these people. They just didn't look like the type of people she would associate with.

He started to place the pictures back into the plain box when suddenly his eyes were drawn to a figure standing amongst the crowd. Ordinarily there was nothing about the woman that would set her apart from the rest. Except for the eyes. She was dressed in an ankle length, pale green halter gown embellished with multi-colored jewels at the empire waist. Her neck was bejeweled with emeralds, as were her ears. Her beautiful curls were swept up into a severe chignon. She looked extremely thin. Her eyes looked much too large as her cheek bones protruded sharply. Gone were the supple curves and softness he appreciated so much.

She was standing next to a man of about fifty. His hair was salt and pepper and he was groomed impeccably. He was handsome but his expression was severe. His eyes looked cruel as his arm held her possessively. He noticed how Shannon seemed to lean away from him. The body language was evident. The caged animal look in her eyes told Seth all he needed to know. She was his property.

Anger and concern consumed Seth as he snatched up the newspaper articles. The headlines were in bold block type:

NEW ORLEANS SOCIALITE KILLS HUSAND OF TEN YEARS

Seth couldn't believe his eyes. 'Shannon killed her husband?' It didn't seem possible.
He read the next headline:

SOCIALITE CLAIMS SELF-DEFENSE

He picked up the next one:

SOCIALITE RELEASED FROM HOSPITAL TO STAND TRIAL

'Hospital?" Then Seth remembered the scar on Shannon's neck.
He picked up the last article:

SOCIALITE ACQUITTED FOR THE MURDER OF HER HUSBAND

Now it was all starting to come together.
Just as he thought he had it all figured out, he picked up a piece of paper that had been neatly folded.

LIST OF THINGS TO DO

1. Learn self-defense
2. Take Art Classes
3. Learn to scuba dive
4. Learn to sky dive
5. Take a cruise to Aruba
6. Learn to Ski, water and snow
7. Learn to ride a motorcycle
8. Buy a motor home
9. Drive across America
10. Travel to Paris and see the Louvre

Everything on the list was crossed out except for number ten, travel to Paris, and see the Louvre. *So she's done all the things on the list, but one.* His fear was realized. She wasn't planning on staying. The Louvre sure wasn't in Sanctuary.

Then down at the bottom of the paper in very small writing as though it were an afterthought:

Fall in love

Have a family

These two items were not crossed out.

Seth suddenly felt like an intruder. He quickly refolded the paper and put it back in the box, took out a couple of pairs of panties and a pair of silky pajamas with little moons and stars on them.

Moving to the small closet, he grabbed a couple of blouses, a skirt, and a pair of jeans. He saw the matching robe to the pajamas and packed that as well, stuffing them all into a large cloth bag.

He took one more look around to make sure that he had left everything just as it was and hurried to his truck.

CHAPTER 6

Shannon had been lying on the couch staring at the fire. Several things were going through her head. *What am I doing here? I should just call Irene and have her come pick me up. No, I can't do that. She probably has her hands full at the diner. I don't know anyone else.... I guess Seth is stuck with me.* Shannon hated putting anyone out. *It was nice of him to suggest I stay, even if it is for medical reasons. Why did I have to reach for that stupid sandwich?* She mentally took back the comment about the sandwich. It was just Irene and Paddy's way of showing they cared and that they were looking out for her.

She realized with a certain amount of trepidation that she had to use the bathroom....badly. Shannon moved very slowly, testing her limits. The last thing she wanted was for Seth to find her sprawled out on his floor. She got up and headed toward what she hoped was the direction of the bathroom. She felt a little light headed but that could be from the crack in her skull. She made her way down a short hallway. *Bingo!*

As she was taking care of business, Shannon looked around at the tiny bathroom. It didn't have a bath tub, just a large shower. *You could fit two people in there at a time,* she thought and a mental image flashed into her head of the two of them lathering each other up, the water cascading over Seth's muscular olive skin. *Stop it Shannon! Don't go there. Even if by some stretch of the imagination we were to get together, how do I know he wouldn't just discard me like yesterday's trash?* She couldn't take it if that happened. She had only been with one man and he turned out to be a monster. She had always thought that love between a man and a woman should be filled with romantic nights of laughter and kisses, not being used and abused.

She would just stay a couple of days and then she would be out of his hair, forever.

Shannon washed her hands as she stood in front of the small sink. Curiosity got the better of her and she opened the medicine cabinet. There was a bottle of Advil, some ant-acids, his razor and a bottle of cologne. Shannon didn't recognize the brand name as she sniffed the top. It smelled woodsy, *like him,* she thought, a slight smile breaking out on her face.

She was halfway back to the couch when Seth walked in holding a bulging cloth bag. They both froze as their eyes met.

"What are you doing up?" Rushing to her side, arms encircling her waist as he helped her back onto the couch.

There it was again, that strange electric shock. She actually stumbled, her legs turning to jelly at the unexpected contact.

Why does he affect me like this?

"I had to use the bathroom and you were gone so long…." Her tone was accusatory as she struggled to control her breathing.

Seth flinched guiltily as he recalled what had caused his delay, "Sorry it took so long but you shouldn't be up. The next time you need to go, let me know and I'll help you," he said as he helped her lie down.

Shannon flushed from her head to her toes at the contact. She suddenly felt too hot.

"You look flushed. Do you have a fever?" Seth placed his hand on her forehead. "How do you feel?"

Irritated at being fussed over, Shannon pushed his hand away. "I'm just a little light headed is all! You don't have to hover over me like some mother hen! I'll be fine!" she lashed out at him. She didn't mean to snap but she hated feeling so helpless.

Seth stepped back as though she had struck him, a wounded look crossing his face. Her words cut him life a knife. He thought of the photos, the trapped look on her face, and he quickly shook off his hurt feelings. She needed him and by God, he was determined to be there for her.

Shannon expected him to get mad and start yelling. Squeezing her eyes shut, she braced herself for the assault. It didn't come. Slowly she opened her eyes and glanced up.

His expression was calm, his tone light and casual.

"I bet you're hungry. I'm going to rustle up some dinner. You can use the shower to clean up and change in my room....if you want." He busied himself, looking for the frying pan.

That sounded like heaven to Shannon. She realized she hadn't eaten a thing. The sandwich was either still in the truck or the tow truck driver had eaten it by now.

She couldn't believe that all of this had happened in just one day. "Thanks, I won't take too long", she said as she got up off the couch. Before she could take another step, Seth was right there, his arm around her for support. She sucked in her breath as little sparks of electricity flowed through her body, making her tingle all over.

"You really shouldn't try to walk too much until the dizziness goes away", he admonished as he tightened his grip.

I probably wouldn't be dizzy if you would stop insisting on touching me, she flushed as the now all too familiar shock took her breath away. You would've thought she'd become immune to it by now, but it still managed to throw her off balance.

Reluctantly Shannon gently moved away from him, breaking his hold on her. "Thanks but I think I need to see if this little bird can fly solo. I can't expect you to bathe me." She started as the words left her mouth. Hoping Seth would overlook the comment, she concentrated hard on walking in a straight line to prove that she could do it on her own.

She turned at the doorway, smiled and gave him the "two thumbs up". Seth smiled back, but as he turned back around, he gripped the edge of the counter. Her words had a staggering effect on him. *Oh Shannon, I would truly love to give you a bath.*

You can't even get this kind of treatment in a luxury spa, she thought to herself as she took full advantage of the eight shower heads that protruded out of the wall in the most strategic places. It felt like a dozen hands massaging her body all at the same time. It was heaven!

Shannon found herself humming softly some old tune as she grabbed the bag that Seth had gotten from her place. The clothes were terribly wrinkled but she took them, hung them up, and turned the shower back on hot to get out the wrinkles.

Seth heard the shower turn off, only to hear it turn back on a few minutes later. He had made a couple of western omelets. *I really need to change out of these clothes. They're filthy.* After setting the table, he decided that he would quickly change in his room and be out of there before Shannon got out of the shower.

He made it to his bedroom and opened the door. Quietly he walked over to his closet and selected an Azure blue chambray shirt that matched his eyes and a pair of blue jeans. He stripped naked, throwing his dirty clothes in the hamper.

Satisfied that the clothes were wearable again, Shannon changed quickly and entered the bedroom. Her mouth fell to the floor! Standing there, in all his glory was Seth. The moonlight shone through the plate glass, enveloping him in a silvery glow. It was breathtaking! She watched, frozen to the spot. Her brain told her to get out of there, but her traitorous body left her staring stupidly at his glorious body.

He pulled on a pair of black boxers, a blue chambray shirt, and a pair of jeans. As he was zipping the fly he happened to turn around. Their eyes locked. They both gasped.

God, would you look at how beautiful she is, standing there in the moonlight in that flimsy shirt, her hair damp from the steam of the shower, her face void of make-up. The freckles were more prominent with nothing to camouflage them. Her eyes were bigger than usual. She looked shocked. He wondered just how long she had been standing there. The thought of her eyes raking over his nakedness was enough to get his blood boiling. Not wanting to put her on the spot, he decided to play it off.

"Oh, Shannon, I didn't see you there." He took in her flushed face and immediately became concerned. "You look like you're going to faint. Here, you better lie down." Seth stepped toward her to help her to the bed. As he reached for her, she did something she had never done before in her life. Rising up on her toes, Shannon tentatively pressed her lips to his.

Seth's reaction was immediate. His hands came up to cup her face as he gently increased the pressure. The last thing he wanted to do was frighten her. It took all his concentration not to throw her down on the bed and give himself over to his passion.

Becoming bolder, Shannon wrapped her arms around his neck, burying her hands in his silky locks. She had wanted to feel the texture of it from the first time she saw him at the diner. Now she was kissing him… and he was kissing her! The feeling was pure bliss!

Seth found it hard to breathe as he ran his tongue between her lips, beckoning her to receive his kiss. His heart soared as she tentatively opened her mouth. He ran his tongue over her teeth, their tongues dancing together as they tasted one another. He could feel his desire growing stronger as the kiss deepened.

Shannon felt his physical desire as he moved against her and gasped in surprise. Feeling her response, Seth immediately broke the kiss, looking down into those bluish green depths, wondering if he'd gone too far. *Damn it! I've scared her and now she'll run away from me as fast as she can. Why didn't I just give her a friendly kiss?* But he knew the reason; he wanted her. He wanted her as he had never wanted another woman. *God forgive me, not even Naome' had sparked such a passion.* But she had been through so much. He had to hold himself back, for her sake. He loosened his hold.

Shannon was surprised and somewhat hurt when he pulled away. She couldn't begin to imagine what he was thinking. *Did I do something wrong? Was it my kissing?* She had never experienced anything so wonderful……or confusing. When her husband kissed her it was to keep up appearances and they were always quick and nonsexual. What he did to her in private never required kissing.

Now, all she wanted was to kiss this man and keep kissing him until she was exhausted.

"I'm sorry, did I hurt you?" Seth's concern was clear on his handsome face.

"Hurt me?" She was confused by his reaction. He so wasn't hurting her. She knew what hurt felt like and this definitely wasn't it. It was more like sweet torture.

He tightened his arms around her and drew her to his chest. Raising his hand he started stroking her hair, rocking back and forth in a soothing motion.

"It's just that I want you so much but considering what you've been through, I don't want to force you into doing anything you don't want to do," he whispered into her hair.

Shannon became rigid. "What did you just say?!" She jerked back from him, pushing away with her hands. "How do *you* know what I've been through?!" The realization hit her in the face. "You went through my things?! How could you?! I trusted you!" She began crying and pummeling his chest. She should have known not to trust him.

"You Son of a bitch, get your hands off me! Let me go!"

Seth was shocked by her violent reaction. *I can't believe I'm so stupid! How did I let that slip?! Now she will never trust me again and I don't really blame her! I know I shouldn't have looked in that box!* Gripping her arms, he tried to explain.

"Shannon, listen, I'm so sorry! I didn't mean to pry. The box fell on the floor! Please don't be mad! I know I shouldn't have looked inside! I don't know why I did. I wish I could take it back! I only want to keep you safe. I would never hurt you and I would kill anyone who did! Don't shut me out, please!" Seth pleaded with her but Shannon only struggled harder.

Suddenly, she collapsed in his arms. Panicked, he scooped her up and placed her on the bed, cradling her head in his arms. "Shannon, wake up." He ran the back of his hand down her cheek.

Shannon looked up, trying to focus. She couldn't seem to get her thoughts together. There seemed to be a fog obstructing her vision. As she strained, an image slowly came into focus. "Oh dear God! Richmond! No! Please, stay away from me!" She feebly beat his chest.

Seth was floored by her outburst. *This guy must have been a real piece of work!* He thought angrily. "Shannon, shhh baby, it's alright. It's me Seth. Please, shhh, you're safe now and I won't let anyone hurt you ever again! I swear it on my life!" He pulled her close and rocked her in his arms.

The fog finally lifted as Shannon realized who was gently rocking her. She could smell his woodsy scent and it was inviting. All of the anger she had felt toward him disappeared with the fog. Her body relaxed and she let him hold her. There wasn't anything sexual about his embrace. He touched her as though she were a piece of fine china. Unable to hold back her emotions, she sobbed against his chest. She gripped him like a drowning person.

Seth held her, letting her release all the emotions that had festered for so long inside her.

CHAPTER 7

Exhausted and spent, Shannon fell asleep in Seth's arms as he continued rocking her. He placed a kiss on her forehead and slipped her under the covers. He turned out the light and closed the door.

Back in the living room, he sat down in his favorite rocker and picked up the piece of wood he had been working on earlier. He looked at its' fine lines and detailing. The subject was one he had never before attempted. He examined the peaks and valleys of the wings. It wasn't like him to carve mythical creatures, but he wanted to do this one for Shannon. In a way, it was like her. The mythical bird creature was known for rising out of the ashes to begin a new life and that is exactly what Shannon had done. He hoped she would like it. He picked up his knife…

Seth didn't know what time it was as he always tended to lose track when immersed in his work, but looking out the window he could see the oranges and reds as the sun began to peek over the mountain tops.

Shannon awoke with Seth's scent all around her. Stretching like a spoiled kitten she looked out the picture window. The sun was coming up over the mountains and the sight was amazing! She walked closer to the window and realized that it wasn't a window but a door that led out to a deck. Opening it, Shannon stepped outside to enjoy the sunrise.

Thinking he should go check on Shannon, Seth walked down the hall and opened the door to his bedroom. The scene before him made him suck in his breath. Shannon was leaning over the deck railing, the breeze blowing her hair out around her. The rays of the rising sun making it practically glow. She was exquisite! He walked up next to her as silent as a cat.

Shannon felt Seth's presence even before he showed up beside her. When he was near, it was as though there was a slight shift in the universe.

"How are you feeling this morning?" Seth asked her hesitantly. Was she still upset about last night?

"Actually I feel wonderful! Have you ever seen such a beautiful sight?" She gestured toward the mountains as they reflected the many hues of the rising sun.

"No, I can't say as I have", Seth answered, his eyes on her. As she turned to look at him, he looked away, gazing out at the majestic vista, seeing it through new eyes, Shannon's eyes. "That's how the Painted Mountains got their name. It seems to suit them."

"I can't wait to start painting them! By the way, about last night…" Shannon began.

Oh great, here it comes. Seth braced himself for the onslaught.

Shannon straightened and turned to face him.

"I'm sorry that I accused you of invading my privacy. It's just that, well, I haven't had to worry about someone getting through my defenses for a long while and I guess I was mostly mad at myself for being so careless. I should have been more careful and locked the box. Shannon reached into her shirt and pulled out a long thin chain with a tiny silver key attached to it. I just didn't think ahead so it's really all my fault."

She sounded apologetic. This confused the hell out of him. Seth took her by the arms, wanting to shake some sense into her but, controlling himself, only rubbed his hands up and down her arms. "Shannon, are you nuts?! Why are you apologizing?! I was the one who went snooping into your private life! Don't you dare apologize! You should be trying to throw me over the railing right now! Listen to me! Don't say a word until I'm done, Okay?" Shannon only nodded her head, her eyes wide.

Loosening his grip, he took a deep breath and let it out very slowly, making his voice steady, "Okay, whether or not the box was locked, didn't give me the right to pry into your business. I only did it because I wanted to know more about you. You fascinate me to the point of distraction. I'm asking you now to trust me. Please. I would never betray your trust." His voice softened to a whisper. "tell me what happened to you?" searching her eyes as he waited for a response.

The natural reaction to his plea would have been to slap him, curse him, or run, but that was too predictable. Instead, she looked closely at him, searching his brilliant blue eyes. Seeing the sincerity on his face, she took a deep breath, "Feed me", she said as she continued to stare at him.

"What?"

"You heard me. I'm starving! Feed me, then you can ask me anything."

Seth looked over at Shannon as she sat at the tiny hand carved dinette table for two. She kept her eyes downcast as Seth cooked another western omelet, having thrown the uneaten ones from last night into the garbage. He placed each on a separate plate and carried them over to the table. Shannon dug in, not lifting her head until her plate was clean.

"Ask me", she said as she pushed her plate away, grabbing her coffee cup.

"Okay," he said.

"Wait," Shannon held up her hand. "I want to know what you found out on your own first."

Seth cleared his throat nervously. "I know that you were in a very abusive marriage. I know that something happened and you killed him in self-defense. I know that you have traveled a lot since then and taken many lovers. I know that you want to visit Paris, I read the list, sorry." Shannon didn't say anything. She continued to look at him with the same penetrating gaze, nodding her head for him to continue.

"I know you used to be very thin, too thin. I know that you must've felt very lonely for a long time…and I know that you love silk pajamas."

She raised an eyebrow at him, ignoring his last comment. "What makes you think I had many lovers?"

"I saw the pictures of all those guys. I don't blame you. You're a very desirable woman. Of course there would be lots of men who'd want you," Seth said begrudgingly.

"Well, we'll get back to that. First I want to tell you a story."

Seth knew this was going to be some kind of breakthrough and he didn't want anything to interrupt her.

"Why don't I clear these dishes and we can go sit next to the fire?"

"That would be nice," she said.

Shannon sat cross-legged, facing Seth on the couch with her arm resting on the back, her fist under her chin. Seth's arm rested near hers.

She took a deep breath and looked toward the fire, losing herself in the flames.

"Once upon a time there was a little girl from Louisiana who lived in the bayou. She had many friends but her family was very poor. They barely survived from week to week. She never thought about those things because to her she was rich. She had loving parents and good friends. Her life was good.

Then, on her sixteenth birthday, her mother came to her with a beautiful box. The little girl didn't have any idea what was inside, but she had never seen such a shiny box in her whole life. The girl's mother held the box out to her with a rather sad smile on her face. "This is for you Cherie. I know you will look simply beautiful in it. Go ahead and put it on, but first we need to scrub the dirt off you. I have made you a warm bath with sweet smelling petals to make you smell like a woman." The girl was overjoyed. What a wonderful birthday present! She thoroughly enjoyed the bath and the way it made her skin glow. Her mother washed her hair with shampoo that smelled the same as the petals. She couldn't help but laugh as she splashed her mother. "Stop playing around and get out of that tub!" Her mother admonished her gently. She never yelled at her daughter, though there were times when she had every right to.

The girl slipped the gorgeous dress over her head and her mother helped her pull her hair up letting only small spirals hang down to frame her young face. She added a little bit of gloss to her lips and mascara to her eyes. "Where are we going ma-ma? Are we going to a party for my birthday?" The girl asked her excitedly.

"Yes, Mon petite, you are going to a party", her voice laced with sadness. The girl was too excited to notice. "Ohhh, goody! Will I be the bell of the ball? Oh I hope so! Maybe Jean Luke will be there. He's so cute. Do you think he will ask me to dance?" She flitted, swinging her arms around animatedly. "No, Jean Luke won't be there, but there will be other…people there." Her mother said. "Now be still and let me look at you", as she turned the little girl so she was facing the full length mirror.

"Oh ma-ma! I look all grown up!" She exclaimed. She turned and hugged her mother tight as she could without breaking her bones. "Ma-ma! You cry because you are happy for me?" Her mother looked at her and smiled feebly, "Yes, Cheri, I am happy for you." "Now get downstairs. There's a car waiting to take you to your… party", her mother pushed her gently toward the door.

She had almost made it to the door when her mother took her in her arms and held her very tightly. The girl, having no idea her life would never be the same again, hugged her mother back. "I love you ma-ma! Thank you for the dress, though I don't see how we can afford it." She waved to her mother, not knowing it was for the last time. The car drove out of sight.

The little girl was taken to a huge plantation on the outskirts of the French quarter. She was very excited about the party as she admired her dress. It was made of a material she had never seen before. The color was gold but there were so many other colors reflected in the dress. When the light shone in certain angles, it was red, orange, and yellow with a touch of pink. It was the most beautiful thing she had ever worn. The bodice was cut low, showing off her budding breasts and her shoes were gold.

When she arrived at the mansion, the door was opened and the chauffeur offered his hand to help her out. As she exited the car she looked straight up to see four extremely large columns and an ornate front entrance door.

Suddenly, she felt very uneasy. '*Who lived here and how did ma-ma know them?*' Someone approached her and led her inside.

The place was immaculate. The girl noticed that there were lots of statues of naked men and women. She looked away quickly, feeling her face flushing pink. There were also many jars with different scenes painted on them. She reached out her hand to feel one close to her… "Don't touch that!" It was a man's voice. It scared her and she jerked her hand back instinctively. "See, I told you she would be obedient. It's from the Ming Dynasty", as he waved a manicured hand toward the vase. He was the most handsome man she had ever seen in her life. It wasn't so much his face that was so handsome, it was his attire. He was impeccably dressed. She held her breath waiting for him to approach.

"Hello my dear. You look beautiful. That dress is perfect with your complexion."

"Thank you very much, sir. Are you here for my party?"

He laughed, amused by her naivety. "You are at MY party, dear one. But you are a very important part of it." He turned to the other man who had escorted the girl inside. "Bring her to the ball room."

"Are we going to dance?" The girl asked the man who took her by the elbow and guided her toward the room. "No, no dancing. But this *is* your lucky day."

"Really, because it's my birthday?"

"No, because it is your wedding day."

"My what?"

"Hush child and be on your best behavior or things will get tough for you."

The girl was very confused. *Maybe they dropped me off at the wrong house. I'm not getting married.*

They entered the ball room. There were only a few people sitting in folding chairs. There was a man in front and that same handsome man was standing to the side. The girl tried to stop but he tightened his grip on her elbow and pulled her down the aisle to the front.

The impeccably dressed man was standing there looking at her in a way that made her very uncomfortable. She seemed to be seeing everything through a long tunnel as panic gripped her.

"No, no, no, this can't be right. It's my sixteenth birthday. I'm supposed to be at my party. I can't be getting married. This has to be a mistake!" she cried as she tried her best to dislodge the man's hold on her arm. It was no use. His grip was like a vise.

"Come Cherie, I have waited for you to turn sixteen for three years. The arrangements were made with your parents and they have been very well paid. They won't have to want for anything the rest of their days. Don't you want them to be happy?"

"My parents made arrangements for me to get married? Why aren't they here?"

"They felt it would be best this way. Now come and say your vows."

The girl went through the motions in a haze. She couldn't believe it was really happening. Could it be that her parents had "sold" her to this man?

When the ceremony was over, the man, Richmond Hilderbrand, took her hand and led her up the stairs to the master suite.

As soon as the door was closed and bolted, he attacked her. Ripping the beautiful dress off her body and grabbing her painfully by her hair, he threw her onto the bed. He was rough and cruel in his lovemaking. She fought him as best she could but she was no match for his strength. It seemed to actually excite him more. Though she was a virgin, she couldn't believe this was the way it was supposed to be. By the time he had satisfied his needs, she was covered in bruises. She wept bitterly over her lost innocence. She was so sore between her legs that she couldn't walk normally for a week. That didn't concern him. He came to her every night and subjected her to all kinds of degradation.

During the day, he insisted she be instructed in the genteel arts....decorating, choosing proper place settings, entertaining, speech lessons, and current events. He wanted his "wife" to be the perfect hostess.

Never, not once in all that time had he allowed her to have friends or hobbies. She was forbidden from leaving the house without him."

Seth continued listening as she recounted the events, her voice completely void of emotion.

"This torture went on for ten years. He never seemed to tire of her, or more to the point, of degrading her. He had a special room set up for his "games". She became depressed, but unable to show her true feelings for fear of his wrath, she buried her depression, going through the motions like a zombie.

She had no appetite and started losing weight. Richmond wasn't happy about it. He complained that her breasts were shrinking and demanded that she start eating more. When she pleaded with him that she just wasn't hungry, he had her strapped to the dinner table every night and wouldn't let her up until she ate every bite of her food. When he was satisfied that she had put on enough weight, he stopped strapping her to the table.

Then one night, everything changed. He had been drinking and on the nights that he drank too much, she usually ended up in the hospital. This particular night he was extremely agitated. One of his partners had made a bad deal and it was going to cost him dearly. He came into the bathroom where she was taking a bath and proceeded to lash out at her. First verbally and then, grabbing her hair, hauled her out of the tub, dragging her naked across the tile floor to the bedroom, all the while, yelling obscenities at her as he threw her down onto the bed. She was too scared to move until she saw him reach behind his back and pull out a straight razor. Practically snarling at her, he advanced, the razor gleamed dangerously in the soft light. She screamed, trying to crawl away from him. Grabbing her hair, he brought the razor to her neck. She stopped struggling. She knew he was going to kill her. She was ready to die. Death would be a welcome relief from the life she was forced to live. He grazed the razor down her neck. Oddly, there wasn't any pain. She could feel the warm blood flowing down onto her breasts. He just kept cursing and calling her names. Unexpectedly, he crumbled to the floor, mumbling, "I've loved you from the moment I saw you playing in the street with the other poor kids. I knew I had to have you. Haven't I made you happy, given you everything you could ever want? Didn't you have the best tutors? And what do you do, you ungrateful bitch! You throw it back in my face! You can't even give me an heir! You drive me crazy! After ten years, I can't take it anymore! I came here tonight to get you out of my life… and my heart, forever!'

Sobbing drunkenly, he dropped the razor as he raised his hands to cover his face. Seeing the razor on the floor, something sparked in her mind. 'Kill him! Now's your chance! Pay the Bastard back for all the depravities he put you through! He deserves to die!' She knew she was probably dying by the amount of blood that was pouring from her wound. She quickly picked up the razor but as she looked down at the broken man before her, she just couldn't bring herself to do it. She wanted to meet her maker without this sorry excuse for a human being's blood on her hands. Suddenly he turned and looked at her, hate pouring from every core. "You Bitch! Give me that!" He reached to grab the razor, but in his drunken haze he stumbled. The blade made contact with his forearm, slicing his arm from wrist to elbow, opening a major artery. Blood poured out of his arm. He looked at her in total shock. Running to the bathroom, she grabbed a towel and tried to staunch the bleeding as his life's blood puddled onto the expensive Oriental rug.

By the time the paramedics arrived, he was dead. She was taken to the hospital and treated for the cut on her neck.

After the trial, because she was the sole beneficiary of his estate, she sold everything he owned and left, never to return."

As she reached the end of her story, Shannon continued to stare into the fire. She blinked her eyes as someone waking from a dream and looked back at Seth.

Seth sat very still. His brain was still trying to process what Shannon had told him.

She was a sex slave to a degenerate asshole! His eyes darkened with anger, making him look dangerous. He wanted to kill the bastard. *Too bad he's already dead.*

Seeing the anger in his eyes, Shannon cringed, *Oh God, he hates me!*

Seth looked into her eyes and saw fear…. fear of him. Realizing she probably thought the anger was directed at her, he reached out, gathering her in his arms.

Her body stiffened as his arms encircled her. How could he stand to touch her? How could any man stand to touch her after everything she did and had done to her? She felt so dirty.

"Shannon!" Seth whispered fervently. "Raise your head and look at me. I'm not going to hurt you!"

Shannon couldn't believe he was comforting her instead of pushing her away in disgust. Her body slowly relaxed as she leaned into him and rested her head on his chest, inhaling his male scent. This was the place she wanted to stay. She never wanted to see this moment end.

Seth began kissing her, first on her head. Then lifting her face upward, he rained soft butterfly kisses on her eyes, nose, cheeks, and chin. Just when she thought she would lose her mind…

"Shannon, open your eyes and look at me." It was a soft command.

Their eyes met. She saw that his were blue flame. He dipped his head and kissed her lightly on the lips.

Passion instantly ignited within her. She wondered at the new sensation.

Burying her hands in his hair, she kissed him desperately. All the pent up feelings she had kept buried for so long came flooding back. She kissed him with everything she had. Her breath became ragged. Her body trembled from the heat of her passion.

"Love me Seth," she whispered as she moved to unbutton his shirt. She wanted this man and the thought shocked her. She had never felt physically attracted to anyone before. She had steered clear of any romantic relationships. But now, all she wanted was to feel this man's arms around her as he whispered words of love into her hair.

At her words, Seth felt his desire growing. He growled deep in his throat. *Dear God, this woman was unbelievable! She is intrusting me with a very precious gift…. her heart.'*He hesitated knowing that once he started down this path there would be no turning back. Who was he kidding? He was lost the minute she stepped foot inside the diner.

He loved his wife and if she were still alive things would definitely be different. Whatever God's plan, he had to believe that he had placed Shannon in his path for a reason and he realized at that moment he would do anything to make her happy.

His mouth moved from her lips to her earlobe as he traced the scar with his tongue. The intimate gesture made Shannon gasp. She seemed to be having a difficult time with his buttons. Moaning as if in pain, he removed her fumbling fingers, impatiently wrenched the shirt off and flung it to the floor. Shannon's breath caught as she heard the buttons fall, clattering to the floor.

She pushed him back as he knelt on the cushions in front of her, his bare chest exposed. "Please, I want to look at you", Shannon breathed as she took in the sight. He was magnificent. His stomach was lean and muscular. She raised her eyes to his hairless chest. *'Richmond was an extremely hairy man.'* The thought was there before she could stop it. She shook her head to clear it.

Reaching out, she touched his face. Her fingers, light as a butterfly's wings, moved over his eyes, nose, mouth, and chin, emblazing his image onto her fingertips. Her hands continued down his neck to his chest.

Seth held his breath for fear of breaking the spell. He knew this was a tenuous moment. The wrong move and it could end badly.

Shannon moved her hands down to his stomach, reveling in the hard feel of him. In response to her touch, his muscles contracted. He sucked in his breath.

"Is something wrong? Am I doing something you don't like?" She asked as she started to remove her hand.

Seth grabbed her hand and put it back on his stomach. "No, it's just a natural response to your touch. This is what it's like when two people care for eachother. There is nothing wrong with it, so please, don't be afraid. You won't hurt me." *That's a lie. She could hurt me very much.*

Seth reached out, removing her flimsy top. She had on a light green flowered bra. The color complemented her skin. His lips once again found her neck, moving down to the roundness of her breasts. Loosening her bra, he slipped it off to reveal her small but full breasts. He noticed that up close, her breasts were also sprinkled with freckles. He leaned back to look at her and she crossed her arms over them.

Seth looked into her eyes. What he saw wasn't fear but modesty. She was shy! After everything she had been through, incredibly, she still had the heart of a virgin.

"Shannon love. You don't have to hide yourself from me."

Shannon glanced up. His eyes were dark blue pools of desire. "Please, will you let me look at you?"

Shannon swallowed and ever so slowly, lowered her arms.

He gazed upon her beauty. "You're so beautiful! His voice husky with desire. "It hurts to look at you."

Her pink nipples hardened under his gaze. It was almost more than he could bear. He had been dead inside for so long and now this woman was bringing him back to life. Seth wouldn't think about what might happen later. Right now, they were here together in each other's arms and he was happy. It would have to be enough.

He gathered her in his arms, crushing her lips to his. Exploring the inside of her mouth with his tongue, he kissed her until she was breathless.

Needing more room to maneuver, he scooped her up into his arms and carried her to his bedroom where he lowered her onto the mattress. Positioning himself over her, he slid her skirt and panties down, allowing himself to feast on her naked beauty.

Shannon didn't move as Seth stood up and shed the remainder of his clothes. He stood before her, his want for her evident. She couldn't look away from the naked wonder of him. He was magnificent!

Neither one moved as they drank in the sight of each other.

"Please Seth. Love me, now!" Her voice cracked with desire.

Seth lowered himself back onto the bed and resumed raining kisses all over her body. "Shannon, I want you so bad! I can't wait any longer!" he cried as he spread her legs to receive him. "I'm sorry," he said as he entered her, sure he had shattered those fragile threads of trust.

He was taken by surprise as her legs wrapped around his hips urging him on. He began to thrust harder, each thrust sending waves of pleasure through to her core. She moaned with every push until, unable to hold back any longer, she felt the spasms of her first orgasm. The sensation was like falling off a cliff, having no control, and then landing in a refreshing pool. She shuddered under his body. As she cried out his name, he joined her in sweet release.

CHAPTER 8

Shannon and Seth lay wrapped in each other's arms. As she rested her head on his chest, she could hear the steady rhythm of his heart.

I never in a million years ever thought it could feel like this, she thought as she breathed a contented sigh. She hadn't been this happy since she was a little girl.

Feeling the old doubts creep up out of her subconscious, she struggled to push them away, but years of systematic abuse were hard to ignore. *What if it was only a ploy to get me into bed? What if he was lying? How can I be sure that he's sincere?* Becoming agitated, her brow creased as she chewed on her lower lip.

Seth stirred, waking from the sweetest dream. He could feel Shannon nestled against his body. He smiled, becoming aroused at the memory of Shannon's supple body moving under his. Tightening his hold, he leaned down to place a kiss in her hair. "Morning", he whispered blissfully. He couldn't remember the last time he felt so light.

Shannon snuggled closer, as if she could get any closer, and raised her head to meet his eyes. "Is it morning? How long did we sleep?"

He could see the puzzled look on her face. He laughed and plucked at her nose with his finger. "Just kidding. It's probably closer to noon. I almost feel like I've got jet-lag."

Shannon could tell by the look on his face that he had every intention of kissing her and, afraid she had morning breath, put a finger over his lips. "Hold that thought. I'll be right back." She jumped out of bed butt naked and ran to the bathroom.

Seth watched her sexy backside and smiled contentedly. She was beautiful and sexy....and his, at least for a while.

Shannon looked in the mirror as she surveyed her face. She had always heard that women glowed when they were in love. She could truly see what they meant. Her hair was mussed and her cheeks were flushed. Her eyes sparkled and her lips were swollen from his kisses. Tracing her fingers around her mouth, she felt her face grow red as she recalled their lovemaking. A huge grin spread across her face.

After using the facilities, Shannon walked back into the bedroom where she found Seth lounging on the bed, the sheet thrown across his waist. He gave her a wicked grin and crooked his finger motioning her to the bed. Shannon practically bounced over as she threw herself on top of him. He let out a "humph" as he felt the wind knocked out of him.

"I'm sorry! Did I hurt you?"

Seth just chuckled, "I think I'll live." He wrapped his arms around her and rolled her under him. "But you're going to pay for that!" as he started tickling her. She giggled. The sound was music to Seth's ears. He looked down at her and something stirred deep within him. He was falling in love with this woman. The realization rocked him. How could that be? They had only just met.

Shannon had her eyes squinted shut as Seth tickled her. She hadn't laughed this freely in a long time. He stopped, suddenly becoming very still. Sensing the change in him, Shannon opened her eyes. He looked shocked and his body had turned to stone.

"Are you alright?" she asked, confused by his sudden mood change. She didn't like the way he was looking at her. No, not looking *at* her, but looking *through* her. She shook him out of his trance and his expression softened. "Tell me what's wrong."

"I don't want to scare you." He sat back on his heels as he looked away from her inquisitive eyes.

"What do you mean, scare me? What's the matter?" She really didn't like the way this was going. How could he scare her unless he was about to drop some huge bomb? What if he was trying to let her down easy? *Sorry Shannon, but we had fun didn't we? or 'Hey, you know, you were there, I was lonely and it had been too long since I had sex so I figured, what the heck?* Her imagination was getting the better of her. She grabbed a pillow and covered herself as she scooted out from under him. Bracing her back against the headboard, she prepared for the worst.

Seth looked down. He couldn't bear to look in her eyes and see her reaction to the bomb he was about to drop. He was a no-nonsense guy and didn't believe in playing games, truth was always the best way to go. He took a deep breath, trying to gather some courage.

Shannon could see the emotions warring on his face.

"Listen, I need to tell you something. Don't say anything until I'm finished, okay?" Shannon just nodded her head. *Oh God, here it comes,* she thought as she took a deep breath. *He's going to try to let me down easy. Well at least he's having a hard time saying it.* She steeled herself for the pain she knew would come.

"I've been alone for three years and I've liked it just fine." He chanced a peek and could see by the look on Shannon's face that he'd said it wrong. He cleared his throat and tried again.

"I'm not the kind of person who rushes headlong into anything. I usually like to weigh my options, think about the consequences. But since you stumbled into my life… (Not the right words)…when I met you, I didn't think at all. I just felt. All my careful planning, building up walls to keep people out, all of it, over, from the first moment I saw you at the counter. We have known each other such a short amount of time, and this has all happened so fast." He realized that he was having a difficult time expressing what he felt so he reached out and cupped her face in his hands. He gazed intently into her eyes and leaned over to gently brush her lips with his.

He pulled away just enough to break the kiss, his lips still resting on her mouth.

Shannon could feel his breath become ragged as it quickened. She somehow knew not to interrupt. Though her heart was beating wildly in her chest, she held perfectly still. It was becoming clear to her that what he was trying to say was extremely difficult. She wanted to beat it out of him. The anticipation was killing her.

"I've fallen for you." There, he said it. Seth let out a sigh as he felt the armor over his heart crack. Now she knew how he felt. No matter what happened from here on, he had exposed his heart, something he hadn't done for a long time. Could he even hope that she would feel the same? Well, if she didn't, at least he had told the truth and he would have to live with the consequences, but he wasn't sure he could live through another heart break.

Shannon couldn't believe her ears. She realized that she had been holding her breath. Trembling with emotion, she pulled away from him. Seth could feel his heart start to break all over again. He sighed, lowering his head so he didn't have to look into her eyes and see the disappointment there.

She put her hands on his face, lifting it to meet her gaze. "Open your eyes, Seth." He did as she told him and looked straight at her, afraid of what he would find there. Tears were streaming down her cheeks. "I never thought that I could ever trust anyone again after my parents sold me into a loveless marriage. Up until then, I loved them more than anything else in the world. My world, as I knew it, crumbled around me. I shut off my heart. After Richmond died, I tried to open myself up, but I felt nothing. I had pretty much decided that my heart was broken beyond repair. Then I saw you sitting at that booth all alone, looking completely lost and I was moved. I felt something! That alone let me know I wasn't dead inside. The feelings came pouring out and I didn't know how to act. I wasn't sure what it was I felt when I looked at you. It was very confusing."

Shannon realized that she was probably rambling but Seth didn't try to interrupt her so she forged on. "Every time you looked at me, my heart would skip a beat. The way your eyes bore into mine, I thought you hated me, but then, when I took a wrong turn and ended up at your place, you showed me nothing but kindness. You even saved my life." Shannon was getting frustrated. It seemed she couldn't get to the point. She clutched her fists and pounded them on her thighs.

Seth placed his hands in hers, uncurling her fists. He entwined his fingers in hers and lifted their hands to his chest. She could feel the heat of his bare chest beneath her fingers. "Shannon, love, just say what you feel. I won't judge you one way or the other", he whispered as he kissed her hands, brushing them across his face.

"I…….I love you!" Shannon blurted, her face flushing dark pink, her eyes wide. "I know that this feeling is stronger than anything I have ever felt. Is that love? I don't know. All I know is that I feel safe with you……and wanted. But how can this be? We've only known each other a couple of days. Is this what they call love at first sight?"

Seth's hands abruptly stopped. Lowering her hands back onto her lap, He leaned forward, towering above her head. Wrapping his arms around her waist, he pulled her to him, crushing her body to his. He still didn't feel she was close enough. He wanted her body to meld with his, to be so close he wouldn't know where she ended and he began. "I love you too, my Shannon." His mouth came down on hers forcefully, claiming her with his kiss. Shannon felt herself floating away as he lowered her back down unto the bed. His hands were maddening as they seemed to touch her everywhere at once. "Please, Seth, make love to me", Shannon pleaded, her breath ragged with desire. He lifted his head and looked down into her eyes. "As you wish".

CHAPTER 9

Shannon and Seth sat in the love seat curled up in each other's arms drinking coffee. They didn't speak as they looked into the fire. No words were necessary. Shannon thought she could stay like this forever. Wearing Seth's blue chambray shirt, she pulled the collar up to her nose, inhaling his woodsy scent. Because Seth had earlier ripped the buttons off, it hung open as she leaned her back against his bare chest. It felt so good to have his arms around her. The sun was setting and the rays cast an orange and red rainbow inside the little apartment. Seth loved the way the sun bounced off Shannon's golden red curls. He seemed to be talking to himself as he finally broke the silence. "I love your hair. The way it feels, as soft and light as down feathers. I love the way it shines, bright as the setting sun," he said in a low hushed tone. Shannon's breath caught in her throat as the huskiness of his voice sent shivers up her spine. He lifted a lock and smelled the gardenia scent. "I love the way it smells, like an exotic and mysterious flower."

"Oh, well, if that's all you like about me, maybe you should just cut some off and put it in your pocket, then you wouldn't need me anymore," she teased as she tried to wriggle out of his arms.

Seth pulled her back down and tightened his hold, laughing good naturedly. Then his voice turned serious. "It is definitely not the only thing I love about you. Would you like for me tell you all the things I love about you?"

"No, you don't have to do that", Shannon pleaded as she felt her face flush with embarrassment. She didn't like other people complimenting her. She wasn't used to it and it made her uncomfortable. Seth figured as much but she was going to hear it anyway. She needed to know how truly remarkable she was.

"I love your eyes. I don't believe I have ever seen that shade of blue except in pictures of the Caribbean Sea. I love your freckles, the way they dance across your cheeks and nose....and breasts." He ran his fingers across her pale mounds.

"Please Seth, I love hearing you speak, but I just wish you wouldn't make me out to be some kind of goddess or something. Can't we talk about something else?" she pleaded.

Seth gave her a squeeze, "I'm sorry, but somebody needs to tell you how incredible you are. It's obvious no one has, so the responsibility falls on me, which, by the way, I consider an honor."

Shannon turned around to face him, straddling his lap. "Okay, turn about is fair play, Mister. Let me tell you what I love about you."

Seth pulled her against his chest and nuzzled her neck with his lips.

"I know I'm perfect so you would just be wasting your time, and I can think of better ways to spend our time together," he whispered suggestively.

His breath on her neck made her dizzy as she felt the desire rising inside her. Seth began to rain kisses on her throat, whispering words of love, his hands coming up to cup her perfect breasts, when his cell phone rang. They both jumped as the shrill sound intruded on their warm and cozy cocoon. Shannon frowned at the interruption. Seth growled as he snatched it from the coffee table.

"Yeah, what?" he growled into the phone. "Oh, Hi Irene", his tone immediately changing as he straightened, "No, don't worry, she's fine. She's making a remarkable recovery...looking better every minute". He winked at Shannon, resisting the urge to laugh. Giving him a dirty look, she stuck out her tongue. "Yes, I'm sure that she'll be able to return to work tomorrow. Yes, she's right here. Hold on, I'll put her on the phone." Seth gave Shannon a wicked grin and shrugged as he handed her the phone.

"Hi Irene. Yes, I'm sure I can be back to work by tomorrow. Um, yeah, Seth has treated me well. He's a wonderful doctor." She gave Seth a devilish look. "He has a great bedside manner," she winked and Seth was tempted to tickle her but controlled himself. He still didn't know how they were going to handle this whole situation.

"Yes, in the meantime I'll get plenty of rest, I promise. Okay, I'll see you tomorrow morning bright and early. Thank you so much for calling. Goodbye." Shannon hung up the phone and tossed it on the floor.

She looked at Seth and said, "Well, I suppose that will be the first lie I've told in years."

Seth looked puzzled, "what do you mean, lie?"

"I promised her I would get plenty of rest", she teased as she wriggled around on his lap. Wrapping her arms around his neck, she buried her fingers in his hair. "God, I love your hair. You should be in a shampoo commercial. It's so soft and thick." She drew his lips down to hers and kissed him, luxuriating in the feel of him.

Seth wanted to get lost in her arms but he reluctantly pulled away, giving her a grave look.

Shannon stared into his eyes, "what's the matter?" she asked puzzled by his sudden mood swing.

"What're we gonna do?"

"Bout what?"

"About other people. How're we gonna act in public?"

Shannon looked crushed, "Are you ashamed of me?"

Seth was dumbstruck, "Ashamed of *you*? I would never be ashamed of you. I want to climb to the highest mountain top and shout to the world how I feel about you! I'm more worried of you being ashamed of *me*."

Shannon felt her heart soar at his declaration, "I don't care who knows. Let them talk. How could I ever be ashamed of the man I love? In such a short amount of time I've felt closer to you than anyone I have ever known. You make me happy. All the adventures I've had, I realize now that I was looking for something. Until now I didn't know what that was. Nothing I've experienced compares to this." She began to cry, the tears glistening on her cheeks.

Seth was so moved by her words; he pulled her close and kissed the salty tears from her cheeks. "Oh, my Shannon, You have brought me such joy!" He pulled her away so he could gaze into her eyes. "Open your eyes and look at me." She did as he said.

"So, when you go back to work tomorrow, you need to act like nothing has happened between us. Just treat me like everyone else."

Shannon looked at him, the question he knew she wanted to ask there in her eyes. He raised his hand to stop her from speaking.

"Though I would love to scream into the faces of those jerks that we love each other, I love you too much to have them outcast you because of me. It makes sense." Seth could tell she was about to protest so he cut her off. "Listen, I know and you know, isn't that enough?" He wanted her to understand.

What if a couple of the miners decided to teach him a lesson by hurting Shannon? He didn't think he could survive it. He was certain they wouldn't.

Shannon looked him square in the eye and with all the courage she could muster, she smiled, "Okay....for now".

He decided it was better than nothing. Sighing, he hugged her to him. Shannon loved the feel of his bare chest on her face as her fingers made lazy circles around his nipple. Just one touch and he could feel his passion rising.

"Well, we have one more night before we have to return to reality so I suggest we make the most of it", she said as she raised her head and started kissing his neck.

Seth felt his blood boil as the heat enveloped him. He moaned as she left a fiery trail of kisses on his neck and chest. "I'm all for that!" He scooped her up in his muscular arms. Shannon leaned into him in anticipation of the soft bed where they had made love for the first time. Instead, she was surprised when he laid her on the fur rug in front of the fireplace.

He released her long enough to slip the shirt from her shoulders, his breath catching as he saw how her skin shimmered in the glow of the fire. She was so beautiful! He felt physical pain just by looking at her. He couldn't believe this magical creature loved him. She had to be magical to melt his heart of steel.

As he brought his mouth down on hers for a long passionate kiss, he thanked God for giving him a second chance at love.

CHAPTER 10

Shannon woke, snuggled in the crook of Seth's arm. He had taken one of the skins and covered their bodies during the night. It was a sweet gesture but totally unnecessary. The heat from his body was all the warmth she needed.

The sunlight streamed through the window, falling across Seth's face. Shannon was awed at the beauty of him. *'How did I ever get so lucky?'* She reached up to brush a lock of hair from his face. He opened his eyes and smiling, looked down at her.

"Morning", he said as he tightened his arm, pulling her closer. It never seemed close enough. He felt like having her surgically attached to his side. She was his Eve, a piece of him. "How did you sleep?"

Shannon answered by stretching luxuriously. The movement was like a panther, totally feline. He wondered if he would ever get tired of looking at her. Shannon froze. "Oh my God! What time is it?" Her voice panicky. She scrambled up, naked as the day she was born and looked for the cell phone she had discarded yesterday.

Seth chuckled softly as he watched her. "You might want to look in the cushions of the couch."

She turned, giving him a dirty look. "It's not funny." She started shoving her hands inside the crevices. "It has to be past 5:30. I am already late! Irene is counting on me!" She jerked her hand out of the cushion, holding the cell phone up in triumph. "Hah, found it." The time on the phone said 6:15. "Oh crap!" She ran down the hall to look for the men's shirt and jeans she wore that first day. She knew they would be dirty but she had no choice. She was unable to locate them and started turning the bedroom upside down. Hearing a noise, she looked up to see Seth in the doorway. In his arms were her neatly folded clothes. They looked freshly laundered. Her mouth dropped open. Looking up, she saw him smirk.

"I thought you might need these so I washed and dried them last night after you went to sleep."

Shannon was so touched. Throwing herself into his arms, she kissed him soundly. "Thanks so much. I thought I was going to have to wear dirty clothes. I'm usually more organized, but for some reason it skipped my mind."

Seth held her, unconcerned that the clothes were getting crushed. "If I'd known that's how you show your gratitude, I'd of washed all your clothes. Oh wait, what's this?" He reached behind him and lifted a laundry basket with the rest of her clothes cleaned and neatly folded. "What do I get now?" his eyebrow arching wickedly.

"Later. Right now I have to motor." She grabbed the clothes from him and made a bee line for the bathroom.

"I'll hold you to that," he said to the closed door.

Shannon emerged from the back of the apartment looking fresh as a daisy. Seth already had her breakfast to-go in a paper bag and a Styrofoam cup of coffee in his hand. "You look beautiful."

Shannon grinned from ear to ear and kissed him as she took the cup and bag.

She turned to grab her shoulder bag and stopped. "What's the matter? Seth asked as he tried to keep a straight face. Noting the humor in his voice, she whirled around to face him. "What's so funny? I just remembered I don't have a truck. How am I going to get there?" her voice panicky.

"You may not have a truck," he said as he held up a set of keys, dangling them in front of her face, "but I do".

"But you said that we were supposed to act casual. How would it look with you driving me to work?" She asked, chewing on her bottom lip.

He stepped around her and headed to the door. "I'm letting you borrow my truck. I don't need it. Besides, very few people even know I have it." He could tell she wanted to protest but what choice did she have?

"Come on or you'll be in even more trouble. Time's a wastin." He tapped his finger on the face of his watch for emphasis.

Shannon had no choice but to follow him. He had to be the most considerate person, let alone man, she had ever met.

He waited with the truck running and the drivers' door open, holding his hand out like she was Cinderella and he was the Prince Charming. Shannon looked at the huge truck with its oversized tires and realized she indeed needed a hand up.

Shannon took his hand and let him help her into the giant truck. She looked down at him with a mix between gratitude and trepidation. Seth didn't release her hand as he stepped up easily unto the running board to stand eye to eye with her. Leaning in, he brushed his lips over hers. She didn't want the kiss to end. Her other hand went around his neck and grabbed his hair as she crushed his lips.

He loved that she wasn't afraid to let herself go as he returned her kiss with equal fervor. Shannon pulled away, touching a finger to his lips. "I better go now or I won't go at all."

Seth kissed her finger. "I'll see you in a few minutes." Jumping down, he shut her door. As she looked into the rearview mirror, she saw Seth waving goodbye, and a flood of emotion came over her.

How will I be able to hide my feelings for him? I don't think I'm that good of an actress, but for Seth's sake, I'll do my best.

Shannon parked the truck on the opposite side of her motor home, away from the diner. She didn't want to chance that someone would recognize the truck. This way, it appeared she had been coming from her place. She ran to the front door just as the crowd drove up. "Oh thank God! She exclaimed. Hey Irene! I'm here!" She ran to put on her apron. Irene came from the back of the diner with a brilliant smile on her face.

"Shannon! I'm so glad you're here. I want to catch up on everything that happened but it doesn't look like we can spare the time right now."

"That's okay. We'll talk later. I am sorry about the truck and about being late. No alarm clock at Seth's."

"Why Shannon, I don't know what you're talking about. You're right on time."

"I can't be. The clock says it's 7:05. Aren't I supposed to be here by 5:30?" Shannon asked as she felt herself becoming more and more confused.

"Yes, on weekdays. It's Sunday morning. We open at 7:00 on Sunday for the church crowd."

Shannon sighed with relief. "Oh, that's great! I was so afraid of disappointing you. It's bad enough I was out for two days but I at least wanted to be on time my first day back."

"Well, if you want to split hairs, you are five minutes late, but we'll let it slide this time." She gave Shannon a little wink. "Better get a move on, the holy rollers get here first, and they don't like to be kept waiting." She laughed as she headed to the kitchen.

Shannon was cleaning the tables after the first rush when Seth walked in. He was carrying himself differently. His posture was straighter and if Shannon didn't know better she would swear he was strutting. He didn't look her way as he settled into his usual table. Setting the tub of dirty dishes on the end of the counter, she walked over to his table. He looked up at her, a twinkle in his eye. Shannon really loved the new Seth. He was practically beaming. She struggled to keep a straight face as she reached up, pulling the pencil from her reddish gold curls. Tapping the pad, she looked at him. "What can I get for you?"

Seth's eyes sparkled as he leaned close, "you".

Shannon blushed deep red. "You already have me. You know, I thought I was a bad actress but if you don't wipe that stupid grin off your face, you're going to blow it. I could care less, but you're the one who wanted to put on this little charade so try to look grumpy and depressed…you know, like your usual self."

"I don't know if I can do that. This might not be such a good idea after all. Maybe I should leave." He started to get up but Shannon blocked his way.

"Oh no you don't. You're not leaving me to deal with Irene all by myself. She already suspects something. I can tell by the look in her eyes. She's dying to get me alone so she can drill me.

"She's not the only one." He wiggled his eyebrows.

"Would you be serious? What am I supposed to say?"

"Let me think about it for a minute. In the meantime, why don't you bring me a B.L.T on toast and some coffee?"

Shannon wrote down the order, stuck her tongue out at him, and walked to the pass-through to give Paddy the order. "Hey, Paddy, how're you doing?"

"Fine thanks. Sure am glad you're back. We really missed you."

"Yeah, me too."

Irene came from behind the bar and went to say hi to Seth. Shannon looked over and saw the two of them deep in conversation. Seth nodded, smiled, and then laughed. Irene laughed then looked over at Shannon who was standing there looking stupidly at them. She gawked as Irene waved her over excitedly. "I don't believe this." She cautiously made her way to his table.

Irene squealed in delight as she pulled Shannon into a bear hug. "Ohhh I'm so happy for you! I had a feeling about you two!"

Shannon gave Seth a dirty look as she peered over Irene's shoulder. He just chuckled. "I've got to go tell Paddy! He's gonna flip!" She hurried to the kitchen.

Shannon leaned over and punched Seth on the arm. "I thought we agreed not to tell anyone," she hissed.

"Owe!" Seth rubbed his injured arm and laughed again. "I think its okay to count Irene and Paddy as exceptions, don't you?"

Shannon couldn't stay miffed at him when he was clearly enjoying himself. "Okay, I guess you're right. I'm sure they can keep a secret. They think the world of you, you know."

Seth's face softened as he looked at the older couple who'd stuck by him during the darkest time of his life. It was only appropriate that they be there to share in his happiness as well.

"They are cute, aren't they?" *Maybe that'll be us in thirty years.* The thought jumped into his head. *Whoa. Aren't you getting ahead of yourself?* Even as he thought it, he knew it was what he wanted. He wanted to grow old with her. *I can't allow myself to think about the rest of our lives. It's too soon. I'll only scare her off. We need time to get to know eachother. No, that's not right. I know everything I need to know, good and bad. I just have to pull in the reins, take it slow.*

It looked to Shannon as though Seth had zoned out. "Seth? You okay?" She shook the arm she had previously punched.

"Huh? Yeah! I'm fine." Seth reached out and took her hand in his. "Do you want to come over when you get off?"

Shannon leaned down and gave him a quick peck on the lips. "I thought you'd never ask. I don't know what time I'm getting off though."

"Irene told me that you get off at 2:00 today. The after church crowd is usually gone by then. She usually closes up for the rest of the day around 2:30." Seth gave her a crooked smile.

"Well, aren't you just a well of information," sarcasm clearly in her voice as she put her hands on her hips and glared at him.

Irene called from the kitchen, "order up!" ringing the bell. Shannon jumped and Seth's grin widened as he chuckled, "Go get my food, woman!" He popped her on the butt as she turned away.

Shannon gasped, turning toward him. She tried to look mad but found it impossible. How could she possibly be angry with him when he was being so playful? "You better watch it Mister! You've seen how I deal with rowdy customers!"

"Sorry ma'am. I just couldn't resist that bodacious booty", Seth laughed. Irene looked toward the young couple and punched Paddy in the ribs. "Would ya listen to that? It sure sounds good to hear him laughing again."

Shannon got to the pass-through just in time to hear Irene's last comment. She smiled to herself. She couldn't imagine Seth going so long without laughing. It seemed an integral part of him. Turning toward the wall, she undid a couple of top buttons on her shirt. She knew she was being wicked but she couldn't help it.

She took his order from the counter and delivered it to his table, bending over so Seth could get an eyeful of cleavage. She beamed at him innocently. He took full advantage as he drank in the sight. Running his tongue over his lips, he imagined his mouth buried between her breasts. Realizing too late how it affected him, he looked away, growling. "You are playing with fire".

Shannon gave a little shimmy before she turned and sashayed back to the counter, swinging her hips seductively. She glanced over her shoulder and batted her eyes.

She's going to be the death of me. She thinks she's innocently flirting but if she only knew what she's doing to me. If I got up now, everyone, including her will know. He grabbed his coffee cup with trembling hands.

Thinking that she had gone too far, Shannon avoided going back to Seth's table until she was sure he had ample time to finish his meal. *He actually looked in pain. I didn't mean for that to happen.*

After about ten minutes, she walked back over to his table. "I'm so sorry Seth! I didn't mean to cause you pain!" She chewed on her bottom lip.

Seth grabbed her hand and brought it to his lips. "I think I'll survive, but even if I don't, what a way to go!" They laughed together. All was forgiven.

Shannon couldn't wait for 2:00. Seth had left a few hours ago and she missed him already. Every chance she got, she glanced at the clock. *Stop it. You know the time crawls if you watch the clock.* It read 1:30. There were only a couple of stragglers left. *If only they would leave!* She kept busy refilling the salt and pepper shakers and sweeping the floor.... again.

Irene stole glances at Shannon as she fidgeted. She couldn't keep from snickering to herself. *That girl is as nervous as a cat on a hot tin roof.* Deciding to put Shannon out of her misery, Irene walked over to the stragglers table. Their plates had been cleared and they were just sitting and talking. "'scuse me," she asked politely, "You folks done? I'd really like to close up early cuz I got to get to the drug store before they close. Old man's outta his medicine." They cleared out fast. Irene beamed at Shannon. "Get your keester outta here and go see that man of yours."

Shannon ran over and bear hugged her. "Thanks so much! I appreciate it! See you tomorrow morning."

"Why don't you come in around noon? I think Paddy and I can handle it til then."

"No way! I will be here 5:30, no if ands or buts about it." Shannon's voice was resolute as she untied the apron, hung it back up, and practically flew out the door.

CHAPTER 11

Shannon couldn't wait to be back in Seth's arms again. She ran to her vehicle and grabbed a small suitcase. Scrounging around in her closet, she put together a few outfits. Taking her small jewelry box, she threw it in with the clothes. After packing her shampoo and bath wash, she zipped it up, grabbed it by the handle, and pulled it to her side. She stood in the middle of her cramped bedroom and looked around at what was her home for the last three years. *Maybe Irene will let me park it in the lot next to the highway and put a "For Sale" sign in the window.* Why did she think that? Shannon knew the answer and the revelation rocked her, *because this isn't my home anymore. No matter where I go, my home is where he is.* But did Seth feel as strongly for her? Could he leave the memory of his wife behind and start a new life with her? *He seems to be happy with me, but my enthusiasm might scare him away. I'll just have to slow things down a bit. We need time.* No, that wasn't true. Shannon knew she wanted to be with him. She'd never been surer of anything in her whole life. He was the best thing that ever happened to her. All she wanted was for him to be happy and she was determined to do everything in her power to see that he was.

Tossing the suitcase into the bed of the truck, she drove impatiently, but carefully, down the winding dirt road toward.... home.

Shannon pulled up under the shelter and parked. Running up the stairs, she started to throw open the front door. It wouldn't budge. Jiggling the knob she realized it was locked. *That's strange.* She called out, "Seth! Are you in there!?' and knocked hard on the door. No answer. Puzzled, she looked in the window, but couldn't see any movement. Panic clutched at her. Where had he gone? Had he had second thoughts? All she could see in her imagination was Seth laughing at her for being such a romantic fool. "Stop it!" She growled. "There you go thinking the worst again! He probably went for a walk or something. There's nothing to get crazy about!" Then an even worse thought replaced it and she felt a stab in her heart. *What if something happened to him on the way back? Maybe a bear attacked him and dragged him into the forest.* Her hand flew to her throat. "I've got to find him!" she gasped.

Not caring that she had no weapon to defend herself, Shannon took off down the stairs and ran around the building. There was no sign of him. Standing in the middle of the front yard, she desperately searched for any sign of him at the edge of the trees. Her eyes went to the blue cabin. She strode up the front porch and through the door.

The inside of the cabin was dimly lit so it took a minute for her eyes to adjust. As her vision became cleared she noticed about an inch of dust on everything. *He never comes in here. Not even to clean the place up.*

As she approached the mantle, a set of framed photographs caught her eye. The dust was so thick she had to wipe it off with the sleeve of her shirt. It was a wedding photo. Shannon gaped. Seth looked incredibly handsome in his black suit, a western bolo around his collar. His unscarred face was angelic, making him look a little too perfect, as he grinned from ear to ear. Her eyes pivoted to the right and she got her first look at Naome's. She was stunning! Her jet black hair hung down to her waist. She had on a white Indian inspired wedding dress. The intricate turquoise beading was delicate and beautiful. Her face glowed as she gazed up lovingly at her new husband. She was so petite, the top of her head barely reaching his chest.

The picture was almost more than Shannon could take. They looked so happy together. Her heart broke for him. She couldn't even begin to imagine what it would be like to lose such a special love. She felt extremely uncomfortable and more than that, she felt like an intruder.

As she turned to go, she spotted movement out the back window. Unnecessarily tiptoeing through the living room, she made her way toward the rear of the house. There was Seth, bending over, taking items out of a box. She wanted to run out the back door and throw herself into his arms, but she knew it would be a bad idea. She had a feeling he might be upset should he find out she had invaded Naome' home.

Making an effort to steady her racing heart, she snuck out the front and walked nonchalantly around to the back of the house.

"Hey." She put on her best smile, hoping he couldn't see the guilt she felt inside. She decided she would keep her investigation to herself. She waved as he turned at the sound of her voice.

"Wait a minute! Don't look yet!" He yelled as he jumped to the side trying to obstruct her view.

Shannon stopped in mid-stride, giving him a confused look. "What?"

"Stop! Close your eyes!" He snapped.

With a shrug did as he asked. "Okay."

"Wait, don't peek! Give me a minute! Don't open your eyes!"

"I get it already! I won't open my eyes!" Irritation creeping into her voice. She could hear him rustling around and wondered what he was up to.

"Okay. Now you can look!" She could hear the excitement in his voice.

Opening her eyes, she stared, shocked, her mouth hanging open as tears welled up in her eyes.

She couldn't believe what she was seeing.

Seth stood looking very pleased until he noticed the expression on her face. Running over, he gathered her in his arms. "What's the matter? Please don't cry!" His voice pained.

Shannon sobbed into his shoulder, unable to hold in her emotions. No one had ever done anything so thoughtful for her. Reaching behind his neck, she buried her hands in his luxuriant hair.

Seth stroked her hair, shhh, shhh, it's alright." For some reason he couldn't fathom, it seemed his gift had obviously upset her. He would take the damnable things and make a bonfire.

Wanting to let him know how much it meant to her, she lifted her head, her lips close to his ear, but all she could manage to croak out was "thank you", before breaking down again.

She's thanking me? Then why is she sobbing? He was unsure how to handle this situation. Figuring he wasn't going to get an explanation until she calmed down, he kissed her forehead. The sobbing lessened. He raised her chin with his hand and kissed her eyelids. The sobbing lessened a bit more. His lips curled up. He kissed her cheek. Just sniffles now. His eyes twinkling, he kissed the tip of her nose.

"Mmm." She craned her neck to give him access to her mouth.

Seth bent his head toward her, but paused before his lips touched hers, waiting.

Shannon panted in anticipation of his lips. She waited, one, two, three, four seconds passed, no kiss. Opening her eyes, she met his gaze. He was frowning, but she could see the glint in his smoldering blue eyes. "You don't like your surprise?" He pretended to be wounded.

She would get to the surprise in a minute. All she wanted right now was Seth's mouth. Tightening her hold on his hair, she jerked his mouth down to hers, bruising her lips with the force. She didn't care.

Seth's reaction was powerful. Sliding his hands down to the small of her back, he grabbed her shirt in both fists, crushing her body to his. She was vaguely aware that her feet were no longer on the ground as she melded to his form.

A war was raging in Seth's mind and in his pants. Should he scoop her up and take her upstairs, or make love to her right there on the cold ground?

Shannon made the decision for him. Without breaking the kiss, she reached back and loosened his hold on her. Just as Seth thought this would be the time to scoop her up, she grabbed his elbows and pulled him down on the ground so he ended up with his full weight on top of her. He pulled his mouth away. "Shannon, I'm squishing you." His voice was full of concern.

Her desire about to drive her mad, she pushed him onto his back, rolling on top of him, straddling his hips. "Better?" Her breath ragged, she sat up, crossed her arms over her waist, and jerking her shirt over her head, threw it a few feet away. Not missing a beat she reached behind her and unsnapped her bra, flinging it in the other direction.

Unable to bear not kissing him, she reached down and ripped his shirt open, buttons flying, baring his chest. Dipping her head to his exposed skin, she pressed her lips to the dip in his collar bone.

"I want you now, Seth", her voice a whisper against his neck.

He cupped her face in both hands and pulled her mouth up to his. She attacked, kissing him with all her might. Her tongue thrust into his mouth to capture his tongue, her breathing shallow and ragged.

He glided his hands down her naked back, over her butt and to her thighs. Grabbing her legs, he began rocking her pelvis against his crotch. Her moan had a desperate quality to it. She thought she would go out of her mind. Trembling with the force of her passion, she tore her mouth away from his and reached down to unfasten his jeans.

As much as Seth wanted to take her right there on the cold dry grass, he had to think of her comfort. Raising himself up, he gently held her wrists still. She looked up at him, frustrated. He smiled. "Do you think you could control yourself for two minutes?"

Shannon gave him a pained expression. "But I wanted to thank you for my surprise", she whined.

"Oh you will." He reached around her waist and cradled her against him. Standing up, he swept her into his arms and made his way up the stairs as quickly as he could.

They never made it to the bedroom. Shannon squirmed in his arms, rubbing her naked breasts against his bare chest, driving him to distraction. He had never known a woman with so much passion. Making a snap decision, he plopped her down on the dinette table. Undoing her jeans, his mouth moved from her face and down her neck. Shannon leaned back, giving Seth's lips access to her breasts as she pulled his head down to where she wanted him. He removed her jeans and tossed them aside. Her panties came off with them. Trembling under his gaze, she sat up and finished the task of undoing his pants.

"I'm going to die if you don't make love to me right now!" She pleaded.

He wanted her so badly. Their previous lovemaking sessions had been passionate but short. This time, however, he was determined to savor her. There were so many things he had been dying to do with her.

Capturing her hands, he gently pushed her back down, her hands now pinned to the table above her head.

"Patience my love", as he bent over, capturing her mouth in a breathtaking kiss.

Shannon's head reeled as he moved his mouth down her neck to her breasts, pausing there, torturing her, before he continued down her stomach, running his tongue over her porcelain skin. She groaned in ecstasy, and her breath hitched as he moved lower.

When she felt his mouth move to the golden triangle between her legs, she gasped, trying to wriggle free. What was he doing?

Seth raised his head, his eyes smoldering.

"What's wrong?"

"What are you doing?" her voice panicky.

"I'm loving you. Haven't you done this before?" He was flabbergasted as he realized she had not. "Oh Shannon, I would never hurt you. Just relax, trust me, and I promise you won't be sorry." She looked at him doubtfully, but wanting to trust him, she laid back down. Her eyes focused on a spot in the ceiling as she waited, chewing her bottom lip.

Seth began kissing her inner thigh, careful not to go too fast. He wanted her to relax, but he could feel her muscles tense under his lips. He continued to kiss her thigh as he moved down to her knee. Lifting her leg, he kissed the back of her knee, her calf, her ankle, and her foot. He felt her slowly relax. Moving back up the other leg, he stopped just inches from her center, but this time she didn't tense up. When he felt the time was right, he blew on her soft womanly hairs. She gasped again, but this time her hands reached down, grabbed his hair, and pulled his mouth to her core. What his tongue was doing to her was pure ecstasy!

Shannon never would have believed making love could be so intimate. She had thought that she and Seth had been as close as any two people could get, but this went beyond anything she could imagine. She felt the fire raging at her core, building, spreading to her whole body. She screamed, "Oh God, Seth!" as a wave of pleasure washed over her, leaving her limp and trembling. Though she had experienced her first orgasm with Seth a couple of days ago, this was stronger, more powerful.

As her breathing slowed, becoming more even, Seth moved his mouth up her body, pausing again to pay attention to her breasts. Her breathing quickened as she realized he wasn't finished with her. His tongue moved over each of her nipples. Already sensitive from her orgasm, the sensation was a mixture of pleasure and pain. She groaned, her fingernails raking his back. He moved up and captured her lips once again, crushing them with his urgency.

Wrapping his arm around her, he lifted her a few inches, scooting her butt to the edge of the table. He groaned as he entered her, not taking his eyes off her face. The sensation was pure bliss. This was where she belonged. *I could die happy right now.* She opened her eyes. The expression on his face alone was enough to send her over the edge. Unable to look away, his eyes locked on hers as he thrust harder. Seeing the passion in her eyes, he knew she trusted him. There was no need to hold back. Lifting her legs around his waist, he drove himself in as far as he could go. Shannon cried out as he filled her. She locked her heels together and urged him onward.

"Shannon!" He cried out as he surrendered himself to her completely. Crying out, Shannon joined him as they collapse into each other's arms.

CHAPTER 12

"I feel like you gave me two gifts today", Shannon cooed as she lathered Seth's back. "Where did you learn to do that?"

"Do what?" Seth asked innocently enough, but his eyes were devilish.

"You know", She didn't buy it as she playfully slapped his soapy backside.

"Oh. I'll never tell!" He turned around to face her, his hair hanging in wet curtains around his beautiful face.

"I don't think I will ever get tired of looking at you." Shannon stated.

Seth was touched by her statement. "You're not so bad yourself", he teased as his hands moved over her naked body. She shivered with pleasure at his touch.

"Or that", she whispered as her body began to smolder. "Definitely not that."

He bent his head and gave her a long lazy kiss, making her head swim and her knees weak.

Seth struggled to regain his composure. "If we stay inside all day, you will lose the light."

Shannon sighed, a resigned look on her face. "Alright, I guess you better leave me alone so I can finish up."

Seth gathered her to him and hugged her close as he quickly kissed her on the forehead. "I'll go wrestle up something in the kitchen."

As he turned to leave the stall, she admired his muscular backside. *He looks like a Greek God, and he has an incredible butt.* Suddenly she picked up the pace as she hurried to finish her shower.

They sat across from eachother, eating the sandwiches Seth had prepared. The conversation was easy and light as they enjoyed each other's company.

"As much as I would love to stay inside with you all day, I've got work to do." Seth said as he scooted his chair back and gathered up the dishes. "I do have bills to pay, you know", he teased, winking at her.

"Let me do that. I need to earn my keep around here." She went to take the dishes from his hands.

"You are a guest", his hands holding onto the dishes.

Shannon felt her heart about to drop when he continued, "I will let you help me around here when you move in, which for me, couldn't be soon enough." He peered at her from beneath his long thick lashes.

Her heart skipped. It was what she had prayed for. "Are you asking me to move in with you?" She held her breath.

"I'm sorry. Did I not make myself clear?" He leaned over the table and kissed her. "Then I will make it very clear so there's no misunderstanding. Shannon my love, will you do me the honor of moving in with me?" His voice serious as his eyes bore into hers.

Shannon took the plates from his hands and walked over to the kitchen sink. Without saying a word she started washing the dishes.

Seth watched her back, a grin on his face. Her butt, covered only by an ankle length skirt made of blue cotton jiggled temptingly as she scrubbed. He found himself enjoying the sight immensely. She wore a striped halter top that tied at the small of her back. Her hair was pulled up, secured with a jeweled comb. Unruly wisps had escaped and were resting against her neck. The affect took his breath away.

With her moving in, I won't get any work done. I'll starve! Seth shook his head. He didn't care. Without saying a word she had agreed. She really wanted to be with him.

He walked up and wrapped his arms around her, pulling her against his chest, molding his crotch to her behind. Shannon froze, the sponge hovering above the plate as her breath caught in her throat. She leaned her head back and wisps of hair tickled his nose as he leaned down to press a kiss on the back of her neck.

"Do you want me to drive to your place and pack your things or would you rather do it?" He whispered into her ear.

Shannon blushed as she confessed, "Uh, I kinda already packed a few things. My suitcase is in the back of the truck." She hurried on. "I didn't plan on you asking me to move in but I was sorta hoping you would let me stay a day or two anyway. I just wanted to be prepared."

Seth chuckled in her ear as he continued grinding his hips. Shannon moaned as she felt him harden with desire. "Well, it never hurts to be prepared." His hands gently caressing her breasts as he nibbled on her earlobe.

In her mind, Shannon could see her motor home sitting by the highway with a "For Sale" sign in the window. Was she dreaming? Could this actually be happening to her? She felt like flying.

"I love you." She whispered. The plate dropped into the sink, forgotten as she turned into his arms. Her fingers ran down the length of his face, leaving sudsy trails. She gazed into his blue eyes, unblinking. She wanted to memorize every inch of his face.

Seth looked into her blue green depths. He felt the intensity of her gaze burning his soul. His breath hitched as he struggled to speak. "I love you too." The words sounded inadequate. He wished the English language had a more powerful expression for his feelings.

He would show her how he felt. He kissed her, his lips tender and soft on hers. Shannon waited for the kiss to deepen as they always did, but was surprised when he continued to leisurely taste her lips. He was obviously in no hurry.

Her knees buckled and she fell against him. Seth supported her weight. He wasn't done yet. His tongue flicked back and forth across her lips. Shannon's breath rushed in and out quickly as her passion flared.

She didn't know how much more she could stand. Her mind became blank, unable to think, only feel. She surrendered completely as he continued manipulating her lips.

Finally, just when she thought she would dissolve into a glob of jelly, he opened her mouth with his tongue, deepening the kiss, his lips hard on hers, his arms tightening, crushing their bodies together. All too soon, he pulled away, breaking contact, leaving her lips feeling empty.

"There." He said triumphantly as he stepped back.

Shannon's eyes flew open, confused, and very disappointed as he stepped away. "Wha...?" She gripped the counter behind her to keep from falling. "What does that mean, 'there'?"

"That's the best way I can express how I feel", a big stupid grin on his face. "You're dripping soap on the floor."

"Oh. Sorry," her voice barely above a whisper, her brain trying to function again. She grabbed the wash rag and started wiping up the mess.

"Well, I've got some work to do in here and it tends to get pretty loud." Shannon knew a brush off when she heard one, but she wasn't upset. They had to come back to reality sometime. She looked out the window at the mountains.

"That's okay. I want to check out my present anyway." She wiped her hands, grabbed her jean jacket, and headed toward the door. As she opened it, she faced his back. "Thank you for my surprise. It was very thoughtful." He turned to tell her she was welcomed, but she was gone.

Shannon hurried to the back of the house to get a closer look at what Seth had gotten her. He had set up a large canvas on an easel. A beautiful cabinet with slots for her paints and brushes stood next to the easel. They were filled with everything she needed. Smiling, she ran her hand over the items, thinking of Seth's thoughtfulness. A tear slid down her cheek. Taking a deep breath, she brushed it away and went to work.

Seth tried to concentrate on his work but his mind kept wandering back to a pair of turquoise eyes and golden red hair. Her body, the softness of her pale skin, her nipples, pink rosettes, her womanhood, reddish gold curls as soft as the hair on her head. He inhaled, still able to smell her scent on his skin. *God, she's unbelievable!* He paused, closing his eyes as he remembered the way she melted in his arms when he had kissed her at the sink. Her total surrender ignited his passion and it was all he could do not to take her right there on the counter. It had taken all his will power to back away from her, but if they were ever going to get anything done, they both had to learn a little self-control. Just being away from her this long was driving him to distraction. *'Get a grip!'* Shaking his head, he leaned over his work bench, concentrating, HARD!

Seth looked up as a ray of afternoon sun shone across the floor in front of him. The sun was setting and Shannon had yet to return. Putting down his tools, he went to look for her.

He found her absorbed in her work. Hesitant to interrupt, he watched as her arm moved the brush back and forth across the canvas, her whole body moving with the motion. It was a sight to behold. He ventured closer, trying not to disturb her. His eyes went to the canvas and he sucked in his breath. It was as though she was taking a picture. The realism was remarkable! He saw her look up toward the sky, Shake her head and lower the brush, sighing. Seth looked up into the setting sun. The mountains, which before were multi-colored now stood black, flat. She had run out of time.

Seth stepped up behind her and placed his hand on her shoulder. She didn't jump. He wondered if she knew he was there the whole time. "Shannon, it's beautiful! So realistic!" Her hand came up and covered his hand. "Thanks, but I lost the light." "Can't you find it again tomorrow?" She leaned her back into him. "Yeah, but I get so involved I don't like to stop once I get going."

He whispered wickedly in her ear, "Yeah, I know." She leaned her head back on his chest, exposing her long neck. Lowering his head, he ran his tongue along the length of her thin scar.

"Mmm", she placed her hands on his thighs, sliding them up to his hips and back down. She did this several times, feeling his desire grow.

"Oh God Shannon, you're trying to kill me!" His voice came out coarse and ragged. Sliding his hands around to her front, he cupped her breasts, grinding his pelvis against her apple shaped bottom. He continued raining kisses over her throat. Wanting to feel her bare breasts, he released his hold on her, moving his hands to her back, under her jean jacket and untied the halter top. Shannon's eyes widened, she moaned deep in her throat as she felt his hands kneading her bare breasts, gently pinching her flesh, causing her nipples to stand erect. Her breath caught. "How do you do this to me?" she croaked. His hands pulled her tighter against his chest as he hissed through his teeth, "I was born to do this to you". He confirmed by thrusting himself against her backside.

Shannon could feel her knees give way as the strength left her.

He whirled her around to face him, kissing her passionately, his tongue exploring, probing. Bending, he swept her into his arms. Shannon let out a little squeak of surprise between his teeth. "Unless you want me to make love to you right here…" He made as though to put her down. Not wanting to break contact, she tightened her arms around his neck, ducking her head to his chest. Seth could feel her head moving in a jerking motion as he carried her to the apartment. He wondered what she was doing when he felt his shirt loosen. *She's unbuttoning my shirt… with her teeth!* Her head ducked lower and he felt the next button come loose.

Unable to lower her head any further, she buried her face into his bare chest, raking her teeth over his skin. Seth stumbled on the top step. Her eyes flew open as he dropped her onto the love seat. Standing over her, he looked down into her round eyes. Shannon was caught in his smoldering gaze, his heavy-lidded stare made her suddenly self-conscious. His mouth turned up slightly, giving him a rakish grin. He looked at her as though she were tasty little morsel. Willing her not to look away, Seth very slowly unbuttoned his shirt, removing it one shoulder at a time until it dropped to the floor. She gasped as his hands moved to the top of his jeans.

Shannon leaned forward to help but capturing her hands, he shook his head, a smile playing across his lips, and pushed her back. She suddenly realized he was stripping for her!

Her breathing quickened as she tore her eyes away from his and looked down at his tanned chest. As he unbuttoned his jeans, she admired the rippling of his muscles. Her gaze slid down to his stomach, so tight and smooth. His thumbs hooked onto the waistband of his jeans and her face became suddenly warm. Moving quickly past his crotch, her eyes slid to his well toned thighs…*wait, that's not right,* her face scrunched up as she tried to figure out what she was looking at. Bringing her hand up to her mouth she struggled to stifle the laugh that threatened to escape.

Seth frowned. Did she actually just laugh at him?

Shannon looked up at his expression and she lost it. Crossing her arms over her stomach, she giggled uncontrollably, tears running down her face.

Seth was furious. "What the hell is so funny?!" his voice thundered through the small house.

Still unable to speak, she struggled to regain her composure as she pointed to the front of his jeans.

Looking down he saw the smeared white handprints, stark against the darkness of his jeans and his anger melted. He started chuckling. The chuckling slowly gaining force until it grew into a full blown belly laugh.

Hearing Seth laughing got Shannon's giggle box turned over and she doubled up clutching her sides. Seth collapsed on the couch beside her.

Laying her head on Seth's chest, she wiped her eyes as the giggling finally subsided. He wrapped his arms around her shoulders and hugged her tight. "Thank you Shannon," he whispered, kissing her forehead. "I can't remember the last time I laughed like that. Too bad it ruined the mood, though."

Shannon raised her hand, bringing his chin down so she could meet his eyes. "Who says it ruined the mood?" Turning herself around so she was straddling his lap, she pulled his lips down to hers, inhaling deeply. God, she loved the way he smelled. She leaned back, discarding her jean jacket and halter top, throwing them on the floor then buried her face in his hair. She could've stayed there for hours, but Seth began to undulate under her, his hands moving all over her body at once. Wrapping his arms around her, he lifted her from the couch. Her legs wrapped around his waist as he carried her to the bedroom so they could finish what they started.

CHAPTER 13

Shannon woke to the rumble of thunder and blinding flashes of lightening. Her hand reached out, touching only an empty pillow next to her. Sitting up, she looked at the clock, 9:30 p.m. *Where could he be?* Leaving the bed, she threw on one of Seth's shirts and a pair of socks and went to look for him.

Seth was praying that the storm wouldn't hit before he could move Shannon's art supplies to safety. He managed to gather everything in his arms just as the first fat drop started to fall. He could tell he would never make it without getting drenched so gritting his teeth, he ran up the back steps of the cabin, not stopping until he was inside. It was very dark so he flipped the light switch next to the back door. He gave thanks that he had at least kept up the payments on the electricity. He looked around at the neglected house. An inch of dust was on everything. He walked to the pantry where food was still stored. Many perishables, having perished long ago, canned goods, and jars of baby food were lined up on the organized shelves. He reached to the left and grabbed a dish rag. Walking to the kitchen table where the high chair still stood, he wiped the seat of a chair so he could sit and wait out the storm. He tried not to look too hard at anything. Just seeing the high chair gripped his heart, making it difficult to breathe. He squeezed his eyes shut and thought of Shannon, her beautiful turquoise eyes, beautiful peaches and cream complexion, the way she surrendered to him and her giggling fit, the way she could bring nature to life on canvas. The pain lifted and he smiled. The thought of her gave him courage. He stood up and walked into the living room, looking around as the memories came flooding back. It hurt, but not as much as he thought it would.

Walking over to the mantle he noticed one of the pictures was wiped clean of dust. He didn't have to guess. He knew it had to be Shannon. Lifting the gilded frame, he gazed at Naome's delicate face. He had loved her. She was a beautiful woman and a wonderful wife and mother. For the first time in years, he willed himself to remember the day of the accident.

They were on the way back from their picnic on the mountain. Naome' was earnestly speaking to him, waving her arms about. He was upset and shaking his head vehemently. He concentrated on what they were saying but the only word that broke through was 'Joseph'.

Seth's eyes flew open. That was more than he had been able to remember from the trial. *What could we have been arguing about?* He remembered what the gossips were saying about Joseph and Naome'. *Could it be that they really were having an affair?* "I still won't believe that!" He hissed as he replaced the photo. He did, however, decide that he had some fences to mend with his childhood friend.

His head suddenly aching, Seth walked over to the arm chair next to the front door and sat down, sending clouds of dust all around him. Coughing, he swiped at his dusty shirt and leaned his head back, the sound of the storm lolling him to sleep.

Shannon couldn't find Seth anywhere in the apartment. Grabbing her jean jacket and pulling on her jeans and boots, she ran out into the freezing rain. The thunder was ear splitting as she yelled for Seth but her cries were swallowed up by the roaring of the wind. Not having grabbed a flashlight, she stumbled around in the pitch blackness. The only way she could find her direction was to wait until the lightening illuminated the area around her, giving her a second to look around.

Shannon didn't know where she was. She was shivering and her teeth were chattering. 'Dammit! Why didn't I have the good sense to grab a flashlight?' She chided herself as she held her hands out in front like a blind person as she felt her way through the pitch darkness, yelling for Seth until her throat was hoarse. The freezing rain filled her mouth every time she opened it to call for him. She was becoming more frightened by the minute. Realizing she was probably getting more lost with each step, she found a tree that offered a little shelter and huddled against its trunk. She began to sob, afraid and freezing. She pulled the collar up on her jacket. "Please Seth, please come find me", she prayed as the cold and exhaustion overtook her and she sank into unconsciousness.

Seth came awake with a start. Something was pulling him from the inside. He jumped up, ran out of the cabin and up the stairs of the little apartment. Throwing open the front door he flew to the bedroom, praying he would find her there. Lightening had knocked out the power so Seth flung his arms out onto the bed. "Oh God!" His heart hammered in his chest as he called her name, frantically searching for any sign of her.

Grabbing a flashlight and his heavy weather coat, he went to search the property. Shining the light on the ground, he found the tiny footprints in the mud. Impossibly, it looked like they were leading into the forest. *Why would she risk coming out in the middle of the storm?* But he knew, even as he asked. *She was looking for me!* Seth felt his heart drop. *What if something bad happened to her? What if she's…?* He shook his head furiously. "No! It can't be!" He cried.

He gave thanks that the rain had stopped so he wouldn't lose her trail. Barreling ahead through the thick brush, he trained the flashlight on the ground.

He had gone about a hundred yards when he came to a clearing. Shining the light on the ground ahead of him, he followed the footprints to a giant oak. Seth sighed with relief as he caught sight of her reddish hair. Running to her, he knelt down, gathering her into his arms. Her eyes were closed tight and she was shivering uncontrollably. "Shannon, honey, can you hear me? It's Seth." He cooed to her, trying to get her to stir. He placed his hand on her forehead. She was burning up! Snatching off his jacket, he wrapped it around her body. Her eyelids fluttered. "Seth? Is that you? Where were you? I couldn't find you." She slipped back into unconsciousness and Seth cursed himself. *Why did I leave our bed? If I hadn't lingered in the cabin, I could've been back in her arms before she even knew I had left!* He picked her up, cradling her in his arms and hurried as fast as he could, back to the apartment.

Once inside he stripped her naked. She shivered violently. Grabbing a thick blanket he covered her shivering body, laying her in front of the fire. He had to get her dry and warm before hypothermia set in. Standing up, he removed his clothes and climbed under the blanket with her. He cooed to her as he held her, rubbing her arms and back trying to get the blood pumping through her frozen veins. "Please forgive me love. I'm sorry I left you alone. I was just trying to save your painting before the rain could ruin it." His voice broke as he choked out the words. He continued to whisper to her, stroking her hair and kissing her cheek and head. Her body was so hot it felt like she was burning his skin. He stayed under the blanket with her, taking his just punishment. "If anything happened to you I don't think I could survive it." His words broke with emotion. As he said the words he knew them to be true. She was his life and nothing else mattered. He would be much more careful with her from now on. He would make sure that he kept a watchful eye on her. She had almost died twice since she met him. Was she always this accident prone? Or was he some kind of jinx? Maybe it wasn't safe for her to be around him. After all, he had lost his parents to a freak car accident when he was sixteen, his car goes over a cliff and kills his wife and child, now Shannon has had a car accident and gotten lost in an unseasonable thunder storm. No wonder people stayed away from him. Would it be better for her if he was out of her life? Just the thought made him feel ill. Whether or not he was a jinx, he knew he couldn't go on without her by his side. *Yeah, that's me, a selfish son of a bitch.* He tightened his grip around her, holding on for dear life, until sleep finally overtook him.

CHAPTER 14

Seth was having a wonderful dream. He was naked in a meadow as little butterflies brushed their wings all over his body. He stretched, opening his eyes. *Oh, this is much better than butterflies.* As he looked on in disbelief, Shannon was kneeling over him, brushing her hair up and down his nude body. The sensation was extremely erotic as he felt himself hardening with desire.

Noticing his arousal, she looked up at him through her hair. "Good morning," she purred as she kissed him tenderly.

Seth sat up and touched his lips to her forehead searching for the heat he felt last night. It was gone. *Well, looks like she feels better, thank God!*

Shannon's lips slid down his cheek to his throat. Moving lower, she teased his nipples with her tongue. Burying his hand in her curls, he moaned, savoring the feel of her lips on his naked body.

Moving lower down his stomach, she nipped playfully at his skin. As she slid further down, her tongue snaked out and licked the lower half of his belly. Seth sucked in his breath sharply. No one had ever done what she was about to do. He had only been with one woman and Naome' had been very demure and conservative.

Flipping her hair away from her face, she looked up into his eyes, catching them in her gaze. She smiled a small wicked smile and kept her eyes on his as she took him into her mouth. Seth was mesmerized, unable to look away as she pleased him. As much as he was enjoying this new experience, he didn't think he would be able to hold off much longer. Sitting up, he grabbed her shoulders. Using only his arm muscles, he lifted her unto his lap. Shannon was awed by his strength. She wasn't a small woman but she felt light as a feather in his arms. He entered her in one long thrust. She gasped as she wrapped her legs around his waist. He rocked her in his lap as they gazed into each other's eyes. She cupped his face in her hands as she leaned in for a long passionate kiss. They climaxed together, still kissing, breathing in each other.

Reclining against Seth's back, Shannon sighed with contentment as she gazed into the fire. "I could stay like this all day but I have to get to work. The sun will be up soon and I don't want to disappoint Irene…. again." She added guiltily.

"You haven't disappointed Irene at all. You had an accident! I'm sure she'd cut you some slack. Besides, I don't think you should go to work today. Call in sick. Play hooky with me", he pleaded as he showered the back of her neck with kisses.

Shannon giggled as he tickled her neck. "As much as I would love to, I really need to get to work."

Seth knew she would probably feel obligated to go in. Besides, he had an ulterior motive. He meant to keep a close eye on her and by God that was exactly what he was going to do. If he couldn't be there to do it, then he had to find someone who would. A plan began forming in his mind.

Shannon hummed a song as she took orders, her soft melodic voice drawing curious looks. She had always been friendly to the customers, but today Irene could swear she was beaming. Her mood was so infectious that even the usual grumps were smiling.

"That Seth sure has been good for her", Irene mused as she observed Shannon flitting from one table to the next. She had a sneaky feeling that Seth was probably humming to himself as well, wherever he was. *Where is he, anyway?* She missed him. He had been coming in three times a day for years, the only exception being when he was out of town on business. Yesterday he had missed lunch and dinner. *But it is good to see him so happy,* her eyes misted over. The telephone rang and Irene rushed to answer it. "Last Resort Café, Irene speaking."

"Hey Irene, it's Seth"

"Oh my! Speak of the Devil! I was just thinking about you. How are ya and what did you do to that girl? She must have weights in her shoes to keep her from floating away! I ain't never seen nobody so happy slopping tables!"

Seth chuckled. "She makes me happy. That's something I never thought I could ever be again."

Irene felt her eyes getting misty again. She sniffed loudly.

"I'm glad my happiness means so much to you… Which brings me to the reason I called."

Irene listened, nodding her head, smiling then frowning. Her expression turned serious, "You better not make me sorry I'm doing this. You know how pissed she would be if she knew what you were up to?"

"She's almost died twice since we met. Either she's accident prone or I'm a jinx. I don't know which, but I can't take any chances. If anything happened to her…" he didn't finish the sentence but Irene heard the emotion in his voice.

"Are you trying to tell me you're in love with Shannon?" Irene could only hope. There was a long pause on the other end of the line.

"Yes, I am. I feel a little guilty about admitting it, like saying it somehow trivializes my love for Naome'. Like our love wasn't real. It was, but I realize now that I loved her with the emotions of a young man, worshiping her as an idol and not a real woman. I have no doubt that if she hadn't died that day, we would still be together, happy with our lives.

He struggled to put his feelings into words and Irene's hand stole up to her neck, holding back the tears that threatened to spill down her cheeks. It was extremely rare for him to vocalize his feelings. *This must be so difficult for him.* Her heart went out to him.

"But what I feel for Shannon is, well, stronger, more powerful. It's……"There was another long pause as she waited for Seth to continue. She heard him sigh raggedly, "Shannon is my soul mate".

The flood gates opened as Irene heard Seth declare his love for Shannon. She chanced a peek in her direction, hoping Shannon hadn't noticed the length of time she'd been on the phone. She was busy sweeping the floor, using the broom as a dance partner, twirling around the floor. "Oh Seth honey I'm so happy for you! Are you gonna pop the question?"

Her question rocked Seth. Was he ready to take that step? Would Shannon be willing to spend her life with him after all she'd been through? "Uh, well, I asked her to move in with me and she said yes." *Sort of,* he thought as he remembered her reaction to his invitation.

Irene snorted, "Humph, it ain't the same thing and you know it".

"We've only known eachother for a few days. Don't you think it would be moving kinda fast to ask her to marry me now?" He wanted Irene to argue with him. If she could convince him it wasn't too soon then maybe it would encourage him.

"Hell, boy, Paddy and I met at a USO dance the night before he was to ship off to war, and we got the Captain to marry us the next morning. Been together ever since. Point is, it don't matter. If you were to wait five, ten years, do you think your feelings for her would change?"

She had a point. "But what if she doesn't want to marry me? You don't know what she's been through and I won't betray her trust, but I wouldn't blame her if she ran screaming, jumped in that RV, and disappeared in a cloud of dust. All I know is that I couldn't take it if she left and....I'm scared!"

"Well, I'll do this favor for you, but you better think long and hard about her feelings. If I were you", she turned as she watched Shannon dance across the floor, "I wouldn't sell myself short. You might be pleasantly surprised." Changing the subject, Irene asked Seth, "You comin in this morning? If you are, you'd better hurry up. Breakfast shift is almost over."

"No. I told Shannon I had some things to do today and that I would see her during the dinner shift. Please don't say anything but I've been thinking about calling Joseph."

"What!?" She couldn't believe what she was hearing.

"I've had a lot of time to think things through and I've decided to let the past go. Besides, I miss him." Seth waited for her to put in her two cents. He wasn't disappointed.

"It might be a good idea to let sleeping dogs lie."

Seth loved Irene like a mother but he couldn't understand her aversion to Joseph. She had known both of them almost their whole lives. She'd watched them grow into men. Joseph was a very well respected attorney and extremely well-liked by the towns people. On the other hand, he got into a lot of trouble growing up and the whole town hated him. Shouldn't she feel just the opposite of what she feels? He shook his head. She had always been eccentric, but he accepted her and loved her.

"Well, I know you're busy so I'll let you go. Thanks for doing me this favor. Bye"

Irene hung up the phone, staring at the wall, lost in thought. She wanted to tell him she didn't think it was such a good idea, but he was always so protective of Joseph.

It wasn't anything she could put her finger on, but it just seemed to her that whenever Joseph and Seth were together, bad things happened...to Seth. Since they were children and got into tussles, the punishment was always severe for Seth while Joseph just had to flash his pearly whites and bullshit his way out of trouble. When Joseph went off to college and grad school, Seth's life became almost perfect. He had Naome' and after graduating from medical school, a great internship at the hospital in Sanctuary. Joseph hadn't been back six months before the accident happened. It was like Joseph was the harbinger of doom for Seth.

You're just being a silly old woman, but she couldn't shake the feeling as a shiver ran up her spine. She knew better than to express her concerns to Seth. As far as that boy was concerned, Joseph hung the moon. The only reason he decked him outside that courthouse was because he wanted to go to jail, punishment for not being able to keep his family safe, but Joseph got him acquitted. There was something else that bothered Irene about Joseph. She didn't like the way he used to act around Naome', always seeming to wedge himself in between the two love birds. Seth never seemed to notice but she could tell Naome' felt uncomfortable. Most people thought her behavior around Joseph was a result of the guilt she felt for sleeping with him behind Seth's back, but Irene never bought it. She saw how Naome' looked at Seth when she thought no one was looking. There was nothing in her eyes but pure unadulterated love. If Joseph had romantic feelings for Naome', it was strictly one-sighted.

And there was one other thing that Irene had kept from Seth. She had already been keeping a sharp eye out because about the time Shannon was hired, Joseph had started showing up at the café. At first she was apprehensive, watching Joseph as he tried to engage Shannon in small talk. She was polite but never encouraging. Once Irene had decided that Shannon was able to handle it herself, she relaxed a little. She never made formal introductions for reasons she still didn't quite understand. She had a feeling that Joseph wasn't there for the peach pie. He was never there at the same time Seth was either. He always seemed to show up a few minutes after he'd left. Irene figured that with their history, it was understandable. But he would linger long after he was finished, watching Shannon wait on other customers and calling her back repeatedly for refills. Irene felt as if someone walked over her grave. The hairs on the back of her neck stood up.

Now with Joseph back in Seth's life, how would it affect his budding relationship with Shannon? She had a really bad feeling about it, but all she could do was wait and see what happened.

She decided she would indeed keep a sharp eye on Shannon, and not just for Seth.

CHAPTER 15

Seth drove into town, parking next to the small red brick building where "Ravenclaw Law Firm" was located. He walked past the shiny brass plaque displaying his friend's business name and into a small reception area. A busty blonde was sitting behind the desk, filing her nails. Her appearance was that of someone who kept the local beauty shops in business. As the chime announced his arrival, she raised her heavily made-up eyes, seeming at first irritated at being interrupted, but as her eyes took in the tall beautiful Indian with electric blue eyes she arched her painted on eyebrows and the corners of her blood red lipstick lips curved up into a seductive smile.

"Hi there." She leaned forward giving him a view of her generous store bought bosom. Seth's eyes didn't waver from her face.

"Hi, I was wondering if Joseph Ravenclaw was in. I don't have an appointment but could you tell him that Seth Proudfoot is waiting to see him?"

"Sure sweetie, just a minute. She motioned to the overstuffed couch. "Why don't you take a load off?"

"Thank you." Seth went over to the couch but didn't sit.

The woman pushed an intercom button. "Excuse me Jo Jo, but there's a gentleman hear to see you."

Over the speaker Seth could hear the irritation in Joseph's voice. He knew he hated to be called Jo Jo. "Well, who is it Millie?"

"Oh, right, wait, what was your name again sweetie?" She asked Seth. He had a funny feeling Joseph hadn't hired her for her brains, unless they were stuffed inside her bra.

The voice sounded really ticked now, "Never mind, I'm coming out!"

A door in the back swung open and Joseph stalked into the room, coming to a screeching halt when he saw Seth standing there. Something flashed across Joseph's face and just as quickly it was gone. Thinking it must've been a trick of the light, he casually dismissed it. As Joseph walked up, Seth half expected a punch in the face, but was shocked when he grabbed his hand and pulled him into a hug.

"Holy Shit man, what are you doing here? Who cares? It sure is good to see your ugly mug." He threw a glance at Millie over his shoulder as he grabbed his jacket off the peg. "Come on, let's catch up." He wrapped his arm around Seth's shoulder and they walked outside.

Some of the townspeople must have noticed when Seth drove up earlier because as soon as their boots hit the sidewalk, they noticed a crowd had gathered across the street.

"Man, news travels fast! I bet they're here for the sequel." Joseph laughed.

"Sequel?" Seth asked, his brows knitting together.

"Sure, the one where I get to punch you out!"

"Oh. Hey man, I wouldn't blame you if you did but does it have to be in the middle of the street like some old spaghetti western?"

Joseph slapped Seth heartily on the back. "Nah, I'm just glad you're back! Let's go celebrate!" Draping his arm back around Seth's shoulder, he guided him to the local bar.

When the pair entered you could've heard a pin drop. It struck Joseph and Seth as humorous and they chuckled as they sidled up to the bar.

"Give me and my long lost best friend a couple of cold beers, Pete!" Joseph slammed some bills on the bar. Pete, walked over, took the money, and shoved it in the cash register.

"So tell me Seth, what have you been up to these days besides carving those funny little animals?"

"Well, I don't know if you've been told but I make furniture now." Seth downplayed his successful business. He wanted his friend to be proud of him but he didn't like to boast.

"You make furniture, huh? Way I hear tell it, you make very expensive, custom furniture." Joseph corrected him, grinning that devilish grin.

Seth looked down at his beer. "Yeah." He cleared his throat, "I also work when they need me at the clinic on the Rez, but mostly I just make furniture". Wanting to shift the attention away from himself, Seth asked, "So how's business? You dating that receptionist or what?"

"I'm never going to make it rich being an attorney in this town, but I make enough from preparing documents, wills, divorce papers, you know, shit like that. And to answer your question, uhhhh, noooo, I'm not dating Millie." He leaned in close to Seth's ear and whispered, "We have an arrangement. Either one of us gets lonely or bored, well…., we make eachother not bored, get my meaning?"

Seth never approved of Joseph's casual relationships. He always thought he should find some nice girl who would calm his wild streak, but Joseph never seemed interested in anyone for more than a couple of weeks. Seth used to tease him saying he had "FADD" short for "Female Attention Deficit Disorder".

Joseph grabbed his beer, drained it dry, and slammed it on the bar. The sound made Seth jump. Waving the bartender over for a refill, he turned a serious face to Seth. "What made you want to see me after all this time?"

Seth took a deep breath. It was the question he had been dreading. Closing his eyes, he exhaled. "I've met someone who has changed my life."

"Did you find Jesus?" Clapping him on the back again, laughing.

Ignoring his question, Seth continued, "She's made me realize that bad things happen but you can't dwell in the past. Life's too short. I knew that before I could move on, I had to try to make things right with you. I've missed you, friend." He glanced over at Joseph who was wearing a strange look he hadn't seen before. He seemed to tense for a second then relax.

That was the most Joseph had ever heard him say at once.

"Wow, where did you meet this angel of mercy?"

"At the diner…. She works there".

Joseph kept his voice neutral, revealing no emotion. He had heard of the beautiful waitress at the "Last Resort" and had been down there to see for himself. Her name was Shannon but she had pretty much ignored his attempts at small talk. Though she was efficient and friendly enough, she seemed to always have a far away, dreamy look in her unusual green colored eyes. He often wondered what she was thinking about....Now he knew.

He was in his office thinking of ways to get her to notice him when Seth had shown up. He decided it might be best to play it cool.

"Well I think that's just dandy! You deserve a break after what you've been through. You still livin' in the same place? Must be hard to look around everyday and be reminded of Naome', huh?"

"Well, actually, I don't stay in the cabin. I fixed up the workshop and now it doubles as an apartment. It's cozy and Shannon seems to like it. Oh, I didn't tell you her name yet. Yeah, it's Shannon. Shannon Mallory. She's from New Orleans. She's traveling across country in a motor home." He added, "Oh, and she paints."

"Damn boy, I don't remember you being such a chatterbox," Joseph said jovially.

"Yeah, well, I feel different. I can't explain it. It happened so fast." He took a big gulp of beer, confessing his feelings in a guy way.

"Well, I've heard there was some cutie working at the diner. I was thinking about going over there and having a look for myself." He looked sideways at Seth.

"She is beautiful, it's true, but it's one tenth of who Shannon is. She's incredible!" Oh how he missed her right now.

"Well, what's she doing driving across country anyway? Strikes me as kind of a hippie, what with the way she dresses in those flowy skirts, from what I've been told." He added hastily. "Okay, so when do I get to meet this little hippie anyway?"

"I'm planning a trip out of town. Just some boring legal stuff. I'll be gone a few days at the most. How about you come over for dinner at our place Friday night? I'll cook steaks on the grill."

"This Shannon doesn't cook?"

"I don't know." Seth realized there were a lot of things he didn't know about Shannon Mallory, but he was going to find out, that is, if they could ever stop jumping each other's bones for five minutes.

"Do you want me to bring a date?"

"Okay, I guess that'd be alright. Shannon hasn't met any women here her own age. I'm sure she would like it. Oh, hey, look at the time.

I have to get over to the diner for lunch. Thanks for the beer. I'll see you Friday, say 7:00?"

"Sounds great, can't wait." Shaking hands they quickly gave each other a manly hug. Seth walked out, leaving Joseph at the bar.

Seth felt elated as he walked down the street toward his truck. Passing a little novelty jewelry store window, he stopped as a bracelet caught his eye. Small and delicate, it was made of white gold links, set with small turquoise stones. The stones were the exact color of Shannon's eyes. He went inside and had them gift-wrap it. He couldn't wait to put it on her wrist.

CHAPTER 16

Shannon's shift was over and she was hanging up her apron when she remembered that Seth had dropped her off this morning which meant she didn't have a way home. An idea came to her and she walked into the kitchen.

"Hey Paddy, do you think that I could have some of those empty boxes out back?"

"Sure, kid. Do you want me to help you carry them?"

"You know, that would be great! Thanks!" She thought about him lugging boxes all the way across the large parking lot. "Wait, Give me five minutes then meet me in the back." Shannon rushed to her RV and pulled into the back alley behind the diner where Paddy waited.

"Smart move Shannon, I told Irene you were more than just a pretty face", he teased.

Shannon laughed as she and Paddy started loaded the boxes into the motor home.

"So Irene tells me you're moving in with Seth. That why you need the boxes?"

"Yeah", she paused briefly, "Actually, I was thinking of selling the "Titanic". Do you know of anyone who might be interested?" Shannon hoped so. She didn't want to go through the process of showing it to umpteen dozen perspective buyers.

"You're selling it?" He paused to scratch his chin. "You know, it's funny but Irene and I was talking about gettin one of those for when we retire. We ain't getting any younger, you know". His voice was casual but Shannon picked up a strange undertone, "so how much you think of gettin for it?"

Shannon couldn't believe her good luck. "I'm sure we can come to an arrangement that will be beneficial for everyone," she said with a little wink. Hell, for Paddy and Irene she'd give it away, but she knew Paddy wouldn't accept charity.

Paddy gave her a sidelong glance. "You know, I been meanin to talk to you alone about somethin. You know I love my wife and I'd do anythin for her…"

Shannon stopped what she was doing and looked at him. "What is it Paddy?"

"Well the thing is, I'm getting old and I'm not in the best shape, as you can see", he slapped his hand on his ample belly. "I've been tryin to talk Irene into retirin. I can tell she wants to, but she won't hear of it unless we can find someone she trusts to buy the diner. That place has been our home for thirty years and she's afraid if she sells it to some conglomerate, they'll level the place two seconds after the papers are signed." He looked down and started wringing his hands.

Shannon didn't know where he was going with this. It was the most she had ever heard him say. He didn't speak unless it was important and she could tell what he had to say was vital. She waited patiently for him to finish.

"I know you don't keep your tips. I've seen you sneak them back into the cash drawer when you think no ones lookin. I would bet my eye teeth that you're gonna tear up your paycheck. The thing is, I don't think you need the money. I just think you do it because you enjoy it." He stopped wringing his hands and ran them through his nonexistent hair. "I got this idea that you don't need to work at all. That maybe you're some kinda lottery winner or the rebellious daughter of a millionaire or something. How you got it ain't none of my business, but I was thinkin that maybe you might want to buy the place, take it off our hands. I can tell you love it here and now that you're gonna be stayin…"He started shuffling his feet. Shannon could tell this was extremely hard for him. There had to be something more to it than just wanting to retire. She laid her hand on his arm.

"Paddy, I know there's something you're not telling me, but I won't pressure you. I love it here, you're right. You're also right about the money. I don't have to work. You're very astute. Nobody has ever even come close. They think I'm some hippie artist living on a wing and a prayer, taking odd jobs wherever I go." Shannon chose her next words very carefully. "Alright, I'll buy the diner, but there are a few conditions."

Paddy's mouth dropped open. He just nodded his head, unable to speak from the lump in his throat.

"These are my conditions and they are non-negotiable", her voice all business. "First, I will buy the diner at the fair market value plus twenty percent. Second, I will only buy the diner as long as you accept the RV as a gift." She gave him a stern look when he jerked his head up to protest. "And third, no matter when it is, you and Irene have to attend my wedding." She offered her hand to seal the deal.

Paddy looked at her outstretched hand for about three seconds before his face broke into a wide grin. He grabbed her hand, pumping it vigorously. "Deal, I'll have to talk to Irene but I'm sure she'll be ecstatic."

"Good. I'll have the necessary papers drawn up by the local attorney. Hey, thanks for helping me with the boxes Paddy." Shannon reached up and hugged him tight.

Paddy could see why Seth loved this woman. She was completely selfless. He knew her price was fair but not extravagant, allowing him to keep his pride in tact.

"Sure, maybe next time I'll get a free boat", he chuckled and they laughed together, comfortable in each other's company.

Shannon was wrapping some newspaper around a coffee cup when she paused, "Paddy, do you...would you...?" She couldn't finish. Paddy put his arm around her shoulder, "What is it?"

Shannon looked at the ground and whispered, "Would you consider giving me away?" It came out in a rush. "I don't have any family to speak of and I've come to think of you and Irene like family. You don't have to, I just thought maybe..." Paddy hugged her to him.

"Of course, it would be an honor", he grinned. His brows knitted together and he grimaced, "Do I have to wear a tux?"

"No. God no! You wear whatever you want. If I have anything to do with it, it'll be a casual affair, what with it being the second marriage for Seth and me."

"Oh, you've been married before?" he asked innocently.

Shannon realized too late, her slip, but as she stood there looking at this man who was so like the father she had always wanted and somehow she knew she could confide in him and without fear of judgment.

"It's a long story. Tell you what; I'll talk while you help me pack, okay?"

Without a word, Paddy reached into the cabinet, taking plates and wrapping them in newspaper while he listened.

CHAPTER 17

Seth pulled up at the diner, parking his truck, his mood light. On the way to see Shannon he thought about everything that had happened in the last few days. It was amazing. There he was, sleepwalking through life, then out of the blue, in walks Shannon, his alarm clock. She had woken him up and now he felt like never sleeping again. He couldn't wait to get up in the morning, each day bringing something new and exciting. His heart felt ready to burst. He looked at the little gift-wrapped box that contained the bracelet, suddenly wishing it was an engagement ring. God, he wished he knew how Shannon felt. He knew she loved him, but was it enough to get her to stay?

He jumped out of the truck and entered the diner. Seeing Irene behind the counter preparing for the lunch crowd, he walked over to the bar. "Hey Irene! How's everything?" unable to stop his eyes from scanning the room for Shannon.

"Hey, Seth! Yeah, looks like my help went M.I.A. on me."

Seth frowned, "Paddy and Shannon aren't here?" his voice even but Irene could tell he was fighting the panic that threatened to surface. She decided to let him off the hook, feeling a little guilty about her deception.

"Don't go gettin all crazy on me. I's just pullin your leg. They're out back. Paddy's helpin Shannon pack." She gave Seth a sly look.

"Oh, Sorry I jumped to conclusions, but you of all people should know that she's a danger magnet and I have a really active imagination, so how bout not doing that again?" He reprimanded her affectionately.

"Do you think it would be alright if I went back there?" He imagined that with Paddy, it was mostly a one-sided conversation. Maybe Shannon needed rescuing.

"I'm sure it would be okay. I'd go back there myself but I'm a little busy right now." Even as the last words were coming out of her mouth, Seth had disappeared into the kitchen. She shook her head, smiling. "That boy has really got it bad." She went back to filling the napkin holders.

Seth was just about to knock on the door of the RV when he heard Shannon's lilting voice from inside. "I love him so much it scares me." Seth's heart swelled in his chest. He heard Paddy respond but couldn't make out the words; Shannon spoke, "How do you think he will react to the news?" Paddy replied, Seth strained to hear him but his voice was muffled. Shannon spoke, "You think? I think it might be better if I waited awhile to tell him. I hope he won't be upset. It will definitely affect us both."

Seth was confused and a little frightened. *Serves me right for eavesdropping.* Not wanting to get caught with his ear to the door, he started to leave when suddenly the door swung open and Paddy came out, eyes wide as he discovered Seth outside the RV. "Humph Hum," he cleared his throat. "Hi ya Seth, Shannon's inside." He stepped past him and went back inside the diner.

Hearing Seth's name, Shannon bounced to the doorway and flung herself through the air into Seth's arms. "I missed you so much! How did it go with Joseph?" Before Seth could answer she kissed him soundly. He melted at her touch. She had her legs wrapped around him as she buried her hands in his silky hair. He returned her kiss with fervor. After a moment he set her feet on the ground, her arms still wrapped around his neck. Eyes half-lidded, she looked up at him adoringly. She smiled a private half-smile, "What time is it?" Seth raised his hand, looking at his watch over the top of her head. "It's 10:50, why?"

She gave a little pout, "Ohhh shoot! That's not enough time."

Seth chuckled as understanding dawned on him. "Do you ever think about anything else?"

"Not lately," she said as her arms came from behind his neck, stealing down to cup his butt cheeks. "Does it bother you?" she asked innocently but her eyes were devilish.

He grinned down at her beautiful round eyes. "It's just one of those things I love about you," he whispered in her ear as he pulled her close for a kiss that left her breathless.

"Are you bringing all that stuff? Why don't you just drive it to my place? That way, everything can stay where it is."

Shannon didn't know how she was going to break the news to him. She thought a minute, "A lot has happened since this morning. I want to tell you everything but it will have to be when I get off work." Lowering her eyes she whispered, "It's… complicated".

Seth raised her chin so he could see her eyes, but she kept them hidden as her head tilted up. "Look at me, baby." Her breath caught as his steel blue eyes gazed down at her, piercing her with their intensity. "Tell me what's on your mind. Good or bad, I need to know." Taking a couple of steps back, he crossed his arms over his chest.

Shannon was awed by him. He looked so yummy in his brown polo shirt, light blue denim jeans and ostrich skin boots. Her hands itched to reach out and touch his gorgeous face. She struggled with herself as to how to break the news. He was motionless as he waited for her to explain, his expression now unreadable.

She decided it would be best to just come clean and let the chips fall where they may. "I'm giving the RV to Paddy and Irene and I'm buying the diner," the words rushed out so fast they almost ran together. She sucked in her breath sharply, staring into his eyes, looking for a sign. What was he thinking? Why won't he say something, anything? The suspense was excruciating as she chewed on her bottom lip, waiting for a reaction.

Seth couldn't believe what he had just heard. *Did she say that she was giving up the RV and buying the diner? No, I heard wrong. There's no way my life could get more perfect.* He stepped forward, grabbed Shannon by the shoulders, and held her at arms length. "Say that again…but slowly this time."

Shannon took a shaky breath and repeated what she had said.

Oh God, he's in shock. Here it is, I drop into his life out of the blue and turn his world upside down. I don't have any idea what his level of commitment is. Does he even want to settle down again? He says he loves me but how will he feel in a year or two or even ten? I knew it was too quick, too soon. I'm forcing him to move too fast and he's going to baulk. It would definitely make for some extremely awkward moments with him coming into the diner everyday, or even worse, if he stopped coming in altogether. Her heart ached at the thought of not seeing him everyday. She wondered if she hadn't made a horrible mistake. *If he wants to keep things the way they are now, I would agree to it. I would do or be anything he wanted.*

Then she saw it, relief on his face. He pulled her into his arms and she nestled her head against his chest.

"You're staying?" his voice barely above a whisper, but she could hear the emotion in his voice.

"If you want me to", her answer muffled by his chest.

Seth tightened his arms around her, suddenly lifting her feet off the ground and swinging her around in a circle. She let out a little yip as her breath whooshed out in surprise. Quickly recovering, she leaned her head back, laughing joyfully.

"You're staying you're staying!" he chanted as he swung her around.

Her feet finally settled on the ground and his arms encircled her once more as he bent his head, pressing his lips to hers in a sweet tender kiss that made her dizzier than being twirled around.

"I have something for you", Reaching into his pocket, he held out the little rectangular box. "It reminded me of you."

Shannon took the gift, her eyes misting over. "You make me so happy!" She ripped off the wrapping impatiently but paused before lifting the lid. Looking up into his beautiful face adoringly, she whispered, I love you, as she opened the box. It was perfect. "I love it! Will you help me put it on?" She was almost jumping up and down with excitement.

"It might be difficult with you acting like a jumping bean", he laughed as he fastened the bracelet on her slender wrist.

She held it up, watching it twinkle as it caught the sunlight. "It's so beautiful. It's the finest piece of jewelry I've ever owned! Thank you. I'll treasure it always."

Seth doubted that it was the finest. He had seen the jewelry she had crammed into the black box he had stumbled across that first night. His was nothing compared to their extravagance. "If you react like this to all your presents, you are going to be one spoiled woman, as he pulled her back into his arms, hugging her close.

"I'll give you a proper 'thank you' tonight," she whispered as her hand slid down between their bodies, cupping the front of his jeans, smiling devilishly as she felt his erection growing.

"I'm going to hold you to that", he sighed, kissing her on the forehead and reluctantly pulling away. "You need to get to work, little girl," as he turned her toward the door and smacked her on the butt.

"Alright. Oh, by the way, don't say anything to Irene about me buying the diner. Paddy hasn't had a chance to talk to her about it yet." And then she was through the door, leaving him standing there as what she said sank in. *She's buying the diner.* It just didn't get any better than this.

Shannon went through the rest of the day in a dreamy state of euphoria. Smiling and responding at the appropriate times, but all she wanted was to get home to be with Seth. She showed Irene and Paddy the bracelet and they commented on how it matched her eyes.

After the lunch shift was over, Shannon went back to packing up her things. She was taking the pictures of her travels off the wall and wrapping them up when Irene knocked on the open door. "Mind if I come in?"

Shannon wondered if Paddy had talked to her. "Sure, come on in", she called.

Irene walked up into the RV and whistled through her teeth, "Wow, this is really nice. Look how homey you've made it." She ran her hand over the padded breakfast bench. "You know, Paddy and I've been talkin bout gettin us one of these but it'd set us back a pretty penny. Maybe we'll get one if and when we hang up our aprons. I worry that Paddy might be workin too hard. He seems to be gettin tired easier these days." She spoke as though she were speaking to herself. "Why're you packin everything up? Why not just drive the whole thing to Seth's?"

Shannon froze, should she tell her? *Oh Paddy, why couldn't you have already talked to her about all this?* She didn't know how to answer and wasn't sure how to stall. As she struggled for an answer, Paddy called from the open door, "Hey Renie, you in there?" Shannon breathed a sigh of relief. "Thank you, Paddy!" she mouthed silently.

"Hey Paddy! Yeah, we're just chewin the fat", Irene leaned up to give him a kiss on the cheek as he entered, his girth taking up most of the cramped little space.

"Renie, honey, there's somethin I need to tell you. I think you'll be happy about it", he looked at her as she raised one dark red eyebrow.

"Paddy, what's goin on? What have you got up your sleeve?" She meant to step away from him, but her backside hit the breakfast table. She crossed her arms and waited.

Shannon thought it was funny how petite little Irene could make a giant like Paddy look like a scolded little boy as he tucked his head down and shuffled his feet. "I know I shoulda discussed it with you before I did anythin, but, well…"

"I'm buying the diner", Shannon spoke up, rescuing Paddy from further humiliation.

Irene's mouth dropped open as she turned that accusatory glare on Shannon. "What have you two been hatching in here? What do you mean you're buying the diner? You're a waitress! How can you afford it?" asking multiple questions at once was a characteristic unique to Irene. Shannon and Paddy waited for her to finish.

"Yes, I am. Paddy and I had a talk earlier and it seems to be the solution to your problem. Besides, I love this place and I would never bulldoze it for a profit." Shannon took a deep breath and continued, "Part of the deal is that you get the RV. I won't need it anymore. Consider it a retirement gift."

"Where'd you get the money? Does Seth know of your plans?"

"I won the lottery", Shannon looked sideways at Paddy.

"Then why do you work at the diner? Why do you work at all? Why ain't you travelin around in a limousine, staying at five star hotels?"

"I like to travel light and I enjoy working. It keeps me grounded", her voice casual. "So, what do you think? You ready to hand over the reins?"

Irene hugged Paddy, tears flowing down her cheeks, "Oh Paddy, we'll be able to see all the sights we've been talkin about all these years. We can go see the kids and visit with our grandbabies!" She looked over at Shannon, "When are we doin this?"

"I have to contact an attorney in town to draw up the paperwork. I was thinking of using Seth's friend, Joseph Ravenclaw. I hear he's the best around these parts. Seth went into town this morning to bury the hatchet so I think he'd be okay with it." Shannon was already making the plans in her head.

"Shannon, there's somethin I need to tell you," Irene hesitated, not knowing how to continue. "You've sorta already met Joseph," she said softly.

"I have?" Shannon racked her brain but couldn't recall being introduced to Seth's longtime best friend.

"I never introduced you but he comes in here a lot. You've waited on him many times." She looked pointedly at Shannon, willing her to remember.

"I'm sorry Irene, but I guess my mind has been preoccupied", her face flushed pink. That was an understatement.

"Well, he has tried to strike up a conversation with you several times but you never gave him the time of day," Irene smiled when she thought back on how his best efforts were completely lost on Shannon. He had tried everything in his "pick up" arsenal. He flashed his pearly whites, showed his wit, and even used his position in the town to attract her attention but it was futile.

"I'm sorry Irene, but I don't remember him. Can you give me a description? Maybe that will jog my brain."

"Well, he's a handsome boy, full blooded, has short dark hair and brown eyes. Oh, and his appearance is very neat, wears fancy name brand clothes." Irene couldn't think of a better way to describe Joseph. Surely love wasn't that blind that she didn't notice the most eligible bachelor in Sanctuary?

"Wait, he was in yesterday, wasn't he? I seem to remember he had the turkey club, hold the mayo, right?"

"That's right," Irene wondered if she should warn Shannon. *Warn her about what? That you've got a gut feeling somethin's "wrong" about him? Your suspicions are unwarranted. It could just be your overactive imagination. You better be careful what you say. If Seth learns that you were saying disparaging remarks about Joseph, he might get very upset.'* She shivered at the prospect of raising Seth's ire.

"Well, if he comes in for the dinner shift, I'll be sure and introduce myself properly. Since Seth has made amends with him, I should make an effort to get to know him."

Irene wanted to say something. She didn't think Shannon should make any kind of effort where Joseph was concerned except maybe to avoid him. She sighed heavily. "Yeah, sure," she conceded, but she would definitely be watching.

By the time dinner shift rolled around, Shannon had everything packed. The boxes were piled up, almost touching the ceiling in the small space of the RV.

As she hurried to ready the diner for the dinner crowd, she found she was excited at the prospect of officially meeting Seth's childhood friend. As she busied herself with refilling the salt and pepper shakers, she mentally counted the minutes until Seth would arrive. *Surely, now that they were buddies again, they wouldn't mind being here at the same time?* She imagined Seth sitting at his booth with Joseph sitting opposite, joking and laughing and telling tall tales like boys loved to do. She smiled just thinking about it when the bell tinkled as the first customer entered. Before she could turn around, arms encircled her from behind.

"Hey good lookin. Whatcha got cookin?" Seth whispered in her ear as he hugged her against him. As he touched his lips to her neck, shivers ran down her spine, and her knees grew week.

"Michael, is that you?" She moaned as her head leaned back against his face.

"Who the Hell is Michael?" Seth released her, jerking away, his voice furious.

Shannon turned around slowly and Seth caught the devilish grin on her face. He relaxed, as he raised his brow, giving her a reprimanding look. "I can't believe I fell for that. You are an evil woman." He refused to make a move towards her.

Shannon closed the distance between them and wrapped her arms around his neck, forcing his head down so she could kiss him properly. "I can't believe that you are still jealous. Don't you know there has never been, nor will there ever be, anyone else for me? You have got to know that by now." She looked into his face, searching his eyes for confirmation.

Seth looked over the top of her head, "It makes me crazy to think that there might be somebody out there who would be better for you. You know that just by loving me, you have alienated yourself from just about the whole town. Can you really live with that?"

Shannon heard the bell again and wanting to prove to him that she could live with it, she grabbed his hair in both hands and crushed his mouth with her lips in a long passionate kiss. She could hear the gasps from behind them but she refused to stop She pressed her body tight against his, kissing him with everything she had.

Seth heard the shocked gasps and tried to pull away, to save Shannon the embarrassment but she refused to let him go. He realized what she was doing for him and it warmed his heart. *She really doesn't care what people think.* His hand pressed against the small of her back, crushing her body tightly to his.

She pulled away slowly and looked up into his eyes, "Yes, I can live with it."

Seth grinned down at her, loving her even more than before. Suddenly applause broke out. Seth and Shannon looked over at the smiling faces of about ten people. One guy hollered, "Okay, if the show is over, we'd like to eat sometime tonight." They all laughed as Seth turned and headed to his booth.

"Okay, I'll be right over", sing-songing as she floated over to their tables.

After Seth had eaten and finished his second cup of coffee, he went up to Shannon who was standing behind the bar. "I'll see you when your shift is over. I love you." There was an audible intake of air as the people who were within earshot heard his declaration. "Okay, I'll see you soon. I love you too", as she leaned over the counter and pecked him on the lips. The people who had reacted shocked before, were practically livid now. They gave both Shannon and Seth dirty looks, turned to each other, and said, "Well, I can't believe it. Guess she doesn't mind getting into bed with a murderer. She'll probably be next. Maybe we should start looking for another place to eat. This place seems suddenly dirty." The venomous words wounded Seth. He flinched, his hands balling into fists at his side.

"Excuse me?" Shannon hissed. "You mindlessly listen to the gossip like a pack of sheep! You wouldn't be saying those things if you even bothered to get to know him! He is the kindest, sweetest, most thoughtful man I have ever met and if you believe all that crap that's been said about him, then maybe you should find somewhere else to eat. I don't want you spreading lies about the man I love in my establishment! Oh, one more thing. Don't worry about the bill. I wouldn't take money from your dirty gossiping hands. Consider your last meal here on the house!" Taking their ticket, she ripped it to pieces, throwing the shredded paper into their shocked and gaping faces.

Seth swung around at Shannon's outburst. He couldn't believe she was standing up for him. When she tore up their bill, he crossed his arms and chuckled as they brushed by him in a huff. A few other people got up and left, mumbling to themselves as the room erupted once again in applause. 'Well, I guess you can't please everyone,' he thought as he smirked at Shannon. "That was quite a performance, but you probably just cut your business by a third."

"I don't care. Let me ask you something Seth. Why don't the Indians from the reservation come here to eat? We only seem to get the miners and the towns' people."

"They don't want trouble and it seems that every time they try to blend with the white people, fights tend to break out."

"Who is usually the instigator?"

"Well you have prejudice from both sides. It all depends on the situation."

"I think we may need to figure out a way to remedy that. We'll talk about it later on tonight."

Seth wondered what she was scheming but decided to let it go for now.

"Oh, by the way, I would've thought that with you and Joseph reconciling, he would've joined you for dinner tonight. There's no need for him to wait until you leave anymore."

"Wait, what are you saying? Joseph eats here? I had no idea", he wondered why Joseph hadn't mentioned that he had seen Shannon when he was with him at the bar this morning.

"Yeah, I didn't notice cause I didn't know who he was, but Irene told me that he waits until you leave and then he comes in. I could understand, what with you two being on the outs but I expected that after today, you'd be practically joined at the hip. It must be different for guys than it is for girls."

She thought about the women she had known who would fight and then make up. They couldn't spend enough time together, giggling and gossiping, happy to put the past behind them. Shannon never felt close enough to any of them to have that type of friendship. They all seemed a bit shallow to her, so she kept to herself. Richmond didn't encourage friendships. He knew that along with friendships came confidantes and he didn't want his wife confiding in anyone about their personal life. He even had spies all around her, ready to report the smallest indiscretion. One of them had noticed her getting too chatty with one particular house maid and before Shannon knew it, she was promptly dismissed. After that, the house staff steered clear of her.

"Anyway, I'll see you back at the house in about two hours. Do me a favor and get that fire stoked up so the house will be nice and toasty when I get there." She walked up to him and hugged him close.

He whispered in her hair, "The fire I feel doesn't need stoking".

Her heart skipped a beat. "Well, I'll just have to make sure it stays that way", as she pressed her breasts into his chest.

His breath caught as he replied, "Oh Shannon. You really will be the death of me." Stepping away, he attempted to compose himself. "I'll see you later then." He turned and left.

Shannon felt a piece of her heart leave with him.

CHAPTER 18

Shannon paid close attention as she waited for Joseph Ravenclaw to enter the café. It was almost closing time when he came through the door. He immediately searched out the room for her as he made his way to an empty booth. He was surprised when she walked up to the table with a brilliant smile on her face, not like the polite but aloof waitress/customer smile she usually used on him. He grinned back, flashing a row of professionally whitened teeth, like a shark. Shannon's smile faltered for a fraction of a second. She saw something in his face but it was a flash and then he was just smiling back at her. *Must have been my imagination,* she tried to shake off the feeling.

"Hi, I wanted to officially introduce myself." She held out her hand. "I'm Shannon Mallory."

He took her hand, but instead of shaking it he brushed his lips across her knuckles. He looked up into her beautiful turquoise eyes, "pleased to meet you, Shannon Mallory". There was something oily about his use of her name. Removing her hand, she resisted the urge to wipe it on her apron. *This was Seth's boyhood friend? He has obviously changed through the years.* Suddenly wanting to get away from him, Shannon came right to the point. "I have offered to buy the diner and I'm going to need some legal papers drawn up and I was hoping you could handle it for me." She managed some semblance of a smile.

Joseph's smile spread into that shark's tooth look again. "Yeah, that'd be great! I'd love to help you with the paperwork." He leaned closer to her. Shannon used all her will power to keep from recoiling from him. She really didn't like this man at all. There was something "off" about him. He gave everyone around him the impression he was the "good ole boy" but there was something dark just under the surface.

"We should exchange phone numbers so we can come up with a strategy. I'll make sure that old bat doesn't take you for a ride." He inclined his head in Irene's direction. Shannon glanced quickly over at Irene and met her eyes. Irene seemed to be trying to send a message with her eyes that was like……a warning? Then it was gone. Shannon looked back to Joseph. He actually thought he was helping her. What could he possibly have against Irene?

Shannon almost bit her tongue off to keep from saying something she might regret. Her voice remained even as she said, "Well, we've already come to a suitable agreement. All I need is your legal expertise."

Joseph looked disappointed. He was hoping that she would jump at the chance to give him her number. *Little bitch is trying to play hard to get. Okay, I'm game. I love a challenge.* "Oh, okay then. Well, you should call my office and make an appointment so we can get the papers drawn up." His shark like smile returned as he pulled out a business card. Taking Shannon's hand he placed it in her palm, holding on just a little longer than necessary.

When he released it, Shannon made an excuse, "Well, I better get back to work. I'll call you." She knew it was a mistake as she said it. His eyes lit up.

"We can talk about it some more when I see you Friday night", he threw at her as she was turning to go.

Shannon froze, a big lump suddenly in her throat. She turned around, the question all over her round face. "Friday night?"

"Yeah, oh hey, Seth didn't mention that we are grilling at his place?" He flashed his teeth. God, she hated his smile. He looked like a hungry lion spying a small rabbit.

"I'm supposed to bring a date."

"Oh, okay. Well, I guess I'll see you then." As she walked off she heard him say in a low voice, "Not if I see you first". Suddenly, Shannon couldn't wait to get out of there. She pulled her cell phone from her apron and dialed Seth's number.

CHAPTER 19

On the way back to Seth's Shannon was unusually quiet. She sat close, snuggling against his side but as close as she was, he felt she was miles away. He was unsure as to what had managed to subdue her usual exuberance, but he decided it was probably none of his business. Still, he racked his brain trying to figure out if it was something he had done…or didn't do.

Shannon wanted very much to discuss her reservations concerning Seth's best friend but she didn't quite know how to go about it. She was afraid that the smallest slip and the warm cozy cocoon they had spun between them would unravel, leaving their emotions exposed and overly sensitive. *How do I get him to understand that his friend has a split personality?* A thought came to her that made her shiver, though she was warm and toasty in Seth's arms. *He reminds me of Richmond. He wore two faces, one for the unsuspecting public and another for the people unlucky enough to be in his inner circle.*

Feeling her shiver, Seth tightened his arm around her shoulder. "We're almost home then you can thaw out in front of the fire." She wrapped her arms around his waist.

Maybe I won't have to say anything. Maybe he'll slip up and Seth will see. She tried to console herself with that thought as they pulled into the drive.

Once inside, Seth pulled Shannon into his arms, running his lips from her neck to her jaw. He pulled away, staring deeply into her eyes. "I know something's bothering you. I can't begin to understand what. Will you tell me?" He sounded a little hurt.

What do I say? She decided on a different course of action. "I'm just a little tired. I think that putting in a full day and packing up all my stuff was maybe a bit much for one day." She wanted to reassure him. "You have done nothing wrong. You could never make me unhappy." She pulled his head down and kissed him softly. His lips were so incredible. She could feel her body respond as she pressed her body against his.

Seth swept her up and carried her to the bedroom. Her breath quickened for what she knew was to come. He laid her on the bed and bending over, began to undress her. Her hands ran up and down his arms and to his face as he removed her blouse and bra. He moved to her jeans and she helped him by lifting her hips so he could easily pull them down. He took off everything but her panties. She was on fire for him as she tried to pull him down to her. He removed her hands but she was too excited to notice until he reached down and pulled the blankets up over her. Her eyes flew open. "What are you doing?" Her voice incredulous.

"My dear Shannon, I am putting you to bed. We don't have to make love every night. Sometimes rest needs to come first." His voice was comforting and reassuring.

"But I want to make love to you, now!" She reached for him again but he held her wrists.

"I'll make a deal with you. You behave yourself and I will spoon with you. We can talk until you fall asleep, okay?"

Shannon couldn't believe how understanding he was and she felt a twinge of guilt for her deception. She wanted him, had wanted him all day, but because of Joseph, she wasn't going to get to have him. She silently cursed Joseph for ruining her evening.

"Alright, I guess I can live with that", she scooted over and held up the blanket. "But you'll have to take those off", she motioned to his clothes as her eyes raked over his body hungrily. He recognized that look.

"Okay, but you have to control yourself......promise?" He undressed down to his black boxers.

"Promise", she sighed.

He climbed under the covers and Shannon felt his arms go around her as he pressed his chest to her back. They lay in the dark listening to each other's breathing. Finally, Seth spoke in her ear, "So how did it go after I left?" Shannon tensed briefly before she answered, "Fine, it went fine". She had a feeling that if she didn't mention seeing him at the diner, that Joseph would find some way to make it look like she was hiding something from Seth. She went on, "Oh, Joseph came in right before closing to get take out." She hoped he wouldn't want details but she wasn't that lucky.

"Great! So you got to meet him. He didn't bore you with stories about our childhood escapades, did he? We used to get into so much trouble, but it was fun." He chuckled a little and Shannon smiled. She loved the different flavors of his laugh. The question he asked was easy for her to answer. "No, he didn't." She turned the subject back to him. "So how did it go with Joseph this morning? I assume it went well considering your mood at the diner, but I never got details."

Seth had totally forgotten he hadn't told Shannon about his reconciliation with Joseph. "Well, I went to his office and he came out, surprised to see me. We shook hands, walked across the street to the bar, and had a beer. Yeah, just a bunch of guy stuff. I teased him about his secretary, Millie. She looks high maintenance, big hair, fake tan, fake nails and too much make-up." He paused to squeeze Shannon, exhilarating in the fresh gardenia scent of her hair. "Not my type, but you'll be able to see for yourself on Friday."

Shannon wasn't upset with Seth but it would've been nice to hear it from him and not that letch, Joseph. She kept her voice even, "Is there something you want to tell me?"

Seth could tell by the tone of her voice that something was bothering her. *What was I supposed to tell her?* Realization hit him. "Oh, did I not mention I invited him to the house Friday?" Shannon kept silent. *Let him squirm a bit. It serves him right.*

"I'm so sorry! I'll call and cancel. I'll think of some excuse." He sounded so pitiful that Shannon had to let him off the hook.

"No, it's okay. I just wanted to be prepared, is all." She started reciting a list, "I'll need to ask Irene if I can get off work early, but I'm sure she'll be okay with it. I need to get to the grocery store and pick up some steaks and this place needs a good cleaning."

Seth stopped her, "Wait, you can't possibly do all that and work too. Tell you what, I'll go to the grocery store, get the supplies and I'll contact a professional cleaning service so all you need to do is get Irene to let you off early."

Just like that, he had taken care of everything. Shannon wasn't used to other people handling the party plans. Even when she was married, it was her sole responsibility to coordinate large dinner parties with as many as five hundred people in attendance. This little get together would've been nothing for her but now she didn't have to do anything. It was a strange feeling. She liked it. Turning over so she was facing Seth, she looked into his eyes. "You really know how to treat a lady."

Seth knew that he should let her get to sleep but she didn't look all that tired to him. As a matter of fact, she didn't look tired at all. She looked delectable. "That's not the only thing I know how to do to a lady", his arms molded their bodies together. He kissed her until she didn't know her name. One thought managed to emerge from her dazzled brain, *Finally.*

CHAPTER 20

The next few days went by pretty fast for Shannon and Seth. The cleaning crew gave the apartment a good scrubbing while he supervised. Before she knew it, Friday had arrived. She was not looking forward to the cook out. Preparations had kept them both very busy so she was pretty sure that Seth hadn't noticed her growing trepidation.

Irene had been agreeable to letting her off early "Actually", she joked, "pretty soon you won't need to ask anyone for permission". Shannon could tell she wanted to say something more, but all she said was "Have a good time, be careful", as Shannon left.

Seth called to see if Shannon needed a ride home but she declined. She had started walking home from the diner for the last couple of days. The first time she mentioned to Seth that she wanted to start walking home, he flat forbade her. It was the first time she felt she was being suffocated by his over protectiveness. They talked, more like debated, and came to a compromise. She could walk home as long as it was light outside and she called him to let him know she was on the way. It wasn't much of a compromise. Shannon had no intention of walking that scary dirt road in the dark, especially after her ordeal during the thunder storm. She enjoyed the walks. It gave her time to herself, time to think, and today she really needed that time. As she turned down the road that led home, she was mentally preparing herself for the night ahead. *How am I going to hide how I really feel about Joseph? Will he do something to reveal his true self? If he does, what will Seth do?* Closing her eyes, she could almost hear the police sirens and see the flashing lights as they hauled Seth and Joseph to jail. "I can't allow that to happen. I'm just going to have to act like everything is okay and handle Joseph myself. I can't let Seth know what's really going on."

Totally lost in thought, she didn't hear the car until it was almost on her. She nearly had a heart attack when the driver tapped the horn a couple of times. She jumped about three feet in the air. "Oh my God!" she gasped as her hand flew up to her heart. Whirling around to confront the asshole who had almost given her a heart attack, the retort froze on her lips as she recognized the driver. "Joseph?" her voice incredulous *Why is he so early? He's not supposed to be here for at least a couple of hours.*

"Hey Shannon!" He laughed as he slid from the car, resting his arm on the top of the vehicle. He had on a pair of sunglasses so Shannon couldn't read his eyes but that hated smile dominated his face. "I didn't mean to scare you." *Yeah, right, I bet,* she thought as she tried to smile. It came out more of a grimace. "That's okay. I was just deep in thought and didn't hear the car." "Car" wasn't sufficient to describe the silver jaguar. *Of course, what else would a man like him drive? It's probably loaded,* she thought as she took in the obscene status symbol. The passenger side window rolled down and a bleached blond head leaned out, "Hey honey! You must be Shannon. I'm Millie. We're early I know but Joseph here was itching to get the party started. I'd be more than happy to help you get things ready." Shannon was shocked by the offer. She didn't expect it from someone who looked like Millie. She chided herself, *Shame on you Shannon. Who are you to judge someone by their appearance?* Smiling genuinely at Millie, she walked the short distance to the car. She leaned down, "Oh that's okay. I'm sure Seth is setting things up. He's been super excited about the party all week too."

"Do you need a lift?" Joseph asked, his smile unchanged since he pulled up. Shannon wondered if he only had one smile. Everyone she had ever met had at least two different smiles, but she had only seen that one predatory grin. She shivered as the hairs on the back of her neck stood out.

"No, that's okay. I like to walk. I'll see you when I get there. Just let Seth know you saw me." She turned to go then turned back around, "It's nice meeting you Millie."

"Wait", Millie called out. "Want some company?" Not waiting for an answer, she grabbed her purse and opened the passenger door.

Shannon was about to protest but realized she might not mind Millie walking with her.

"Sure, that'd be great!" Shannon smiled at her. She didn't know why, but she really liked this woman, with her heavy make-up, fake nails, and big boobs.

As Millie walked toward her, Shannon noticed the heels of the six inch stiletto pumps, sinking deep into the dirt. She was rethinking her invitation when Millie reached down and pulled them off, holding the straps between her fingers. She curled her toes into the dirt. "Ooh, I haven't walked barefoot in the dirt in a long time. I love the way it squishes between my toes." Giving Shannon's Nikes' a disapproving look she said, "Come on Shannon. Take off your shoes and let them tootsies breathe." She laughed as she kicked up some dirt playfully.

Shannon couldn't help but laugh too, completely oblivious to Joseph until he cleared his throat loudly. They looked at him then as he grumbled, "Well I'm going on ahead. You girls don't go lollygagin." He slid behind the wheel and sped down the road, leaving a dust cloud in his wake.

Shannon coughed and waved the dirt from her face. As she looked at Millie, she saw something flash across her face, but a second later it was gone and Millie was grinning at her. Shannon could swear it was fear. She had seen that same fear when she used to look in the mirror. It was all too familiar and it sent a stab of anger through her. *He mistreats her.* She felt an instant connection with this flamboyant woman. "You're right, Millie. It feels wonderful!" They laughed again as they walked barefoot down the dirt road like two little kids.

"Millie, when did you meet Joseph?" Shannon threw the question out casually. It was a question anyone would ask an acquaintance or potential new friend.

Millie looked out at the forest line and replied, "I met Joseph at the local bar. I know what you're thinking but it wasn't like that." She glanced at Shannon sideways, surprised to see that Shannon's expression was open and sincere. *She's not just being polite. She's really interested. It seems like she really wants to know me.* Millie liked this girl. *She could use a bit more make-up and a manicure, but she is pretty in a "girl next door" kinda way.* She continued, "I was working as a waitress and he started talking to me. Not like pick up lines, but personal questions about my life. I explained to him that I had a couple of quarters of secretarial courses from the local tech school and had planned on getting a certificate but the money got tight and I had to drop out. He offered me a job as his secretary and I jumped at it. Nobody had ever offered me anything... but a good time." She laughed nervously. "Anyway, he's good to me." The tone of her voice changed. It was very subtle but Shannon caught it.

"Is he?" Shannon asked, keeping her voice neutral. Millie's head shot up, cutting her eyes at Shannon suspiciously. "What do you mean by that?" her voice cautious. *What had this girl seen?* A horrible thought came to her. If *she can see behind the charade, can everyone else?* If Joseph ever thought that their secret was in danger of exposure....she didn't want to think about what he might do. She could lose her job...or worse.

Shannon decided it might be time to lay her cards on the table. "Millie, even though we just met, I feel a connection between us. Without going into the gory details, I was in an abusive relationship for years." Shannon stopped and put her hand on Millie's arm, "stop".

Millie halted and turned toward Shannon, tears welling up in her eyes. "You were abused?"

Shannon nodded her head, "I was....but I got out". She looked pointedly into Millie's heavily lined golden brown eyes.

Millie was awestruck by the intensity in her gaze. *It's like she can see into my soul. Do I want her to see?* She dropped her eyes and looked at her dirty bare feet. "You don't understand. It's....complicated."

Shannon reached up and put her index finger under Millie's chin, tilting it back to meet her gaze, "explain it to me then", she whispered.

Millie had no choice but to look back into those incredible blue green eyes as she blinked back the tears that threatened to ruin her carefully applied make-up. She took a deep breath. She couldn't believe she was going to confide in this girl, telling her the one thing that she could never bring herself to speak of. She was so afraid Shannon would judge her or worse....pity her. She was used to being judged on her looks, but she never wanted pity from anyone. *We really could've been friends.* Jerking her chin out of Shannon's hand, she looked at her defiantly.

"He makes me do things, weird things. I've never been a saint or anything, but the things he makes me do, they're....sick! He does things to me too." Her face went blank. "I don't care. If it means keeping my job....I just zone out so I don't have to think about it." She searched Shannon's eyes, looking for the shocked expression she knew would be there.

Shannon looked evenly at Millie. "I did the same thing when it was happening to me. I would close my eyes and think of some exotic place I wanted to travel to or I would imagine lying on the beach, the sun kissing my bare skin. It made things....bearable." She gripped Millie's arms. For a split second Millie thought Shannon was going to shake her or push her away, but when Shannon embraced her, she was totally shocked. Choking back the tears, she hugged her back.

Pulling away, Making sure no tears had actually shed, Millie's fingers dabbed at the underside of her eyes. She was afraid that if he noticed she'd been crying, Joseph would come to his own conclusions about the conversation she'd had with Shannon.

Satisfied that she was still intact, she smiled brightly at Shannon, "I think we're going to be great friends. I don't know about you, but I could really use some girl time...and a beer." Approaching Seth's home, they linked arms as they walked into the open field.

Seth and Joseph were relaxing in lawn chairs, each holding a beer. As Shannon and Millie approached, Seth jumped up and ran to Shannon, scooping her up into his arms. "God, I missed you!" He kissed her soundly, hugging her tight. Shannon mentally thanked God for him. Putting her down, he beamed at her, grinning from ear to ear. Shannon couldn't help but glance over at Millie who had stepped away. Meeting her eyes, Shannon smiled sweetly at her. Seth followed Shannon's gaze to where Millie stood looking at them, the envy clearly written all over her face.

Shannon looked back at Seth, "I know you've already met but I wanted to properly introduce you two. Seth, this is Millie...my friend." She turned toward Millie, a big smile on her face. Millie was touched. No one had called her "friend" in a very long time. She stuck out her perfectly manicured hand, "pleased to meet you hon--Seth" catching herself. She never bothered to learn people's names. She figured they probably wouldn't remember her anyway so why bother? "You have beautiful blue eyes", she beamed at him. All men loved to be complimented. It made them feel good.

"Uh, yeah, thanks. Anyway, who wants a beer?" He walked over to the ice chest and grabbed one in each hand, holding them up.

"I'll have one." Shannon looked at Millie who looked confused. "You want a beer Millie?"

"Yeah, sure, why not?" She couldn't understand Seth's reaction. She was just trying to be friendly. She didn't think he liked her very much. If Seth didn't like her, it was going to be difficult to be friends with Shannon. She had been there before and it always ended the same. The boyfriend or husband managed to put an end to any potential friendship.

Shannon walked over with Millie's beer and motioned her to a couple of lawn chairs that Seth had set up for them. Suddenly she got an idea, "Millie, I want to show you my favorite place, come on!" She grabbed Millie's hand and they walked around the back of the cabin. "Don't worry about Seth. He's not used to compliments. You caught him off guard, that's all. He just has to get to know you." She draped her arm around Millie's shoulders as they rounded the back of the house. "Close your eyes!" Millie immediately did as she was told. This disturbed Shannon. *'She's used to obeying without question, the typical reaction of a victim. I'm going to have to work on her.'* She placed Millie in the best spot for optimal effect. "Okay, you can open your eyes now." She stepped back as Millie opened her eyes.

"Wow!" was all she said as she leaned her head back, trying to take it all in.

"Pretty amazing, huh?" Walking around in front of Millie, Shannon stretched out her arms and twirled around in a circle. "The day I saw these mountains was the day I fell in love. I don't think I'll ever see anything more beautiful. Their majestic splendor is breathtaking! Kinda makes you rethink your place in this world, doesn't it?"

Millie was mesmerized. "Yeah, I can see that."

They stood there gazing up at the mountains, arm in arm, admiring their beauty.

"Hey ladies, it's time to eat!" Seth called.

"I guess we should get something to eat", Shannon sighed as they returned to the "party".

Shannon walked over to Seth and wrapped her arm around his waist as she listened to the two men talk about their exploits together. She smiled, laughed, and frowned at the appropriate time but her mind was on a completely different track. *He is so slick! How could anyone keep up this charade without making one mistake? He is so like Richmond, but even Richmond slipped up once in a while.* She glanced over at Millie, who was sitting on the edge of the lawn chair. She was also reacting, but in a more animated way, her laugh as fake as her nails. Shannon knew because she had experienced her genuine laugh during their walk. Her heart went out to her. *Maybe if I keep working on her, she will find the courage to quit her job and get away from him.* Her skin crawled. She suddenly felt filthy. *I really need a shower and a change of clothes,* she thought as she pulled away from Seth's embrace.

"I think I'll go get cleaned up. I smell like hamburger fat."

"Okay babe. Don't take too long. Everything will be ready in just a little while." He kissed her on the head and watched her climb the steps to the apartment.

Once inside, Shannon went straight back to the bathroom. Shedding her clothes as quickly as possible, she stepped into the giant shower stall. It wasn't just the hamburger fat she needed to wash away. She turned the hot water on until it was almost scalding as she thought of the way he had leered at her when she and Millie had walked up to the house.

"Hey man, I don't see any mustard on the table. You know how much I like to eat mustard on my steak."

Seth looked over at the table. "Oh, I'm sorry. I guess I forgot. I'll go get it". He started to peel himself out of the lawn chair.

"Nah, that's okay. I'll get it. Give me a chance to check out your crib", he smiled as he practically pushed Millie off the chair. If she hadn't been a regular at the gym, she would've ended up on the ground but her leg muscles were strong so she did a squat and jumped back up, a disapproving frown on her face. "Where's the fire?" Joseph didn't acknowledge her as he rushed up the stairs, two at a time.

"Hey, are you alright?" Seth moved quickly, thinking she was falling but came up short as she pulled the Pilates move on him. "That's impressive," his voice shocked. Millie gave him a sweet smile as she slapped her butt, "stair master". Seth couldn't help but laugh. Millie laughed too. He could understand why Shannon had taken a liking to Millie. *If you get past the outside packaging, she really is a sweet girl.*

"Hey Seth," Millie looked down at her feet as she suddenly became uncertain. "Sorry about the whole 'beautiful eyes' thing earlier. Shannon told me how uncomfortable you are with compliments." She glanced up at him to see his reaction.

"Oh, that's okay. Don't give it another thought." He reached down into the ice chest and pulled out two more beers. "You want another beer?"

"Sure", she smiled, reaching out her hand.

Joseph cracked open the door and peered inside the small apartment. He didn't see Shannon in the front room so he went inside and wandered down the hall until he came to the master bedroom. "So, this is where they do the nasty." Moving over to the bed, he leaned down and sniffed the pillow case. It smelled of sweet gardenia. His pants became tight as he felt his excitement growing. He reached down and pulled at his crotch, the movement making him stiffen with desire. *Oh, man, I can just imagine her lying here, completely naked.* He wanted so badly to lie in the spot where she usually slept. He thought better of it. He didn't want to get caught pleasuring himself. That would make for a very awkward situation and he hadn't been careful all these years just to botch things up now. Cocking his head in the direction of the bathroom, he could hear the water running. *'She's still taking a shower. I wonder...'* He went to the bathroom door and tried the knob. It was unlocked. Grinning wickedly, he slowly cracked the door open. *I wonder if she left the door unlocked for me.* The shower stall was completely glass, and huge! The water had steamed up the glass, but he could still see her silhouette. She was so curvy! Becoming bolder, he entered the bathroom and walked closer to the stall. Just then, Shannon turned to rinse her hair, giving him an almost unobstructed view. His breath caught in his throat. 'My God, she's hot!' He licked his lips. "Oh shoot!" Shannon exclaimed as soap got into her eyes. Squeezing them shut, she opened the shower door and stepped out, grabbing a towel.

The sight of her fully naked just inches from him was almost more than Joseph could bear. He reached out his hand, coming just short of touching her. His other reached down to cup himself. He could see them entwined in a lustful embrace. He knew she would be a wildcat in bed. He let out a low groan.

Shannon froze. She thought she heard someone. Her eyes flew open, causing them to sting painfully. She squinted, trying unsuccessfully to see through the tears that had sprung up. "Is someone there?" she asked timidly as she swiped the towel over her eyes. *Come on Shannon,* she scolded herself as her search revealed she was the only one there, *get a hold of yourself!* Wrapping the towel around her, she went into the bedroom to get changed.

Joseph came down the stairs, holding up the mustard bottle like it was a fishing trophy. "Found it. took me awhile though. When was the last time you cleaned out your refrigerator?"

Seth looked up and waved back, "Sorry, I thought I put it on the table. Shannon must have put in the fridge." He gave Joseph an apologetic shrug.

"That's alright," he said as he walked over to Millie, pulling her against him in a possessive hug. His desire needed to be released. He ground his hips against her butt. He was really going to enjoy himself the next time he and Millie were alone. Maybe he would have her wear a strawberry blond wig. The thought made him want to adjust himself.

Millie felt his erection through her pants. *What could possibly have made him so randy? All he did was go get mustard.* She tried unsuccessfully to wriggle away from him. He pulled her back and growled in her ear, sending shivers down her spine. She remembered what usually happened when he got in this kind of mood. She looked down at the nearly faded marks around her wrists. She had suddenly lost her appetite.

Shannon stood in front of the mirror in the bathroom, staring at her reflection. She just couldn't shake the feeling that someone had been there. Looking around the room, she searched for evidence but came up empty. She shrugged, chiding herself as she checked her hair in the mirror. "I wish I could take more time with it, but, oh well, it is what it is." Twisting her hair up around the top, she grabbed a jeweled comb and secured the curls. Taking a cursory look at her face, she stood back and turned sideways. She had chosen a flowered halter sundress made of cotton. The hem was a little too short for the weather so she pulled on her skinny jeans as she had seen in the fashion magazines. The 'v' neck of the halter showed off her full bosom without being too revealing. She put on some garnet dangle earrings to match the roses in the print. Slipping into her leather boots, (an indulgence she allowed herself a couple of years ago) she grabbed her jean jacket, and rushed outside to be with Seth and Millie.

Seth caught his breath as Shannon bounced down the steps, adulation evident on his face. The look he gave her made Shannon blush. She smiled tentatively as she made her way over to where he stood next to the grill.

"Steaks are ready, honey. I've set the table and I think we are ready to eat." He held up a giant steak, "I hope you're hungry."

Joseph watched Shannon descend the stairs with hunger in his eyes. When she walked past him, he abruptly let go of Millie, stepping away from her. Caught completely off guard, Millie stumbled but quickly regained her composure. He was careful so no one saw a thing. Millie glared at him but he just shrugged, flashing that cruel smile.

Shannon made an 'o' with her mouth as she looked at the humongous slab of beef. "Wow, that's a lot of cow flesh!" she exclaimed. Joseph whistled low, "you expectin an army?" He looked over at Shannon and winked, a secret hidden in his dark brown eyes. She cringed. Catching a movement, her eyes slid down to his other hand which had moved down, brushing against his crotch. Her eyes flew up to his and that predatory smile was back on his face. She quickly looked away, her face turning deep red. Shooting a look at Seth, she prayed he had seen the exchange, but he was busy setting the steaks on the picnic table. Keeping her eyes cast downward, she quickly made her way to her seat. *Did I do something to encourage that lecherous look? I've barely looked at him the whole time.*

Seth sat next to Shannon, who was staring at her steak like it might start doing a jig. It hadn't escaped him that for the last few days she had been acting strange, aloof, preoccupied. He kept telling himself it was just his imagination. That he just couldn't relax and enjoy his good fortune, always waiting for the bomb to drop, but as he watched her expression, he felt a stab of apprehension. Suddenly, the bomb didn't seem such a stupid, paranoid idea. Wanting to reassure her, and himself, he reached under the table to hold her hand. Shannon's mind wasn't a thousand miles away, but just a couple of feet, to the man sitting directly across from her. She was racking her brain. Something seemed very unsettling about that look he gave her. She jumped from the unexpected touch. Her hands which had been fisted together under the table jerked upward and hit the underside painfully.

"I'm sorry, are you okay?" Seth grabbed her hands, examining the damage, concern mixed with disappointment. She had never reacted like that before to his touch.

"Yeah, I'm fine." She looked at his profile his jaw muscle working, his forehead creased. She noticed his concern and her heart ached. She pulled her hand from his and cupped his chin, bringing his face level with hers, but he wouldn't raise his eyes. "I'm sorry, I must've been daydreaming." She gave him a tentative smile, "It wasn't your fault, Seth". She was careful not to glance across the table. Steeling herself, she tightened her grip on his chin, making him look her in the eyes. His eyes locked with hers. The intensity of her gaze burned into his soul. Before he could apologize again, she pulled his face close and kissed him, putting aside any doubts he had been having for the last few days. He placed his hands on each side of her face, running his thumbs along her cheeks. They had completely forgotten they weren't alone. Shannon leaned into Seth, her hands reaching behind his neck. He loved the way her fingers glided through his hair. It was one of the small signs of affection she displayed.

Somewhere, from faraway, they heard someone clearing their throat. The sound was soft and feminine. Embarrassed, not because they had gotten caught kissing, but because they were about to get carried away, they broke away, their faces flushed and their breathing labored. If Millie hadn't interrupted them....Shannon didn't want to think of the spectacle they would've witnessed. A shiver went through her as she imagined how Joseph would respond. *He wasn't going to interject. I bet he would've loved the scene.* She snatched a quick glance at Joseph. He wasn't smiling and the look on his face was....anger, envy, jealousy? Maybe all three? She quickly looked away from him and back into Seth's eyes which had been watching her every move. She smiled, trying not to look guilty. *Guilty? For what? I didn't do anything wrong!* That was it, the last straw. She made up her mind.

Tonight, she was going to have a serious talk with him about his best friend, until then, she would try to have a nice time, for his sake.

The conversation was flowing as the men talked about hunting and fishing and golfing. Shannon didn't know Seth did any of those things. There was so much about him that she didn't know.

"Shannon has been skydiving." She jerked her head toward Seth as he shoved a spoonful of mashed potatoes into his mouth. Why would he tell them that? She had pretty much kept the conversation away from herself, now all eyes were on her.

"Wow, Shannon. That must've been a rush, huh?" Millie gasped. "I couldn't do it. I'm afraid of heights, always have been. I can't even climb a four foot ladder to change a light bulb without getting vertigo. What did it feel like?"

"It felt like"…Shannon's mind went back to that glorious but anxious day, "freedom", she sighed at the memory of the wind whooshing past her as she threw herself out of the plane with abandon. Once she was falling, she didn't worry about the chute malfunctioning. She just enjoyed the feeling of letting go. It was the most exhilarating experience she had ever had, well, up until now anyway. She didn't even notice the tears that had escaped her misting eyes, under Seth reached out and brushed them away from her cheek. She turned her face toward him. The love she felt was almost a physical ache.

Seth looked into her eyes as he brushed away her tears, wondering what had brought them on. *Maybe she was thinking about her years of marital hell.* He hated that he had mentioned the skydiving. It had made her sad. *Stupid asshole! You made her cry.* He was busy mentally punishing himself, when Shannon reached over and took his hand. Leaning close so no one else could hear, she whispered into his ear, "but even skydiving is nothing compared to how you make me feel. I love you." She squeezed his hand and turned her attention to her plate. "I'm starved!" She picked up her knife and fork, carved off a large hunk, and shoved it into her mouth.

"Well, you're quite the daredevil." Shannon froze in mid-chew at Joseph's voice. "Looks like you got yourself a real adrenaline junkie, son." He grinned, showing most of his too white teeth. "So, are you into extreme water sports too?"

Shannon glanced up to find him looking at her intently, that hated smile on his face, but it was his eyes that gave her a start. *He was in the bathroom!* She knew it. Somehow she just knew. She gasped as the realization hit her in the face, causing the half-chewed piece of steak to get sucked down her wind pipe. Her eyes bulged out as she gasped for breath.

Seth immediately jumped up. Positioning himself behind her, he wrapped his arms around her waist, placing his fists in the Heimlich maneuver. Shannon's breasts strained against the material as Seth jerked, trying to dislodge the food. Shocked, Millie's hands flew to her face, worried for her new friend. Joseph managed to look shocked, but it was an act. His eyes were hungrily devouring Shannon's exposed flesh as every jerk seemed to reveal more of her creamy breasts. *A couple more jerks and they'll spill out over her top,* his tongue almost snaked out to lick his lips in anticipation.

"Come on Shannon, breathe!" Seth cried as he jerked harder, though he was worried the force would break her ribs. Shannon was turning a dangerous shade of blue. Realizing that it wasn't working, Seth reached down and swept his arm across the table, sending food and dishes flying. He dumped Shannon onto the table. He raised her eyelids. Seeing no change in her pupils, he began to pray out loud. "Please God; don't take her from me now. Please baby, don't leave Me." His voice cracked with emotion. "Millie!" he shouted as he opened Shannon's mouth wide to look down her throat, "Do you have a pair of tweezers in your purse?"

"Huh?" Millie asked slack jawed, not comprehending. He took his eyes off Shannon long enough to look Millie in the eye. *He really has the most incredible eyes.* His voice was soft but compelling, "tweezers? Please hurry." She nodded her head, rifling through her purse until she felt the hard steel of the tweezers she kept for touch-ups. She handed them over to Seth.

He positioned them over Shannon's open mouth and then they disappeared down her throat. *He must have them jammed all the way down,* she thought as she fought to find enough saliva to swallow.

Seth was careful not to touch the sides of her esophagus as he inserted the tweezers as far as they would go. It felt like a dangerous game of "Operation". He was praying that the food hadn't gotten lodged too far down or he was going to have to perform a tracheotomy. Suddenly he felt an object and praying harder than ever, gently extracted the tweezers from her throat. Quickly throwing the offensive chunk on the ground without bothering to look at it, he leaned his face close to her mouth. Unable to determine she was breathing, he turned to Millie once again. "Millie, I need your compact mirror." Acting faster this time she snatched it out and practically shoved it in his face. "Thanks." He held it to Shannon's mouth. She wasn't breathing at all. Holding himself together for her sake, he tilted her head back and started C.P.R.

Millie realized that she had been holding her breath. Seeing Seth administer the breath of life was like a trigger, releasing the sobs she had been holding back. Joseph just sat there, watching Seth, who, between blowing into Shannon's mouth and pumping her chest, was praying fervently. Seth's composure was crumbling. He struggled to hold back a sob as he blew into her mouth. Shannon's body lay motionless. Her face had gone deathly pale. He had seen death many times while working in the emergency room and he knew she was standing on the brink. Snatching her up into his arms, he shook her violently. "Don't leave me dammit! Do you hear me? Fight Shannon! Breathe!" He reared his hand back and brought it across her face. The sound of the slap broke his heart and made Millie jump. Hugging her tightly, he whispered in her ear, "please baby, please, forgive me. I didn't mean to hurt you."

Seth felt her body spasm, sucking in precious air. "Oh God, thank you, thank you, thank you." He rocked her like a small child, tears streaming down his face.

Shannon's eyes fluttered open. "Hey," she said, looking up into his red rimmed eyes. "Why are you crying?"

Seth looked down as the color began to return to her angelic face. "Hey," he croaked as he half laughed, half sobbed, refusing to loosen his hold. "You had me a little scared there for a while."

Shannon smiled and glanced over to see Millie's make-up running down her face. Her eyes went to Joseph and he looked back at her, his face unreadable. She looked down and noticed she was on the table. Her eyes full of questions, she looked back to Seth. "Why am I on the table and why are you two crying?" Seth's mouth worked, trying to find the words to tell Shannon that she had died. Unable to utter the words, he drew her to him and kissed every part of her face, leaving her lips for last, lips that had been cold and unresponsive only a moment ago.

"Oh honey", Millie leapt out of her seat and ran around the table to hug Shannon which was proving difficult as Seth refused to release his hold even a little.

Their behavior was bizarre. Holding her hands out, Shannon gently pushed away from Seth's smothering hold. "Somebody better tell me what happened, and I mean now!" Seth couldn't meet her eyes. She looked at Millie who burst out in another bout of sobs. She wasn't scared anymore. She was pissed. "Tell me!"

"You died." Joseph stated evenly. "Yeah, you choked on a big ole hunk of beef."

Seth, Millie, and Shannon snapped their heads around to look at him. "What?" She couldn't have heard him right. "I died?" she asked incredulously.

Millie intervened, her voice shaking with emotion, "But Seth did some fancy C.P.R., and brought you back".

Shannon jerked back around and locked eyes with Seth. He looked at her sheepishly. "You saved me…again?" He always seemed to be close by to rescue her, like her own personal knight in shining armor. She wondered how long her lifespan would've been if Seth hadn't been there? She probably wouldn't have lived very long.

Seth wondered how long her lifespan would've been if they had never met. She would probably live to be a hundred and five.

Shannon climbed down from the table and sat in one of the folding chairs. Putting her head in her hands, she tried to remember what could've possibly made her choke. Realization hit her in the face. She jerked her head up and locked eyes with Joseph. He looked back at her and winked. Her eyes almost bugged out of her head. *That's how I choked. He had looked at me like that, but why?* She racked her brain trying to remember.

Seth knelt down on one knee and gently took her hands in his. "Shannon love, look at me." Shannon looked into blue pools that were swimming with emotion. "Marry me."

Shannon gasped, unable to look away. His face was dead serious and his voice had an edge of desperation. "I don't ever want to lose you like that again." The words cracked as he buried his face into the nape of her neck. She couldn't breathe. It was everything she had ever wanted, the love of a good man who wanted her despite her past.

"Yes", she whispered so low that he didn't really hear her as much as he felt her exhale. Lifting his head, he looked deeply into her eyes.

"Was that a "yes"?" His breath caught as his heart fluttered, ready to take flight.

She smiled down at him and he saw the look from his dreams in her eyes. "Yes, I will marry you Seth Proudfoot. I have waited for you my whole life." The tears spilled over her cheeks as she spoke the words that made his heart take flight…and Joseph's turn to stone.

CHAPTER 21

"Congratulations you two!" Clapping her hands, Millie jumped up and down excitedly. "Oh Shannon! You have to let me coordinate the wedding!"

Shannon turned to look at Millie and grinned, "Uh, okay, I guess so, but you have to promise me you'll keep it small and simple". She gave her a reproachful look.

"Sure, sure, okay, whatever," waving her hand dismissively. She could hardly contain herself. "I'll get on the phone first thing Monday morning. I know this really cute bridal shop on Main Street...

Shannon looked at Seth sheepishly, wanting him to rescue her.

"Don't look at me. I already did the hard part."

"Oh, you!" Shannon slapped him playfully on the arm. He grabbed her, pulling her body close as he chuckled good-naturedly, Shannon's brush with death slowly receding from his mind as he gazed into her eyes.

Languishing in his warm embrace, Shannon sighed contentedly as she closed her eyes.

Seth gave a little chuckle as Shannon fell asleep in his arms. "Looks like she's had a very eventful day. I better go put her to bed." Scooping her into his arms, he took her inside for some much needed rest.

Millie cleaned up; making sure everything was back in order. Knowing they were left alone, Joseph grabbed her around the waist and pulled her onto his lap. He bit her earlobe, almost drawing blood. "Ouch! That hurt!" She struggled to get up but he tightened his grip. "Don't get any ideas," he growled in her ear. "Just remember who writes your paychecks." To prove his point, his hand came around and savagely pinched her nipple. "You belong to me, to do with as I please."

Biting back the tears, Millie straightened her back and tossed her blond hair. "Well maybe I don't want to work for you anymore, maybe I….I quit!" Managing to disengage herself she spun around to face him, "I want what Seth and Shannon have. You don't love me so why are we doing this?"

Joseph looked at the mascara running down her face and crinkled his nose like he smelled something disgusting. He waved his hand dismissively. "I do it because I'm bored and you're there."

Millie was a practical girl. She knew he didn't love her, but the way he dismissed her like a pesky fly drove it home for her. "So I'm nothing but a….booty call?"

His laughter held no humor, "That's right darlin, a booty call. You didn't think I hired you for your proficiency in dictation did you? Besides, you get a paycheck, a mighty generous one I might add, and a very nice apartment to live in, which I pay for, so I figure it's a fair trade. You might find it very hard to walk away from all that just to save your precious pride."

"Oh yeah? Well, Shannon was in the same position and she got out. She says I don't have to put up with it. Maybe I'll talk to her about going to work at the diner", she said as she snatched up her purse and headed for the car.

Joseph waved his hand dismissively. He wanted to hear more about Shannon's past. Crossing his feet in front of him, he blocked her escape. "Where do you think you're going?" He crossed his arms, giving her a dangerous look. She'd seen that look before. He was on the verge, his rage barely below the surface. "You're not going anywhere until you spill it."

Millie looked blankly at him, "spill what?"

He raised one eyebrow. She didn't even know she had slipped. He smiled but there was no humor in it. He spoke slowly like he was explaining to a child why the sky was blue, "Tell me everything Shannon told you about her past".

The realization of what she had blurted out in a fit of anger hit Millie like a slap in the face. Without even meaning to she had betrayed her new friend's trust. She looked at Joseph and knew she would find no peace until she confessed. She lowered her head, her shoulders sagging in defeat.

Joseph rejoiced. Reaching out, he pulled her onto his lap as he waited for her to begin. When it seemed she was taking too long, he reached up and gripped her chin painfully. "Tell me Millie," he whispered savagely.

Hanging her head dejectedly, she recalled her conversation with Shannon as fresh tears mingled with old, making new tracks in her smeared mascara.

When she had told him everything, Joseph pushed her off his lap and walked to his car without so much as a backward glance.

"Aren't you going to drive me back?"

His voice heavy with contempt, "I'm sure you can find your way home. You're a resourceful girl. Just don't be late to work come Monday." He climbed into the car and leaned his head out the window. "I'll want to be updated regularly on your friendship with Shannon." She opened her mouth to object but he held up his hand, cutting her off, "and if you don't agree, you can say goodbye to that fancy apartment you're living in. Oh, and if you mention this little conversation to anyone, you will be very sorry. Think about that while you hitch a ride home." And with that, he sped down the drive, leaving her in a cloud of dust.

Not knowing anything else to do, she just stood there. *How am I going to get home?* It was getting cooler outside and shivering, she thought about what she had just done. *How could I betray Shannon like that?* But more importantly, *why is Joseph so interested in Shannon?* She had seen how he watched every move Shannon made. She started getting goose bumps and it wasn't from the chill in the air. Straightening her shoulders, she walked upstairs to ask Seth for a ride home.

"Sure, no problem," Seth agreed. "Shannon was totally beat so she'll probably be out for awhile. I'll just write her a note, but, can I ask you why Joseph left without you?"

"Let's just say we had a little tiff." She reached out and put her hand on his chest. Seth looked at her suspiciously, *Oh God, please don't let her be making a pass at me,* he silently prayed. He didn't want to hurt her feelings but there was no way anything was going to happen between the two of them. *I mean, Jeez, I'm engaged!* 'He opened his mouth to speak, but she cut him off, "I know you've been friends with Joseph for a long time, but… He's changed." Still a little frightened of what Joseph might do to her if she divulged too much, she leaned forward, close to Seth's ear, "Looks can be deceiving". She dropped her hand and stepped away from him.

Seth looked at her, his brows creased. *What's that supposed to mean. It almost sounds like she's warning me, but what of?* He wanted to question her to find out exactly what she meant but he could tell by the set of her lips that she wouldn't explain herself further. He hadn't witnessed any such behavior from Joseph. *She's probably just lashing out because they had a fight, trying to get back at him for leaving her stranded.* He thought it a lame effort on her part.

As they got into the truck, he decided it might be best to humor her.

"I'd appreciate it if you'd keep this just between us." He saw something flicker in her eyes.

They rode the rest of the way in silence.

A little while later they pulled into her apartment complex. The entrance was elaborately decorated with exotic shrubs and plants. The apartments were upscale, expensive, and relatively new. As they pulled into the parking space in front of her unit, he heard her say under her breath, "I guess I better start looking for a cheaper place." He decided to act like he hadn't heard her. "Well, here we are."

"Thanks for the ride Seth. Tell Shannon I'll call her tomorrow so we can make plans. Congratulations again."

"Thanks Millie. I'll let Shannon know. Have a good night." He watched her walk to her door and didn't pull away until she disappeared inside.

Seth quietly undressed and crawled under the covers, pulling Shannon against his chest. She felt so good. Instinctively, she snuggled up, resting her head on his chest, a little sigh escaping her lips. He smiled as he laid his cheek on the top of her head, breathing in her familiar fragrance. Closing his eyes, he drifted off to sleep, the smile still on his face.

CHAPTER 22

Seth woke the next morning in a panic. Something was wrong. He had reached for Shannon, only to feel the empty space where her body should've been. Sitting bolt upright in bed, his eyes searched the still dark room for any movement. Hearing the water start up in the bathroom, he breathed a sigh of relief. Leaving the now cold bed, he walked into the bathroom and straight into the shower. Shannon was distracted, her mind going over the events of the night before and her suspicions about Joseph. When Seth wrapped his arms around her, she cried out, her heart jumping to her throat. She relaxed as he pulled her backside up against his pelvis, letting her feel his growing desire. His hands cupped each breast as he buried his face in her neck, nipping her flesh with his teeth. Shannon raised her arms and grabbed his head. Arching her back, she pushed her backside against him. His breath caught in his throat. He wanted her now. His urgency awed him. He pressed her against the shower glass as he entered her from behind. Shannon groaned deep in her throat as she felt him fill her with every thrust. Her moans spurned him onward as he let his animalistic nature take over. Burying his left hand in her hair while his right gripped her hip for support, he rode her with abandon as she urged him on. Shannon cried out as spasm after spasm racked her body. Feeling her clench around him, Seth felt his own release. Afterward, he turned her around, showering her face with kisses. She clung to him as if her life depended on it, loving the sweet soreness she felt in her core.

They took turns lathering each other's bodies. He reveled in the softness of her curves while she marveled at the hardness of his muscles. They both realized it probably wasn't such a good idea to wash each other when their bodies began to respond to the others' touch. Shannon looked meaningfully into Seth's darkening eyes, "Don't get any ideas. I have to get ready for work."

"I'm kinda resenting your job right now." He looked at her from beneath his impossibly thick lashes. "I really wanted to spend as much time with you as possible before I have to leave."

"Leave? What do you mean, you're leaving?" Shannon froze at his words. "Where are you going?"

Seth cursed himself. Did he forget to tell her he was going out of town? How could he forget? He cleared his throat, "Yeah, I have to see my financial adviser in New York, but I'll only be gone a few days. I just need to take care of some legal matters." He pulled her into his arms. She refused to look at him for fear he would see the disappointment in her eyes. "Hey, don't be mad, okay? I'm sorry I forgot to tell you. I guess with everything else that's happened…"

"I'm not mad," Shannon whispered, "just, disappointed."

Seth lifted her chin. "I'll be back before you know it." He kissed her, feeling her relax against him as he waited for her to open her eyes. When she did his gaze made her skin burn. "I'll miss you every second." She was dumbstruck by the intensity of his expression. She fought the tears that threatened to spill over her cheeks. Suddenly they both jumped as cold water stung their skin. Forgetting for the moment, they laughed as they ran from the freezing water. Seth grabbed a towel and wrapped it around Shannon's trembling body. With no thought for himself, his body shivering, he painstakingly began to wipe the droplets from her skin. Shannon took the towel from him and ran it down his muscular chest. "It's not fair that you get to have all the fun", she pouted as she knelt to run the towel down his long legs. He looked down at her, the expression on his face soft. Sinking to his knees so he was on the same level with her, he looked questioningly into her turquoise depths, "What makes you think I'll be having any fun?" It was Shannon's turn to look puzzled, "You don't look at drying me off as fun?" He realized with a start that he had misunderstood her first comment, "Oh, I thought you were referring to my boring trip to New York." He sighed with relief, "Of course, drying you off isn't exactly what I would call fun. It's more like sweet torture." Taking the towel from her hands, he wrapped it around them both, using the towel to pull her against him. Her breasts felt incredible against his chest. She looked into his eyes and saw the desire in his darkening pools. She felt it too as her body molded to his. "Take the day off. Spend it with me…just me." She could hear the wanting in his voice. It would be too easy to say yes and to hell with everything else, but Shannon had made a commitment and it wasn't like her to shirk her responsibilities. "You know I can't. I have a responsibility to the diner. What's going to happen when it's mine and I have to be there most of the time?" Feeling suddenly claustrophobic, she stood and walked out of the bathroom. She needed air. Walking over to the balcony door and sliding it open, Shannon stepped out into the frigid cold. The freezing wind was an assault to her naked body, but she just stood there, her body looking more like a statue than a warm blooded woman.

Seth stood gazing at her through the glass. What had he said to make her risk pneumonia? He had only asked to spend time with her before leaving on his business trip. He never meant he wanted her to give up everything for him. Her words rang in his ears.

Grabbing the blanket off the bed, he joined her on the deck, draping it over her shoulders. "Shannon love, I never meant for you to give up on the diner. I just wanted to spend time with you so when I'm in New York, I can go to bed every night with the memory of you in my arms. I don't know how I'm going to handle being there without you. I know I'm being totally selfish."

She turned to look at him, her eyes filling up with tears, "I panicked. That old feeling of being smothered came rushing back. I was afraid you were becoming like….him." She choked back a sob.

He took the blanket and wrapped it around both of them, letting his body warm hers. "I would never keep you from your dreams. I only want to be a part of your life…no matter how small that part may be." His eyes searched hers, "Please, forgive me?"

She melted, feeling suddenly too hot under the blanket. "There's nothing to forgive. It's just that I have these demons that are with me all the time and sometimes they show themselves unexpectedly. I don't know when, or if, they'll ever go away." She buried her head in his chest, her next words almost unintelligible, "I'm damaged goods".

Seth wrapped his arms around her waist, pulling her close to him. Shannon felt his body shake before she heard the chuckle low in his throat. She looked up at his face and saw the strangest expression. He seemed amused. She felt the heat on her face as the anger began to rise, "What the hell is so funny?" Placing her hands on his chest, she attempted to push him away.

Seth gripped her tighter and looking down into her eyes, all humor gone, he whispered, "I was thinking how silly you were for thinking you were damaged. You managed to take a horrible experience, one that would break a weaker person, and use it to turn your life around. Look at all the things you've seen and done. Then I thought of how damaged I was before I met you and how, with your love, you put my heart back together piece by piece. You made it whole again." He lifted her chin with his fingers, rubbing his thumb along her jaw. Shannon trembled from the heat of his touch and his words. "So from now on, instead of thinking of yourself as "damaged", why don't we just say you're…reconditioned?"

That was a good word for Shannon. She was damaged but Seth's love had repaired her, "reconditioned" her. Yeah, that fit perfectly. Rising up on her tiptoes, she brushed her lips against his. "Okay, I'll try, but I have really got to hurry or I'll be late." She escaped from his arms and ran back inside. After a minute of watching her scramble into her clothes, Seth walked into the bedroom to get dressed.

Seeing the suitcase on the bed made Shannon's heart sink, "When are you leaving?"

"This afternoon. I'll call and let you know when I get there." Seth busied himself, throwing clothes and toiletries into the suitcase but his mind was on Shannon. He had told her he didn't know how he was going to handle being away from her for three days but the realization made his stomach clench, suddenly making him feel nauseous. *I just need to eat something.* Even as he thought it, the prospect of food wasn't especially appealing to him.

"Do you need a ride to the airport? Cause if you do, I could ask Irene to let me off." She was pulling her hair up off her neck in a haphazard ponytail, making her look like a teenager. Seth knew it was silly, but he felt that if he allowed her to take him, he would never get on that plane.

"Nah, that's okay. I'll call Joseph. I'm sure he wouldn't mind taking me. Besides, I'm not sure Irene could spare you during the dinner shift." He felt guilty for the small lie. He wasn't planning on calling Joseph. He was just going to take a cab, well, *the* cab. Old Tony had the only operating cab company in town since he'd opened in 1976.

Wanting to change the subject, Seth suggested, "Why don't you call Millie and you two can have a girl's night out? I'm sure she'd love to spend time with you. You could talk about wedding plans or go out and see a movie or something."

Shannon cringed at the mention of Joseph's name. She was positive it had been him in the bathroom last night but without proof it would be better to keep her mouth shut, though the thought of him ogling her as she stood there stark naked made her skin crawl.

She thought about Seth's suggestion and realized it might not be such a bad idea. She sure didn't want to stay there alone, all by herself. A picture of Joseph standing on a ladder, peeking through the windows was enough to creep her out. "You know, that's not a bad idea. I think I will." Seth sighed with relief.

"Good, though I don't like the thought of you being out here alone."

"I'll ask her if she wants to have a sleepover. I haven't had one since I was little. It might be fun." She smiled though she began to feel nervous. It wouldn't do to let Seth see how anxious she was. 'What if she had other plans? What if she went back to Joseph? What if she was just being friendly last night and didn't mean anything she said?"

Just then Shannon's cell phone rang. She rushed to answer it. "Hello? Oh hey Millie." She smiled with relief. "I was just about to call you." She looked over at Seth who winked at her, "Seth is going out of town for a few days, and I was wondering if you want to hang out with me. We could go over wedding plans or go to a movie or something. You would? Great! I get off at 9:00 tonight. Do you want me to pick you up or do you want to meet me at the diner and follow me back here? Okay. See you then. Yeah, me too." She hung up the phone and grinned at Seth. "See, all taken care of. Now you don't have to worry."

Shannon knew she needed to get to work but she found herself dawdling, not wanting to leave. Seth noticed her reluctance. They talked about trivial things while she sat on the bed watching as he finished packing. She was afraid to take her eyes off him. Getting up from the bed, she walked over to him as he was pulling out a pair of socks from the bottom drawer and touched his arm.

He straightened up and she wrapped her arms around his neck, running her hands through his hair. He looked down at her, touched by the familiar caress. His arms went around her waist as he gazed down at her. "I love you," Shannon whispered, her eyes confirming her words.

No matter how many times he heard those words, they never failed to fascinate him. She loved him. It just didn't seem possible. Smiling, he bent his head and brushed his lips across hers. "And I love you." She rose up, recapturing his lips for a passionate kiss that left Seth dizzy…and hard.

Reluctantly, she pulled away. "I really have to go. Do me one favor?"

Seth hated letting her go, but he knew he couldn't hold her 24/7. If she knew he was even thinking like that, she'd bolt. He had to let her go if only for a little while. Putting on a cheery face he gave her his best smile, "Anything for you love."

"I just want you to be careful…and hurry back." She kissed him one more time then left.

Seth stood in the middle of the empty room, feeling more alone than he'd ever felt in his entire life. When she left, it was as though all the air had been sucked out of the room. He found it hard to breathe. Grabbing his cell phone, he walked outside onto the balcony. The crisp cold air helped to clear his mind as he punched in the number to Tony's Taxi Cab.

CHAPTER 23

Shannon couldn't wait for her shift to be over. She was nice enough to the customers, always smiling and quick to refill a glass when required, but she was running on automatic. She was miles away, daydreaming of a pair of electric blue eyes, running her hands through silky black hair, reveling in the scent of woods and musk. Irene couldn't help but notice Shannon's odd behavior. She walked up to her when she was placing a ticket on the wheel, "Shannon?"

"Hum?" Shannon replied, completely preoccupied.

Irene reached out and touched her arm. Shannon seemed to shake herself, her eyes focusing for the first time as she turned to look at Irene. "Oh, I'm sorry Irene. I guess I'm a little preoccupied."

"Honey, that's an understatement! What's gotten into you? Did you and Seth have a fight?" Irene pressed her for an answer.

"No, nothing like that. Seth went out of town for a few days. I miss him already and I still have two more days left." She struggled to make her voice steady. It wouldn't do to break down in front of Irene. She knew she was being silly but she just couldn't seem to help it.

Irene gave her a knowing look and nodded her head. "I know just how you feel. It may not have been that long that you've known each other, but it feels like forever, am I right?" Shannon just nodded her head as Irene continued. "Now that you're separated for the first time, you feel like half of you is missin?" Shannon gaped at her. She hit the nail on the head. "And now you're frettin that something will happen to him and you'll never see him again. You feel like you can't breathe."

"That's right. How did you know?"

"Cause the day Paddy sailed away to go risk his life in the war, everyday I fought to breathe. The only thing that kept me goin was the letters that came, however infrequently, in the mail. I don't think I took a normal breath until I saw him walking down that gang plank, coming home for good." She looked back into the kitchen and her eyes misted over, "I haven't let him out of my sight since."

Shannon was so moved she flung her arms around Irene's neck. "You are so lucky to have such a love."

Irene patted her back comfortingly, "Ah, but you have that same kind of love for Seth, now don't you?"

Shannon released her and stood back, "Yeah, I guess I do. It's frightening in a way, knowing now that it won't diminish with time, but maybe I can eventually get used to it."

Irene laughed good naturedly, "Girl, you just don't get it. It's true the feeling won't diminish with time. What you don't seem to grasp is that it will only get stronger. So, you better fasten your seatbelt." She turned away and walked into the kitchen, leaving Shannon to gawk after her.

"Oh my God! It gets stronger?" It just didn't seem possible. *The love I feel for him is almost more than I can bare now! If it grows stronger, my heart might just explode!* She had to reach out and grip the counter as the thought staggered her.

Just then Millie floated through the front door and up to the bar. "Hey girlfriend! You ready for some fun?" She took some sweetener packets and slipped them into her purse. Shannon just rolled her eyes.

"Yeah, I get off in about fifteen minutes. You want something to drink?"

"Sure. How about a coke?"

Shannon tapped the counter, "coming right up", as she turned and filled a glass from the tap. Setting it down, she winked at Millie, "on the house".

"Cool, thanks!" Millie took a sip.

"I'll be back in a few. I just need to bus these last few tables and sweep the floor then we can go."

Millie watched her head over to one of the tables and saw Joseph enter the diner. Her smile froze on her face, "Oh crap", she whispered to herself. Before she could look away, he met her gaze and grinned at her. He knew she was there. Had he followed her? Maybe it was just a coincidence, but somehow she couldn't make herself believe it. *He's stalking me?* but that didn't make since either. She shook her head, totally clueless. She saw him wave at Shannon as she bussed the tables.

Oh, God, not him again. Smile Shannon. Act natural...for Seth. She braced herself as he grinned at her. *I really hate that smile,* she thought as the hair stood up on the back of her neck. She waved the rag she was using in greeting, "Hey Joseph, I'll be right with you".

"Oh, that's okay. Take your time. I'll just go sit at the bar with Millie. Just give me the usual. I'm planning on eating it at home so wrap it up for me, would you?"

"Sure", she wrote a ticket and walked to the pass through.

Millie gave Joseph a wary glance, "Are you following me?"

He looked at her as though she had two heads, "As if! Don't flatter yourself! I come in here almost every night and get take out on my way home. I had no idea you'd be here." He looked at her profile. "Why are you here, anyway?" He saw her cringe as though he had slapped her across the face. He watched her face reddening. "Is there something you want to tell me?" Leaning close to her ear so no one would be able to overhear, he whispered, "Remember our arrangement".

"Believe me, as much as I'd like to forget it, I remember," she mumbled.

Shannon came up and placed the take out box on the counter, "Here you go, your usual. That'll be $5.35."

Joseph reached into his pocket, pulling out his designer alligator wallet and handed Shannon a ten dollar bill. "Keep the change", his voice low as his thumb rubbed her hand. It was all Shannon could do not to snatch her hand away like it had been burned. "Thanks," she mumbled. "I better go sweep up, it's closing time." She hurried away, rubbing her hand on her apron. Joseph watched her retreat, his eyes slowly sliding down her body to her butt. He let out an audible sigh.

Millie had been studying the bubbles in her glass, watching them fizzle when his sigh caught her attention. She glanced over at him. He was watching Shannon, his face guarded. She hated that look. He was obviously hiding something but she knew from experience not to question him. He didn't like questions. If he wanted her to know something, he'd tell her. She turned back to stare at the bubbles but the coke was going flat. He suddenly leaned close to her again, "Do you two have plans tonight?"

She wanted to lie to him but thought better of it, "We're having a slumber party while Seth is out of town".

Without a word, Joseph grabbed the take out container and marched out the door. Millie was surprised but not shocked. She knew he could be very unpredictable. She breathed a sigh of relief as Shannon made her way over, "Hey, you okay?" she asked Millie. "Yeah, I'm fine. Hey, I brought some junk food and a few chick flicks."

"Sounds like a plan. Let me tell Irene I'm leaving and we can go." Shannon went back to the kitchen where she was met by a very worried Irene. "What's the matter Irene?"

"Do you have a minute?" Irene was worrying her apron with her hands.

Shannon became alarmed, "What's the matter? Is it Paddy?"

"Oh no. Everything's fine with Paddy. Can we step out back?" Without waiting for an answer, Irene headed out the back door of the kitchen.

Once outside, Irene turned to face Shannon, her arms crossed over her chest. "I have to tell you somethin but I don't want to scare you." Too late, Shannon was already there.

"Just spit it out for God's sake! You're freaking me out!" She thought Irene would be quick to reassure her but she just stood there with her arms crossed, her brows scrunched together.

Taking a deep breath, she finally spoke. "Remember I told you the story of Seth's childhood and his friends, Joseph and Naome'?" Shannon just nodded. She had a funny feeling this had something to do with Joseph.

"Well, what I didn't tell you was how when they used to come in here after school and even when they were grown, the way Joseph acted around Naome'." She took another deep breath and Shannon could tell it was going to be a long conversation so she sat on the little chair propped next to the door. Irene leaned against the truck.

"I always thought there was just somethin not right about Joseph. He would somehow manage to be the one sittin next to Naome' at the booth or he would wedge himself between them when they would stand around talkin. Most folks didn't notice it, but I did. It wasn't just the way Joseph acted. It was the look on Naome's face whenever he was around. She tried to hide it but I could tell. She was scared! The only thing Seth and Naome' ever argued about was Joseph. On the rare occasion when they were here without Joseph, I would see her lean over, whispering to Seth, waving her arms around like she was trying to get him to unblock his mind or somethin and he would sit there and give her a look like she was crazy or sometimes he'd look at her with a "talk to the hand" attitude. She would get frustrated and then give up and apologize. I ain't stupid. I know she was tryin to tell Seth about how Joseph was when he didn't think anyone was paying attention. I never did understand Seth's loyalty to him. He didn't want to believe anything bad about his best friend even from the woman he loved." Irene gave Shannon a pointed look before continuing, "Sometimes I would catch Joseph when his guard was down, and let me tell you, it made my skin crawl." Irene looked directly into Shannon's eyes, "I've seen that same look… when he watches you."

Shannon sucked in her breath. At last someone else who saw it too. Thinking Shannon was shocked, Irene leaned forward, "He's got some kinda obsession with you. I feel it in my bones. Keep your distance from him. He's bad news. If you can, find a way to keep Seth away from him. He will only get him into trouble." She pushed away from the truck and leaned close to Shannon, "I know not to try to dissuade Seth from havin anythin to do with Joseph if I want to continue to be his friend but I will tell you this…he's *not* Seth's friend". She waited for Shannon's reaction.

"Irene, I couldn't agree with you more." She related the events of the cook out. When she was done, Irene nodded her head.

"You go with your gut. If you think he was there, then he was. God! It gives me the heebie jeebies to think that he was just inches from you in that bathroom." She gave a little shiver. "You're welcome to stay here tonight. We can set up a cot for you in the living room."

Shannon looked at her, affectionately, "Thanks for the invite, but Millie is going to stay with me while Seth is gone, his idea. He felt bad about leaving me alone with no company. I don't think he was concerned about my safety so much as he didn't want me to get lonely." Irene smiled at the dreamy look on Shannon's face when she mentioned Seth's name.

"Okay then. Just remember, you always have a place to stay. This is gonna be yours soon and you can either rent out the upstairs or move in yourself, though I don't see that happenin with Seth havin a perfectly livable place for the two of you. Not to mention the view from his place." Her face became serious again, "Just be careful and let me know if anything weird happens. Paddy will be over there lickety split."

Shannon hugged the older woman and assuring her, went back inside.

Irene said a silent prayer for Shannon. She had a bad feeling, like someone had walked over her grave.

CHAPTER 24

"Make yourself at home while I go freshen up. I smell like hamburger grease. Why don't you put the movie in the player?" Shannon called over her shoulder as she headed down the hall to the bathroom.

Millie grabbed the popcorn bag and nuked it in the microwave. The 42 inch flat screen television was on a half wall directly across from the love seat. She kicked her shoes off and settled down while she grabbed the remote for the disc player. As she hit the power button, classic rock ballads played out of unseen speakers. "Surround sound. Cool." She pressed the button for the DVD player and the music was replaced with full bodied theatre sound as she watched the previews. The microwave beeped and Millie got up to take it out when she was startled by the ringing of her cell phone. She rushed to her purse and looked at the caller I.D. Unknown. She answered it, "Hello?" She recognized the smooth voice at once. It was all business, "Where are you?" "Oh hey," she answered, her voice dropping to a whisper. "Why are you calling?" He laughed. There was no humor in it, "I'm keeping tabs on my *lady*". He said the last word sarcastically. It made her cringe. She knew she wasn't a lady but it hurt to hear it anyway. "Seriously, we just got here and were sitting down to watch a movie." She heard his breath hitch, "Is she right there with you?"

"No, she's in the shower. If you must know, she said she smelled like hamburger grease and wanted to freshen up", her voice was caustic.

"Careful. I don't like it when you get uppity", but he couldn't seem to sound mad. He remembered sneaking into the bathroom while she showered. He thought about how she had looked, the water streaming over her voluptuous body. He reached down and cupped his growing erection. "Okay then, good night." He hung up the phone quickly and went to his computer. He couldn't wait to try out his new toy.

Shannon stepped out of the shower and wrapped a towel around her wet hair. Grabbing one of Seth's plaid robes, she cinched the waist and walked into the bedroom where she dug through her suitcase for her boy shorts. After towel drying hair and rolling the too long sleeves up, she walked into the living room. Picking up her cell phone, she slipped it into the pocket of the robe and plopped on the couch. "Man that felt like heaven! I love working at the diner but sometimes I feel so grubby!" She reached her hand into the popcorn bowl and shoved a fistful into her mouth. When she had swallowed enough that she could talk she reached over and picked up the margarita wine cooler that Millie had set on the coffee table. "How did you know these were my favorite?" She took a long swig. It felt so good and cold on her parched throat. "So what movie did you put in?" It really didn't matter to her, she was just glad to have the company.

Millie had never seen Shannon so at ease. Was it because there were no men around or was it that Joseph wasn't around? "Blood and Chocolate. It's one of my favorites. Have you seen it?"

Shannon was surprised by the title. "Never heard of it. What's it about?"

"It's a love story between a human and a werewolf," Millie said dreamily. "Their love beats the seemingly insurmountable odds. It's very romantic, you'll love it." She pressed the play button.

Shannon hated to admit it, but Millie was right, it was really good. When the credits rolled, she turned to Millie, "You're right, it was very good. I loved the chemistry between them."

Millie stretched her arms over her head, "Do you believe in love at first sight?"

Before she met Seth, Shannon's answer would have been a definite "no", but how could she deny it when she had met her soul mate? "Yes, yes I do." She blushed a little at her admission.

Millie turned toward her, the T.V. totally forgotten, "Tell me how you knew Seth was "the one"."

Shannon got up and went to the refrigerator for another wine cooler. "Do you want another one?"

"Yeah, sure." Millie took the bottle Shannon handed her and popped the top.

Sitting down, she quickly drained half the bottle at once. She had to admit, she was getting a little tipsy. She never could hold her alcohol. That's probably why she wasn't much of a drinker. Her face became flush from its affect. "When I walked into the diner and saw him sitting alone, looking like he didn't have a friend in the world, I felt sorry for him but when he looked at me and our eyes locked, I couldn't catch my breath. It was like the electricity was a physical thing, you know? I guess I knew right then." She paused to take another sip then continued, "I didn't recognize it then. I had never felt that strong an attraction to any man….ever. It was very confusing and I was so scared that he didn't feel the same." She sighed, "but the first time we kissed…" her face took on a dreamy quality", It was like…. skydiving. Just letting go." She turned looked at Millie and saw the tears welling up in her eyes.

"Oh Shannon! That's so romantic!" The tears spilled over, "Why can't I find someone like that?"

"I'm sure you have plenty of men beating down your door. Look at you, you're beautiful." Shannon touched her shoulder reassuringly.

"Thanks Shannon. I have had plenty of men beating on something but it's never been my door." She gave a little dry laugh, "Seriously, I seem to attract the wrong kind of guys. Why do you think that is?"

Shannon didn't want to hurt her feelings. Millie was a great girl if anyone took the time to find out, but she gave off the wrong signals. Steeling herself, Shannon looked directly into Millie's eyes, "Do you really want to know what I think?"

Millie was floored by the intensity of Shannon's gaze. She tried to swallow the lump that suddenly formed in her throat, "Yeah, I guess I do. I respect your opinion." She braced herself for the criticism.

"I think that you are very sweet and trusting and your heart is bigger than Texas." She looked at Millie, a soft smile on her face, "I also think that you are extremely open and certain types of men hone in on that. I'm not saying that you should become hard hearted, that's just not you, but it might be a good idea to maybe not be so eager to open up to men you've just met." She let out a long breath, searching for Millie's reaction.

"Is that it?" Millie laughed and took another swig of her drink. "God, I thought you were going to start ripping me apart, Millie you wear too much make-up, you wear slutty clothes, you flirt too much, your hair is too blond and too big, you don't need to be wearing a push up bra, you know, that kind of stuff." She plopped back against the couch and laughed. "You have to be the sweetest person I have ever met." She reached out and gave Shannon a bear hug. "Well, I think I'll go take my face off and get comfortable. I've got another movie for us to watch. I'll be right back."

Shannon sat eating popcorn and drinking her third wine cooler, feeling the effects. She found herself wishing Seth were there. Her arms ached to hold him. She leaned her head against the back of the couch and closed her eyes imagining him there. Suddenly her cell phone rang. Startled, she fumbled as she tried to pull it out of the pocket of the robe, sending it flying across the floor. She scrambled after it, praying she could get it in time. "Hello? Hello?" her voice almost panicky.

"Hey, are you alright?" Seth's voice was anxious.

She breathed a sigh of relief, "I am now". They both relaxed as he told her about his day. She loved the huskiness of his voice. She told him a little about the movie she'd just watched. She heard him chuckling, "Why are you laughing? It was a love story, not a romantic comedy."

"I was worried at first but I've got it figured out now... you're drunk!"

Shannon tried to sound indignant, "I am not! I just had a few wine coolers. Millie brought them. Do I sound different?" She hadn't noticed she was slurring her words.

"It's not anything obvious, but I can tell."

"Well since I'm drunk and can't be responsible for anything I say..." She lowered her voice to a sexy whisper, "I wish you were here with me right now, kissing me, holding me against your gorgeous body while we do wicked things to eachother".

Seth's breath caught in his throat. His breathing becoming uneven, his voice ragged, "I wish I were there with you. I would bury my hands in your golden red hair, kiss you until your knees buckled and as you collapsed I would carry you to the bed and peel your clothes off... slowly. I would then kiss each one of your nipples and taste them with my tongue. Sliding my tongue down further, over your soft stomach and then I would take you into my mouth." His erection was getting painful but he continued, "Mmm, You taste like honey on my tongue. I would lick your button until you grabbed my hair, urging me on until you came in my mouth."

Shannon's breathing became labored as she imagined Seth there doing to her all the things he was describing. Her wanting was painful. Somehow she knew it was just as painful for him. Bold from the liquor, she decided to try her hand at it. "But before you make love to me I would bring your mouth up for a passionate kiss. Then I would run my tongue down your neck and nibble on your nipples, swirling my tongue around them until they became hard as rocks. Then I would slowly run my tongue and teeth down your chest to your stomach as my hand rubbed up your thigh and my mouth and hand would meet at your crotch. I would wrap my mouth around you Can you feel my mouth on you?"

Seth thought he would explode with desire. The pain was excruciating but also extremely pleasurable. "Yes", he managed to croak.

She smiled at the affect she had. Becoming bolder she whispered, "Touch yourself Seth. Imagine it's me touching you, pleasuring you. Let me hear your passion."

Seth closed his eyes and did as he was told. He groaned as his need for her became a burning inferno. "I can smell the wonderful gardenia scent of your hair. Oh God Shannon! I love you so much!" His body shook with his release.

"I love you too," she whispered, her unspent desire still boiling inside her.

"That was incredible! Did you get off too?" He would have loved it if they had come together.

"No, I'm not alone. Millie is here. She just went to get ready for bed. I'm just happy I could do something for you. I can't wait until you're here with me." She felt her heart flutter.

"Oh, I was hoping that you were pleasuring yourself as well. I guess I'll just have to make it up to you when I get home", he teased, his voice husky smooth again.

Just then Millie came bouncing into the living room. She stopped when she saw Shannon's face all flushed. "What's wrong? Is Seth okay?" concern clearly in her voice.

Shannon used all her will power not to burst out laughing, "Uh, everything is fine. Seth's great. He says Hi."

"Hey Seth!" Millie shouted toward the phone.

"I will talk to you tomorrow. Get some sleep and dream about me, okay?"

"Don't worry, I will. I love you, hurry home." She tried her best to keep her voice even. She could feel the ache working its way to her heart. "Bye." Raising the lapels of his robe, she breathed in his woodsy scent. There would be no sleeping tonight without a little help. She raised the fourth bottle to her lips and took a long pull. If she was going to get through the night, she would have to be drunk. "Put another movie in, Millie." She leaned back and put her feet on the coffee table, enjoying her buzz.

Shannon was out before the movie was halfway over. Millie pulled her up and helped her to the bedroom. Laying her gently onto the bed, she pulled the covers over her but Shannon kicked them off, her robe coming untied, leaving her body bare to the night air. Millie blushed as she averted her eyes and turned out the light, closing the door behind her.

She grabbed a pillow and blanket out of the hall closet and lay down, waiting for sleep to overtake her.

Joseph panned the camera toward the bed where Shannon lay exposed. *This is so good! I can't believe I didn't think of it sooner.* He licked his lips hungrily as the infrared lens turned Shannon's light skin to dark, her rosy nipples to light. It wasn't as good as being inches from her in the bathroom but it would do in a pinch. He had been disappointed when earlier he had just missed catching her changing her clothes. He could feel his lust engorging his pants and reaching down, unzipped his pants.

Shannon tossed and turned as the nightmare unfolded. She was walking on the trail near Seth's when she realized someone was following her. She found her feet quickening as panic set in. The footsteps behind her grew closer as she tried to put distance between them. She began to run as she felt the person gaining on her but it didn't matter how fast she ran, he was going to catch her. Suddenly, she felt hands grabbing her arm, snatching her backward. She tried to scream but a hand clamped over her mouth. She was helpless. She kicked and struggled but it was no use, his arms were like steel traps, holding her motionless. Suddenly, he twisted her around to face him and she looked into the eyes of Richmond, her departed husband. He replaced his hand with his mouth. She fought him with everything she had but to no avail. When he pulled his mouth away to look at her, his face had changed into Joseph's and he was grinning, that evil shark's tooth grin she hated so much. "Oh God Joseph!" She shrieked in her sleep as she writhed on the bed.

Joseph was stunned to hear his name. "She's dreaming about me!" he exclaimed with delight. "And by the way she's thrashing around, I bet it's a wet dream. Why wouldn't she want me, look at me?" He strutted around the small computer room, doing a little victory dance. He collapsed into the desk chair, "I knew she didn't love Seth. It's all an act to make me jealous! All that pretending she was doing at the diner, treating me like everyone else, when all the time she was just playing hard to get. Well I guess the next time we're together I'm going to have to put my theory to the test." He went back to watching his private home movie.

Shannon sat bolt upright in bed. 'Dear God that was a horrible nightmare,' she thought as she turned on the bedside lamp. Looking down she saw that her/Seth's robe had come open and feeling like she was on display even though no one else was in the room, she quickly shed the robe and pulled on her flannel pajamas. Feeling less exposed, she climbed under the covers and turned out the light. Determined to have sweet dreams, she filled her mind with thoughts of Seth.

CHAPTER 25

Sunday morning came way too early. Shannon knew she didn't have to be at the diner until 7:30 but she forgot to change the alarm clock. Rolling over, she hit the button, groaning as the shrillness pounded inside her head. *I should never drink wine coolers ever again.* She plopped back onto the bed and clutched her head between her hands trying to stop the pounding. Just about the time she started to doze off....

"Hey sleepy head, time to get up!" Millie bounced on the bed and hit her over the head with one of the throw pillows. The pounding started back up but this time it was more intense. "Ohhh, please, let me die in peace!" Shannon moaned as she tried to cover her head.

Millie jerked the pillow away from her, "come on, I've got the full proof remedy for a hangover. Believe me, it works every time." Taking Shannon's hand, she pulled her off the bed and down the hall to the kitchen where a strange green liquid was sitting ominously in a glass on the dinette table. Millie swooped it up and handing it to her, encouraged Shannon to drink it all without stopping.

"Oooh that is so...disgusting", she laughed as she let out a loud belch. Millie laughed too. "Gotta make sure you have fuel for work today." Shannon sat down at the table and looked at Millie. "Wow, I believe my headache is letting up. What's in that stuff?"

"Oh, just a bunch of things you find in the kitchen, but I can't tell you what they are." She crossed her chest, "I crossed my heart and hoped to die. It's a family secret."

"Okay, I wouldn't want you to divulge family secrets, but hey, it does work. My head has completely stopped hurting. As a matter of fact, I feel pretty darn good." She finished her omelet and went to take a shower.

Shannon offered to take Millie home but she declined, saying she wanted to hang around if it was okay with Shannon.

Shannon got off work at 2:30 and drove Seth's truck into Sanctuary for some groceries. She was on the phone with Millie when she happened to pass by a used car dealership and something caught her eye. She decided to check it out and turned into the parking lot. "I gotta go. I'll call you in a little while." She parked and looked out the windshield, smiling at the sky blue convertible Volvo. She jumped when someone tapped on her window. Instead of rolling the window down, she opened the door and stepped outside. The salesman flashed a toothy grin at her and asked if she saw anything she liked. Introducing herself, she walked over to the car and ran her hand along the hood. *It's about the exact color of Seth's eyes. I really need to get my own transportation. We can't keep using only one vehicle.* She asked the man if she could test drive it. Smiling, he excused himself and disappeared into the showroom, returning promptly, the keys dangling from his hand. She asked him about the mileage and the history of the car. He told her it had belonged to the owner's wife and that it had very low mileage. She had it about one year and then she had seen a BMW convertible she wanted so the owner had put it up for sale, not confident it would get sold because the folks in Sanctuary liked to ride in trucks and SUVs so there wasn't much of a demand for $70,000.00 convertible cars.

"I'd like to take it for a test drive. Do you need to be with me?" She wasn't sure what their policy was but sometimes they just made a copy of your drivers' license.

"Not necessary. Just bring her back in one piece." He tossed the keys to her and she slid behind the wheel. The interior was beige leather, with a state-of-the-art stereo system and blue tooth. She pushed a button and the top peeled back soundlessly then disappeared inside a secret compartment. She pulled out and headed toward Seth's.

Pulling up into the driveway a few minutes later, she honked the horn exuberantly, waving as Millie poked her head through the curtains. "Jeez Shannon, this is beautiful but it looks familiar. Did you get it at the used car lot in town?"

Shannon nodded, "The salesman told me it belonged to the owner's wife but she had gotten bored with it. It's only a year old and it has really low mileage. Did he feed me a load of bull hockey?"

Millie laughed and jumped into the passenger seat, not bothering to open the door. "If that's the only thing stopping you from signing the papers, let me ease your mind. Everything he told you is true but I know for a fact they were asking $55,000.00 for that car." She looked at Shannon as though seeing her for the first time, "How can you afford it? Did you inherit a bunch of money, rob a bank or something?"

Shannon shook her head, "Millie, remember the conversation we had on the first day we met? I told you I had gotten out of an abusive relationship? Well, I'll tell you all about it on the way. I need you to drive Seth's truck back here while I drive my new car but first we need to hit the grocery store for some party food."

"Okay, but you were saying about the reason you can afford this fabulous automobile...?"

Shannon sighed and started from the beginning.

By the time they had bought just about everything in the little market, it was starting to get dark.

"We better head on over to the dealership. He's going to think I stole the car." They both laughed and though Shannon started feeling the chill of the night air, she left the top down. They pulled into the parking lot and Shannon could have sworn she saw the salesman's shoulders relax when he spotted them. Composing himself, he ran over, "Well, how did she ride?" What was it with guys calling cars "she"? Shannon winked at Millie, "pretty good, actually. I think I'll take it."

He breathed a sigh of relief, "Well come on in and we'll set up the financing."

"Alright", Shannon agreed as she and Millie followed him into the little office. When they were seated he excused himself. A couple of minutes later, Shannon and Millie heard a commotion just outside the door, some whispered words and then the door was flung open and a large man wearing a Stetson hat and sporting designer cowboy boots entered, his bulk filling up the space in the door. "Howdy", reaching for her hand he pumped it vigorously. "I'm Billy Bob Tanner, owner of this here establishment." "Very nice to me you," she replied, her teeth rattling. "Well, my boy here says you're wantin to buy my wife's purty little convertible." He looked Shannon over speculatively, taking in her usual diner uniform, white men's shirt and faded Levi's. "We gonna have any problem gettin financing?"

Shannon looked at him levelly, "Actually, yes, we are."

He started to bluster but she cut him off, "I'm paying with a wire transfer so this will be a cash sale".

He narrowed his eyes but seeing the serious look on her face, smiled broadly, "Well, that's just dandy! I'll have my boy here draw up the paperwork."

"Sounds great"

"You know I bought that little beauty for my wife's birthday last year." He shook his head, "she gets bored easily". He smiled sheepishly at Shannon and she knew that cars weren't the only thing his wife got bored with. She felt sorry for him. "Don't worry, I promise I'll take really good care of… her." She reached out and took his hand. He seemed surprised by the gesture and cleared his throat, "Well, see that you do. I don't want to turn on the T.V. and see it wrapped around a tree or something."

"Don't worry, she's in good hands."

He started to leave and then turned and looked at her seriously, "Why did you buy her, if you don't mind me askin?"

"She's beautiful and I love that shade of blue."

"Well, it was nice meetin ya. If there's ever anything I can do for ya, just give me a holler, you know, in case she starts acting up." He pulled out a business card, but before handing it to her, he wrote on the back of it. She accepted it, flipping it over to find his private number written on the back.

"Gee, thanks", she commented and slipped it into her purse. He gave her a pointed look then broke out into a grin. "Well, better get on home to the little lady. She hates it when I'm late." Shannon could tell he was very much in love with his wife, even if the feeling wasn't mutual. She found she liked him more than she thought she would.

A few minutes later his "boy" came back into the office with the paperwork. He explained that the tag would be mailed to the dealership in about two weeks, and that he'd call her so she could come pick it up. Shannon shook his hand and he handed over the keys.

The wind was picking up as Shannon and Millie walked to the car. "You know, it might be a good idea to put the top up for the night," Millie suggested as she pulled her jacket tighter. "You're probably right," Shannon agreed.

Sanctuary looked totally different when the sun went down. The inconspicuous buildings Shannon had passed earlier were lit up with bright neon signs advertising every sort of alcoholic beverage. Shannon had assumed that they rolled up the sidewalks at dusk, but there were more vehicles parked along the streets than there were during dinner rush at the diner. "This place sure is hopping."

Millie's face lit up, "Hey, when was the last time you went out dancing?"

"Never," she replied distractedly. She was still trying to get over the number of people milling around. Where did they all come from?

Millie gaped at her, her eyes practically bulging out of her head. "Change of plans. Let's go to my house."

"Why? What for?" Shannon looked at her suspiciously.

Millie beamed at her, "just trust me. You won't regret it."

Knowing she was fighting a losing battle, Shannon turned down the road that led to Millie's apartment.

"Oh, you look so hot!"

Millie exclaimed as she inspected Shannon in the full length mirrored closet doors. Shannon looked at her reflection but all she saw was a stranger looking back at her. She had fiercely protested when Millie revealed her plans, but a part of her wanted to experience an honest to God honky-tonk. Now she was questioning her decision. She blushed as she turned sideways, inspecting her ensemble. Millie had dressed her in a hot pink, tank top mini-dress that hugged her body. It was made of some stretchy material, spandex, Millie called it, but the top layer was little iridescent beads. It looked sort of like a flapper dress from the twenties, but the hemline was far too short. She finished it off with matching hot pink stiletto pumps. If the dress wasn't bad enough, Millie had insisted on doing her make-up and hair. Squealing with delight at the results, she had bowed dramatically, giving Shannon the hand-held mirror. Shannon sat stunned as she looked at her face. Millie had insisted she put on false lashes. Shannon had never worn anything false, not even hair extensions, but she couldn't help but be pleased with the results. Her eyes practically popped from beneath the heavy lashes and the make-up was applied heavily, yet tastefully. She thought she would look quite natural walking across a stage in some local beauty pageant. She breathed a sigh of relief when Millie decided to forgo putting on heavy foundation, electing instead to let her freckles show. She finished off by applying a sparkling pink tinted lip gloss that stated on the tube, guaranteed to last up to twelve hours. Millie put her hands in Shannon's hair, "Wow, your hair is soft as a baby's. How do you keep it like that?"

"Oh, I just wash it and condition it. Most times I just throw it up into a ponytail. Why?"

"Have you ever dyed your hair or permed it or straightened it?"

"No. I never really thought about it. Richmond wanted it pulled back all the time. He said it gave me a more classic look. So, when I….left I decided to wear it the way I wanted."

Millie noticed she cringed a little at the mention of her dead husband's name and decided to change the subject. Grabbing a couple of jeweled barrettes, she pulled a couple of pieces of Shannon's hair away from her face and twisting them around, secured them with the barrettes. The affect, though subtle was striking.

"You look beautiful! Okay, now you just sit there and try not to mess anything up and I'll be ready in two shakes." Shannon watched as Millie grabbed a low-cut black sequined halter top and a pair of red spandex pants. She slipped on a pair of red and black sequined stilettos and refreshed her make-up. The whole process took less than ten minutes. Shannon was shocked when Millie breezed into the room looking like she had taken hours of preparation rather than mere minutes.

"Okay, let's go, we ain't gettin any younger." She linked arms with Shannon and they walked together to the car.

Millie's directions put them in front of a large warehouse building with a neon sign that simply said, "Warehouse 5". If not for the flashing sign, it would have looked like a factory. The parking lot was almost full but Shannon managed to find a spot in the far back corner away from the building. She was about to express her reservations but Millie had jumped out of the car as soon as it stopped. Sighing, Shannon followed her to the entrance door. There was no line outside and except for the cars, the place looked empty. Shannon gave Millie a quizzical look, "Are you sure about this? It looks creepy." "Have a little faith." Millie knocked on the large steel door. Not two seconds later it swung open and a very large, muscular black man stood in the doorway, his arms crossed in front of him. His face was serious until he caught sight of Millie. A broad smile appeared as he reached out and gave her a bone cracking bear hug but Millie just giggled and slapped him on his huge upper arm. "Behave yourself Marty!" He gave her a reproachful look, "Hey, you know I don't like it when you call me that." His voice was almost whiney. *So much for the macho man impression,* Shannon thought as she struggled to keep a straight face. "Oh, alright, *Martin,*" Millie conceded. "This is my friend Shannon."

He looked Shannon over appreciatively, "Very nice to meet you, Shannon". He reached out, grabbed her hand and bowing low, lifted it to his lips. Shannon almost lost it at the overly dramatic gesture. "Thanks, same here." He straightened up and flung his arm out gallantly, "Ladies, welcome to Warehouse 5". Shannon and Millie walked past Martin and into another world.

The place was decked out in full 70's glamour. There were disco balls, lighted dance floors and "purple rain" purple on the walls. The tables were clear glass with hidden colored lights glowing from beneath. There was a live band playing, of course, disco music. Couples were dancing to the "disco beat" as Shannon and Millie made their way to one of the empty booths that lined the walls on each side of the large space. A waitress with a classic Farrah Fawcett wig and hot pants rolled up to the booth on skates, "Whatta ya have Millie?" she yelled over the music. Shannon was about to order a wine cooler when Millie interjected, "Two shots of tequila, a couple of limes, and some salt…and keep em coming", slipping the waitress a $50.00 bill". "Sure thing", the waitress skated away. Shannon was awed at the way she managed to maneuver through the crowded room. As Shannon looked around, she recognized several people from the diner. A table full of her regulars waved and she waved back self consciously. Why had Millie insisted on using her as a life sized Barbie doll? She pulled on the hem of the too short dress. The waitress returned with their tequila shots. Millie showed Shannon what to do and Shannon winced as the liquor burned her throat. After a couple of shots, a warm feeling spread to her stomach. She closed her eyes and leaned back on the hot pink velvet seat.

"Would you care to dance?" Shannon was shocked by the masculine voice so close to her ear. Her eyes flew open. She looked up into the face of a boy of about eighteen. He had been one of the guys who had waved at her earlier. She made her mind push through the alcoholic fuzz, trying to remember his name. "Hey Jared," she decided to be polite. By the look on the faces of the others, he had obviously lost a bet. They were waiting for her to shoot him down. Feeling for the boy she beamed up at him, "Sure, that'd be great!" His expression changed from anguish to triumph. He took her hand and they found a small space on the lighted floor. The tempo changed to a slow song. Shannon thought Jared turned a shade redder than his already sun-kissed skin tone. She held her arms out in front in an invitation. He beamed again and pulled her against his body. She couldn't help but compare his bony boy-man body to Seth's athletic muscular frame. He was clearly half her size but he could dance quite well. She was surprised to find she was enjoying herself. No sooner had he thanked her when another of the men asked if he could cut in.

Shannon lost all track of time. As much as she wanted to sit down, (Millie's shoes were beginning to give her blisters) she didn't have time between dances so she took them off and held them by the straps while she was whisked around the dance floor. Managing to peek over the shoulder of her partner, she searched the room for Millie. She found her, laughing and twirling on the arm of a cute blonde guy. She raised her voice to be heard above the noise, "Man, Millie's got some moves!" He yelled back, "Yeah, she's won like a zillion dance contests." Shannon couldn't believe it. Why hadn't she mentioned it? She leaned over close to her partner's ear, "I really need to sit down. I have to get something to drink, but thanks for the dance!" Excusing herself, she weaved her way through the crowd, back to her table. She thought she was going to have to call the waitress over for refills, but when she got to the table, there sat two more shots of tequila, and some fresh lime slices. She drank them down in succession and tried to ignore the room swaying. 'Whoa, those pack some kinda punch.' Sitting back against the plush bench she closed her eyes.

She was enjoying the rhythm of the music when suddenly she felt a finger slide down her arm. "Hello Shannon," Joseph cooed as he slid in next to her. Her eyes flew open in shock at the sound of his voice. She thought about trying to slide out the other side but the combination of booze and too much dancing weakened her. So, knowing there was no escape, she plastered on a fake smile. "Hello Joseph," her speech slurring a bit. He leaned close, *much too close* and whispered in her ear, "Sorry but I didn't get that. What did you say?" his lips were actually touching her ear. She felt light headed from the alcohol, but no amount of booze could keep her skin from crawling. Leaning away from him, she took another shot from the table. *I thought I drank the two that were here already.* Shrugging her shoulders she downed the tequila, licked the salt she'd poured on her hand and sucked on the slice of lime. Joseph laughed and held up two fingers to the passing waitress. *He's trying to get me drunk! Too late!* Shannon fumed. "Sorry Joseph but I have to use the ladies room." She started sliding toward him so he would let her out but he paused for just a few seconds too long and her breast rubbed against his arm. Her face was inches from his and he could smell her perfume. It smelled of some sort of exotic flower. It suited her and made him burn with lust. "I recognize that dress but I must say it looks much better on you", as he peeked down the front of her dress. She thought she might just throw up in his lap. She really wished she would but she had never thrown up from drinking. "Thanks, excuse me?" He slid off the seat and Shannon jumped out and scooted by him, not giving him another chance to pull her back down, perhaps on his lap.

On her way to the bathroom she caught Millie's eye and motioned toward the restroom. Millie made an excuse to her dance partner, and met Shannon inside. "Millie, I can't believe Joseph is here! How did he know we'd be here?" How was she going to escape his clutches? She spied the window in the back of the room and wondered how much damage would be done to Millie's dress if she managed to wriggle out of the small opening. "Joseph, oh, this is his usual haunt on weekends." She stared at Shannon, "Didn't I tell you?" Shannon just stared dumbfounded. "This is where we met." Shannon gaped at Millie, "Wait a minute, isn't this the same Joseph you told me about? The humiliating sex play, the S&M? I seem to remember you wanting to get out from under his control." Shannon's voice was getting louder as she became more certain that Millie had rationalized herself back into that destructive relationship. Staring into Millie's guilt ridden face she threw her hands up, "You've gone back to him, haven't you?"

At the accusatory look from Shannon, Millie's back straightened stubbornly, "Well, I got to thinking about it and I weighed the pros and cons. The pros won." She gave her a tight smile, shrugged and turned to check her face in the mirror, "That doesn't mean you and I can't be friends." She looked at Shannon in the mirror, "Right?" Shannon saw her smile falter just a bit and realized that even though she was acting nonchalantly, underneath she was sweating.

Shannon wasn't about to let Joseph ruin her friendship with Millie. She liked Millie. Millie was funny and fun to be with. Shannon pulled her into her arms and hugged her, "of course we can still be friends. You're still planning my wedding, right?" She felt Millie's body relax as she returned the hug. They parted and Millie went back to checking her face. Shannon caught her reflection and did a double take. She just couldn't believe she was looking at herself. She made a play at checking her eyelashes as she commented, "I still think you can do better. What about your dance partner. He's really cute." Millie giggled, "His boyfriend thinks so too". Shannon's mouth hung open, "Oh. Well, there has to be someone here who's shown interest in you. Look at how great you dance!"

"Thanks, but other than Thad, my gay dance partner, No one has the nerve to approach me as long as Joseph's around." Shannon saw her flinch. "What is it Millie?"

"Well, there was this one time…some guy who was passing through bought me a couple of drinks and we danced a little. Joseph walked in and was real nice to the guy. I thought he was cool with it. I mean the guy didn't try to pick me up or anything, he just wanted some company before he moved on." She looked down at her fingernails as she continued, "The next day I saw an article about him in the paper. He had been rushed to the hospital. The police said he was a victim of a hit and run. They did a preliminary investigation but his blood alcohol was pretty high so they figured he wandered into the road at the wrong time. I went to see him but the minute he saw me he started yelling for me to get out, like he hated me. I turned and ran out of the room. I figured Joseph had something to do with his "accident" but he never said another word about it and I sure as hell wasn't going to nag him. It was like it never happened." She looked up and locked eyes with Shannon, "I think he did it because he was jealous. That has to mean he cares, right?" her eyes were begging for reassurance.

Shannon was torn. Part of her wanted to scream at Millie and shake her until her teeth rattled in her head, but part of her wanted to be the supportive friend. Not wanting to lie, she answered, "I have heard of men doing crazy things when they're jealous".

Millie beamed at Shannon, "Are you ready to get back out there? I don't know about you but I'm parched. Let's go have a drink." She linked her arm with Shannon's as they walked back into the main room.

The music seemed to be louder after being in the almost soundproof bathroom. Shannon resisted the urge to put her hands over her ears. They walked back over to their table, Millie jabbering excitedly, Shannon dreaded every step that brought her closer to Joseph. Her eyes swept the area. The table was empty! She breathed a sigh of relief. Two more shots were waiting for them. They looked at eachother, picked up the glasses, and knocked them back, slamming them back onto the table. Shannon felt the liquor burn a path to her stomach. She pulled out her cell phone to check the time and found she had four voice mail messages. "Oh shit! Millie, I have to step outside and check my messages. I'll be right back."

After getting her hand stamped, she walked outside into the night air. It did wonders for clearing her head. She called up her voicemail and listened, her heart beating faster with each one. "Shannon, hey, it's Seth. I just wanted to talk to you. Call me back, okay?" Then the next, "Shannon, it's me again. Where are you? Call me back." Then the next, "Shannon where the hell are you? Why aren't you answering your phone? Shit…call me." Then the final one, "I'm really worried now! Please, call me the minute you get this. I'm packing up tonight and catching the red eye. I'll be home in a few hours." Shannon felt the blood drain from her face. She dialed his number but got his voicemail. "Hey Seth, I'm so sorry I didn't answer. Millie took me to a local dance club. I guess the music was so loud I couldn't hear my phone. No need to worry so if you get this message don't cut your trip short. I'm fine, really." She was about to end with "I love you" but ran out of time. God, she hated voicemail. You practically had to talk shorthand. She looked back to see the time of the last message. 9:30 p.m. It was 12:30 now. That would mean that his plane landed and he's on the way home.

Rushing back inside, she located Millie at the table with Joseph. 'Oh, great.' She hurried over and leaned close to Millie, ignoring Joseph, "I have to leave. There was some kind of miscommunication and Seth is on the way home. Do you think you could find a ride ….?" She looked over at Joseph, "or I can take you". Millie leaned toward Joseph and said something in his ear. He nodded and Millie said, "Joseph has agreed to drive me home so you go be with your Seth. I'll talk to you later." Shannon didn't know if she should insist on taking Millie home or let Joseph take her. Thinking back on their conversation in the bathroom, Shannon opted for the latter.

She hugged Millie and said good bye to Joseph who laughed and held his arms out for a hug. Not wanting to seem like a coward, Shannon stepped around the table and quickly hugged him, sliding out from under his arms before he could get a good grip on her. She said her goodbyes to Millie and hurried outside to her car, her heart racing at the thought that soon she would be in Seth's arms.

CHAPTER 26

Shannon raced back to Seth's place, praying she wouldn't get pulled over by the police. She knew if she was given a breathalyzer test, she would never pass. She had lost count of how many shots she'd had. The ring of her cell phone startled her and she almost lost control on a sharp turn. "Hello?" "Are you still at the club?" She could tell he was struggling to keep his voice even. "No, I'm on my way home. I'm so sorry I worried you. I guess I lost track of time." Seth took a deep breath, "Have you been drinking?" Shannon didn't feel drunk but she knew she'd had too many. "Yes, I had tequila shots." He didn't respond and Shannon was beginning to think she had lost signal. "How many?" his voice broke the silence, cold steel. Suddenly Shannon felt claustrophobic. Pushing the button to lower the top, the frigid wind whipping through her hair, she took a sobering breath of night air. "Shannon, answer me, how many tequila shots did you have?"

"Too many to count", her tone crisp as she felt her anger rising. "But if I had to guess I'd say....ten."

"Are you driving?" He was on the edge, His concern translating into possessiveness. Surely she wouldn't be that reckless, but what little hope he had was swiftly crushed.

"Yes, I'm pulling into the driveway now. Why don't you come see for yourself?" She pushed the end button on her phone and tossed it unto the passenger seat. She didn't have anything to be sorry about. She wasn't going to let him bully her. She'd had enough of that with Richmond. She pulled the convertible to a stop. Before she could take the keys out of the ignition, Seth was beside the car. He grabbed her around the waist and lifted her into his arms where he held her tightly, raining kisses all over her face.

Shannon's anger floated away with the night breeze as she melted in his arms. "Oh God Shannon! I thought something had happened to you! You scared the hell out of me!" He felt so good, his muscular arms squeezing tighter than he ever had before. Leaning her head back, she gazed into his beautiful eyes. They were fraught with worry. She reached up and smoothed away his frown. "It's okay. I'm okay. There's no need to worry," she cooed as she rose up on her tiptoes to place a kiss on his trembling lips.

His reaction was surprising. He groaned as he hungrily devoured her lips, his tongue shoved its way deep into her mouth. Shannon felt her knees buckle under her. Lifting her up, he placed her onto the hood of her brand new car. He pulled away for a moment to remark, "Nice car". She murmured, "Thanks", and he was kissing her again. His mouth ran down the length of her neck until his tongue was blocked by the band of pink material at the top of her dress. Snaking his hand around, he found the hidden zipper. He took it in his hand, sliding it down until the flimsy material bunched at her waist, leaving her breasts bare to the night. Shannon thought she would be cold but the heat from both their bodies was warmer than any electric blanket. He twirled his tongue around each nipple, suckling the peak between his teeth. Shannon moaned and grabbed his hair, keeping him from pulling away. He worshiped her breasts as though they were the most precious thing in the world. His hands slid down her back to grasp her butt, and in one swift motion he pulled her against him. Her body caught fire as she anticipated the feel of him inside her. She was shocked when he made no move to undress himself or take off the small bit of covering over her womanhood. Shannon blushed as she recalled the gleam in Millie's eye as she held up the next to nothing sheer hot pink thong, coaxing Shannon to try them on. They had felt sinful. Now, all she wanted was for Seth to tear them from her body, but instead, he started grinding his pelvis against hers as he continued to lave her nipples, driving her to the point of distraction. The combination of his mouth worshiping her breasts and his pelvis grinding on hers was having a maddening effect on her. She leaned her head back, gazing at the millions of stars hanging in the velvet sky. It was intoxicating.

Seth moved his mouth, while grinding his hips, up her neck and back to her lips. His kiss was brutal and exciting. He moved to her ear where he nipped her lobe, "Tell me what you want me to do to you". Shannon was beyond shame, the effects of the alcohol combined with her desire made her bold but she wasn't accustomed to voicing her wants so she hesitated, moaning and moving her hips instead, keeping rhythm with him but he wasn't going to be put off, "Say it," his voice husky as he rubbed her lobe between his teeth. "I want you to take me, now!" she breathed raggedly. She was almost at the brink. Sensing she was about to climax, he stopped abruptly, "No... not yet." Her eyes fluttered, not quite understanding what had just happened. Shannon whined as a child who had had its favorite toy snatched from its greedy little hands. "Wha...what are you doing?"

He grinned at her as his hand went under her dress. As though he were reading her mind, his hands gripped the piece of lace on each side of her hips and yanked them hard. Her heart rejoiced as she heard the fabric tear away from her body. "Oh yes, Seth. Yes, make love to me!" She didn't think it was possible to feel this much heat without turning to ashes. Now surely, he would make love to her, releasing her from this sweet agony. Closing her eyes in anticipation, she waited for him to fill her up with his erection. Unexpectedly, she felt his mouth on the inside of her thigh and a moan escaped her lips. She quickly tried to wiggle away. *He couldn't do that now! I've been dancing all night in a sweaty club and I'm not very fresh.* Seth held her captive with his hands as his mouth traveled upward. She reached down, gripping his hair. He looked up puzzled, "I thought you enjoyed this", he sounded disappointed.

"Oh, I do, it's just that, well..." her voice trailed off as her face flushed. He continued to hold his heated gaze on her. She knew she had to say something so when the words came out they were fast and breathy. "I'm all sweaty from dancing all night so I don't think it would be a good idea to....to do that." Not wanting to hurt his feelings she quickly added, "Maybe later, after I've had a shower?" She thought that hearing her explanation, he would jump away like he'd been bit by a rattlesnake but he just smiled, "You smell like gardenia and honey. I would live between your legs if it were possible." He gave her a reproachful look, "Now lay back and enjoy...I know I will."

His mouth found her core and she arched her back as little sparks of light flashed in front of her eyes. She could feel herself teetering on the precipice, her body stiffening as wave upon wave of pleasure shot through her like lightening. She barely had time to bask in the afterglow when suddenly she found herself being lifted up and turned onto her stomach. She felt the cold wind as it danced across her exposed behind. Her breath caught in her throat as she heard him unzipping his pants. As he leaned over her, his voice was raspy with desire. "Do you have any idea how crazy you make me?" She didn't have time to answer. Still wet from her own orgasm, he slid easily inside of her, his hips thrusting, his manhood filling her. It felt like he was trying to crawl up inside her. The sensation was explosive.

Grinding her butt in a circular motion, she could feel his member grow even more than before as the blood rushed to his center, making him lightheaded. He realized he was drunk…. with lust. Whispering love words in her ear, he massaged her breasts. "Oh Shannon, my love, you feel so warm. I could stay like this for eternity. If we didn't have to eat or sleep, I would be content to make love to you forever." Shannon was almost too far gone as he lunged one more time, freezing as he climaxed; her name on his lips.

Shannon joined him, arching her back, no longer feeling anything but the ecstasy of the moment.

Seth wrapped his arms around her pulling her against him, his breath slowly returning to normal. Shannon sighed contentedly in his arms. "Did I tell you I missed you?" her voice soft and intimate warmed his heart. He wondered how he could have lived this long without ever hearing her voice. It had the power to touch him as nothing else had. He whispered in her ear, "You didn't have to. I could tell." She shivered as his breath tickled her neck. Thinking she was cold, Seth zipped up her dress, swept her up in his arms, and carried her up the stairs to the apartment. Shannon didn't protest. She was right where she wanted to be.

CHAPTER 27

Shannon knew as the sun's rays penetrated her foggy brain that she was in trouble. The sound of the birds screaming, the wind roaring, and the clock's banging was enough to drive her mad, but how could the sun shine so bright without burning up the world? Moaning loudly, she grabbed a pillow and drew it around her head, trying to block out the cacophony. It was of little comfort. She raised her head to see the time and the room suddenly tilted sideways. Jumping out of bed, she ran for the bathroom, just making it to the toilet. Falling to her knees, she proceeded to throw up everything she had ever eaten or drank in her whole life. At least it seemed that way to her. Moaning loudly, she wanted nothing more than to rest her head on the cool ceramic rim and wait for death to release her from her suffering. Suddenly she felt a cold washcloth pressed against her forehead. "I'm here baby. It'll be alright." He knelt beside her and pulled her hair back, running the cold cloth over the back of her neck. It felt like heaven and she sent up praises to the porcelain God.

Shannon didn't know how much time had passed before the heaving subsided but she felt Seth's arm cradling her the whole time. He was a very good doctor. She looked at him apologetically, "I'm so sorry. You must think I'm a lush, but I swear I've never drunk like that before in my whole life." He looked at the pallor of her skin, "Do you feel like you can drink some juice?" She nodded feebly.

He picked her up and carried her back to the bed. She noticed he had closed the curtains. "Thanks for taking care of me." She felt extremely foolish. How could she have been so stupid? She just wanted to go out and have fun, and she did, but was it really worth it if this was the price she had to pay? "I'm sorry," she said simply.

"About what?" his brow creasing.

"About making you worry and cutting your trip short. I really didn't want that."

She was surprised to hear him chuckle, "I was leaving this morning to come home anyway. What's a few hours, give or take?" He leaned over and kissed the tip of her nose, "now you just lay back and let me take care of everything". He turned to leave but froze when Shannon sucked in her breath, "Oh my God! Look at the time! I'm going to be late. I have to get dressed." She made to get up but Seth put his hand on her shoulder, holding her down gently, "Don't worry about work. I'll call Irene and let her know you're feeling a little "under the weather".

"No, I have to go to work!" Shannon pushed, trying to get up but it was like trying to move a brick wall. "Seth, let me up!"

"I don't think that would be a very good idea", but he released her and stepped back, his lips curving up, a knowing look in his eyes.

Shannon stood up and realized too late it was a mistake. The room began to spin and she crumpled. She never hit the floor. Seth caught her and laid her on the bed, pulling the covers over her. "I'll go get some juice. Stay put!" he shook his finger at her reproachfully.

As much as she wanted to tell him to stick it, Shannon knew he was just looking out for her well being. Nodding her head, she complied. "okay, maybe you're right. Maybe I should rest a little while and go in later." He regarded her with a stern look, "No going to work today," he emphasized the word "today".

Shannon started to protest but knew it would be a losing battle so instead she snuggled under the covers.

"That's better. Now, I'll go get that juice." He leaned down and pressed his lips to her forehead.

A few minutes later he came back with a large glass of orange juice, two Advil, and a fried egg sandwich on a breakfast tray, balancing it in one hand.

Her eyes widened in surprise as she recognized the strange green liquid he held in his other hand. He set the tray down on the foot of the bed. "Uh, I found this in the refrigerator. You don't by any chance know what it is, do you? Cause it really stinks!" he wiggled his nose in disgust as he took another whiff of the obnoxious liquid. Shannon couldn't help but giggle.

"That looks like the concoction Millie made for me after I had too much to drink that first night. Believe it or not, it made me feel better right away." She was tickled by the way he was holding it out at arms length, like it was a pissed off skunk. "Don't be such a baby. Here, give it to me." Reaching out, she snatched it from his hand. He gawked as she downed the liquid in one gulp. She couldn't resist smacking her lips, watching as he crinkled his nose, "Yuck! How can you drink that crap?"

"It's really not that bad. She made it from things that were in the kitchen." She could already feel the miracle brew working. Her head stopped spinning and she felt her strength coming back. "I feel better already."

Seth looked doubtful, "Okay, after you eat everything on your plate, I'll help you take a shower. Then, if you still don't feel sick or weak, you can ride with me to the reservation."

At the mention of the reservation, Shannon became excited. She'd been curious to see it ever since Seth and Irene had told her about it. Grinning at him, she grabbed the sandwich and took a huge bite. He raised one dark brow, "Every last bite".

Shannon answered him with her mouth full, "No probwim". She took a healthy swig from the juice glass and shoved the sandwich into her mouth again.

Seth tried his best to keep a straight face. She looked like a little girl, her legs crossed Indian style, devouring the sandwich, her eyes twinkling. She was adorable.

"Also, if you're up to it, I thought we could take a drive, let me show you the sights?"

"Dat woud be gweat!" she said around a mouthful of food. He laughed, "Hey, slow down. You're going to get indigestion or choke or something." His mind suddenly went to the cook out where she had choked on a piece of steak and had to be resuscitated. His hands suddenly felt clammy. He quickly sobered, "Seriously Shannon, slow down", all the humor gone from his voice.

Puzzled by his sudden change of mood, she lowered the food from her mouth and concentrated on chewing what she already had. When she had finished her sandwich she upended the juice, draining the glass and set it down on the tray. "There, now can I get my shower? I feel grungy." Seth moved quickly to help her into the shower. He shed his own clothes and joined her. Her heart began to race at the sight of his nakedness. She never tired of his body or the things he could do with it.

When she reached out to him, he smiled and gently lowered her hands. "Not now my love. Now we need to get you scrubbed clean as fast as possible." She gave him a pouty look as he lathered up the luffa sponge. He was thorough as he ran the sponge all over her body. As much as Shannon tried to detach herself from what his hands were doing, her body reacted instinctively. He turned her around to lather her front, his hand guiding the sponge from her neck down over her breasts, her stomach until he was between her legs. She closed her eyes, moaning. Seth could feel his self control slipping as her body responded to his touch. He steeled himself but when she looked into his eyes, he saw her hunger and it set him on fire.

Shannon looked up to see his eyes dark with desire. She fought to keep her legs from buckling as she tilted her head back, inviting him to kiss her. Unable to resist, Seth crushed her mouth, expressing with his lips his need. He replaced the sponge with his hands, moving them over her body, making her breath catch in her throat. He reached down, his hand sliding along the back of her thigh. Lightening quick, he hitched her leg up, his pelvis grinding against her. Bracing her back against the tiled wall, he lifted her other leg so she was straddling his hips. He continued kissing her as he slipped easily inside her. She moaned in his mouth, her body straining against him. He broke the kiss, whispering raggedly into her hair, "Good God woman! You are incredible! He continued grinding his hips until his ears roared with his climax. Shannon had never known this much happiness. It was a little frightening. She couldn't believe God had showed her such favor as she melted in Seth's arms.

CHAPTER 28

Shannon sat tucked in the crook of Seth's arm as they rode to the reservation. They didn't talk much. When Seth asked her about her night out, she told him about dancing with her regulars from the diner. When he smiled, she didn't see the slightest hint of jealously. When he asked who else was there she failed to mention Joseph's presence at the club. She just didn't want to think about him or have to lie to Seth if he asked for details. Her body stiffened at the memory of how he had touched her and undressed her with his eyes, sneaking a peek down her dress. Seth picked up on her body language immediately but kept silent, not wanting to pry. *If it's important, she'll tell me when she's ready.* "Well, I'm glad you had fun." He squeezed her shoulder and kissed her hair, smelling the flowery scent. He loved the way she smelled! Other than Seth pointing out a landmark once in a while, they were quiet for most of the trip.

Turning down a dirt road that dipped and weaved around the rocky terrain, the all wheel drive truck climbed an exceptionally steep hill with little trouble. Seth put the truck in park at the top and Shannon got her first glimpse of the reservation. She didn't know what she expected, certainly not teepees, and bonfires but she was shocked at the smattering of run-down shanties that lined each side of what appeared to be the only street. In the open space behind the houses was something resembling a playground, though it didn't look safe for children. The equipment was in desperate need of repair. No, not repair, replacement. A small school house was situated at the end of the road. They drove straight through the town. Shannon looked around for the hospital. "Seth, I don't see the hospital. Shouldn't we have seen it from the top of the hill?"

Seth sighed and patted her shoulder. He then pointed in front of the truck and Shannon understood. "The school house doubles as a hospital?" She was shocked that they had to live in such conditions. Every town should have its own hospital. As they came closer to the school house, Shannon saw the people lined up with small babies and children.

"It's time for their inoculations. That's why I'm here today." His tone was sullen. He concentrated on parking the truck. As he reached for his medical bag, Shannon touched his hand. "Do you think it would be okay if I helped?" She wasn't about to stand idly by while he treated these unfortunate people. She looked out the window and caught the eye of one pretty little girl. She hid inside her mother's skirt as Shannon lifted a hand and waved at her. "You're wasting your time. They don't take to strangers…and sometimes not even their own." He was retreating into himself again and she wasn't going to let that happen. Taking his face in her hands, she made him look at her, "That happened a long time ago. You're their doctor now. You will never change their attitude towards you until you change your attitude towards yourself. Besides, they are damn lucky to have you." Her eyes burned into his. "Now, let's go stick somebody." He smiled slightly as she jumped from the truck, watching as the desert breeze whipped the baby blue gauzy skirt around her. His heart ached with tenderness. Maybe she was right. Maybe if he were more approachable the people wouldn't treat him like he was the one with the disease.

Shannon walked over to the little girl she had waved to and introduced herself to her mother, then proceeded to introduce herself to everyone standing in line, lingering a few minutes with each person, asking questions about their lives and their children. She was a most gracious host.

By the time Seth had set up the make-shift exam room, he could hear laughter filtering through the door. Smiling, he felt his spirits lifting as he opened the door, determined to take her advice. He smiled at his first patient and was shocked when the old man gave him a toothless grin.

The rest of the day went surprisingly fast. Seth found himself joking and laughing along with Shannon and the patients. He watched her as she mingled with his people as though she were one of them. He had to laugh at that. She was as alike to them as black was to white, with her red hair, freckled sun-kissed skin and those turquoise eyes. He found himself staring at her, his heart filled with so much pride he thought it would burst. A couple of the younger women had their heads pressed together, whispering, and snickering as they looked at him. When it was time for them to be examined they both said in unison, "So you and Shannon are getting married?" They both giggled. Seth was taken aback by their question, "Uh, yeah, we are." They giggled again, "Shannon invited us to the wedding". From somewhere in the line, he heard someone interject, "She invited all of us!" Seth felt like he was having an out-of-body experience. They've *never accepted me before. Why would they want to be a part of my second wedding when most of them blame me for what happened to Naome'?*

He looked over at Shannon as she beamed at him, "Isn't it wonderful? They're all coming! It will be such a beautiful wedding!" Seth was dumbfounded, "They're all coming?" He looked at them and they smiled genuinely at him. He felt his eyes tearing up. Thinking they may see his tears as a sign of weakness, he cleared his throat. "Sure, yeah, of course you can come. It will be at my house. We haven't set a date yet but it will be soon." Shannon bounced over to where he was and wrapped her arms around his neck, hugging him tightly. A round of applause went up from the group. Seth knew he should feel embarrassed, but he felt only pride. "I love you more everyday, if that's even possible," he whispered in her ear. She squeezed him tighter, "I love you". She slapped him playfully on the arm in feigned shock, "Why Doctor! Behave yourself! That's not a very professional thing to say!" She looked at him and winked conspiratorially. He was confused until he heard the laughter and realized she was putting on a show. Figuring he'd play along, he swatted her behind when she turned around to call the next patient and was rewarded with another round of applause and fresh giggles from the young girls.

When everyone had been seen, Seth busied himself dismantling the fold-away table. Carrying it outside, it almost dropped onto his foot. The people were still hanging around the front of the school house, laughing and joking with Shannon. Seth stared, his mouth agape at the scene before him. She was sitting in the middle of a crowd with her white peasant blouse draped low on her shoulders, a child on each knee, looking like a queen conversing with her people. Even the elders were enamored of her, standing around puffing on their pipes, hanging on her every word. She was telling them stories of all the places she'd been to and the things she'd done. Seth knew that most of the people had never been past the Sanctuary city limits, unable or unwilling to venture out into the world.

Shannon was in the middle of recounting the first time she put on a pair of snow skies and mistook the advanced slope for the bunny slope, when she saw Seth. Waving at him, she excused herself, kissing each child on the head, and handing them back to their mothers. "Hey, do you need any help putting that in the truck?" Seth thought it a weird question, "I think I can handle it". He started to lift the table but felt the weight get suddenly lighter. He started to tell Shannon he didn't need her help but stopped when he spotted her standing off to the side, a small smile on her beaming face. Looking over the top of the table, he saw that two brawny young men were practically pulling it from his grasp. Standing there, looking at them in shock, he looked back over at Shannon and she was beaming. When they finished, he reached out to shake their hands in gratitude. They accepted, grinning from ear to ear. Shannon leaned her head out of the window and waved to the crowd, "I'll see you guys at the diner! Remember, kids eat free!"

This was certainly turning out to be one surprising day. Seth patted the small square bulge in his left pants pocket…and it was going to be one surprising night.

CHAPTER 29

Seth could tell that Shannon was excited about something. She kept fidgeting in her seat like a mischievous child in church. He gave her a sidelong glance, "What's on your mind? You're acting twitchy." Putting his arm around her shoulders, he pulled her close to his side. She snuggled under his arm and kissed his neck. "I've got some news that I think you're going to like. At least I hope you're going to."

"Well, what is it?"

Shannon squeezed his arm, "Okay, I'll tell you." She took a deep breath, "You remember that I'm going to buy the diner? Well, when it becomes mine, I'm going to hire people to run it for me."

Seth smiled with satisfaction, "That is good news! Then you and I can travel. There are so many places I want to see with you." Shannon continued to fidget. Seth could tell that wasn't the only news she had. "You're not telling me everything. What else happened?"

She swallowed hard, trying to find her courage. "Well, um, I sorta hired the extra help already."

"Oh, did you take out an ad or something?" Shannon was quiet for what seemed like a long time. Seth was just about to repeat his question when she finally whispered, "I hired a few people from the Rez."

Seth hit the brakes, skidding to a halt, "What?" He couldn't believe his ears. What could she possibly be thinking?

"I think it would be good for everyone. They get a job so they can provide for their families and I get help so I can spend more time with you. What could be wrong with that?" she felt her defenses go up and pulled away, looking at his stoic expression. "I don't see what the harm is. It would increase business to have people from the Rez start patronizing the diner and it would give the town's people a chance to reconcile their differences." She started chewing on her lower lip, "Well, they're willing to give it a try. Look how they warmed up to you. That's got to be a good sign, don't you think?" she knew she was reaching but her mind was made up and it was imperative she get Seth to see her point of view.

He looked at her, saw the determination in her eyes and though he had his reservations about the whole thing, he could tell it was important to her. Cupping her head in his hands he kissed her lips.

"If this is what you want....but, I have to warn you, it may not turn out like you want it to. My people are very proud and extremely stubborn." He let out a small chuckle, "maybe even as stubborn as you, my love".

Shannon squealed and kissed him soundly, "Okay then, I just need to call Millie and see if the papers have been drawn up, then I'll start hiring". She pulled out her cell and pushed speed dial. "Hey Millie, how are you? Great. Listen, has Joseph drawn up the paperwork yet? He has? Great! I'll let Irene know and call you back when we can coordinate our times. Okay, see you then." She started to hang up but paused, listening, her face suddenly flushing pink, "Yeah, he got in last night. He's right here. Oh, okay." She handed the phone to Seth as she started worrying her bottom lip again.

"Hello Millie. Fine thanks." His face was stoic as he listened. Finally, he said goodbye and hung up the phone. He cranked up the truck without another word and gunned the engine. Shannon looked at him but he just kept his eyes straight ahead, the only sign of emotion was the jaw muscle that was twitching as he ground his teeth.

She couldn't bear the silence. Her imagination running wild, she tried to sound casual, "So, what did Millie have to say?" She noticed that muscle working a bit harder, "Seth? What's the matter? Are you upset with me about something?"

Seth was seething. Millie had been babbling about their night out and he wasn't really paying attention until she happened to mention Joseph's name. Why hadn't Shannon mentioned it? What was she trying to hide? What had really gone on while he was out of town? Is that the reason she couldn't or wouldn't answer her phone? Had she asked him to meet her there? Suddenly the cab was stifling. He had to get some air. Hitting the brake, he jumped out, leaving Shannon to gawk after him.

Walking briskly away, he didn't stop until he was standing on top of a hill that looked down into the valley below, his eyes misting over as he clenched and unclenched his fists, struggling to get his temper under control.

Shannon came up behind him and reached out to touch his arm. Something about his rigid posture made her stop, "Seth?" her voice tiny and scared. He just stood frozen, refusing to answer. He was really scaring her. She could feel the tears stinging her eyes as she tried to keep her voice even, "Please, talk to me."

Seth whirled around to face her, his face showing everything he was feeling all at once. When he looked into her eyes, she felt like she was looking into his soul, his tortured soul. "Why didn't you tell me that Joseph was at the club last night?" his voice accusatory and full of pain, gaining volume as he interrogated her, "and that he sat at your table? He saw her expression change to horror as she realized he knew everything, and his heart broke into a million pieces. Unable to look at the guilt written on her face, he brushed past her and headed to the truck.

Shannon raced after him and grabbed his arm, her nails biting into his flesh, desperation in her voice, "No, you don't understand! I didn't go there to meet him! I didn't even know he was going to be there!" He lifted his hand to extract her fingers but she grabbed him with her other hand, "Please, stop! Let me explain!" She was sobbing. He felt his anger trying to give way, but squared his shoulders and closed off his heart. The fact that he loved her so much, made the pain almost unbearable. She suddenly released him and he looked back as she collapsed on the ground, sobbing, "I love *you*! Please believe me!" she trembled all over as the sobs racked her body.

The wall he had started to rebuild, crumbled at the sight of her anguish. He reached down and pulled her up where she buried her face in his chest. He felt unyielding, like hard marble, but he stroked her hair, shushing her.

Shannon was torn. She wanted to tell him about the real Joseph but Irene's warning kept screaming in her head. Did she tell him her suspicions or did she make something up. His love was more important than anything. Pulling out of his embrace, she hugged herself. When she looked up and saw the pain in his eyes, she quickly lowered her gaze, opting to stare at a pebble on the ground. Taking a deep breath, she decided to tell him…part of the truth. "Joseph was at "our" table. He wasn't with me. Millie knew he would be there but she didn't tell me because she thought I would feel like a third wheel and not go." She looked up at him then, her eyes steady. Pushing away from him, she placed her hands on her hips, "Ask Millie if you don't believe me". It was her turn to be mad. He had no right to assume that she would have anything to do with Joseph. Why couldn't he trust her? Pushing past him, she headed toward the truck. Turning around, she yelled at him, "Besides, I didn't even dance with him!" Instead of climbing into the truck, she turned and headed down the road on foot.

Seth realized what an ass he'd been. Of course nothing happened between the two of them. How could he have been so stupid? "Hey Shannon, wait!" he yelled as he ran after her. She was talking to herself and waving her arms around dramatically. When he got close enough, he heard the words "stupid, blue eyes, kissable lips". Reaching her, he pulled her to a stop. As mad as she was, her heart leapt at his touch, "What is it now? Did you want to accuse me of sleeping with the bartender?" she tried to sound pissed but it sounded more like a whine.

He pulled her to him and hugged her tight. She fought him off half-heartedly but in the end, relaxed against his chest, sobbing quietly into his shirt. He held her, stroking her hair until she had cried herself out. Scooping her up, he carried her back to the truck and carefully placed her in the passenger seat.

Shannon napped the whole way back in her favorite place, snuggled up against Seth. When they pulled into the drive, he leaned down and placed a kiss on her head. "Wake up sleepy head. We're home." She didn't want to wake up. What if he wanted to continue the interrogation? She hated lying to him, but she was afraid he wouldn't believe her. Look how he reacted with little else but suspicion. She pretended to be extra groggy, hoping Seth would carry her upstairs. She thanked the heavens when he gathered her into his arms. Once inside, she conveniently "woke up". Setting her down on the love seat, he pulled her gently into his arms. "I owe you an apology," he whispered as he stroked her hair.

"For what?" "For accusing you of having feelings for Joseph." He kissed the top of her head. "You have to understand, when it was Joseph, Naome' and me, I always held a secret jealousy toward him. He was always the smooth one. He could talk his way out of anything. All the girls were gaga over him but he never had a steady girlfriend. I guess he played the field a lot, but I always had the impression he felt more for Naome' than just friendship. I mean, who wouldn't. She was the girl everyone wanted and for some unknown reason, she chose me. Who knows, maybe she regretted her decision later." Shannon felt him shrug. "Then, after the accident, everyone started saying that I ran the car off the road on purpose because I found out they were having an affair." He took a deep breath then released it. "So I have to live everyday with the suspicion that my best friend and my wife were secretly in love since we were kids and that I could have intentionally murdered my wife and son." Shannon's heart ached as he bared his soul. "So I guess I overreacted when I found out that Joseph was at the club with you....and Millie." He lifted her face and looked into her tear filled eyes, "Why did you fail to mention it?"

Shannon felt her treacherous cheeks turn red. "Okay, I'm going to tell you something and you have to swear to me you'll keep an open mind."

His eyes narrowed as he tried to read what was behind her eyes. "I'll try".

"No, your mind has to be open. What I'm about to tell you is going to rock your world. You will have to rethink your whole life", her voice somber.

He wanted to laugh, her cryptic statement sounded overdramatic but the look on her face was enough to keep him sober. "Alright, I'll keep an open mind." He waited for her to continue.

Shannon knew that she was treading on very thin ice but her love for him would never be complete until she could be totally honest with him. Moving away, she turned to face him, her legs crossed Indian style under her skirt. "Before I say anything, you need to know that there are a couple of people who will back me up so if you don't believe me when I'm through, you can ask them yourself." She took a deep breath and began. "It is true that Joseph felt more than friendship for Naome'."

Seth looked disbelievingly at her but before he could interject, she held up her hand, silencing him. "Remember, you're supposed to keep an open mind." He nodded, miming his lips sealed and throwing away an invisible key.

"I was told that he found every opportunity to stand between the two of you. It has been speculated that he was obsessed with her. Granted, no one has ever actually heard him confess it but did you ever wonder why he never tried to squash rumors of his affair with Naome'? I mean people respected him and he could get them to believe it if he really wanted to....unless he wanted it to be true?" She paused as she saw the tinniest bit of doubt on his face. "Okay, now this is when you will have to swing those doors in your mind wide open. These are my own observations."

She steeled herself. What she was about to say would either make or break their relationship. "From the moment I met Joseph, I felt something wasn't quite right about him. When I would lean over to refill his glass, I would catch him sneaking peeks down my shirt. He says things too, and....he touches me." She looked at Seth to see his reaction. He was working that jaw muscle again and his hands were fisted. Suddenly she didn't feel like going on, but she knew she would only get this one chance, "When I went to take a shower on the night of the cook out...I could have sworn he was in the bathroom with me". Seth bolted from the couch and went to stand in front of the fire, "Go on", he whispered so low Shannon barely heard him. He was obviously struggling to stay in control.

"The thing that's the most troubling of all is that when I look at him he reminds me of Richmond. There's something "off" about him. It's like he wears a mask so no one will see his real face. I know you think he's your friend....but he's not."

"Is that it?" his voice even as he turned to look at her.

"No. There's one more thing. Millie told me about a guy who danced with her once at the club. When Joseph came in and saw them, he acted like everything was fine but later on that night, the guy was a victim of a hit and run and ended up in the hospital. Millie said that when she went to the hospital to visit him, he freaked out and yelled at her to leave him alone and she also told me...." Shannon was about to break a promise but she felt she had to make him see the truth; "He and Millie have kinky sex." Seth raised an eyebrow, a gesture she missed but heard in his response, "So they're kinky, so what?"

Shannon braced herself, "Not just kinky, he does things to her, hurtful things involving whips and chains. I know what you're thinking but you're wrong. He abuses her, uses her like a toy and…… he beats her and he blackmails her. He got her used to the expensive gifts, her apartment, her car and then he threatens to take it all away if she doesn't do what he asks. It's like he's a drug dealer and she's the addict."

Seth walked over and knelt down in front of Shannon, taking her hands in his. She looked in his eyes and knew she had gotten through to him, if just a little.

"Well, if half of what you told me is true, I can't allow you to go to his office alone to sign those papers."

She couldn't believe her ears. He believed her. She met his gaze, "Why aren't you half way to his place, determined to smash his face in?"

He smiled at her, "I really would like nothing more than to beat him to a pulp. It's because of you that I'm not. I would rather be here for you than rotting away while sitting in some jail for aggravated assault." He pulled her into his arms, holding her tightly, "You are more important to me than anything. But I will tell you this, if Joseph ever lays another hand on you…" he let the words die on his tongue.

"Don't worry about me. Now that you know everything, I will handle Joseph in my own way." She buried her face in his neck, inhaling his masculine scent.

"There is one thing you haven't told me."

"What's that?" Shannon whispered, relieved that he was taking everything so well.

"You never told me what happened at the club."

She looked into his eyes and saw only curiosity. "Well, Millie and I were dancing but after awhile I needed a break so I went over and sat down. I drank another shot of tequila and leaned my head back on the seat. Then I heard him whispering in my ear, "Hello Shannon", and then he rubbed his finger down my arm." She gave a little shudder at the memory, "It was bad enough, but when I caught his expression….it creeped me out. I excused myself, said I had to use the restroom but he had slid into the booth next to me and I couldn't get out the other way so I had to make him let me out by scrunching up against him. I hated the satisfied look in his eyes. I had to practically climb over his lap before he would budge. I noticed him looking down my dress and I suddenly wanted to take a shower. I ran to the bathroom, making Millie go with me. I confronted her in the bathroom and she told me that Joseph frequented the club on weekends and that it wasn't surprising to see him there. He actually gave her a ride home. I was checking the time, hoping it was late so I would have a good excuse to leave when I saw I had voice messages. I excused myself and went outside to check them. When I heard your voice, I went inside and told Millie I had to get home and I left.... You know the rest." She chanced a glance at Seth. He seemed to be taking it pretty well. "The problem is he's very careful. He never does anything if he thinks there might be witnesses. He waits until everyone around is preoccupied and then he looks at me, undressing me with his eyes and grins, oh God that grin, I hate that grin. It makes me think of sharks, right before they attack." She stifled a sob, her eyes looking haunted by something from her past, "He scares me". She grabbed Seth's collar and made him look into her eyes, "Please, you have to swear to me that you won't go all Rambo on me. He isn't worth it. After I sign the papers there won't be any reason for me to be around him so it shouldn't be a problem, right?"

Seth stood up and walked back over to the mantle, staring into the fire, his voice was calm...too calm. "Right, 'but if an occasion should arise, I'll just have to keep a sharp eye out." *How could I have been so blind all these years? Did he have an affair with Naome' or was it just one sided on his part? Was he obsessed with Naome' back then....and now Shannon?* "I feel like such an idiot! Thinking all these years that he was my best friend only to find out he was using me to get to Naome'. His mind went back to all the fights he'd had with Naome' over Joseph. She tried to tell him but he refused to listen, thinking she was being ridiculous. She would get so angry with him for defending his friend and not believing her, and then she would concede, agreeing that he was probably right and they would reconcile, and for a little while things would be great again. *And what about the day of the accident? Had we been fighting over Joseph again when the car hit the guard rail?* His hand pressed against his forehead, straining to remember but only getting bits and pieces. "Dammit!" His fist came down hard on the mantle, causing the figurines to shake from the force.

Shannon went to him then, and wrapped her arms around his waist, her chest pressed against his back, "I know it's a lot to deal with, but you don't need to do it alone, I'm here now and I will never hurt you… again. I swear!"

He turned in her arms, catching her face between his hands, "What do you mean, again?"

"I've hurt you by telling you about Joseph", she choked back a sob.

He smiled down at her, "You haven't hurt me, my love. You can't blame yourself for my bull headedness. It's my fault for not listening. If anyone's to blame here it's me." His face suddenly sobered, "but I can tell you this….if he steps out of line with you ever again…" He couldn't finish his threat. What would he do? What was he capable of? Contrary to popular belief, the thought of hurting another human being, even Joseph Ravenclaw, was repugnant to him, but would his need to protect Shannon make him lose control?

Leaning down, he captured her lips with his, taking his time, relishing the way she surrendered to him without reservation. His hands fisted the material of her shirt as he squeezed her tighter against him. She could feel his desire through the flimsy material of her skirt, causing her breath to catch. His need for her increasing with each ragged breath, he whispered against her hair, "I want you so much right now. Can you feel it?" he punctuated by sliding his hands down to her butt, grinding her against him.

Shannon wondered why she didn't pass out from sheer ecstasy. He crushed her lips as her hands gripped the hem of his shirt, jerking it upward. He broke away long enough to jerk the shirt over his head and toss it away carelessly, then resumed violating her mouth. She ran her hands slowly over each muscle, her touch like fire on his skin, leaving a trail of desire in their wake. He pulled her shirt from her skirt, his hands sliding under the thin material to cup her breasts, manipulating the sensitive nipples through her lacey bra. Unable to stand one more second of torture, Shannon unbuttoned his jeans and slid them down his muscular legs. Her lips traveled down his neck, past his stomach until her face was close to the center of his desire. She hovered close, blowing on the little hairs that revealed the path to his manhood. Seth gripped the mantle, moaning as he felt her hair graze across his skin, every nerve in his body on fire. As he felt her mouth close around him, he inhaled sharply, sucking air between his teeth. Reaching down, he buried the other hand in her hair. She was gentle, taking her time, worshipping his body with her mouth.

Feeling close to the edge, Seth knelt on the floor, pulling Shannon into his arms. He finished undressing her, his mouth following the path of his hands. Laying her back onto the fur rug, he entered her in one long thrust. She arched her back, moaning. Seth changed position, lifting her up unto his lap. Capturing her mouth, he intensified his thrusts. Shannon leaned back, presenting her breasts to his lips. Hungrily, he devoured her erect nipples, tonguing the ultra sensitive flesh. He took one between his teeth, gently nibbling the tip. Shannon saw bright bursts of light as her body exploded, floating away on a sea of desire. Seth felt her clench around him and together they road the waves of ecstasy until they collapsed into each other's arms.

CHAPTER 30

Lying naked together, the fire warming their bodies, Shannon sighed contentedly. "Can we stay like this forever? Just us?" Seth ran his hand down her curvy waist, coming to rest on her hip, "Ah, my love, I would wish it too." He smacked her on the rump, "but you need to get up and get dressed. I'm taking you out tonight." Shannon squealed, "Really? Where? What are we going to do?" He chuckled at her enthusiasm, "It's a surprise….wear something dressy". She rose up and kissed him on the nose. "Alright, I'll get a shower." She paused and Seth looked up, "what is it?" She blushed, Seth thought it was amazing that she was still capable after all they'd shared, "It's just that if I'm going to get all dressed up for this, well, it would be better if….if it were like a date, you know?" He was more confused than ever, "what are you suggesting?" She sighed and rolled her eyes, "that you not see me until it's time to go". He smiled and nodded; "Now I get it. You want it to be like a date, like a "first" date." Jumping to his feet, he quickly threw on his clothes. "I just need to grab what I'm wearing and I'll get ready in the cabin." He started to walk down the hall but Shannon reached up and grabbed his hand, "Wait, are you okay with that? I mean, isn't it hard for you to go in there?" Seth looked down into her liquid blue green eyes and saw the concern on her face. She didn't want him to do anything that might cause him pain. He was also surprised to find that he wasn't at all bothered at the thought of entering the abandoned cabin." Smiling, he reassured her, "I'm fine, really." He pulled her up until her body was flush with his and he whispered in her ear, "I'll see you at 7:00 sharp." He kissed her quickly and headed down the hall.

Singing an old rock tune as she showered, Shannon took her time, enjoying the shower heads as they worked out the tension in her body. She was so excited about the evening Seth had planned. She had never been on a date before and found that she had butterflies in her stomach. Paying special attention to her hair, she used the expensive shampoo and conditioner and shaved under her arms, applying the debilitating cream to her legs and bikini area. Satisfied, she wrapped a towel around her waist and walked to Seth's closet where she had previously hung up her dressier clothes. She decided on a black halter dress with empire waist that flared into a short flouncy skirt. It had lime green satin piping on the bodice and hem. She had spied it in a store front window a month ago and, though she didn't have an occasion to wear it, she just had to have it. She slipped on a pair of matching stiletto heals and a silver anklet. Taking great care with her hair, she pulled it up and secured it with a marcasite embellished clip. No matter how she manipulated the strands, errant curls fought their way free, framing her face with delicate tendrils. Grabbing a pair of emerald drop earrings, she stared at her reflection in the bathroom mirror. Looking at her reflection, she suddenly felt nervous. *I hope he will be pleased*, she thought as she prepared to tackle her hair one more time but was interrupted by a knock on the front door. Her heartbeat quickened and her mouth became dry. She took her perfume bottle and sprayed her wrists and neck. Raising her wrist to her nose she licked at the fragrance. It was an old Creole trick she had learned years ago.

Seth stood at his front door, nervous as a school boy on prom night. His hand went up self-consciously to the piece of rawhide securing his long raven hair. It was shaking. *I can't believe it! I'm actually nervous!* He chuckled to himself and straining to compose himself, knocked on the door.

Taking one last quick glance at herself, she grabbed her beaded black purse, and flew to answer the door. Her hand hovered over the knob, frozen. Taking a deep breath, determined to squelch the butterflies that had somehow turned into a flock of black birds, she grabbed the doorknob....

Seth was dumbstruck by the vision in front of him. The look on his face relieved all the built up tension in Shannon. She smiled as she spotted the bouquet of gardenias by his side, "are those for me?" Her voice seemed to break his trance, "Huh? Oh yeah, here." He shoved them in her face. What was wrong with him? "Thanks, they're lovely. Would you like to come in while I put them in water?" She walked back into the room. Seth watched her walk away and his heart swelled with pride. She was a goddess and she was his. "O…Okay," he stammered as he stepped inside. He caught himself fantasizing, of sliding his hands up under the dress to her underwear. What kind was she wearing? Was she wearing any at all? He felt the bulge in his pants growing and was about to act when she turned around, "Well, shall we go?" Fighting the urge to take her in his arms, using all his will power he took her hand and raised it to his lips. "After you my love", motioning to the door. She blushed, withdrew her hand, and walked past. Her behind put him in a trance as he watched it sway from side to side. She paused at the door, looked back over her shoulder from under her thick lashes, smiling coyly, "You coming?" Seth realized he'd been licking his lips, "Uh, yeah", his eyes were smoldering as he came up behind her. Shannon felt she may have pushed him too far. As he reached around in front, she held her breath, expecting him to pull her against him. *Oh well, it was fun to play the first date game, even though it didn't last long.* Her eyes widened in surprise when he opened the door for her, "ladies first," his voice smooth as silk. Shannon's breath caught in her throat as he placed his hand on the small of her back. It was only for a moment but his fingers left her skin burning.

The drive to the restaurant was awkward. Seth couldn't think of a thing to say. His mind was preoccupied by the sight of Shannon's bare legs. He had decided to take her new car for their date and with the top down the wind blew across her lap, causing the gauzy material to inch up her thighs. His eyes kept wandering to them every few minutes, lingering, fantasies running wild. Frustrated, he gripped the steering wheel, squeezing until his knuckles were white. All he wanted to do was pull off the road… "Seth, look out!" Shannon yelled and he jerked the wheel in time to avoid hitting the oncoming truck. "Shit!" he growled, grinding to a stop. "Are you alright?" his brow furrowed with concern. Shannon gulped, pushing her heart back down into her chest, "Yeah, I guess." She turned to him, intent on reprimanding his driving skills but, seeing the fear in his eyes, her anger evaporated. "That was close," she whispered.

Seth touched her bare shoulder, the electricity was palpable, "I'm so sorry, my love…I was distracted". His face flushed red. "What distracted you?" She looked at him innocently. His eyes flitted to her lap and Shannon blushed as she realized she was the source of his distraction. Reaching out, she cupped his chin, "You've seen my legs before….and a whole lot more". She couldn't figure out why her legs had almost been the death of them. Seth took her hand from his face and kissed her palm. "What can I say? You drive me to distraction…. especially the way you look tonight." He hated how corny he sounded, but it was the truth. "You're exquisite! I want nothing more than to ravish you right here in this car, with the moon shining on your pale naked breasts." He let out a ragged breath, "but I have to behave. This is a very special night." He leaned close to her, "but I would like one kiss?" Shannon realized she'd been holding her breath, her voice barely a whisper as she fought for air, "I'd like that…very much". Their lips met, exploring each other's mouths as though for the first time. Seth used all his control to keep from dragging her onto his lap. Pulling away, he looked intently at her face, memorizing it. She still had her eyes closed, her chin lifted, waiting for him to kiss her again. Smiling to himself, he gently ran his knuckles across her silky cheek. "We'd better hurry. I made reservations". Her eyes fluttered open as Seth pulled back onto the road. Watching his profile as he looked straight ahead, she couldn't believe how breathtakingly handsome he was, the wind lifting his silky black locks. Without taking his eyes off the road, he entwined his fingers in hers, a slight smile appearing on his face.

"You are radiant tonight," Seth murmured as he poured Shannon a glass of wine. "Thank you," She felt her face flush as he gazed at her, his eyes like molten lava. Averting her eyes, she glanced around the dimly lit room. It was filled with booths, the backs high enough to provide adequate privacy. Tiny twinkling lights were strung everywhere, giving everything a dreamlike quality. Soft stringed music wafted down from the carefully hidden speakers. They sat side by side, his leg inadvertently bumping against her leg. She was very aware they were secluded as she reached over and ran her fingers up and down his thigh. Seth felt the electricity run up to his groin. When he felt her fingers move up to his crotch, he sucked in his breath. Grabbing his glass of wine, he downed it in one gulp. "Shannon, what are you doing?" He looked over at her and saw the glint in her eye, "nothing", she lifted her glass and took a sip innocently, all the while her other hand continued to act as if on its own accord. "Please," he growled as he leaned in close to her, "You have no idea what you're messing with. If you continue to do…that, I will not be responsible for my actions…He growled low in his throat, his voice raspy, "I hope you don't particularly like this restaurant because I'm afraid we're going to get kicked out for lewd behavior," and then she was in his arms, one hand at the small of her back, crushing her breasts against him, the other moving up and disappearing beneath her skirt. His lips were burning fiery trails down her throat when suddenly his eyes flew open, "You're not wearing panties!" he hissed through his teeth. He thought he would lose it completely. Shannon's lips curled up, "I'm wearing a thong". Somehow the thought of her wearing that little bit of lace was even more erotic than her wearing nothing at all. Moaning, his lips crushed hers as his hand moved around to cup her bare buttocks…

"Humph hmm" Shannon jumped. Seth growled and turned toward the source of the interruption. The waiter looked down his nose at the couple. From his bored expression, Shannon had a feeling it wasn't unusual for him to catch couples "other wise engaged" on a regular basis. "Are you ready to order or do you require more time?" Shannon slapped her hand over her mouth to stifle the giggles. Seth turned red and sat up straight, trying to concentrate on the menu in his hands. The sight of Seth trying to look composed while still sporting an erection was enough to send her into a fit of laughter. "Excuse me; I need to visit the ladies room. Please, order for me?" she scooted out of the bench and knowing Seth would be watching her, she couldn't resist sashaying seductively as she walked away, smiling from ear to ear. What she didn't notice was the turning of every head in the room as she walked by, but Seth did and his heart burst with pride. She had chosen him, and after tonight, he patted the breast pocket of his sport jacket, everyone would know she was his and his alone. He looked up at the snooty waiter and taking his hand, stuffed a wad of bills into it. The waiter's eyes widened for a second and then he beamed at Seth, "Is there something the gentleman would like? I am at your service." Seth crooked his finger and the waiter leaned in……

Shannon looked at herself in the mirror and was shocked at her reflection. She was glowing. Her make-up was still fairly fresh but her lips looked swollen from Seth's kisses. She checked her eyes. She decided that she liked the effect of the false eyelashes Millie had made her wear, so she had worn them. Her eyes were the color of the Caribbean Sea. Her hair had managed to come loose from the barrette and stuck out everywhere. She blushed, "I look like I just had sex". She repaired her make-up and tackled her unruly curls. Satisfied that she'd repaired most of the damage, she composed herself and walked back to their booth.

After they had managed to finish their appetizers of oysters and escargot and entrees of steak and lobster without jumping eachother, Shannon leaned back with her third or fourth, or was it fifth glass of wine. She felt full and satisfied as a spoiled kitten. Seth turned toward her, leaning close to her face, "Did you enjoy your dinner, my love?" She looked lazily back at him, her eyelids heavy, "Oh yes, very much, thank you". She leaned up and wrapped her arm around his neck, "Would you like me to show you how much?" he felt her foot sliding up his leg. Looking down he noticed that the hem of her dress had ridden up high on her thigh, giving him a peek at the lime green lace barely covering golden blond curls. The effect was immediate. His erection strained against his pants as his breath caught in his throat, "Oh God, Shannon! Everything you do makes me crazy for you. You have absolutely no idea what effect you have on me..." he swept the room with his gaze, "and every other male in this room". She pulled his head down until it was just a breath away from her own, "I don't see anyone else but you." Becoming bold from the wine, she attacked his mouth, kissing him with wild abandon. Seth stiffened briefly, taken off guard by her aggressiveness but her passion ignited him and he matched her kiss with his own. Reluctantly, he pulled away and looked deeply into her eyes, "The best is yet to come." He held up his hand and snapped his fingers twice. Suddenly, the snooty waiter appeared with a plate covered by a silver dome. Completely confused, Shannon looked at Seth, "What's this?" Seth looked at her and purred, "Dessert". She shied away, patting her stomach, "I don't think I could eat another bite. Please, take it away." Seth looked up at the waiter for help, "I can assure you madam, this dessert is practically fat free and completely non-filling." With a grand flourish he lifted the dome.

Shannon stared, not quite believing what her alcohol soaked brain was seeing. There, sitting on a beautifully decorated dessert plate was a little black velvet box. She reached out with trembling hands and lifted the lid. Tears streamed down her face as she looked at the most exquisite ring she had ever seen. "Oh Seth, it's beautiful!" She held it up to the light, marveling as the stone glittered, giving it a rainbow affect. He took the ring from her hand, "Shannon Mallory, would you do me the honor of becoming my bride and making me the happiest man alive?"

Looking at him with all the love she possessed, she took his face in her hands, "Yes, of course I will." He knelt on one knee and took her hand, "You brought me back to life. What more can anyone ask?" Her hand covered her mouth as he slipped the ring on the third finger of her left hand. She held it up to the light once more, "It's so unusual. What kind of stone is it? It can't be a turquoise even though it's the same color." Seth watched as she moved it around, loving the way it reflected the light. He could tell she was trying to figure it out. Reaching up, he pulled her hand down to the table. She turned and he looked into her eyes, "I had it specially made. It's a man-made turquoise diamond." He waved his hand dismissively, "the clear ones on either side are just for balance". Shannon's eyes widened in surprise, "It's a diamond?"

"Yes, I don't believe in diamond mining. It's inhumane how they treat those workers." He wondered how she felt about the subject. They never seemed to get around to talking politics or religion. Shannon looked into his eyes and found another reason for loving him. He truly cared about the plight of the underprivileged, not just his own people, but all mankind. "I will cherish it always and remember that no one had to suffer to produce it." Seth shrugged, "Well, I think the jeweler suffered a little bit. I practically drove him crazy until he finally finished it." They both chuckled. Shannon wrapped her arms around his neck, drawing him close to whisper in his ear, "I love you Seth Proudfoot, and I can't wait to take your name as mine". His heart soared as he kissed her tenderly, but Shannon deepened the kiss, her tongue exploring the outer rim of his lips, nibbling with her teeth. "I think it's time to go," he hissed between his teeth. If she didn't control herself, he wasn't sure he could either and he certainly didn't want to ruin a perfect night by being thrown out onto the street.

He threw a wad of bills on the table. Shannon looked down as he pulled her out of the booth and saw nothing but hundred dollar bills, several of them. Sliding his arm around her waist, he escorted her out of the restaurant and out to the car.

He was trying to find the right key when she moved to stand in front of him. Without a word, she unbuckled his belt and unzipped his pants in one fluid motion. Dropping to her knees, she took him into her mouth. Seth quickly looked around at the deserted parking lot, and then turned his full attention to Shannon. He reached down and pulled the barrette from her hair, burying his hands in her soft curls. She licked and laved his erection until he thought he would explode. Pulling her up, he sat her on the hood. Reaching up under her skirt, he made short work of the flimsy bit of lace. Savagely, he ripped it from her body as he drove his shaft to the hilt. She cried out in pleasure as he thrust in and out with an animalistic urgency, grunting as his seed spread inside her. There were no whispered love words or declarations of love, this was raw animal lust….and she loved it.

His senses returning, Seth looked around to make sure their tryst wasn't witnessed. Looking down at Shannon, he started to apologize for being so inconsiderate, thinking only of himself and not her pleasure, but the satisfied look on her face stopped him short. "Did you enjoy that as much as I did?" He asked incredulously. She pushed herself against him, her ankles locking around his waist, "I can't believe you kept me waiting this long." She kissed his nose. "But I think it might be best if we continue this at home."

He growled, burning her with his gaze, "I couldn't agree with you more."

Seth concentrated on keeping his attention on the road, but couldn't resist glancing over at Shannon's sleeping form. She had fallen asleep before he'd even left the parking lot. The wind whipped through her hair, giving it a wild appearance, while the moonlight shone on her face, reminding him of some magical mythical creature. She was breathtaking. She was reclining in her seat, her breasts straining against the fabric, allowing him to drink in her womanly curves. The hem of her dress floated around her legs.

Seth smiled. This time he didn't have to wonder what was under the gauzy material. He'd taken care of that back in the restaurant parking lot. As he recalled their savage lovemaking, he felt his desire growing, *What is wrong with me? I can't seem to think about anything else but making love to her, touching her, tasting her soft, pale, gardenia scented flesh.* He couldn't think with her around and when she wasn't around, he could think of nothing else. She was like a drug to him. The more he had her the more he wanted. He didn't even feel this way about Naome'. He found his hand reaching for her as if it had a mind of its own. Running his hand up and down her leg, he marveled at the softness of her skin. Shannon moaned in her sleep. Seth slid his hand up higher and she wriggled, her legs separating. He was beginning to think she was awake until she turned her head toward him, her eyelids closed, her eyeballs moving back and forth. *She's dreaming,* he thought with satisfaction, *and she still wants me.* His hand continued to move higher until it disappeared beneath her skirt. His pants strained against his growing erection. Her legs spread even wider as his hand brushed across her golden curls. He massaged her sensitive flesh, her core hardening with each stroke. His breath became ragged as he struggled to keep control of the car. She moaned again, her tongue flicking over her lips as he slid his finger in and out of her warm wetness. Her lips clutched around his fingers as her body spasmed. Suddenly Shannon's eyes flew open in surprise. Seth looked at her and smiled mischievously, his hand resting on her thigh. She sighed contentedly, taking his hand in hers. "You are insatiable, do you know that?" He gave her a slight smile, "It's your fault for looking so ravishing". She laid her head back and smiled, "I love you, you know?" He chuckled, "yeah, I do."

CHAPTER 31

The next few weeks flew by as Shannon prepared for her wedding day. With Millie practically taking over as wedding planner, Shannon was able to concentrate on hiring help for the café:. Irene was thrilled to hear that they were going to be getting in some "new blood" as she put it and Millie had acted as liaison regarding the purchase of the diner which suited Shannon just fine. She wanted as little to do with Joseph as possible.

When the day of the signing came around at last, Seth insisted on being present. Shannon had put up quite an argument, but he wouldn't budge an inch. He didn't want her in the same room with his "best friend" unless he was there. They both agreed it would be best if Seth acted ignorant of Joseph's ulterior motives. Shannon had her reservations as to whether or not he could pull it off but as they entered the boardroom, Seth and Joseph shook hands and chastised eachother for waiting so long between visits. They both seemed sincere. They made plans they both knew would never come to fruition. Shannon was amazed at Seth's acting abilities. No one had a clue that Seth was studying every move Joseph made, every glance, every gesture, but Joseph was all business. The meeting went off without a hitch and Shannon was given the deed to the "Last Resort Café".

As Shannon was training two new girls, the same girls who giggled at Seth that day at the reservation, she heard Irene and Paddy chatting away excitedly about their upcoming trip in their recently acquired RV. Since Shannon had purchased the place, Irene and Paddy were like a couple of newlyweds. She smiled as she recalled catching them kissing in the walk-in refrigerator. Paddy seemed younger, less stressed and Irene was practically glowing. Shannon was also on the lookout for a new chef and asked the girls if they would inquire around the Rez. Everything seemed to be coming together nicely. Even Joseph stopped frequenting the diner which put Shannon more at ease. Millie would come in now and then but it was to consult with Shannon on wedding details.

It was on one of those days, Millie had rushed in, all in a thither about how many gardenia center pieces to order, "You know, Millie, if you wanted to, you could open your own wedding planner business. You're extremely thorough and you've definitely got the outgoing personality for it… If you wouldn't mind a silent partner, I'd be happy to back you financially, if you want," Shannon offered. Millie was dumbstruck, "You would? Oh Shannon, you are the best!" She hugged her until she thought her ribs would crack, "I've got the perfect place in mind. I saw this quaint little house with a white picket fence and a wrap around porch for sale that would do perfectly! I'll call about it today! Oh, thank you, thank you!" She hugged Shannon again and floated out the door. Shannon smiled to herself, *I love taking Richmond's foul money and using it for good. Now Millie can get out from under Joseph and be a strong, independent woman.*

Things are definitely looking up, she thought as she felt her stomach do flip flops. Irene had nagged her for a week to have a doctor look at her but Shannon had way too much to do to take the time. She sat down at the bar as a wave of dizziness swept over her. *I just need to eat something.* Her stomach rebelled at the thought but Shannon took a pack of complimentary saltines from the basket and shoved them into her mouth. One of the new girls, Hannah, saw her and asked if she could get her anything. "Thanks Hannah. I would love a coke, if you don't mind." Hannah looked at her with a strange expression as she placed the coke in front of her. Shannon took a few sips, ate another pack of saltines, and felt better. *I've just been so preoccupied with everything that I haven't been taking care of myself, that's all.* She used the same explanation with Seth when he noticed her clothes starting to hang on her. "Shannon my love, you're wasting away". *My wedding dress will have to be taken in, again!* She hated the pensive look on his face as he worried, she thought, unnecessarily about her. Every time they were together he tried to get her to eat something. He brought her breakfast in bed, went in town to pick up her favorite foods, even had catered meals delivered to the house but she would just look at it and shake her head. She was beginning to resemble the thin girl in the photographs Seth had discovered in the little black box. Though she could keep down what little she did eat, food just wasn't appetizing to her.

As she started across the floor to show the other girl, Leah, how to bus a table, spots flashed in front of her eyes and the room began to sway under her feet. Shannon felt something cold and hard under her as she shivered, struggling to open her heavy lids. "What…. happened?" she wanted to sit up but felt a heavy weight on her chest. Her eyes opened wide and looking down, she discovered the source of her discomfort. She was strapped to a gurney, being lifted into an ambulance. Someone was holding her hand. She looked up into electric blue eyes, brimming with tears. She started to reach out and place her hand on his cheek but the restraints wouldn't allow her "Seth? What's going on? Why am I strapped to this gurney? I don't understand." He stroked the back of her hand with his thumb, "You fainted my love, and they weren't able to revive you so they called 911…and me". He leaned over and kissed her forehead, "everything will be alright. I'll be with you the whole way, don't worry." She wanted to tell them to let her up, that she didn't need to go to the hospital but she didn't have the strength. She looked into his eyes and he suddenly looked uncomfortable, "What is it Seth? What's wrong? Is there something you're not telling me?" He cleared his throat, "Shannon, I don't want you to freak out……we won't no for sure until we run tests……" She looked at him alarmed, "What? Spit it out!"

"Well, what was the date of your last menstruation?"

"What?" she asked incredulously.

"When was your last period?" he sounded nervous but his expression was unreadable.

Shannon's brow creased as she struggled to remember. She had never been regular so it wasn't something she really thought about. Richmond had pronounced her barren when she failed to provide him with an heir. She considered herself lucky. She prayed she was so she would never have to bear his children. When she had given herself to Seth, she never gave "birth control" much thought. No, it wasn't possible. There had to be another explanation for her illness. "I can't be pregnant." She looked at him evenly, dashing both their hopes. He leaned close to her ear, "You know it would make me extremely happy if you were pregnant with my child, but if you aren't, I will find out what's making you ill, I promise". She smiled at him. It would be wonderful. She could just imagine a baby with his eyes and his raven hair.

Shannon surfed through the channels as she waited for Seth to bring her news. Frustrated, she flung the remote, hitting her foot. "Owe!" she cried out, "Great work Shannon." She threw her head back on the pillow. "This waiting is driving me mad!" She was under strict orders to stay in bed or she would have thrown the covers off and marched down the hall, determined to find someone who could tell her something. Normally she would have disobeyed those orders but she had to think about her baby, if there was one. She wasn't about to take another spill and risk hurting it/he/she. Just as Shannon thought she was coming out of her skin, Seth walked in.

"Well, what's the verdict?" she practically screamed at him.

He noticed she was nervous and wanting to reassure her, he walked calmly to the bed and took her hand. Looking at her tenderly, he leaned over, and kissed her cheek. *That was odd. Why didn't he kiss me on the lips? Do I have bad breath or something?* He was beginning to scare her. "Seth Proudfoot, if you don't tell me what's up, I'm going to strangle you!"

"You're not pregnant", he was using his doctor voice again. Shannon knew there was more. At the worried expression on her face, he squeezed her hand. "You have a virus. It's commonly found in poor areas where the bacteria run rampant." He looked at her pointedly, "like reservations".

The realization hit her like a ton of bricks, "I caught a virus from the Rez?" she gazed into his eyes, seeing the guilt reflected there.

"Yeah, seems you caught the virus I was inoculating the tribe against." Balling up his fist, he struck his forehead, "how stupid can I be? I surrounded you with it, and never thought you wouldn't be immune. White people get inoculated before they start grade school. How come you weren't?"

Shannon looked at Seth and saw how he was beating himself up about something that clearly wasn't his fault. She touched his cheek, "I came from a very poor neighborhood, remember? I told you that.

We didn't have access to treatment there and when I was married to Richmond I was never allowed to go anywhere so he never thought to immunize me against viruses or diseases. Seth, look at me. This isn't your fault so stop blaming yourself. You couldn't have known." She looked into his clear blue eyes, "now, tell me the rest. How bad is it?" She steeled herself for the bad news. How long did she have? There was still so much she wanted to do and see. *Oh well, at least I had the love of a lifetime, even if that lifetime was cut short.* She saw surprise flash over his face and then…relief?

"Oh Shannon my love, you're going to be just fine. All you're going to need is complete bed rest for a couple of weeks. Your immune system just needs to recover and you're a little anemic and dehydrated from not eating. We'll inoculate you before you leave the hospital and we've been pumping you with vitamins through your I.V. You'll be back to your old self in no time." He kissed her on the forehead.

She glared at him, "If I'm not going to die then why do you insist on kissing me on the cheek or forehead? How come you don't kiss me on the mouth? Am I contagious?"

Seth chuckled, "You silly, silly girl. I didn't kiss you on your mouth because I didn't think you would want me to. I know how you are about oral hygiene but if it doesn't bother you then…." His lips came down on hers for a long lingering, make your toes curl, kiss. He pulled back, smacking his lips. "Ah, you still taste like honey".

Shannon looked up into his smoldering eyes. His comment had been casual, light, but his eyes betrayed the desire that kiss had awakened. She rose up to pull him back down but a wave of dizziness caused her to suck in her breath and she slumped back onto the pillow.

"Shannon, are you alright?" he touched her neck and looked at his watch, checking her pulse. She tried to slap his hand away, thinking he was overreacting but her hand flip-flopped feebly. She was alarmed that she was so weak.

"Oh Seth, why do I feel like I just ran a marathon?"

"I told you, you're immune system was weakened and you needed to rest and by God that's exactly what you're going to do. No arguing!" He tone was resolute. That was okay. Shannon didn't feel much like arguing anyway. She nodded her head and closed her eyes.

The next few days were a blur, a boring, routine filled, blur. Shannon woke every few hours or was woken, so nurses could get vitals, change IVs, or shove food down her throat. She hated the monotony of it all. The boredom was broken now and then when she would get visitors but Seth never let them stay long, worried they might tire her out.

Millie brought fresh flowers and a cute little stuffed unicorn. She filled Shannon in on all the happenings in Sanctuary. Shannon's ears perked up when she told her how Joseph had left town for a couple of weeks. He told Millie he was scouting for a replacement since she had decided to venture out on her own. Shannon was extremely surprised, no, shocked, that Joseph hadn't made it tough on her. Millie smiled, her eyes twinkling, "He seems genuinely happy for me." Shannon smiled back, keeping her opinion to herself. Irene and Paddy came by as well, volunteering to postpone their trip until she had made a full recovery which was a welcome relief. Several of her regulars came by, and the new hires sent her a "get well" card with some tin foil looking balloons but it was Seth's visits that she looked forward to the most. He made sure he kept their visits purely platonic. He would fluff her pillow, sit and talk to her until she fell asleep but he never repeated the kiss from that first day, the kiss that had frightened him. He treated her as though she were something fragile. She counted the days until she could feel his arms around her in a passionate embrace.

After a few more days of staring at the popcorn ceiling, Shannon had had enough. She argued, threatened, begged, and pleaded to be released, until finally, Seth came to her room pushing a wheelchair. He wheeled her out spouting off rules that she would have to swear to abide by or he'd make sure she was promptly returned to her hospital bed for the duration of her recovery. Shannon readily agreed with his demands, excited for the first time in days. The sun felt good on her face as he wheeled her to the truck. She noticed a chill in the air, hinting that winter was almost upon them, and hugged herself. Suddenly a coat materialized around her. He didn't miss anything, did he?

On the drive home, Shannon couldn't help noticing that Seth was acting strange. Well, not strange exactly, more like a woman with a juicy secret she couldn't wait to share. He kept looking over at her with a stupid grin on his face. By the time they pulled unto the dirt road that led up to the house, he was practically squirming in his seat. "Okay, close your eyes. I have a surprise for you." *No shit Sherlock*, Shannon rolled her eyes. He gave her a sad little puppy dog look and she sighed, "alright, have it your way". Her lips curved up just a little, enjoying his excitement.

"Okay, don't open them yet", he came around and helped her down from the truck. She expected to be lifted into his arms so he could carry her up the stairs but was surprised when he tucked her close to him for support and just stood still. "Okay, now open them!"

Shannon opened her eyes, blinking several times, her eyes getting used to the sun's rays. She stood with her mouth open. This couldn't be Seth's place. She looked around the yard and noticed everything was as it was except for…turning back around, a smile slowly blossomed on her face. "Seth! It's beautiful! But how, when?" He beamed down at her, "Well, I knew you would need a place to recuperate and I figured it would just get tiresome running up and down the stairs. Besides, I thought you might like a place where you can hone your craft, when you're feeling better. Come on", he urged her forward. Shannon was flabbergasted at the work he did in such a short time. He had taken the bottom level of the garage apartment and enclosed it. There was a bright red entry door, on one side a large picture window with flower boxes filled with all types of flowers. She stepped across the threshold and into a cozy living area with a fire roaring in the fireplace. "Where does the smoke go?" "It's a faux fireplace. The logs are electric. No fuss, no muss."

The open floor plan was tastefully decorated, the walls painted a subtle blue against dark wood trim. It was beautiful. Her paintings were displayed on the walls in modest wood frames. It had Seth's influence but it was definitely made for Shannon. She could feel the tears streaming down her face. She turned in his arms and he looked down into her turquoise eyes, "Wait, the best is yet to come." He walked her to the back, past a modest bathroom to the master bedroom. Shannon felt her knees go weak. Seth's grip tightened, "Oh Seth, it's lovely". She couldn't think of any other word to describe it. The walls were an exact match with her eyes. The large picture window was bordered by white gauzy sheer curtains. The hand crafted head and footboard was made of knotty pine and left raw, with several layers of clear polyurethane. The bed was covered with a white comforter. A quilt of pastel hand-embroidered flowers was folded across the foot and her miss matched throw pillows were scattered across the head against fluffy white pillow shams. The furniture matched the bed. There was an armoire in the center of the opposite wall and end tables on each side of the bed. She smiled as she felt her feet sink into luxurious white carpet. The whole place was so light and airy. "I can't believe this!" She looked at him and he thought he would explode with joy, "You really like it?" She punched him as hard as she could. He merely chuckled. *Damn, it sucked being weak!* Wanting to do nothing more than crawl into the softness of the fluffy comforter, she attempted to take a step but Seth held her back. Confused, she looked up at him. He wasn't done yet. "You have something else to show me?" He beamed at her, "I saved the best for last".

He turned her around and walked back into the hall then stopped in front of what Shannon had thought was the door to the linen closet; it being directly across the hall from the bathroom. He reached down and turned the knob, swinging the door open. Shannon peeked inside and Seth had to literally hold her to keep her from falling. It was an art room. No, not room, more like a studio. The entire back wall was glass. The sun's rays shone unobstructed into the bright space. He walked her to the glass wall and Shannon looked out to see a breath taking view of the Painted Mountains. She leaned against him, her heart racing. She could just imagine spending hours here, being inspired. The floor was covered in terra cotta tile. He had set up her easel and the white walls were lined with her sketches, framed once again, in hand carved wooden frames but these were left raw, the natural wood grain complimenting the paleness of the walls. It was the best present she had ever gotten. She turned in his arms and looked at him, tears streaming down her face, "You are incredible! I love you so much!"

Scooping her up in his arms, he marched to the master bedroom. Her heart fluttered as she pressed her lips against his neck. Seth felt the electricity down to his toes. Growling in frustration, he placed her gently down on the bed. He started to pull away but Shannon still had her hand around his neck. He reached up to loosen her hold but, using her arm as leverage, she pulled his lips down to hers. She actually whimpered as she felt his lips crush hers. Seth had taken every precaution, making sure they were never alone for more than a few minutes at a time, not touching her intimately, keeping his eyes off her body, only looking at her face. That was hard enough. He knew it wouldn't take much for the smoldering embers to burst into a firing inferno but what he felt was so much more than that. It felt more like a molten volcano erupting in the deepest pit of hell. His body was enflamed. Ripping her blouse off, he buried his face in her mounds, inhaling her scent as a drowning man gasps for one last sweet breath of air. She was like air. Without her, he couldn't breathe. He stripped his shirt off and tossed it aside. The sight of his bare chest made Shannon's breath catch in her throat. She started to swoon, her head feeling like a lead ball on her shoulders. Suddenly,she went limp in his arms. Seth felt the change in her immediately. He looked down, alarmed, "Shannon? Oh Shannon! My Love! I'm so sorry! I couldn't help myself!" He moved away from her and sat on the side of the bed.

Shannon's eyes fluttered open, "Seth?" she whispered as she laid her hand on his arm. Running his hands through his hair he shook his head, "I'm scum! I'm nothing more than some sex starved pervert! I should go." He started to rise. Shannon gripped his arm feebly but it might as well have been a steel vice. He stopped short. "Please Seth! Don't leave! Stay with me!" she paused… "Just hold me, okay? Lie here with me. We don't have to do anything. I'll behave." Her voice faded out. She had worn herself out. She didn't have anymore strength so she waited…Seth looked over his shoulder and saw the dark circles under her lovely eyes.

"Oh Shannon, you've done nothing wrong. I'm the one who's behaved badly, not you." Smiling, he laid back, wrapping his arms around her waist. She placed her hands over his and drifted off to sleep.

Shannon awoke as the sun was rising over the mountains. She luxuriated in the softness of the comforter. Flinging her arm across the bed, she expected to feel Seth's warm body but felt only the coolness of the sheets, the heat of his body long gone. She sat up, puzzled, as she looked around the room. An electric fire was crackling in the faux fireplace, giving the room a cozy feeling. She wanted nothing more than to snuggle under the covers with Seth. Sighing heavily, she threw the covers off and walked to the bathroom. She was pleasantly surprised. The bathroom was painted to match her bedroom. The towels were white and there was a white shower curtain with embroidered pastel flowers just like the quilt on her bed. She made a mental note to ask Seth if he'd hired a professional designer. Turning the shower on, she stepped inside, letting the warm water cascade over her body, as she took her time, relishing the first shower she'd had in over a week. She noticed her favorite shampoo had been placed within her reach and thanked Seth silently.

After her shower, she brushed her teeth, making sure to gargle several times. She felt wiped out before she could finish her toiletries. Cinching the robe around her, she walked slowly back to her bedroom. She stopped short when she saw Seth sitting on the edge of her bed, a breakfast tray sitting next to him. Ignoring the food, she flung herself into his arms. His eyes widened in surprise but he smiled and embraced her. "Good morning my love," he whispered as he kissed her chastely. "I brought you breakfast." He looked at her barely covered state. Reddening, he asked hoarsely, "Do you need help getting dressed?" She gave him a pouty look, "I'd rather have help getting *undressed*". He lifted her off his lap and stood up, leaving her to look up at him quizzically. He turned and went to her closet, moving the hangers back and forth, back and forth. The sound of the squeaking hangers was grating on Shannon's nerves. "What on earth are you doing?" He turned to her, his face contorted with pain, "I can't allow myself to be close to you while you're….like that!" he motioned to her robe. The front had fallen open at the bust and she looked down, seeing for the first time her disheveled appearance. She walked over, his eyes never leaving her, and stood in front of him. Looking up at him defiantly, she loosened the sash and shrugged her shoulders. The robe fell in a heap at her feet. His panicked expression incensed her. Running her fingers along her naked stomach, up along the sides of her breasts and up through her hair, she tilted her head and arched her back, looking seductively at him through her thick lashes, "Is this better?"

Seth was gritting his teeth as she teased him, flaunting her curvy body like a temptress from Greek Mythology. "Please, don't. If you continue tempting me, I won't be responsible for my actions," he hissed through his clenched jaw. Shannon had been starved for him. She was determined as her tongue snaked out and licked her bottom lip sensually. It was too much for Seth. Grabbing her around the waist he crushed her body to his. She gave a little triumphant shriek as he captured her lips, kissing her passionately, his hands moving down to cup her buttocks, grinding her hips against him. She moaned as she felt the hardness rub her enflamed womanhood. He grunted in her ear, "Argh!" He lifted her up, carrying her over to the dresser, her legs wrapped around his waist. Sitting her on the polished wood, he pulled away, looking sternly into her half-lidded eyes, "Are you sure you're up for this?" She didn't answer him but he felt her hands on the waistband of his jeans, fumbling with the buttons. Growing impatient, he brushed her hands aside and within seconds he was naked in front of her. His arousal made her gasp, as her breathing quickened. He cut off her breath with another passionate kiss, entering her carefully, mindful of her delicate condition. She bucked under him, groaning, "I've missed you so!" He responded by whispering into her hair, "I haven't been able to breathe, wanting you so badly! I am truly a heartless bastard." He continued to rock in and out of her, sending her over the edge as they both climaxed. She slumped against him fully satiated. Cradling her against him, he carried her over to the bed and tucked her under the covers. She reached out to him, not wanting him to leave, "Please don't go. Stay with me". She scooted over and patted the spot beside her. Seth smiled, "First you eat". He placed the tray across her lap. "At least sit beside me? I think I will be able to eat as long as you're here", the pouty look was back on her face. He chuckled, "Is it possible to say "no" to you?" He climbed in next to her and picked up the fork. "Now open wide." The pouty look was replaced by a genuine smile as she did as she was told.

CHAPTER 32

Shannon wasn't a very good patient. Seth had to be on guard every minute. He would put her to bed, giving her strict orders not to get up. She would give him an assuring nod but as soon as he left to get some work done, he would find her cleaning the house or cooking supper. "Shannon, you are going to be the death of me," he would exclaim, totally exasperated. She would give him that pouty look, "I'm going crazy! I have to do something! I hate this! It's like being under house arrest!" Seth wasn't so sure it was coincidence when he would come inside and she would happen to be in a state of undress. He would stop dead in his tracks, his mouth gaping open. She would look completely innocent. "Shannon! For God's sake, put some clothes on!" He would growl.

She would sidle up to him, flaunting herself in front of him. He would utter a few choice words and storm out of the room.

One night Shannon walked from her bathroom, down the hall to her bedroom, with only a towel wrapped around her head, and literally bumped into Seth in the hall. "Oh!" Shannon shrieked. Upon impact, Seth raised his hands up to catch her and mistakenly grabbed her breasts. Shannon sucked in her breath and leaned into him. His breath hissed through his teeth, "What do you think you're doing?" "It was too hot and steamy in there," she purred.

Shaking his head, he gripped her arms, setting her delectable body a couple of feet away from his aching one. "My love, you have to stop trying to seduce me. Until you are completely recovered there will be no more sex. Stop walking around half naked. Stop "accidentally" running into me. It's hard enough keeping my hands off you. Why do you insist on torturing me?"

Shannon realized that she had been selfish, thinking only of her own pleasure, but she couldn't help it. She would want him even if she were paralyzed from the neck down. Her desire ran far deeper than the flesh. It was a need to just be with him.

"I'm sorry Seth. I didn't realize I was making things hard on you. I promise from now on, I will behave, cross my heart and…."

Seth put his fingers on her lips, stopping her from finishing the vow. "Don't say it. I'm a little superstitious when it comes to vows. I believe you if you say you won't." He wrapped his arms around her, pulling her to him, "but I will promise you that as soon as you get a clean bill of health, we are going to make up for lost time". He kissed her on the forehead and turning her toward the bedroom, smacked her round bottom, "Now get to bed and stay there. I'm going to take a shower and then I'll be joining you."

Hearing the shower running, Shannon couldn't help but smile. Yes, she was frustrated that her ploys didn't work but she was comforted by his promise to her. She closed her eyes, dreaming of the things they would do together when she recovered.

She was running through the forest again. Something or someone was gaining on her. Seeing a clump of dense brush, she huddled down, trying to become invisible. Her pursuer ran past, then, sensing her, stopped, turned around, and walked back until she could see his cowboy boots. She had seen those boots before, but where? Her breath was ragged from exhaustion and fright. She clapped her hand over her mouth to keep from screaming as he came within inches of her hiding place. Suddenly he leaned down and the brush parted….

Shannon screamed, sitting bolt upright in bed. "Shannon, are you alright?" Seth wrapped his arm around her shoulders and she sobbed into his chest, her hair sticky from perspiration. He didn't ask her any questions, just held her, stroking her hair, until the demons faded away. "There there, feeling better now?" Her sobs finally reduced to sniffles, Shannon hiccupped a couple of times. "It was so real," she whispered between hiccups. "Do you want to talk about it?" He cupped her face and tilted her head up so he could look into her red rimmed eyes. Giving him a half smile she waved her trembling hand dismissively, "It was just a nightmare. It seems kinda silly now. I just want to forget it, okay?" He kissed the tip of her nose, "If you say so, but you know you can tell me anything". He looked deeply into her eyes, "but I have to ask….was it about Richmond?" He knew he shouldn't have asked. He desperately wished it wasn't. He was hoping his love was strong enough to completely wipe that bastard from her mind. It was egotistical of him. "No….I don't know, maybe. I couldn't see his face, just his boots. Richmond never wore cowboy boots, so, I don't think it was him." He frowned, "I wear cowboy boots". She laughed at his statement, thinking how absurd it was. He warmed as her mood lightened, "It was just an observation, but I'm glad that you think it's ridiculous". Shannon smiled and hugged him tightly. He could feel her warmth against his bare chest and his body immediately responded. This moment of intimacy was more powerful than the strongest aphrodisiac. Shannon felt his arousal and remembering her promise, she moved away from him, "Sorry, I didn't mean to…" she whispered guiltily.

"Don't be sorry. It was my fault. Even the most innocent touch makes me want you." He sighed dramatically, an evil glint in his eye, "but it's just a burden I'll have to live with". She laughed and he reached out and touched the tip of her freckled nose. Her color was looking much better and he noticed how luscious she looked, her black tank top clinging to her ample breasts while her long shapely legs curled under that round bottom he loved so much. This was not working out, he realized. *I have to find some way to stay away from her so she can make a full recovery. If I stay here much longer, I won't be able to resist her.* He had plans to make.

Sliding out of the bed, putting distance between them, he mumbled, "I've got some errands to run. I'm going to call someone to come and sit with you while I'm gone." Shannon didn't like the way he said "gone". It sounded final somehow. "It's really not necessary. I can look after myself." She didn't want anyone intruding on their little world. She knew she was being selfish but she couldn't help it.

Seth gave her a stern look, "You know I won't allow that. You could have a relapse at anytime." His look forbade any argument, "I've got to take care of some business out of town, and I need to make sure you'll be okay…so I don't want to hear how strong you think you are".

Shannon's mouth dropped open, "You're leaving, again?" I don't want to be all clingy but I would feel better if you could stay." She looked into his blue eyes, seeing his resolve wavering. She felt guilty for pressuring him. Letting out a sigh she told him what he wanted to hear, "but I realize you have business to see about, so, I'll be fine", her voice steady, fighting the tears that threatened to spill down her cheeks. Pushing them back, she smiled bravely back at him.

Seth saw the brave front she was trying to put on and his heart ached for her. He wanted to gather her into his arms and comfort her but he had to resist. He squelched the desire welling up inside him. Steeling himself, he made his voice sound casual, "You get some rest. I'll check in on you later." With that, he turned to go, leaving a piece of his heart behind.

CHAPTER 33

Shannon awoke late in the evening to the smell of heaven coming from the kitchen. Rousing herself from the bed, she put on Seth's robe and walked down the hall to the front of the house. She stopped dead in her tracks. There, standing in front of the sink, humming a lively tune, was a squat Native American woman. When Seth had told her he was going to have someone come and sit with her, she thought he would hire a homecare nurse, not one of the women from the reservation. Just then, the woman turned around, a steamy bowl of chicken soup in her hand. Spying Shannon, she beamed at her.

"Hello Miss Mallory. I was just about to bring you some chicken soup. It's good for what ails you." Shannon met the woman's soft brown eyes, "Hello. It seems you have me at a disadvantage." The round woman's brows knitted together, "huh?" Shannon smiled and the woman smiled back, her generous mouth showing strong white teeth. "You seem to know my name, but I don't know yours." Placing the bowl on a breakfast tray, she laughed, "Sorry, I'm not used to people not knowing who I am. My name is Anna Maria, but most people just call me Manna." Shannon looked at her curiously. "It's a mix of Anna and Maria. My granddaughter started calling me Manna and it just stuck." She looked at Shannon, sizing her up. She could see that she was ill but on the mend. "I hope you don't mind but I gave myself a tour of the house while you were sleeping. Did you do those beautiful paintings?" Shannon nodded, "Well, they are so rich with color. You would think they were photographs, the images are so realistic!" Shannon was flattered.

"Thank you very much. I have to admit, I've been dying to get back to it, but Seth thinks that painting will make me tired and I might have a relapse." She was amazed that she was opening up to this stranger, but for some reason she felt very comfortable around her. Manna made a shooing gesture with her hands, "Pooh, that's just silly. Doing things we enjoy helps bring the color back to our cheeks." Picking up the breakfast tray she asked, "Well, where would you like to eat supper, the bedroom or the living room?" Shannon was shocked, "You mean I can eat in here?" Manna beamed at her, "Why of course. What difference does it make where you sit? All you're going to be doing is eating. Now, go have a seat and I'll bring your dinner." Shannon grinned and plopped down on the couch. Manna placed the steaming brew in front of her and Shannon took a long whiff. "It smells delicious. Thank you." She patted the seat next to her, "Please come sit down, talk to me. I've been dying for some female companionship." Manna looked between the couch and the kitchen, "I really should be cleaning up…"

"Well, you're here to look after me, right? So I would have to say that means the dishes come second." Manna smiled, "I guess it wouldn't hurt to sit a spell".

Shannon found she liked Manna very much. The old woman kept her entertained for hours telling stories of her ancestors. She spoke of how the tribe had been in the valley for centuries and how the government stole their land and sold it to large companies who came in and raped the mountains of their treasures. Surprisingly, there was no trace of bitterness in her voice. "Why don't you hate the white men who did all that to your people?" Manna patted her on the hand, "Life is a gift. While I am on this earthly plain I want my life to be happy, not dwell on the past." Shannon nodded her head, "I agree with you." When she didn't elaborate, Manna took her hand, "You have had much unhappiness in your past". Shocked that she could just look at her and know, Shannon felt her face flush. Finding just enough voice to utter, "Yes", she lowered her eyes. "Oh my dear, don't be embarrassed. What happened to you wasn't your fault. We can only hope to learn from our experiences, good and bad."

"Oh, I'm not embarrassed exactly. I just don't like to dwell on it." She gave herself a small shake, "Like you said, leave the past in the past". Her eyes wandered to the empty bowl, "Thank you so much for the soup, it really hit the spot". She looked at Manna conspiratorially, "Since we're throwing all the rules out the window, do you think

I could work in my studio for awhile?" Manna clapped her hands together with delight, "Oh that would be wonderful. It's such a beautiful day. The leaves are turning, you know."

"They are? Wow, I have really been out of it. How long have I been sick?" Manna wrung her hands, "Gee, I don't really know, but it only takes a few days for the cold to turn the leaves".

After visiting with Manna for a little while longer, Shannon excused herself. "I really could use a shower." She ran her hand through her tangled mess of hair. "I must look a fright." Manna smiled sweetly, "You look like you've been sleeping", then throwing her head back, she laughed heartily, "I just wish I looked the way you do upon waking". She found her laughter contagious and joined her, suddenly feeling better.

After languishing in the bathroom, Shannon dressed in warm-up pants and a baby blue thermal undershirt over a black tank top. Entering the sunny studio, she grabbed her smock hanging from a peg on the wall. "Seth thinks of everything." Her heart fluttered at the thought of him. She missed him terribly. "Well, if he can't be here in the flesh, I'll just have to be content with a likeness of him." Nodding her head, she picked up a large canvas......

Shannon lost all track of time. She had been concentrating so hard she didn't hear Manna tell her she was going home for the evening. "Miss Shannon?" She rapped on the door as hard as she could. Shannon jumped. It was just pure luck that she happened to be dipping the brush into the paint. She shrieked and spun around, "What?"

Manna recoiled at her shrill tone. Shannon saw that she had upset the old woman. "I'm so sorry, Manna. I guess I wasn't paying attention. I didn't mean to sound upset. What was it you were saying?" Manna smiled and walked into the room. Shannon could tell she was craning her head, trying to get a look at her progress. "I was just saying that it's getting really late. If you think you'll be okay, I need to check on my family." Shannon felt guilty for taking this lovely woman away from her home. "Of course, I'll be fine. By all means, go take care of your family." She walked over to her and hugged the woman affectionately. "Thank you so much for staying with me. I really enjoyed your company." Shannon gave Manna a warm smile, "It's not quite finished but if you would like to see it…"

Manna's eyes widened, "Oh could I?" "Sure", as Shannon turned the easel around Manna clapped her hand over her mouth in wonder, "Oh, it is truly wonderful! The way you have captured the color of his eyes." Shannon felt her heart swell at the woman's praise, "It isn't quite done. I still have to finish the face." Manna was drawn to the clear blue eyes looking back at her. "Mr. Seth will surely love it when you give it to him." She said her goodbyes and left, leaving Shannon alone in the tiny apartment.

After cleaning the brushes and hanging up her smock, Shannon went to the kitchen for a bottle of water. It was after midnight and the wind was howling outside, or was it a lone wolf pining after an elusive female? She pulled the oversized sweater tighter around her, feeling the loneliness down to her soul. Why hadn't Seth called her? It wasn't like him to go even a whole day without talking to her. She shook her head, trying to dispel the ominous feeling in the pit of her stomach. She knew she should probably get some sleep but she was too wound up. Plopping down on the comfortable couch, she flipped through the channels, sneaking glances at her cell phone, willing it to ring but the screen remained black as the moonless night outside the picture window. *Why haven't you called me Seth? Don't you know I can't sleep without hearing your voice?* She tossed the remote on the couch and marched to the refrigerator. Standing with the door open, she looked for something to occupy her time. Even though it was filled to overflowing with all her favorite foods, thanks to Seth, she just couldn't think about eating. She found a couple of wine coolers left over from her "girls' night in" with Millie. Popping the top, she kept hearing a small voice in her head warning her about mixing alcohol and certain prescribed medicines. Shrugging, she took a couple of swallows. The liquid burned a trail down her throat and into her stomach, warming her at once. Taking another swig, she grabbed the remote from the couch and turned the stereo on. Soft rock drifted through the apartment. She frowned, she couldn't dance to that. She pushed the search button until it landed on a pop music station. The Black Eyed Peas "Boom Boom Boom" blared from the speakers. Smiling, she began to sway to the music, every now and then taking a long pull on the wine cooler.

By the third song, and her second wine cooler, she was feeling pretty good when movement outside caught her eye. Was it a trick of the light? Was she just imagining things because of the mix of alcohol and drugs? Flipping off the lights, she stared across the yard into the trees. There it was again, a light flickering through the woods. Shannon crouched down and watched as it moved farther away, dimming, and finally disappearing into the dense brush. Her heart hammered in her chest. *Someone was out there! He was spying on me!* She crawled on her hands and knees to the front door and turned the dead bolt until it clicked. *Oh God Seth, I wish you were here!* What should she do? She sat with her back against the front door, her mind racing. *I should call someone...but who?* She looked at the clock on the wall. It was almost one o'clock in the morning. Everyone would be asleep. Should she disturb them? What for? The intruder was long gone. *What would be the use in getting everyone upset when whoever it was had already left?* Steeling herself, she got up and walked over to the picture window. Pulling the sheer curtains back, she looked out into the yard, *Nope, not a soul around.* Breathing a sigh of relief, she decided it was safe to go to bed. Crawling under the covers, she pulled them up to her chin. Shutting her eyes she said a prayer, "Please God, don't let anything happen to Seth. I love him so much! Please don't take him away from me. I don't think I could bear it." As she fell asleep, a single tear drop slipped from under her lid, slid down her cheek and finally came to rest on her pillow.

Shannon was in the middle of the same nightmare. She huddled down in a thicket, hiding from the man in the cowboy boots. He passed by but stopped and turned around, sniffing the air as though he could smell her and drew closer to her hiding place...

She forced herself to wake, only to come out of one nightmare and into another. A hand clapped over her mouth. She could taste something vile in the back of her throat. She tried to struggle but felt like she was clawing through a room full of cotton. As quickly as she had awakened, she succumbed to the blackness, fading into unconsciousness.

CHAPTER 34

Seth couldn't wait to get home to Shannon. His business meeting ended up being a little longer and more in-depth than he had initially planned. He kept looking at his watch as the meeting dragged on, wanting to call her, to hear her sweet voice, but he knew that any interruption would make it last that much longer.

Now he stood frozen with the cell phone in his hand, his heart beating faster with every unanswered ring. *That's odd. Why isn't she answering? Maybe she's in the shower or sleeping.* He closed the phone, disappointment turning his gloomy mood, darker still.

After packing up his toiletries, he tried calling her again but there still wasn't any answer. He left a message on her voicemail, straining to keep his voice casual. He had overreacted when she was at the club. *I don't want to alarm her. I know she gets upset when I try to be overprotective,* but something was eating at him. It just felt wrong. He tried calling her several more times on his way to the airport, electing to hang up before it went to voicemail. She would only get angry if she checked her phone and there were ten messages from him. He dialed a different number. "Hey Manna, it's Seth." He heard children playing in the background. "Hello Seth, how are you?" Seth tried to keep his voice even as he felt the panic bubbling up inside him, "Is Shannon there? She doesn't seem to have her phone on her." There was an uneasy pause on the other end of the line as he heard her shushing the kids, "I'm home. Miss Shannon said that she would be alright for the night and told me to go see about my family." He heard her gasp into the phone, "Oh no! You don't think something happened to her, do you?" The panic was getting very close to the surface, "I'm sure everything is fine, but would you mind going over there just to check? It would make me feel a lot better." Manna assured him she would and hung up the phone.

The next hour was excruciating for Seth. While waiting to board his flight, he kept checking his watch, scowling, grumbling to himself, *Time couldn't possibly drag like this.* As he paced back and forth, people who happened to walk near gave him a wide berth. He looked crazed, and dangerous. Hearing his flight number over the speaker, he became torn. Should he board his flight which would make it impossible to answer his phone if Shannon called or should he skip his flight and wait for her to call? If he boarded his flight, he would be there in less than two hours but if he stayed behind, he could continue to try to reach her by phone. "Shit!" he exclaimed as he ran to catch his flight. Something was pulling him. He could feel it, like an invisible thread attached to his insides, propelling him forward.

CHAPTER 35

Oh my God, I've gone blind! Shannon thought as she opened her eyes and was met by pitch darkness. She tried to bring her hands to her face but found that she couldn't Move. *Am I paralyzed too?* Her breathing became shallow as she felt the panic rise up, making her nauseous. Something was shoved into her mouth. Feeling completely helpless she let out a small whimper. It felt like she was on a bed of some kind. The mattress was thin and lumpy and the springs squeaked when she moved. Suddenly, the brevity of her situation hit her like a slap in the face. Someone had taken her. She struggled futilely to break her bonds. Exhausted and nauseous, she became very still, listening. Except for the squeaking of the bed, there was no sound….at all. The gag was wedged so far back in her throat that she couldn't push it out with her tongue. Tears of frustration and terror slid past the blindfold and down her face. *Please Seth, come find me* The thought of never being in his arms again was enough to refuel her determination. Jerking on the rope that bound her hands, she thrashed around on the squeaky bed, oblivious to the racket she was making.

"Well, I see we're finally awake." That voice. Shannon ceased her efforts. Even blind she could clearly see the shark's tooth grin. She felt hands running slowly down her arms until they were resting on her wrists. Stilling herself, she waited for the moment when she could make her escape but almost moaned with frustration as he only untied the rope that bound her feet to her wrists, allowing her to sit up but not giving her the freedom she desperately wanted.

He leaned down close to her face, "Now, I'm going to take out the gag, but you have to promise me you'll be good and not scream,

228

not that anyone would hear you out here anyhow. I just don't like my women to be screamers.......at least until I make them scream." He chuckled at his personal joke. Shannon felt a shiver run down her spine. She knew from experience she was dealing with a Psychopath. How many women had he brought out here, to play with at his leisure? And more importantly, what did he do with them when he tired of his games?

She made her voice sound as emotionless as possible, "Hello Joseph". He clapped his hands in delight, "I knew you would know it was me. I'm sorry that I had to go to such lengths but that Son of a bitch was always stuck to you like glue so I figured this would be the only way we could be alone....really alone." The insinuation wasn't lost on Shannon. She felt the bile rise in her throat, "I could really use some water. That gag was really jammed in there."

"Of course, I'll go get you a bottle."

"Wait!" Shannon's voice revealed a tiny bit of the panic she was feeling.

Joseph looked back at her, his voice sounding suspicious, "what is it? You don't have to be afraid. Just think of this as a preview to our honeymoon." With that, he crossed over to her and before Shannon knew what was happening, he grabbed her hair painfully and crushed her lips, shoving his tongue down her throat. It took all her will power not to vomit in his mouth. She endured his assault. The thought of what Seth would do to him being her only comfort. He released her and stood back, "Wow that was intense! I have to admit, I am pleasantly surprised. I thought you would put up more of a fight...... I knew you liked me." She could hear the triumph in his voice.

"Uh, Joseph, I really don't think this blind fold is necessary, do you?" Not waiting to hear his reply, she rushed on, "I mean, its not as if I don't know who you are, right?" She let out the unused air she had built up, waiting for his response.

He laughed, "You have a point there". He reached down and removed the blindfold. Shannon had to blink several times, as the light pierced her eyes. "There now, isn't that better?" She looked up into the grinning face of the madman. If she didn't know better, she could swear he was posing for her. His clothes were impeccable and fit like a glove on his tall muscular frame. His raven black hair, cut close to the scalp, was shiny, every hair in place. She could see how women would be attracted to this man but when she looked at him her blood ran cold. He could almost pass for Seth's brother except for the eyes. Seth's were electric blue and Joseph's were dark brown, almost black. Shannon looked into those eyes and felt nothing but cold. There was no warmth there. It was like looking into a bottomless pit. Here was the stuff of nightmares, for she had seen that very same look before, in Richmond's eyes. He actually thought she was okay, being trussed up like a Thanksgiving turkey. Keeping her voice light, Shannon pointed to her throat, "water?' She croaked.

He snapped his fingers, "Right, I'll be back in a flash", as he walked out of the room, locking the door from the outside.

Shannon looked around the room. The walls were wood. She could tell she was in a log cabin, but unlike Seth's, this one was dark and dingy. No pictures adorned the walls. The only furniture in the room was the squeaky bed, dresser and a table with a rustic looking lamp on top. With no visible window, it was the only source of light in the room. Even the cover on the lumpy bed was white, generic. It was as though he didn't want this room to reflect anything about him, but Shannon knew that the absence of personality was in effect, a perfect representation of his real self, completely void. She had to get out of here. She struggled vainly with the rope again, refusing to give up. Painfully aware she wasn't wearing a bra, the position of her arms caused her breasts to strain against the stretchy material of her black tank top. What happened to the blue thermal top she had on earlier? She hated to think that he had taken off her while she was unconscious and totally helpless. What else had he done or seen? Shaking herself, she knew there was nothing she could do about it as long as her hands were tied behind her back. Remembering a movie she had seen, she laid down on the bed, pulling her knees up to her chest while sliding her hands over her butt, down her legs and over her feet until her hands, though still tied, were now in front of her body. Wasting no time, she reached down and started working on the knots around her ankles. She heard a key rattle in the door, signaling Joseph's arrival and knowing there was nothing she could do to hide her progress, she decided to use it to her advantage.

"Hey, I brought you some water." He was grinning until he saw what she had done. "How did you do that?" He shrugged his shoulders. "Doesn't matter. I was planning on replacing those nasty ropes anyway... with these." Shannon's eyes widened as he dangled a pair of silver handcuffs he had pulled from his back pocket. With his other hand he deftly pulled out a hunting knife and laid the cold blade on the side of her face. "Don't make me use this on your lovely freckled face." Shannon's heart beat wildly in her chest. "You're going to behave?" Unable to respond for the knot in her throat, she nodded. "Very good. Now, lie back on the bed." Shannon did as she was told. This was not the time for heroics. He kept the blade close to her neck as she positioned herself. Satisfied, he grabbed her wrists, loosening the ropes just enough to move them so he could attach the handcuffs, wrapping the chain around the slats in the wrought iron headboard, making it virtually impossible to escape. She was totally helpless and at his mercy. If that wasn't bad enough he removed the rope from her ankles, leaving them free. She clamped her legs together. Joseph chuckled at her vain attempt. She squelched the bile rising in her throat, once again threatening to gag her. She had to keep a level head.

"Don't worry my dear. I don't plan on compromising your virtue. When I finally make you mine, you will be begging me for it." He waved his hand around, "I have all the time in the world...... and I am a very patient man". He put a straw in the water bottle and pressed it to Shannon's lips. She took a tentative sip but once the cool liquid slid down her parched throat, she sucked it greedily, bringing a smile to Joseph's face. "There now, isn't that better?" He got up and tossed the bottle into the trash can on the other side of the bed. "I'll be back in a while with your supper. You must be famished." He leaned over to kiss her. She jerked her head away, "Don't touch me you pig!" she hissed.

Surprise flashed across his face. Quickly recovering, that hateful grin returned as though it had never disappeared. "It's alright. I know you get a little cranky when you're hungry He quickly gave her a peck on the cheek and left the room, locking her in again. It was more than Shannon could bear. She let the tears flow freely down her cheeks, surrendering to her fear.

Shannon looked up at the nondescript ceiling, *I have to think. Get a hold of yourself. You have to think of a way to get free and somehow get to Seth.* Just the thought of him almost made her come undone. *No,*

I have to keep my focus, bide my time, wait for just the right moment. She knew if it came right down to it that she might have to do things that repulsed her. She had to get him to let down his guard, just once. She wasn't fooling herself. She was dealing with a sick psychopath and if he caught on, her goose was cooked.

Joseph returned a little while later with a breakfast tray and another little surprise. Shannon's mouth fell open as he knelt and attached a manacle to the leg of the bed. Taking the other end, he snapped it onto her ankle, his hand running up to her knee. She kicked at him viciously. He laughed, "Now there's the spirit I was expecting". He released her wrists from the handcuffs. Moving so fast, his hand a blur, he pulled the hunting knife out and waved it at her. "Don't try anything or I'm afraid you might get hurt." The sight of the knife made Shannon freeze. He placed the tray on the side table. Shannon looked at the sandwich and soup and felt her stomach rumble. He had placed the sandwich on a paper plate and the soup in a Styrofoam cup. He was careful not to give her any flatware. Shannon picked up the sandwich and took a tentative bite. She recognized the flavor at once. He had ordered it from the diner. How many times had he come by on his way home and gotten a sandwich to go? Her heart clinched at the thought of him walking into the diner and ordering his usual while she was possibly drugged and lying in the trunk or back seat of his car. She took a sip of the home made vegetable soup Irene was famous for.

Joseph watched her eat, his eyes roving over her body. His gaze lingered on her breasts. His breathing quickened, but he restrained himself. He knew that the longer he resisted, the sweeter the prize. He could feel himself harden and reveled in the pleasure pain. Oh yes, she was going to give him hours and hours of pleasure.

Shannon wiped her mouth and took a swig of the bottled water, "Joseph, I was wondering…" He looked at her expectantly, "Yes my dear?" She knew there was no easy way to broach the subject, "How am I going to…you know, go to the bathroom?" She hated that her face flushed red, letting him see how embarrassed she was.

Joseph smiled as she blushed. He loved the way it spread down to her chest. His eyes followed the trail to the "v" between her breasts. He wanted to reach out and pinch a nipple. "Oh, well the manacle is long enough to reach the bathroom." Shannon pulled on the chain, gauging the length and looked doubtfully at him. His shoulders shook with mirth as he walked over and opened what had looked to Shannon like a closet door. *Surely he's not going to make me do my business in a closet.* Relief flooded over her when the room revealed a toilet, sink, and small bathtub. "All the comforts of home", Joseph bowed extravagantly and waved his arm, "Nothing but the best for my lady". Shannon wasn't so sure she was going to be able to keep her food down. He picked up the tray and once again left her locked in. She immediately dropped to the floor. Looking at the legs of the bed, her heart dropped to her feet. They were bolted to the floor. She growled in frustration, "Arghhh". Walking to the bathroom she wasn't surprised to see a pedestal sink. There were no storage units or cabinets, no drawers where a discarded pin or nail file could be hiding. She pulled back the shower curtain hoping to find something that would help her get loose but found only her special brand of shampoo and conditioner. *Well, he's thought of everything.* Wrenching the shower curtain back in place, she could feel the rage building up, making her hands tremble. Just as quickly, it was replaced by abject sorrow. Her body shook as she sobbed, crumbling into a heap on the bathroom floor. Looking up toward Heaven, she begged, "Please God, help me find a way back to Seth." Suddenly she spotted something she hadn't noticed before. She climbed up on the rim of the tub and examined the curtain hooks. They were designed to look a little like diaper pins and made of some type of steel. She unhooked one and tried it in the keyhole of the manacle. It slipped in easily. Her heart soared and she thanked God for answering her prayers. She moved it around but before she could make any headway, she heard the bedroom door opening. Thinking fast, she closed the door, pulled her pants down and sat on the toilet, just as Joseph knocked on the door. "Shannon my dear, what are you doing in there?" She called out, "I had to use the toilet. I'll be out in a minute!" Quickly flushing, she went through the routine of washing her hands. Looking into the mirror, she hardly recognized her reflection. Her eyes were red and puffy and mascara was streaked down her face. Her hair was sticking out every which way. She was a hot mess. *Good. Maybe he will think me unattractive and let me go.* She almost laughed at the absurdity of the thought. She attempted to calm the rat's nest that was her hair but failed miserably. *What do I care how I look anyway?* She frowned at her reflection and steeling herself, opened the door.

"Ah, there you are. Is everything alright?" He asked anxiously. "I thought you fell in or something." He laughed at his own joke and Shannon realized that he really wasn't concerned at all. It was just an act. Psychopaths made the best actors. They had to play the ultimately role...being human.

"No, I'm fine. I just feel a little weak. I think I need to lie down." She started past him and he grabbed her elbow, "Here, let me help you". She had to play it cool. She wasn't quite sure what might set him off, "Thank you", she whispered.

"Can I get you anything?"

"How about a key to these....?" Shannon held up the chains that bound her.

Joseph threw his head back and laughed as though she had just told the funniest joke he'd ever heard. Then he looked her straight in the eye, all the humor suddenly gone, replaced with mock concern, "We can't have you getting lost in the woods, now can we?"

Her blood ran cold. *We must be in some hunting cabin up in the mountains.* Her shoulders slumped as she felt the blood drain from her face. They were miles away from civilization. He was right. Even if she screamed, there was no one within earshot. He walked up to her and leaned in close. She could smell his breath in her face. The smell of cinnamon almost stifling, and fought back the nausea. His eyes searched hers, looking for a specific emotion. She refused to give him the satisfaction and kept her face blank. He gazed at her for what seemed an eternity. He must have thought he found something in her eyes. Imagining it to be desire, his face broke into that hated grin. Grabbing her chin so she couldn't pull away he attacked her lips. Her instinct was to claw his eyes out but just as her hands shot out, she felt the cold blade of the hunting knife against her neck. She froze; flashbacks of Richmond springing into her head. He pulled away, wanting to look into her beautifully strange eyes but Shannon had them squeezed shut. *She must want me to kiss her again, the little slut.*

He pinched her chin. Shocked by the pain, Shannon's eyes flew open. He scowled at her for a split second, then grinned, "You have the most beautiful eyes I have ever seen". He moved the knife along her chin and up to her cheek. Shannon sat completely still as the tip rested just under her bottom lid. "Maybe I'll pluck them out and keep them as souvenirs." He chuckled when he saw the panic on her face. About to step away, he stopped as he noticed the thin scar on her neck. "Tell me how that happened?" It wasn't a request. The last thing Shannon wanted to do was confide in this madman. He saw her hesitancy and increased the pressure on the knife. She felt the blood trickle down her neck as it pricked her skin. She knew it would be dangerous to make something up. He would know if she lied. Looking into his eyes, she sighed, suddenly exhausted. "It was a parting gift from my dear late husband", her eyes challenging him. Comprehension crossed his face and he laughed dryly, "You must have pissed him off something fierce! I love a woman with spirit... a wild filly that I can break." Reaching out, he traced his finger along the scar. Shannon felt sick and this time she didn't think she could keep down her food. Clapping her hand over her mouth, she sprang from the bed. Joseph was caught off guard and stumbled backward. Tripping on the chain he went down, hard. She saw the small window of opportunity but abandoned the idea as the nausea overtook her. She ran to the bathroom and threw up into the toilet.

After heaving up everything she'd eaten, she sank to the floor, curling up into a ball. Joseph yanked on her chain, jerking her awake. "Hey, you done? Come on back in here." He yanked on it again, harder this time. "Don't forget to flush, and brush your teeth! I hate the smell of puke." Shannon forced herself up off the floor and walked on unsteady legs back to the bed. She collapsed face first onto the bed, completely oblivious to Joseph. Her head was pounding like a jack hammer as she moaned into the pillow. Joseph turned her over and she flopped around like a ragdoll. Her shirt twisted up under her breasts. He reached out and exposed one pale mound to his greedy eyes. His breathing became labored. Before he even knew he had done it, he cupped her breast, roughly kneading the soft flesh. His tongue snaked out to lick his upper lip, imagining his lips there instead of his hand. As his erection became painful, his other hand ducked down to squeeze himself...hard, sending shivers up and down his spine. His eyes traveled over her body, taking in the curve of her waist and her ample hips. Leaning over, he captured her lips with his mouth. This time, however, she responded to his embrace.

He was pleasantly shocked. His confidence growing, he lay down on the bed and pulled her into his arms. She responded by wrapping her arms around his neck, pulling his body close, forming her body to his. As his lips traveled down her neck and over the paleness of her breasts, she moaned, and he smiled. "Seth", she breathed as she tangled her fingers in his short hair. Jumping up, he roughly pushed her hands away. "Son of a bitch!" he growled and stormed out of the room.

Shannon moaned in her sleep. She was having the most erotic dream. Her fingers traced the outline of her lips. Imagining they were Seth's lips, she moved them down her neck and over her taut nipple. "Oh yes, Seth. Make love to me!" Her fingers continued their descent, traveling over her stomach and disappearing beneath the waistband of her pants. She felt as though her loins were on fire. As her fingers explored her wet heat, her tongue snaked out, licking her lips. She thrashed around on the ratty mattress, as spasm after spasm wracked her body. The instant it was over her eyes flew open and she looked down with horror as she realized what had just happened. *God, what did I do? How could I do that….here?* She felt sick again but having nothing left in her stomach, curled up into a fetal position, and cried herself to sleep.

CHAPTER 36

Joseph's Pov

"Dammit! She fell asleep on me! I must've put too much of the aphrodisiac in her food. And it was going so well too. Not a big deal, there'll be plenty of time for us to get to know eachother." He mentally patted himself on the back at his cleverness. "It was just so easy. All I had to do was wait for Seth", he said the name with venom, "to leave her alone". He crossed over to the monitor, staring at the blank screen. "He just had to go and build that private little apartment for her and then hired that fat old witch as her nurse maid." He sat down in the desk chair and pulled a pencil from the holder, running his fingers up and down the shaft absently, thinking of that night he had followed her home from the club. He smiled when he remembered the little porno show she had put on for him on the hood of the little blue convertible. She was incredible. He thought of how her face glowed in the moonlight, caught in the throes of passion. He had imagined himself in Seth's place. It was a fantasy he played over and over in his mind. "Soon, it will be a reality." He picked up the remote and hit the replay button. Kicking his feet up on the desk, he watched the recorded image of Shannon walking around the apartment upstairs, unaware of the hidden camera that had followed her every move.

He sneered as he remembered the first time he had laid eyes on Shannon. He knew then he had to have her. His mind began to work, hatching a plan almost on instinct. It was quite simple, really. All he needed to do was wait for the right moment. He had shadowed her, following her to work, home, pretty much everywhere. He had even followed her as far as the entrance to the reservation but had turned back. He didn't want to take the chance of someone recognizing him and mentioning it to Seth.

Following her that night when they had driven to the next town, he had sat in his car a long time, waiting for them to leave. Getting antsy, he slipped into the restaurant, hoping to spot them, only to growl in frustration. The place had private booths so it was virtually impossible to see where they were sitting. Just as he had given up and started to leave, he saw her. His mouth watered at the memory of her sashaying across the floor to the ladies room, every guy in the place watching her. The bitch was putting herself on display. Just like all of them, strutting around, teasing. He would teach her not to play with people's feelings. He considered following her into the bathroom but noticed there was too much traffic, so he elected to wait in his car for them to leave. He chuckled to himself as he remembered Shannon's exhibition in the parking lot. The bitch was insatiable! He couldn't wait to get her alone in the cabin, her long shapely legs wrapped around *his* waist.

He paid cash for the cabin a few years ago, right after Naome' died. He gritted his teeth, "That Son of a bitch husband of hers had ruined everything back then, and he was trying to ruin his plans now with Shannon. I know if I can get her to trust me, she'll realize that I'm the man she really wants. I plan on keeping her for as long as it takes, even if that means holding her for weeks, months or years. "You will love me Shannon Mallory." He gripped the pencil and hearing it snap in two, grinned. It was going to be extremely interesting breaking her spirit. Throwing the pencil on the desk, he decided he should check in on his very special guest.

CHAPTER 37

As soon as his plane landed, Seth tried Shannon's number again. "Dammit! Shannon, where are you?" He gritted his teeth together, his jaw working furiously. He couldn't imagine why she wasn't answering her phone. He called Manna, too anxious to wait for her to call him back. "Have you been able to reach her?" He didn't bother with formalities, his heart constricting in his chest. "I'm sorry Mr. Seth, but she isn't here. I have looked all through the house." Her voice was panicky. He knew there was something she wasn't telling him. "What else?" he asked, trying to keep his voice calm, all the while his jaw working furiously. She hesitated for what seemed like an eternity, "Her clothes are still here…" she choked back a sob. Seth ran to the waiting cab, "What? What is it you're not telling me?" He jumped into the backseat, "Step on it Joe!" The urgency in his voice was enough to make the old man step on the gas. "Her car and your truck are still here. I don't think she would be strong enough to walk anywhere. Oh Mr. Seth, I am worried for her." Seth could hear the concern in her voice and his heart warmed, *that's my Shannon. The old woman barely knew her and already cared for her. And why not? She made it so easy to love her.* "Manna, calm down. It's very important that you do exactly as I say until I get there. Don't call the police yet and don't touch anything." Though Shannon could be stubborn, he felt sure she wouldn't jeopardize her health by walking into town. He hung up from Manna and rang Millie's number.

"Hey Millie, it's Seth." By the tone of his voice, Millie gathered it wasn't a social call. "What's wrong?" She had a feeling it was about Shannon. "We can't seem to locate Shannon. I am about a minute from the house and Manna is already there." "How can I help?" Millie asked.

Seth took a deep breath, trying to keep the panic out of his voice, "Do you by any chance know where Joseph is?" Millie was taken aback, "Joseph? But what does Joseph have to do with...? Oh my God!" realization hit her in the face. "Do you know? Millie!" Seth shouted in the phone snapping her out of her trance. "Yeah, uh, I mean no." Seth's hand shook as he struggled to keep his cool.

Millie went to the front window of the little house she had renovated and looked out. Joseph's office was across the street and a couple of buildings down but the parking lot was clearly visible. "I don't see his car. Hang on." She rushed outside and down the street, the cell phone dangling from her hand. Seth waited impatiently.

"Okay, he's definitely not here. The building is locked up tight." She heard Seth utter an oath and panic crept up her spine. Would he actually do something to Shannon? He had certainly made it plain to her that he was interested. Millie said a silent prayer. If Joseph had become obsessed, there's no telling what he might do. If anyone knew how cruel he could be, it was her. She shivered as she thought about the "special" time she had spent with Joseph.

"Millie, listen to me carefully. Can you recall anywhere he may have gone? Did he ever tell you about a certain place he liked to go? Did he ever take you someplace secret, private?" Millie wracked her brain, "No, we usually went to a hotel, motel, or back to his place." She gasped, as she suddenly got a mental image of Shannon in the secret room, his "playroom".

"What is it, Millie? Did you think of something?" He couldn't hide the hope in his tone and Millie felt very guilty for what she was about to do but she couldn't let him know about the secret room. What would he think of her? What would the whole town think of her if this got out? She had to handle this herself. "Seth, why don't you check out the local hotels and motels to see if he has rented a room and I'll go check out his house? I'll let you know if I find anything."

Seth hesitated, "okay, that actually sounds like a good idea." He was surprised she'd thought of it. "That's going to take awhile. I'll try to get some people to help so we can cover more ground."

Millie heard the surprise in his voice at her suggestion. She shrugged it off, "Sounds good. I'll call you later."

Seth wished he could call Irene and Paddy but they had left to visit their family a few days ago. He looked at the useless phone in his hand. He didn't have anyone he could call. Suddenly an image of Shannon sitting in the center of a circle with babes on each knee came to him. Jumping in his truck, he headed out to the reservation. Maybe there was someone he could ask after all.

CHAPTER 38

"Alright, you men come with me. The rest of you, comb this entire area. We have to find her." Seth felt his heart swell at the response he got when he had driven at break neck speed into the middle of the Rez. The out pouring of love for Shannon was impressive. He decided not to involve the town sheriff who was an alcoholic and never did an honest days work in his life but having connections so it was no wonder he kept getting re-elected.

Seth straightened his spine. It was going to be hard for him to approach the people who had condemned him but he would do it…. for Shannon.

Millie took out her key to Joseph's house. She took a deep breath. What would she do if she found evidence that he had kidnapped Shannon? If anyone came here they would eventually find out all his dirty little secrets and she would be ruined in this town. "Well, let's get this over with", she turned the knob and stepped inside…

Joseph's house was opulent. Expensive furnishings covered the rooms. One of a kind artwork adorned the walls while oriental rugs blanketed the cherry wood floors. Millie tossed the key carelessly in an antique glass bowl sitting atop the antique table. She walked with purpose to the hidden doorway behind an antique rug, depicting Indian life, hanging on the wall. The door had no lock. There was no need for one. It was well hidden. She turned on the light and stepped boldly into the room. "Hello?" she called out as she walked past the strange devices. She brushed against a chain hanging from the ceiling and swiped it away. It made a tinkling sound. After checking the three interior rooms, she sighed with relief. Shannon wasn't here. By the look of it, nobody had used these rooms in quite sometime. She ran her finger across the long table in the center of the room and looked at the dust on her finger. "Yuck!" She wiped her hand on her mini skirt. "Joseph hasn't been here for awhile." He had to be somewhere else. She left the room and started for the door when a thought occurred to her. Making a left, she passed through the kitchen and stood outside the only room Joseph had forbid her to enter. The door was double padlocked. It was the only door in the house that locked. Going back into the kitchen, Millie looked through cabinets and drawers until she found a flat head screwdriver. "This ought to do." She studied the locks for a minute or two. Taking the screwdriver, she tried to fit the end into the key hole of the lock but it was too big. Standing back, she looked from the lock to the screwdriver, once, twice, three times. Suddenly, a light seemed to come on and she jammed the end between the door and the jam and worked it back and forth. She succeeded in getting the door unlocked but the padlocked remained intact. Shrieking in frustration, she stomped her foot. "Dammit! I know there's a way in, I just don't know how!" Her eyes tearing up, she walked back into the kitchen and sat down at the table. Putting her hands on each side of her face, she proceeded to slap her temples, "Think Millie. What would Daddy do?" A memory started forming in her mind. She concentrated really hard. Jumping up, she ran over to the utility drawer and brought out a hammer. Taking the screwdriver, she placed it under the screw to the jam and hit the handle with the hammer. The screw loosened and soon, "plink", it fell to the floor. "Yes!" She made short work of the other two and opened the door from the wrong side. "Thanks Daddy."

The room was littered with electronic gadgets. There were video monitors everywhere. Millie noticed a metal file cabinet in the corner. Walking over, she pulled on the door. It was unlocked and swung open easily. Millie's hand flew to her mouth. It was filled with video tapes and DVDs. Each one was labeled meticulously. That was just like Joseph. Even his obsessions were O.C.D. but that's not what made her heart drop into her chest. It was the names and dates on the labels. There were at least a couple dozen different names. The dates went back at least five years.

She looked closer and noticed that only two names showed up multiple times. "Oh my God!" Millie's hand went to her throat. There were at least five or six discs with Shannon's name on them.

She recognized the other name immediately, Naome'. These were much older and some were even on VHS tapes. She took one from the collection and slipped it into the VCR. The picture was grainy from age but she recognized the timid but beautiful smile of Seth's dead wife. There was candid film of her doing daily chores around the house. She watched as Naome' piddled around in the kitchen, cooking a meal while the baby sat in the highchair banging a spoon. She sucked in her breath as a slightly younger Seth strode into the room and wrapped his arms around his wife, kissing her on the neck, then walking over and lifting his little baby into his arms, twirling him around. The baby squealed with delight.

Millie hit the fast forward button. A different scene came on the screen. At first she couldn't make out anything from all the fog…. no…steam in the room. A shadow walked up and flipped on the exhaust fan, at least that's what Millie guessed it was from the sound it made. She watched in horror as Naome's beautiful face floated out of the fog. She watched as Naome' walked from the bathroom, a towel wrapped around her petite body. The scene changed again, Naome' was in the bedroom. Dropping the towel, she was naked for the entire world to see.

Millie ejected the tape and went back over to the cabinet. With a shaky hand, she took the disc with Shannon's name on it and slipped it into the player. Oh, the miracle of modern technology. There were four parts on the screen, the yard, the front room, the bathroom, and the bedroom, all being recorded simultaneously. She watched as Shannon walked from one square to the next. She felt ill. "Think Millie!" What should she do? Seth certainly needed to know what Joseph had been doing but should he see the footage of his former life? She ejected the disc and put it back on the shelf. She was about to close the cabinet and call Seth but she saw a box shoved to the back of the cabinet. Getting down on her knees she pulled the box from its hiding place. It had a tiny lock like the kind you would find on a teenager's diary. She made short work of it and flipped open the lid. It contained one disc. Unlike the others, this one was unmarked. Curiosity getting the better of her, she slipped it into the player.

"Seth, I need to see you." He didn't recognize Millie's voice at first. It sounded so strange, not like the bubbly lilt he was used to.

"Millie?" He asked doubtfully. "Yes it's me. Come to Joseph's house."

Panic sprang up in his voice, "What is it? What did you find? Oh God Millie! Don't tell me…"

"Will you please shut up and get over here……NOW!" She hung up on him.

Seth broke all kinds of laws on his way to Joseph's. He was about to knock when Millie swung open the door, giving him quite a start.

"Come on in." She disappeared into the interior of the house as Seth cautiously stepped over the threshold. He quickly surveyed the expensive compliments as he followed Millie into the kitchen.

"Millie? Where are you?"

"In here", came her reply. Seth followed the direction of her voice and found himself standing in the doorway to a surveillance room. Millie stood in front of an open cabinet and if Seth didn't know better, she was purposely blocking his view.

"Seth, sit down. I have something to tell you, well, actually, it's more like show you. Wait, no, it's show and tell you really." She shifted from one foot to the other nervously.

Seth clinched his fists, his nails leaving indentions on his palms, as he struggled to keep his composure. "Slow down Millie, breathe."

She took a deep breath, "Okay, here goes. I am almost definitely sure Joseph has Shannon." Seth clinched his jaw and Millie became frightened by the look in his eyes. There was no cruelty there, just pure unadulterated rage. He took a couple of steps toward her and she backed away until the back of her knees hit the chair. She promptly sat down, looking up, his face looming above her, his eyes blue fire.

She cringed, putting her hands protectively over her face. The sight of Millie cowering before him, snapped him out of his rage. His eyes softening, he knelt down beside her and gently touched her shoulder, "I'm sorry Millie. I didn't mean to scare you. It wasn't you I was angry with." She looked at him, tears brimming in her eyes, "I understand how mad you are but unfortunately, that's not the worst part, and I don't know if I want to be here when you see this…" She held the disc up in front of Seth's face. He stared at it, "What's on it?" She looked him square in the eye, "the world", as she slipped it into the player. Joseph's face appeared. Millie turned up the volume and her words, which had seemed nonsense, suddenly became crystal clear.

Millie reached over and pressed the eject button. Seth was frozen, his expression stoic. She wasn't sure if she wouldn't rather he been enraged. This new look was beyond rage, he looked deadly.

"Okay now. This is the worse part." She stood up in front of the metal cabinet and waved her arm like one of those models on "The Price Is Right". Seth looked in the direction of her hand and saw that it was filled with tapes and discs. He looked closer and the blood drained from his face. He looked helplessly at Millie, unable or unwilling to comprehend.

Millie looked at him and seeing the pain etched on his face, reached out, touching his shoulder, "Seth?" He jerked as though from a dream, "Huh?"

"Listen to me. I don't want you to see these. You don't want to see these, believe me. But there is one I have to show you. She took the last one on the top shelf marked "Shannon" and slid it into the machine. Seth felt the strength sucked out of him as he sank to the floor, never taking his eyes off Shannon's beautiful image. As he watched the recording of her, his heart hurt so much he thought he would die. Tears fell unnoticed down his face. When the screen showed Seth and Shannon making love, something inside him snapped.

Snatching up the untitled disc, he walked over to the table and grabbed a pen and a piece of paper. "Millie, I need you to take this disc to this address. Make sure you give it to him personally."

"Who is this Seth?" He put his hands on her shoulders. "He's an old friend and customer of mine. He's also a state senator. He will see to it that it gets to the proper authorities." She started to protest, to say that she could still be of help to him, but he shooed her out the door. "Don't worry, we can handle it from here."

Millie glanced over her shoulder at the video cabinet, her eyes pleading, "Promise me you won't watch anymore of the tapes". She looked to him for reassurance but he all but forced her out the door, locking it behind her. Millie turned and beat on the front door. She searched her pockets and cursed as she remembered she'd left them in the antique glass bowl. Having no other option, she walked to her car, the disc and the address clutched tightly in her hand.

CHAPTER 39

Joseph was becoming very agitated with Shannon's lack of cooperation. It had been a week since she had refused to eat and he was actually beginning to see the outline of her ribs. "Shannon, come on, you know you'll have to eat soon", as he lifted her head and tried to force the spoon into her mouth. Shannon jerked her head away, clinching her jaw, refusing any nourishment he offered. She couldn't take the chance of him drugging her again. The thought of being drugged into having sex with him only strengthened her resolve.

He gave her a pitying look, "You know that if you don't eat, you will leave me no choice but to force feed you". He smiled sweetly as her eyes widened. "Have you ever been force fed? I can assure you it isn't pleasant. A tube is inserted down your throat and into your stomach. Then a protein cocktail is pushed through the tube. The insertion is very unpleasant but when the tube is removed, the gag reflex sometimes wins out, making the patient vomit what was in the stomach, and the whole procedure has to be repeated." He leaned close to her face.

She picked up the faint scent of alcohol as his breath moved little strands of her hair. "Please honey, I promise I'm not drugging you. Won't you please eat something?" Shannon glared at him but refused to answer. That was another thing she had decided after her humiliating experience, she wouldn't speak to Joseph. She knew that because he was a psychopath, she was dancing with the devil but she didn't care anymore. The absence of windows in her little cell, because that's what it was, a prison, made it difficult to track the passage of time, but she guessed she had been Joseph's prisoner for about a week. "Still giving me the silent treatment I see. Well, if you refuse to speak to me then you leave me no choice", his voice deadly calm.

Oh Seth, where are you? Why haven't you found me? She frantically held on to the hope that he would rescue her. In the meantime, she wasn't going to make it easy on Joseph. Why should she? If he thought that he could kidnap her, chain her to a bed, and slip her a mickey, expecting her to cozy up to him, well, he had another thought coming. She looked defiantly at Joseph, murder in her bloodshot eyes.

"Have it your way," he hissed, pushing her head away so he didn't have to look at the expression on her face. Shannon gave a little grunt as her head hit the pillow. She heard Joseph ranting as he slammed the door, but not before he took the only source of light from the little room. Her heart flip flopped as he wrenched the small lamp out of the wall, smashing it to pieces. Left alone in the dark, Shannon closed her eyes and prayed.

Joseph stalked into the living room and snatched up the remote. Clicking on the local news, he plopped down into his favorite leather chair. "What's the matter with her? I know she's just teasing me, playing hard to get, but my God, does she have to take it so far? Why doesn't she just give in? It is, after all, inevitable. She's really starting to piss me off." He leaned forward, elbows on his knees as he ran his hands through his short black hair. Suddenly, he froze, lifting his eyes. His image stared back at him through the television. They were sending out an all points bulletin. His jaw went slack as Shannon's beautiful face appeared next to his. There was a man hunt and he was the target! The state and local officials had teams of law enforcement personnel and volunteers combing the entire area, searching for her. *This has to be Seth's doing, damn him!* Joseph slammed his fist down on the coffee table, making the ice in his glass of whiskey tinkle lightly. Picking up the glass he marched over to the bar to pour himself another drink when the sound of Seth's voice made him jump about two feet. Spinning around, he was captured by Seth's drawn face as he pleaded for information to the whereabouts of his fiancé. "Well Seth, you're not as dumb as you look after all." He knew they would figure it out eventually, but now that the heat was on, he wouldn't be able to come out of hiding for awhile. He had stocked up on supplies so he was ready to hole up at the cabin until spring. By that time, Shannon would be his and they could reappear with no fear. She would say that they had run away together to be alone and get to know each other better. He may even get her to say she disappeared because she was afraid of Seth's temper. That would be the feather in his cap.

As he started to pour his third drink from the decanter, he froze as he heard another name added to the broadcast. Suddenly Joseph roared with rage and flung the decanter across the room where it shattered against the stone hearth. Pacing back and forth, his breathing ragged, he wasn't finished. Striding over to the bar, he threw his arms out and sent the crystal decanters and goblets flying. *Think man, think.*

What do I do now? He sat on the edge of his recliner and pressed his hands against his eyes. He would definitely have to wait until spring but he could nix the plan to just show up with Shannon on his arm. He was now wanted for the murder of Naome' Proudfoot. He would have to escape and somehow manage to get out of the country. *How did they find out?*

He thought about how careful he had been, leaving no proof behind. Besides, it was an accident. He'd meant to kill Seth. He had planned it out to the finest detail. He was so confident his plan was foolproof that he had recorded it on video. He would make a small cut in the brake line, just enough to ensure the fluid leaked out slowly. He had checked with the hospital to make sure Seth was on duty that day. Seth would have an "accident" on his way home from work and he would be there to comfort Naome' and step in as husband to her and father to the little baby. It was the perfect plan until Seth decided to call in sick and take his family on a picnic. He had ruined everything. The head injury was a stroke of luck. Because he couldn't remember the last few moments before the accident, he couldn't tell anyone the brakes had failed.

Joseph smiled as he remembered the agonized look on Seth's face during the hearing. Seth wanted to be convicted; therefore, Joseph was determined to have him acquitted so he could wallow in his misery. It was the ultimate revenge. It was even worth the left hook he received outside the courthouse, the cherry on the top. His actions had solidified his guilt with the townspeople.

He was shocked to find out he had been trumped by Seth when Shannon started working at the diner. "Bastard is a thorn in my side, always has been." Now it was up to him to do damage control.

But if it was foolproof then how......the video tape! They had found the tape. That means they found the surveillance room and the other tapes as well. He chuckled to himself as he imagined the look on Seth's face when he realized his most intimate moments had been recorded. *I bet that burned him up!* Feeling better, he walked behind the bar and grabbed another bottle of whiskey. Not bothering to look for a glass, he took several long pulls straight from the bottle. It was time to show Shannon who was the real man around here.

Shannon woke to pitch darkness. She didn't know how long she slept but she desperately needed to pee. Being careful not to ram her toe into the furniture, she got up from the bed and started to make her way to the bathroom. Suddenly, she cried out in pain as she stepped on a piece of broken glass. Reaching down she felt the jagged shard. Taking a deep breath, she yanked it out. Air hissed through her teeth at the pain. Getting down carefully on her hands and knees, she slid her hands very slowly from side to side, pushing the broken pieces against the direction of the door and away from the path to the bathroom. Taking no chances, she crawled across the floor to the entrance. Running her hand along the wall she found the light switch and flipped it on. Nothing happened. She moaned in frustration. *Joseph must have turned off the breaker for the bathroom.* She stumbled over to the sink and turned the handle, again, nothing. He was punishing her. She couldn't even get a sip of water from the tap. She knew the toilet wouldn't flush but there was nothing she could do about it. Before dipping her foot into the toilet to rinse the blood off, she scooped up a handful and drank. It was cool and refreshing. She just had to block out of her mind that she was drinking toilet water. She felt around for the towel rack and snatching the towel down, wrapped her injured foot as best she could. Hurriedly she emptied her bladder. Unable to flush, she felt behind the back of the toilet and fished out the shower curtain hook she had hidden there a few days ago. Hoping against hope that Joseph didn't have infrared cameras in the bathroom, she jammed it into the lock attached to her ankle. She almost whimpered with frustration, *it looks so easy in the movies. I must be doing something wrong. It can't possibly take this long to figure out the mechanisms.* As she worked on the lock, her mind was preoccupied with Seth. She could almost feel him next to her, his hands gentle and loving, caressing her cheek as he whispered words of love into her hair. The hole inside her was growing. The longer she was separated from him, the more the pain ate her alive. She knew if she didn't eat soon, she would be putting her health in danger. The thought of never being in Seth's strong embrace again was killing her. Until she figured a way to escape or Seth somehow managed to find her, she had no choice but to succumb to Joseph's wishes. Maybe if she played along, he would slip up, giving her an opportunity to escape. Fighting back the nausea that threatened to make her gag, she pulled herself up and limped back into the bedroom.

If he decided to punish her until she agreed to eat, this place was going to get pretty rank, and without fresh water, she was going to get pretty rank as well. She wondered just how far Joseph would go to get his way. Would he really force a feeding tube down her throat? She was running out of time…and tricks.

CHAPTER 40

Seth was going crazy. He had Shannon's kidnapping broadcast on all the local and major networks hoping to flush Joseph out. He made sure to add the murder of his wife Naome' and his baby boy to the news story. The thought of Joseph being a murderer while pretending to be his best friend made Seth want to kill him. He had wasted three years of his life, walking around like a zombie, the guilt of their deaths poisoning his soul while all along it had been Joseph.

And now Shannon. His heart twisted painfully in his chest at the thought of her helpless against that madman. What had he done to her? What was he doing to her right now? His eyes narrowed, "I swear, if he lays a hand on her, I will rip out his heart and feed it to him," he hissed, his knuckles tightening on the steering wheel. He pretty much lived in his truck now, going from house to house, seeking answers that would somehow, miraculously lead him to Shannon. "I will find you, Shannon my love."

Suddenly, his cell phone rang. Picking it up, he looked at the caller I.D. "Hey Millie, whatcha got for me?" "Nothing much really," disappointment heavy in her voice. "I just wanted to let you know that I heard Irene and paddy are on their way back. Seems they saw last night's broadcast." Though Seth was glad to see them again, he didn't know how much more they could do to help in the search. He had called in every favor, used every resource to intensify the search. "Word is, they left the RV at their kid's house and hopped the red eye so they'll be here in a couple of hours. I could meet them at the airport if you have things to do."

"That's okay Millie, I'll do it, but thanks anyway." He had to admit he had been impressed by her tenacity. When he'd seen her earlier, she was wearing the same outfit she had worn the day before and her face, which was usually made up perfectly, was scrubbed clean. The effect was astonishing. She looked like a teenager, especially with her bleached blond hair pulled back into a ponytail.

"Oh Seth, by the way, I thought of something that might help us. I don't want to tell you too much, it might be a dead end but I'm going to check it out. Call you later."

"Okay Millie. Good luck and call me the second you find anything." Seth hung up the phone, pushing down the hope that threatened to bubble up inside him. He had run into so many dead ends, he didn't think he could take more disappointment. He turned the truck toward his house. He needed to take a shower and shave before meeting his adopted parents.

Walking into his apartment for the first time since Shannon's disappearance, Seth expected it to be dreary and cold. His mouth fell open when he entered to the smell of fresh baked bread and a roaring fire. He felt some of the weight lifted off of him as he spotted Manna in the kitchen, washing dishes and humming a lullaby. "Manna, what in the world are you doing here?" She gave a little squeak of surprise and wagged her finger at him, "Don't you scare me like that, Seth Proudfoot! I am an old woman after all!"

"Oh, sorry, I just didn't expect you to be here. I don't believe I hired you to clean my house while I'm gone."

"No, of course you didn't. I am here as your friend." She gestured to the table, "Now sit down and have some of my famous home baked bread and preserves".

Seth plopped down into the chair.

She came over, placing the bread and preserves in front of him. When she placed a large glass of warm milk in front of him, he stared at it like it was going to sprout a mouth and start talking to him.

"Eat; you can't go on like you've been. You will be no good to Shannon in the hospital suffering from dehydration and malnutrition." She admonished him with a stern look, "and while you eat I'm going to tell you what you must do".

Seth couldn't believe how good the bread and milk made him feel but halfway through he lost his appetite. "You want me to what?" He asked incredulously.

"I didn't stutter, did I? You need to go to the reservation and see the old medicine man. He will prepare you for your journey."

"But I can't track. I don't even hunt!" Seth believed the old woman had snapped under the strain of Shannon's kidnapping.

"You heard me. Go to him. He will show you the way. You do want to find her don't you?"

"Of course I do. I'd give anything."

"Would you *do* anything?"

The woman was clever, he'd give her that. "Yes, I'd do anything." He knew he'd just been manipulated. She smiled sweetly and pushed the plate closer to him, "Then eat up, you have a date with the medicine man".

Seth remembered that he had agreed to pick Irene and Paddy up at the airport, "Wait, I have to pick up the old couple who owned the diner from the airport. Can it wait until I get back?"

Manna looked into his eyes and saw the war raging within, "Yes, I suppose it can. I will wait here." And with that, she picked up his plate and took it to the sink.

"I came back to get a shower and shave." He pushed away from the table and headed to the back bedroom where he and Shannon had shared so many pleasant moments making love. A scowl creased his brow. He walked over to the bed and started looking around at the ceiling. Finding his mark, he addressed the hidden camera, "Joseph, if you are watching this, just know that I found your secret surveillance room and I know you killed my wife and son. For that I will kill you." He pointed his finger as he stepped closer to the hidden lens, "But, I swear by all that is holy, if you harm one hair on Shannon's head, I will make it slow and painful. Before it's over, you will be begging me to end your suffering, you Bastard!" He reached up and yanked the grate out of the wall. Clutching the tiny camera in his hand he threw it to the floor and crushed it under his boot. He then went to every room, destroying each one until none were left. Then he stripped naked and shaking with rage, walked into the bathroom.

"Seth, my Lord, what's goin on? Irene hugged him tightly and Seth fought back the tears that threatened to slide down his gaunt cheeks. She frowned as she pulled back and gazed at him intently. "Why, you're wastin away! When was the last time you ate a real meal? How come you didn't call us? Didn't you think we would be worried?" Seth couldn't help but chuckle at Irene's usual multiple questions. The action shocked him and he quickly grew solemn again. He had no right to feel humor while Shannon was being subjected to "who knew what". Irene gave him a stern look, "You know, it doesn't diminish your love for her just because you smile once in a while. You look dead on your feet." She wrapped her arm through his, "but that's okay, Irene's here now." She motioned for Paddy and without speaking he picked up their bags and followed them to Seth's truck.

Paddy climbed into the driver's seat while Irene pulled Seth up beside her. Seth was so exhausted he didn't even protest as they made the trip to the diner. Irene held his hand while she spoke softly to Paddy. The sound of her voice was soothing and leaning his head against the window, Seth closed his eyes and dreamed of reddish golden hair and turquoise eyes.

She was crying out his name. He couldn't make out where she was. Her voice seemed very far away but determined to reach her, he made his way through the thick fog. Hacking his way through the dense forest, he called her name over and over. It felt like he had been walking for hours but incredibly, was making no headway. Just when he thought the forest and fog would go on forever, the trees thinned, and the fog started to lift. Straining, he was able to make out a faint outline in the mist. His heart leapt as the figure in the fog drew closer. "Shannon my love, is it really you?"

"Seth, wake up, we're here." Seth started awake at the sound of Irene's voice.

"You were dreamin. Must have been a doosey. You were moaning in your sleep." She studied his face, noticing the dark circles under his eyes, "Somethin tells me you've had similar dreams lately. Wanna talk about it?"

Seth looked into Irene's eyes and saw the genuine concern there, "It's strange. I'm looking for Shannon through the woods and I can hear her calling my name. Just when I think I've found her, I wake up."

Irene saw the pain and suffering in his eyes. She reached out and touched his face tenderly, "We'll find her, don't you worry". He captured her hand and patted it affectionately.

"I hope you don't mind if I drop you off. I have somewhere I need to be." He jumped down and helped Irene out of the truck.

Giving her a hug, he then walked over to the driver's side and shook Paddy's hand. "Thank you both for being here." Paddy pulled Seth into a bear hug, "You do what you have to do, but be careful."

Surprised by Paddy's sudden burst of affection, Seth clapped him on the back, "I will. Listen, don't let Irene worry but I am headed to the reservation to meet with the old medicine man. I don't know why, but Manna seems to think it's something I should do if I want to find out where Shannon is." He smiled nervously, "Hey, if it means getting her back, I'll try anything". They said their goodbyes and Seth sped off down the road.

CHAPTER 41

Seth made his way through the middle of the reservation. People who were outside stopped and waved as though he were a life long friend. A few even shouted encouragement to him as he drove by. He was extremely touched by the outpouring of love for Shannon.

Coming to the edge of town, he turned off on an old dirt road that disappeared behind two tall peaks. On the other side stood a small adobe shack with smoke curling up from the roof. He parked outside and approached the weather-worn door. Before he could knock, it swung open and a terribly slouched, wrinkled old man stood in the doorway. Though he slumped from age, his presence was formidable. He was easily over six feet. Seth had no idea how old he actually was but he hadn't changed since Seth was a little boy. It seemed he had found the secret to longevity but just a little too late.

"I have been expecting you." He gave Seth a pointed look, "but I thought you would be here earlier".

Seth gave the old man a questioning look, "Well, I had something to do….for a friend."

The old man looked into Seth's strange blue eyes. Satisfied, he nodded and stepped aside for Seth to enter.

The first thing Seth noticed when entering the small one room shack was the heat. It must have been at least one hundred degrees. The source of the heat and the only light was a campfire burning in the middle of the room. There were authentic headdresses lining the walls and the smell of sage and something else he couldn't identify permeated the cabin.

The medicine man walked over and knelt in front of the fire. Taking a pinch of something from a bowl, he tossed it into the strange smelling fire. Multicolor flames shot high into the air. He motioned for Seth to kneel across from him.

Seth knew that it would be insulting not to obey the old man, but he was anxious to continue his search for Shannon. Sighing, he knelt, looking at him through the multicolored flames.

"Do you want to find your true love?" The old man whispered through the fire as he again tossed the strange powder into the flames. Seth was starting to feel a little disoriented.

"Yes," he croaked. The smoke was messing with his voice and his head felt too light.

"Then you will need to reach inside yourself and discover your true strength. Only then will you be able to find her. Close your eyes and let the spirit guide show you the way."

Seth felt himself being carried away by the sound of the old man's voice. Suddenly, the recurring dream of him in the forest with the mist all around, came flooding back. This time however, everything looked and felt real. He actually felt the moistness of the mist and smelled the pine as he again followed the sound of Shannon's cry. He was surprised to find that when he looked down, he was wearing only a pair of doe skin pants and carrying a tomahawk. He turned as he heard the bushes rustle and came face to face with the biggest wolf he had ever seen. The blue eyed beast seemed to be communicating with Seth as they stared at each other for what seemed like an eternity. Finally breaking eye contact, the wolf turned and disappeared into the dense forest. Hearing Shannon's voice getting closer, Seth made his way through the fog until he again saw the ghostly outline of her body. His heart skipped as he called out her name, "Shannon! Where are you?" Just as he thought he was getting closer, she started to fade like an apparition. "No! Come Back!" He ran toward the quickly fading figure, reaching out his hands, but she disappeared altogether, as though she had never been. He dropped to his knees, staring at his empty hands. Unable to contain the pain and despair, he threw back his head and howled like a wounded beast.

Seth came awake with a start. At first he thought the old man had splashed water on his face to wake him, but reaching up, he felt the moisture on his cheeks and realized he'd been crying. He stared at the man through the fire, rage in his eyes, "How could you bring me here just to relive the same dream that has haunted me every night?"

The old man did something so unexpected, the rage melted from his face, replaced by shock…he laughed, not some small little chuckle but a full on belly laugh, tossing his head back and howling with laughter. Seth frowned at the crazy old man. *He is old. Maybe he has finally lost it.*

The medicine man stopped laughing and locked Seth in an intense glare, "Not the same dream, I think. There was something different, no?"

Seth was about to disagree when he paused, there was something different about it this time. He looked into the old man's eyes and found himself recalling the details of the dream. When he was done, the old man got up and went to a shelf where he retrieved a tomahawk. Turning around, he held it up for Seth to see. It was the exact same one from his dream…vision. For Seth knew that's what it had been. He then moved over to a box and Seth somehow knew he would pull out a pair of doe skin pants. "You must fulfill your destiny and become a great tracker, like your father and his father's father. You have the gift, use it." As Seth rose, the old man placed his hand on his arm, "You must not take anyone or anything with you but the items I have given you. Look inside yourself and you will find her…and your destiny. Leave now, go into the mountains, your spirit guide will lead you."

Seth nodded, turning to go, but the old man touched his arm again, "Wait, there is one more thing". He walked over to the counter and brought back a jar of dark liquid. Seth looked at it doubtfully, "What's that?" "It will make you strong for the journey." He thrust it into Seth's hand.

Holding the jar up to the fire light, he could swear he saw something swimming around inside the disgusting looking brew. He glanced at the medicine man who smiled, a twinkle in his aged eyes, "I take a glass of it everyday and look at me, still dancing".

Seth grabbed the jar and holding his breath, tipped the jar to his lips. As the thick liquid coursed down his throat, he could feel his muscles tightening as though he were pumping iron. As he felt the power coursing through his body, the dark circles under his eyes disappeared. He felt energized. "Wow, this stuff is great! I feel so strong!" The old man shoved the jar into a leather pouch and handed it to Seth. "This will give you the strength required to make the long journey. Take a couple of swallows every morning and you will be able to travel faster, longer, as the animals in the forest."

Seth slung the leather strap over his bare chest then gripped the old man's forearm. Thank you. I don't know why you want to help a half-breed like me but I am grateful."

Gripping Seth's forearm in return, the old man looked intensely into his eyes, "You have the spirit of the wolf in you, as your father had and his father's father before him. Just remember, trust your instincts and you will find the happiness that has eluded you, and beware of the serpent's strike."

Seth felt the old man was giving him valuable advice. He just wished he wouldn't speak in riddles. "Thank you again. Please let everyone know where I've gone. I wouldn't want to worry them unnecessarily."

When Seth walked outside, he was almost blinded by the brightness of the sun's rays. Shielding his eyes with his hand he noticed a black and white horse tethered to an old fashioned hitching post. The saddle on its back was straight out of a western movie.

The old man walked up behind Seth and motioned to the pony, "She is yours. A gift from the people of the reservation to help you in your search." Seth walked up to the filly and stroked her neck, his heart tight with emotion. The people who had ostracized him his whole life were giving him a most precious gift. The gift of a pony was considered a great honor and a sign of respect from the tribe. He was now one of them. He finally belonged and it was because of Shannon, her love and compassion had changed not only his heart but the hearts of his people.

Jumping up into the saddle, he looked down at the old man. "I won't return without her." With that, he dug his moccasins into the pony's side and galloped away, across the plains. If anyone had chanced to see him, his half clad body on the black and white pony, raven hair caught up by the wind, they would think they had somehow crossed through a rip in time, back to the old west.

CHAPTER 42

Hearing the key in the lock, Shannon sat up in bed. The time had come to implement her plan. Light spilled into the room as Joseph opened the door. He had a covered tray with him and Shannon's stomach growled at the prospect of food. "Good morning Joseph, or is it afternoon?" Joseph was surprised by her greeting. Was she actually being civil to him?

"Hello Shannon." She cringed inwardly at his evasive answer. He refused to even let her know what time of day it was. This was going to be harder than she thought.

"I'm starved!" she clapped her hands together. "What did you bring me?"

Joseph looked at her suspiciously, "Why, you won't eat it anyway, right?"

"I have decided that the thought of a feeding tube is rather distasteful to me. So, stop torturing me!" allowing a little whine to creep into her voice, she pursed her lips for effect.

He grinned at her and it took all her willpower to smile back, but not too much or he would see through her ruse. "Well, I'm glad to see that you have come around. I would hate to see all this delicious food go to waste. Well I'll just put it here and leave you to it then." He placed the tray on the foot of the bed and turned to leave.

"Please, you don't have to go, do you?" Shannon affected the whine again. He seemed to like it. He turned around and she saw hope glittering in his eyes. He really was delusional.

"Okay, I'll stay if you want. Wait right here, I'll be right back."

"Yeah, like I can go anywhere", she called out. She heard his laughter as he retreated down the hall. 'What is he up to?' she wondered. 'Did he buy it or was I too obvious?' Chewing on her bottom lip, she barely breathed until he entered the room, a straight back chair in one hand and a lamp in the other. She couldn't help but smile. He was going to allow light in her room again. Did he also turn the breaker back on in the bathroom? Well, there was one way to find out.

"Thank you for the lamp. I am sorry my bad behavior caused you to destroy the other one. Was it very expensive? It looked like it was part of the whole ensemble." She knew she was babbling but Joseph seemed to enjoy her humbleness.

"Actually it was mine when I was a little boy. As a matter of fact, the bed you're lying on is also from my childhood. I had the furniture brought over when I purchased this place." He stood up and walked around the room, lovingly running his hands over the dresser. "You know, you are the first guest who has taken an interest in the furniture. It is quite dear to me." He waved toward the tray. "Eat up before it gets cold."

Shannon removed the silver dome and was shocked at the contents of the tray. There was a whole roasted chicken with potatoes, carrots, and stuffing. She felt drool forming at the side of her mouth. Jerking her head up, she looked wide eyed at Joseph's confident smirk. He knew she was going to cave and the thought enraged her. She quickly lowered her gaze for fear he would see her reaction. Taking a deep breath she managed to compose herself, "It looks delicious, but it's just too much. If I eat it all I will be sick."

She heard him snicker, "You are far too thin. That nice ass of yours is disappearing. You will eat every bite, I insist. We have to fatten you up. I don't like holding on to skin and bones." He sat in the chair and waited for her to begin. When she made no move, he reached over and taking the napkin, placed it in her lap, his fingers lingering on her hips. Shannon held her breath as she felt his lips close to her face. Refusing to look up for fear he would get the wrong idea, she whispered, "Thank you, I think I can handle it from here." He sighed and leaned back in his chair.

Tearing off a leg, she shoved it into her mouth. It was surprisingly good, seasoned just enough. She devoured the meal, her stomach protesting loudly on the last few bites. She had to eat everything with her hands as he had not provided her with eating utensils.

Joseph felt his desire growing as he watched her ravage the chicken, licking her fingers of the juices. It was very erotic. He leaned over and taking the napkin from her lap, wiped her hands. Her lips glistened with chicken juice and before he knew it, he captured her lips with his. The suddenness of his kiss took her completely by surprise. Shannon froze. Taking her stillness as acceptance, he deepened the kiss, shoving his tongue deeply into her throat. The spell was broken and Shannon twisted her head away. *Oh no, I've ruined it. He'll never trust me now.* When she gathered the courage to look at him, she was shocked to see that he was grinning widely.

"Ah, that was wonderful! I knew that deep inside you felt something for me." Taking the tray, he walked out, locking the door. Shannon jumped from the bed and raced to the bathroom. Turning the handle on the facet, she sighed as blessed water poured over her trembling hands. She lathered them liberally and washed her face, scrubbing as hard as she could. She brushed the soap brutally across her lips, the memory of his sudden kiss almost making her gag. Tears mingled with water as she rinsed the soap off her skin. Covering her face with a towel, she muffled her sobs of outrage. His kiss was clumsy, bruising, and utterly disgusting.

She thought of how Seth's lips had felt on hers, allowing herself this one moment of pity. She knew that if she indulged in memories of Seth, she would never be able to trick Joseph into believing she had feelings for him. She sighed as she remembered the first time she'd seen him, his hair reflecting the ray's of the rising sun. Oh how she loved his beautiful hair. She clutched her hand over her heart as the pain literally drove her to her knees. Burying her face in the towel, Shannon sobbed, an emotion so deep with despair it seemed to come from her toes.

Shannon dried herself off and brushed her teeth. She didn't need a magnifying glass to see the puffy purple circles under her eyes. Her cheeks were sunken from her weight loss, and she couldn't remember ever crying as much as she had these past days, however many days it was. Her hair was lack luster and lank from not being shampooed and she sniffed her underarms, "Ewwww gross". She smelled like a lumberjack. Ripping the material of her tank top, panties, and warm up pants in order to get them off because of the manacles on her ankle and wrist, she tossed the ruined clothes into a corner. What would she wear now that she had destroyed the only clothes she had? Oh well, the damage was done. All she wanted was to wash the grime from her body. Climbing into the small bathtub, she turned on the hot water, melting under the luxurious feeling. She winced as the soap ran under the shackles, burning the irritated skin beneath. With some difficulty, she managed to shampoo her hair and wash herself fairly well with the burden of the shackles but not without ripping out clumps of hair that got caught in the chains.

Stepping out, she dried herself off, wrapping the towel around her. She wished she had another change of clothes. The idea of Joseph seeing her in just a towel made her skin crawl. Walking into the bedroom her eyes widened in surprise. Laid out on the bed spread was a halter dress made of gauzy material with a small floral print pattern, a clean pair of lacy bikini underwear and bra to match. Snatching up the dress, she wanted to throw it across the room and stomp on it until it was nothing but a crumpled mass of material but as she grabbed it, preparing to ball it up, she heard a "ping" as something fell onto the floor. Looking down, she couldn't believe her eyes. Bending over, she picked up the small silver key. Could it be? Did Joseph actually give her the key to her shackles? Trying to crush the excitement building inside her, Shannon held her breath and tried the key. She marveled as the manacles clicked open and fell from her wrists. Reaching down she unlocked the ones on her ankles, rubbing the angry red whelps. Why had he done this? What was he up to? Keeping her thoughts on Seth, she picked up the dress and put it on. The gauzy material made her feel like some kind of porcelain doll, extremely feminine and altogether vulnerable. If he wanted to, he could certainly take advantage of the flimsy underwear. One tug and they were sure to rip like tissue paper, but what choice did she have? Flimsy underwear compared to no underwear. The decision was simple. At least it was some protection, though that didn't seem to reassure her in the slightest. She towel dried her hair and brushed her teeth, the mundane tasks helping to blank out her thoughts for a little while. She was inspecting the purple baggage under her eyes when something in the corner of the mirror caught her eye. Her heart skipped a beat. Whirling around, she rushed to the bed and looking underneath, found her cloth bag containing her make-up and art supplies. Hugging the bag to her breast, she plopped on the bed and dumped out the contents. He had been thorough, taking out anything she might use as a weapon or escape tool. The color pencils were gone but her oil pastels remained. The tweezers she carried in an overnight satchel were missing, as were the small scissors used to trim nails or snip off price tags.

"Oh well, at least he left me something to do. It's more than I expected." She took out her make-up case, "Well if I'm going to go through with this plan, I guess I better look the part". She applied a small amount of make-up to her face and finished it off with lip gloss then thinking twice, she grabbed the tail end of the bed spread and wiped off the gloss. "No need to tempt him. I don't think I could bear to have his disgusting lips on me again." But even as she said it, Shannon knew that if it meant she would once again feel Seth's embrace then she could bear anything.

Shannon had just pulled out her sketch pad only to find that Joseph had ripped out every drawing she had done of Seth. "I wonder what he did with them, throw them away, burn them or….hadn't destroyed them but kept them for 'inspiration'?" She found her iPod in her bag and quickly shoved it under the pillow. It would be nice to have some music to help her fall asleep.

Hearing Joseph's footsteps in the hall, Shannon shoved the items into her bag and tossed it under the bed.

"I thought you might like a little cappuccino after your shower." He came in carrying a tray with a lavish setting of cappuccinos', strawberries dipped in chocolate with a vanilla orchid in a small vase. It would have been perfect if it were Seth holding the tray.

"Oh, that looks delicious, but I don't think I can eat another bite after that last meal", Shannon patted her swollen belly. He looked at her, his face turning petulant. "Awww, I went to a lot of trouble to get these strawberries. They come from a farm in South Carolina and they are the sweetest you will ever eat." He walked over and slammed the tray on the dresser making Shannon jump. "And after I released you from your chains, you'd think you could be a little more grateful!"

"Well hey, why don't I have just a little bite then? I'm sure I could make room for just one and the coffee smells divine." She hoped to keep him from having a tantrum.

He whirled around, that nasty grin on his handsome face, "Okay then". He bounced back over to the bed, sloshing the mocha liquid all over the tray. Placing the tray gently on the foot of the bed, he took a succulent strawberry, and popped it in his mouth. Looking heavenward, he scrunched up his shoulders, "Mmmm Mmmm good!" Smiling at Shannon he took another and held it out for her. Having no other option, she reached up to take it from his hand. Snatching it back, he gave her that petulant look from before, "No. You have to take it from me with your mouth. That's the way they do it in the movies." He offered it to her again and having no choice, she opened her mouth, knowing she would never like eating strawberries again as Joseph squeezed the fruit against her lips, running his thumb over her bottom lip, spreading the juices. "Oooh, you look good enough to eat." He leaned in, his tongue snaking out to lick the juice from her lip. Shannon felt her stomach heave. Pushing him back and over the chair, she rushed to the bathroom and threw up in the toilet.

Joseph frowned, *why did she get sick? Is she allergic to strawberries? Was the chicken too much food for her stomach?* His ego wouldn't let him contemplate the notion that Shannon had been made physically ill by his advances. Standing in the doorway, he looked at her, a disgusted look on his face. "Be sure to brush your teeth, and use the mouthwash." He turned and left without another word. Shannon heaved up everything she ate, the strawberry making the first appearance before the chicken and stuffing. Was it his touch that made her vomit? She didn't know if she bought that. She had lived with a maniac for ten years, been humiliated for his sexual pleasure and not once had she hurled like she did at the slightest touch from Joseph. It didn't make sense. Or had he poisoned her food again? When would he realize that her body rejected the drugs?

When she emerged from the bathroom with a cool cloth over her face, Joseph was no longer in the room, neither was the tray of strawberries and cappuccino. "Oh thank God, he's gone. Probably couldn't handle the whole throwing up thing." She noticed a note lying on her pillow. Angling it toward the small lamp, she read it, her eyes disbelieving. He had stocked the chest of drawers and dresser with clothes. She knew he had an ulterior motive but not really caring, she collapsed on the bed. Her stomach rumbled, protesting the misuse it had endured, demanding she replace what she threw up. Tightening her arms around her waist, she curled up into a fetal position and tried to drift off to sleep. Remembering the IPod and earphones she had stashed under the pillow, she pulled them out and placed them in her ears. Soft rock ballads drowned out the growling of her stomach as she concentrated on catching some sleep.

It was the same dream. She was walking through a thick forest heavy with fog, calling frantically for Seth. The roots and vines were almost alive, tearing at her clothing, trying to trip her up but she muddled through, determined to emerge from the moist fog. Suddenly, she could see a figure in the fog. The silhouette was tall and definitely masculine. She could just make out his clothing, or lack of. He was half-naked. But before she could call out, he suddenly morphed into a large wolf. A scream caught in her throat as she watched the transformation. The beast shook from head to toe. Becoming aware of her presence it turned towards her and she looked into its electric blue eyes.

Shannon woke with a start. She never seemed to get past that part. She felt the dream was trying to tell her something but she just couldn't figure it out. It was extremely frustrating. Grabbing her bag from beneath the bed she leaned over the sketch pad.

CHAPTER 43

Seth rode into the mountains, not stopping until the sunlight had faded from the tops of the giant pines. Finding a small clearing, he made camp. Once he was settled in front of the small campfire, a small rodent roasting on a stick, he leaned back and stared into the flames. His mind drifted away, remembering the smell of gardenias and turquoise eyes. He could almost see her face, hair as bright as the fire. He closed his eyes and thought of the silky softness of her skin. He groaned, "Oh Shannon my love, you are so precious to me, like a gift I never deserved." His eyes flew open and he chucked a fistful of dirt into the fire, "I swear I will hold you in my arms again. Nothing on this earth is going to prevent that. We will be together and I will never let you go." Relaxing, he closed his eyes again as he imagined their future together, the many children they were going to have, her belly round with his seed. No matter what had happened in her past, he knew she could bear children, his children. They would have her hair and eyes and her generous heart. "Please God; send her peace that she will know I haven't given up hope. I will never give up. Shannon love, sleep, and dream of me tonight. Lying on his back, his hands behind his head, Seth drifted off to sleep.

He awoke the next morning, grabbing the jerked rodent that he had forgotten about last night. Stripping the flesh off, he ate it, chasing it down with the strange black brew. Feeling a hundred times better, he quickly packed up and headed into the thick forest. Somehow he knew he was headed in the right direction. He wanted to push the pony harder but afraid she would collapse, took care to stop frequently, keeping a slow but steady pace. There were times when he had to lead the pony on foot. Several times he wondered if he should let the pony go to find its way back to the reservation but something told him he would need her later so he drudged on, helping her over the uneven terrain. He had to admit, he was glad for the company, even if it was just a horse. He kept himself occupied, telling the pony his thoughts and dreams and the life that waited for Shannon and him. He knew the animal couldn't understand a word but it made him feel better anyway.

Night came faster and the weather became increasingly colder. Seth encountered snow on the peaks of the mountains and only wearing doe skins was definitely not enough comfort. He fashioned a trap and used the rodents he killed to snare some larger game for food and clothing. He had to admit, he was getting pretty good at this "Grizzly Adams" life style, though he wouldn't mind a long soak in a hot tub.

The dreams were always waiting for him when he collapsed, exhausted as another day proved fruitless. The fog, forest, Shannon's voluptuous silhouette in the mist and the wolf, ever present in the dream. What did it all mean? He decided that tonight he would try an old Indian ritual. What the hell, he didn't have anything else to do.

Making the necessary markings in the dirt, he sat, legs crossed, in front of the fire. Emptying his mind of everything else, he concentrated on Shannon and only Shannon. Willing the stress and tension to leave his body, he allowed his mind to drift, up over the trees and around the mountain side. He could almost hear the flapping of wings as he sailed across the night sky, using his keen eyes to search....

Still in the cross-legged position, Seth came awake with a start, "Whoa! That was intense!" He thought back on how long he had flown. On horseback the distance to the cabin was going to take at least three days to reach but now that he knew where it was he was determined to get there as soon as humanly possible. Had he really astral-projected or had it been a dream? No, he had to believe that he'd really flown miles over the trees and seen the rooftop of the cabin nestled in the thick forest. It would be almost impossible to see from a plane or helicopter. The roof was the same color as the top of the pines, totally camouflaged from view.

A thought came to him. If he could astral-project, then perhaps he could reach Shannon telepathically? Determined to try, he closed his eyes again. This time he let his whole being think of nothing but Shannon. He thought of her eyes, her smile, and the feel of her skin under his caresses.

Reaching out his hand, he imagined touching her face, running his fingers down the line of her jaw, his thumb lightly touching her bottom lip. Keeping his eyes closed, Seth could feel her skin and his heart leapt. He whispered into the night wind, "Shannon". His fingers moved down the side of her neck as he traced the thin scar, so much a part of who she was, and he lovingly stroked her neck, daring to slide his hand down to the swell of her breast. She was wearing a gauzy little halter dress. Leaning closer still, he untied the ribbon at the back of her neck. The material fell free and his mouth replaced his hand. He captured her nipple between his teeth and suckled there. Groaning, he felt her arch into him, giving him full access to her delights. He rose up and whispered into her ear, "I'm here Shannon my love. No distance can keep us apart. Oh, but you feel so good. I missed you. Now relax and let me worship your body." He saw her smile, her eyes closed, as he laved her neck, working his way back to her breasts. Her nipples were dark pink with desire. The sight was excruciatingly pleasurable. He lifted the hem of her dress and studied the lacy panties. "Very nice," his voice husky, "such a shame", as he grabbed the piece of lace and pulled. Shannon moaned as he ripped the material from her body. As he buried his hand in the golden red curls, using his other to gently push her legs apart, he could hear her suck in her breath, her hips automatically pushing against his hand, "Oh Seth that feels so good. Please, don't make me wait anymore. I want you now!" Seth's fingers disappeared into the warmth of her womanhood, rubbing the skin around and over her cleft. She began to thrash around on the bed, her head shaking back and forth as the heat built inside her. She reached out and gripped his behind, kneading the softness of the doe skin over his derriere. The shock of actually feeling her touching him broke Seth's concentration and he was abruptly brought back to the campfire. He howled with frustration, for now he was convinced he was actually there. Exhausted from his efforts, he collapsed on the ground. It felt as though all his strength had been sucked out of his body, leaving him weak as a kitten. Desperately wanting to go right back, he tried to concentrate but just trying to sit up took every bit of his strength. He barely made it back to his sleeping bag before he felt sleep overtake him.

CHAPTER 44

Shannon woke slowly from a very delicious dream. She stretched, the air making her exposed breasts tingle. Her hands ducked down, feeling bare skin. Her eyes flew open wide as she looked at her disheveled appearance. "Oh my God!" she reached under her dress and was shocked that she wasn't wearing the lacy underwear anymore. Sitting upright, she felt around, locating them on the very edge of the bed. She dangled the destroyed piece of lace in front of her face, twisting them around, awestruck at the damage. "When did that happen?" She couldn't believe it was a drug or that Joseph had somehow seduced her while she slept. No, it felt like Seth. The way he touched her, played her body like a finely tuned instrument. Only Seth would know how to make her body sing. Could the dream have been so strong that his touch felt especially real? *What was the deal with the deer skin pants?* "Okay Shannon, it's official, you've gone nuts!" She righted her clothes and lay back on her side. Closing her eyes she thought about the all too real dream, of the way his hands felt on her body, his lips laving her breasts. She touched herself between her legs, feeling the warmth where his hands had been just moments before. Her heart ached with a need like nothing she had ever felt. Bringing her hands up, she buried her face in her hands, crying herself to sleep.

Joseph watched the DVD, conflicting emotions on his face. Shannon was having an erotic dream but something wasn't right. He scanned in close, once again studying how the dress had somehow gotten untied and the bodice pulled down to expose her pale breasts. Hitting the pause button, he moved closer to the screen. When he hit the slow motion button, his eyes grew wide. It couldn't be! He could see her nipples being suckled but no one was in the room! And who was she talking to? He shook his head as he watched the hem of her dress slide up to her hips and thought he had gone insane when the underwear was ripped from her body by unseen hands. It was impossible! But nonetheless, no matter how many times he watched, it was the same. And just before the show was over, he watched bug eyed as she reached up and started kneading the air with her hands as though someone was on top of her. "What the hell is going on here?" He studied the monitor and saw Shannon's body curled in sleep. How did she do it? How did she make that stuff happen? Did it have anything to do with being chained? He had heard of people doing extraordinary things under duress. Like the mother who lifted the truck off her baby or people who saw into the future or those that could make things move with their minds. That had to be it. She was one of those "special" people. It was definitely getting interesting around here.

Coming awake for the second time, Shannon felt it was time to change into something comfortable. She turned on the lamp and jumped out of bed. Suddenly, she felt nauseous and ran to the bathroom, gagging into the toilet. Did she eat something bad? She was sure that after the last time, she wouldn't have anything left in her belly but here she was, throwing up again. Maybe she never quite got over the virus. That had to be it. The stress of being kidnapped and held hostage was making her have a relapse.

As she was dressing in a pair of black workout pants and bright turquoise tank, her mind wandered back to the surreal dream she'd had. She could close her eyes and practically smell his woodsy scent. She had refused to shower so she could revel in his scent. It was torture, she knew, but there was pleasure in the pain. Since she was now free of the chains, Shannon decided she could use a little workout. Putting on the earphones, she hit the play button and went into her workout routine. She felt compelled to keep herself fit. *Never know when the opportunity to escape will present itself.*

Wiping her sweaty brow with a towel, Shannon realized a shower was unavoidable. Seth's scent had been replaced by her own sweat. Feeling somewhat disappointed, she stepped into the shower, scrubbing until her skin was a pinkish hue. It felt good to be able to wash her hair without getting it caught in the chains.

Changing into a pair of stretch denims and a button down men's shirt, she plopped onto the bed and took out her sketch pad. She thought about her recurring dream as she took out the oil pastels. She was really getting into it when the door opened and Joseph walked in carrying the food tray. Her stomach growled at the sight. She felt like Pavlov's dog, being conditioned to salivate at the sight of the silver domed tray. "Oh great, I'm starved!" He didn't look up at her or say a word. Putting the tray on the bed, he turned and left, locking the door behind him. Shannon was taken aback by his weird behavior. "What did I do?" Her stomach growled louder, and dismissing him from her mind, she lifted the dome. Her hand flew to her mouth as the bile rose in her throat. "Oh my God!" The nausea was replaced by rage as she screamed, flinging the tray, sending it and the dead rodent crashing against the far wall. "Damn him and his stupid sick games!" She realized with a sinking feeling in her empty belly that she had made a horrible mistake. She had become complacent in her little prison, dependant on the kindness of the jailer when the jailer was a twisted psychopath who got his jollies from torturing his prisoners. And she had fallen for it. She went crazy, ripping off her bedding and upturning the dresser drawers, slinging clothes around the room until it looked like a small tornado had touched down. Far from being finished, she attacked the bathroom next, taking the toiletries and shampoo and pouring them down the drain. "I will not bend to his will. I will not brush my teeth or take a shower or fall for anymore of his tricks." She was as mad with herself as she was with Joseph. He couldn't help it; he was, after all, crazy, but she should have known better. Completely exhausted, she sat on the cold tile floor and buried her face in her hands, but this time she didn't cry. She was through with crying. It was time to buck up and put on her armor. She was not going to make it easy for him. Kicking the toilet bowl with everything she had, she smiled to herself with satisfaction as it moved just a bit from the assault. Standing, she scooped up a handful of toilet water and drank. She could do this. Gathering her courage, she walked into the bedroom to straighten up the mess she'd made.

By the time she had righted the room, she was hungry and exhausted. She curled up on the bed for a nap but just as she started to fall asleep, Joseph burst into the room. He stormed over to the bed and before Shannon knew what was happening, she felt the sting as he stabbed her arm with the needle. She tried to fend him off but darkness soon overtook her. When she awoke, she felt the weight of the shackles. Her head was splitting and she felt the nausea overtake her. Stumbling to the bathroom, she dry heaved into the toilet. She splashed water on her face and walking into the bedroom, collapsed on the bed.

She didn't know how long she lay there looking up at the ceiling when Joseph made another visit. This time, he came in, pulled up the straight back chair, and sat next to the bed. Not wanting to give him the satisfaction of scaring her, she sat up and glared at him. He looked at her as if she were a bug he was studying for a science project. "What the hell are you looking at, you Son of a Bitch?!" she spat at him. He continued to look at her, no expression on his face. She felt the rage boiling up in her. "I am not going to lie down and let you manipulate me anymore. I was kidnapped and I'm chained to a bed in a room with no windows so I don't even know if it's night or day and have to wait for you to decide when and what I can eat! I am here against my will and if you think that by torturing me, that I will somehow fall madly in love with you, you are sadly mistaken! I love Seth!" She felt triumph when Seth's name made him flinch, "That's right Seth Proudfoot! We are engaged! We are going to get married! He's my soul mate!" She leaned over, inches from his reddening face, driving home her point, "I will *never* love you! You are *nothing* to me! You will *never* be anything to me! So, if you don't like it you can go to hell!" She turned over and showed him her back. She ground her teeth as he chuckled. "There's that spirit I've missed so much. I was wondering where it went." He slapped her on the butt, but before she could turn over and tell him what for, he exited the room, locking the door behind him. "Ohhhh!" She grabbed the pillow and viciously threw it across the room. Taking a deep breath, she wrapped her arms tightly around her. Knowing Joseph would look at her art work; she grabbed her sketch book and drew a picture of the face behind the mask. "Edgar Allan Poe would be frightened of this face." She suddenly felt a breeze against her hair, but that couldn't be, there were no windows. She sucked in her breath. She could've sworn she just heard someone say her name. Suddenly she felt like she wasn't alone. *Don't be stupid. You must be getting cabin fever or something.* She stashed the pad away and grabbing the pillow off the floor, curled up, clutching it to her chest. "Seth, I am begging you, please come get me….and make it soon before I go crazy!"

CHAPTER 45

Seth woke with a start. Something was wrong. He could swear he could feel an emotion separate from his own...Rage. He felt rage, and despair and he knew in his heart it was Shannon. No matter what, he was going to intensify the search. He could feel something pulling him, like a magnet being drawn to its polar opposite. He cursed under his breath. The pony snorted anxiously at her master's sudden anger. He stood up and went to her, running his hands over her satiny nose, "Shhh, it's alright girl. Everything's okay." He had taken several large skins and covered the pony. The snow had started falling steadily by mid-afternoon. Now the clearing was covered in virginal white. It was beautiful and Seth couldn't help but think how Shannon would love to paint the perfect scene. Thinking of her made him want to try the astral projection thing again.

Making the sacred symbols in the hard dirt floor, he sat cross legged in front of the fire. Once again, he thought of Shannon and within a few minutes felt himself being transported again. This time however, he found her awake and sketching. Hovering above, he looked down at the pad. It was hard to make out but it looked like a monster's face. He reached out and touched her hair. She didn't seem to feel it. He whispered her name, "Shannon", but she didn't seem to hear him either. *It must be because she's not asleep so she isn't open to the experience.* Sighing, he thought he would look around at the room she was being held in. There was only one small lamp, no windows, a small bathroom obviously made from a closet and a couple of pieces of furniture. He looked down at her again, his heart aching to be with her. Suddenly she shifted and he saw the shackles on her ankle. She was chained to the bed!

He howled with rage and the intensity of the emotion yanked his spirit from the room and back into his body. The pain he felt was unlike anything he had ever experienced before. Though his body was too weak to react, his heart broke as he lay on his back, tears of helplessness and rage falling from the corners of his eyes, "Oh Shannon my love, just hang on, I'm on my way.

CHAPTER 46

The following day, Seth took four swallows of the energy brew. He was going to need the extra boost if he was to get to the cabin by tomorrow. The weather had worsened in the night and a real blizzard was raging. Wrapping every one of the furs around himself and the pony, he set out.

It wasn't long before he realized no matter how much of the disgusting brew he drank, he wasn't going to make it over the mountain in the blizzard. Resigning himself, Seth concentrated on finding shelter in the mountains for the both of them. "I'm sorry Shannon, but it looks as though it may take a little longer than I had planned but please darling, don't lose hope." He looked up through the white haze and saw a large wolf standing on an out crop of rock. It seemed to be looking at him. When he made a move toward it, the beast continued to stand there like a proud statue. Something inside him told Seth to follow the giant wolf. Climbing up through the thicket, he got to within about fifty feet from the animal when suddenly it turned and disappeared over the ridge. Continuing in the direction of the wolf, he came upon a cave big enough for him and the pony to stay while they rode out the storm. Luckily, there were no bears. Checking out the cave, he discovered dry kindling toward the back which looked exactly like old bedding for a family of wolves or bears. He just prayed that the family had moved on and weren't just out hunting. Getting a raging fire going, he hunkered down in the furs as the wind howled outside. Just as he did every night before he went to sleep, he said his prayers and sent his love through the mountains to Shannon.

The next few days, Shannon thought she had died and gone to hell. Joseph took perverse pleasure in torturing her. Oh, he didn't put her on the rack or stick bamboo under her fingernails; he just never gave her a moment's peace. The harder he made it on her, the harder she made it on him. Every time he would hold back food in an effort to break her spirit, she would spit in his face when he tried to get her to eat.

Refusing to bathe and brush her teeth really got on his obsessive compulsive nerves. They had literally had a wrestling match as he tried to haul her bodily to the shower. She kicked and scratched with every ounce of strength she had. "Shannon stop fighting me. You stink and your breath smells like toilet water!"

"Good! Then you won't want to touch me! I would go the rest of my miserable life without bathing if it will keep you away from me!" She batted at his hands, trying to find a vulnerable spot so she could scratch his eyes out.

Whining in frustration and anger, Joseph pushed her away and left the bathroom. She smiled to herself but the victory was short lived as she heard him call over his shoulder, "If you don't bathe then you don't eat! Let me know when you're ready to be reasonable!" She heard the door slam extra hard, like a petulant child who couldn't have its way.

Lying on the floor of the little bathroom, Shannon felt the fight drain out of her body. She was resisting with all her might, but the sad truth of it was, Joseph was slowly chipping away at her resolve. "I just don't know how much longer I can hold out." She tightened her arms around her waist, her body wracked with hunger pains. Steeling herself, she went to the sink and splashed water on her face. Looking at her reflection in the small wall mounted mirror, she was shocked at what she saw. Her hair hung limply around her gaunt face. The circles had gone from purple to grey which matched the color in her sunken cheeks. Her hands slid down her neck, over her collar bones that protruded prominently from under the dirty tank top. Unable to see past her shoulders in the small mirror, she allowed her hands to help her see. Running them down her rib cage, she was appalled. She could actually count each one. *Boy, this is some diet plan. I bet the people in Hollywood would pay a fortune for a month at this fat camp,* she thought dryly. She didn't even realize she was laughing until she felt the tears running down her face. The laughter turned to crying and she had to clutch the sink with both hands to regain her composure. "Stop it! You can't afford to get hysterical! It's exactly what he wants!"

Gritting her teeth, she walked into the bedroom and climbed under the covers. *You know you're going to have to eat soon or you will die.* "Shut up! She grabbed the pillow and pulled it over her ears as if she could actually block out the nagging voice in her head. *You need to keep up your strength for when Seth rescues you. It's not like you're fifteen minutes from civilization. You are in a cabin in the middle of nowhere and the snow has probably fallen by now. How are you going to be anything but a burden to Seth while he carries your sorry ass through the forest?* "I know but I don't want to give Joseph the satisfaction." *What do you think he is going to do when he realizes you aren't going to budge? Didn't he say something about a feeding tube?*

Not wanting to think about it anymore, she grabbed her earphones and turned up the volume. Staring at the ceiling she had counted sheep to every night, Shannon felt the tears slide from her eyes. She would try to hold on for Seth. He was the only one in the whole world who could keep her from slipping away, but she was tired and so hungry.

Suddenly the door swung open with a crash and Shannon jumped. Joseph walked in like he had done before and grabbing the chair he pulled it next to the bed. Shannon braced herself for the physical and emotional battle but felt Joseph's hand gently on top of hers. *Are you serious?* She snatched her hand away and showed him her back.

"Shannon please, you have to eat something. You're wasting away. I'm really worried about you", trying to cajole her, his voice was soft and pleading. "I tell you what, why don't we make a truce? I won't make you bathe but you have to promise me you'll eat something, okay?"

Shannon turned over and looked warily into his handsome face. Was he serious or was this just another form of torture. Get me to agree and then laugh in my face, scoring one for him. All she saw in his eyes was concern and sincerity. "Do you mean it?" she almost choked on the words, her tongue feeling too large.

Smiling from ear to ear, he pulled a bag from behind his back. "Look, to show you I mean it, there's a sandwich, chips and a Dr. Pepper in here." He put the bag on the night stand. Shannon felt her stomach clinch. Could she believe him? She looked suspiciously between him and the bag, "You know, I'm not stupid. I remember the rodent under glass. How do I know there's not a snake in the bag or the severed head of a squirrel?" He chuckled at what he thought was a joke but sobered when he looked at her expression.

"I'm sorry about that, but you made me so mad! It was juvenile and I'm sorry I scared you." Taking the bag, he opened it and dumped the contents onto the bedspread.

Shannon jerked her legs close to her body, putting as much space between the bag and her feet as possible, but there was nothing creepy or gross, just an innocent sandwich, chips, and her favorite soda. She could feel the saliva building in her mouth, her eyes stared, too large for her face, giving her the appearance of one of those sad looking kids in those old cheap velvet paintings. Embarrassed by her reaction, she closed her eyes and struggled to resist snatching up the sandwich and devouring it right in front of him. The image of his gloating face gave her the will power to hold out.

Taking a deep breath, Shannon opened her eyes and held his gaze. "Thank you for the food." She half expected him to snatch it up, and do a victory dance around the room, but he just nodded his head and left, locking the door behind him, of course.

Shannon waited at least two excruciating minutes before she ripped the plastic wrap off the sandwich and shoved it into her mouth. She nearly choked on the dry bread, realizing too late she had literally bitten off more than she could chew. Taking a large swallow of the cold soda, she sighed, feeling the liquid burn a trail to her empty stomach. She made quick work of the rest of the meal, having little trouble though she hadn't eaten anything in days, weeks?

The food acted as a drug. Her lids felt as though they weighed a ton and she was just too satiated and tired to fight it. She sighed, allowing herself to drift off to sleep, free of the hunger pains that had of late, become her constant companion.

Coming out of a delicious dream where she caught the woodsy aroma of fresh cooked bacon and the sweet smell of maple syrup, Shannon stretched languidly. Blinking her eyes, she realized the smells had not been a dream. Sitting up, she noticed the plate on the bedside table, brimming over with bacon, eggs, and pancakes smothered in maple syrup. She looked hesitantly around for Joseph. Getting up off the bed she went to the bathroom.

After Shannon had eaten as much as she could of the banquet, the little voice in her head made its appearance once again. *You know, you could give a little. It seems that he really wants to make amends. Besides, aren't you feeling just a little bit nasty? Let's face it girl, you stink!* "I know, but how can I trust him? He's tricked me so many times and even drugged me!" *Well, what if Seth comes to rescue you and has to hold his nose? That doesn't paint a pretty picture, now does it?* "Oh alright, I'll do it! Just stop nagging me!"

Shannon had to admit, she felt like a new woman. Her hair glistened under the bare light bulb in the tiny bathroom but she would have to eat a lot of food to put the weight back on. Plus, she never knew when Joseph would get bored or worse, horny, and ruin everything, and then starve her again for his own amusement. Her frequent conversation with the voice in her head warned Shannon that she really needed to get out of this room, even if it was just to walk around the rest of the house. She imagined that if there were any mice around, she would have made pets out of them by now. She thought about that movie "The Birdman of Alcatraz" and felt a shiver run down her spine. She decided the next time he brought her her food, she would broach the subject. Maybe he would agree to let her get some air since she had obeyed his wishes and cleaned herself up.

CHAPTER 47

Seth felt like he was losing his mind. All he wanted was to get back out on the trail that was quickly becoming impassable. The snow had continued to fall for seven straight days. He only ventured out long enough to check the traps he had set out and forage for some whittling wood to help keep himself occupied. With nothing to do in the small cave, he passed the time carving statues, keeping his hands busy, but nothing could keep his mind off Shannon.

He didn't want for water. The snow was cool and refreshing. He melted some in a pot, filling his canteens. Seth's spirit was restless, even the pony was getting twitchy. "I know girl. I feel the same way." Looking up to the heavens, he sent a prayer up to God, "Please God, just let it stop snowing long enough for me to get through that trail. It drove him crazy that he was less than two days from reaching the cabin. Even if the snow stopped now, it would still be an arduous journey, fraught with peril. One slip on the snow while climbing the mountain would surely lead to injury or death. Seth struggled to remain patient but in the quiet of the night, with the wind roaring at the mouth of the cave, all he could think about were the moments he was fortunate enough to share with Shannon. Oh, what special memories he had and he was determined to spend the rest of their lives making many more. Grabbing his saddle bag, he stuffed another finished statue into the already crowded satchel.

He stared into the flames of the campfire. Shannon's hair had always reminded him of fire, the ever changing nuances of golden blond to reddish to almost orange as the light danced over it. He remembered the morning he had awoken from a dream of butterflies to find her brushing those gorgeous curls down his body.

He groaned and shifted as his pants became tighter at the memory of how much she had pleased him that morning. He looked down the length of his body and imagined her there, looking up at him sweetly, her turquoise eyes smoldering with desire. "Dammit to Hell!" He jumped up and started pacing around the cave, mumbling to himself, causing the pony to neigh nervously. He hadn't tried to astral project since the failed attempt on the second night in the cave. Concentrating as hard as he could, he had expected it to work as it had the first couple of times, but he soon found no matter how hard he tried, he just couldn't seem to keep his concentration.

As he knelt down by the fire, he thought about what the reason could be. Suddenly it came to him, "I am too agitated, but how can I calm down? All I can do is curse the snow and the time I'm wasting, stuck in this Damn cave!" He got up and stalked around. In the days of being trapped inside, he had worn a path in the hard-packed earthen floor.

CHAPTER 48

"Hmm, let me think on that a minute." Joseph was rubbing his chin thoughtfully. Shannon had mustered up her courage, her voice anxious and excited all at once. She knew she had to ask but had trepidations about what his answer would be. Would he laugh in her face, yell at her, punish her or worse yet, try to bargain with her? She didn't care how stir crazy she was, she would never make the kind of bargain she knew he wanted, so she started a conversation with him when he brought her meal. She asked about the weather and asked if he had heard from Millie. He was open to most questions but skirted quickly around the ones he was reluctant to answer. "We're pretty isolated out here aren't we?"

Joseph looked at her with questioning eyes, "yeah, we're in the middle of nowhere. There aren't any phone towers out here so even the cell phones don't work." His eyebrows cocked, his eyes narrowed suspiciously, "Why, you wanting to make a phone call?" Shannon quickly pressed on, "No, of course not. It's just that I'm getting a little stir crazy in here and just thought that since there is absolutely no way I can escape, that maybe I could start going outside, get a breath of fresh air, maybe? She knew she had to walk on egg shells. His mood was subject to change without notice.

"You can supervise me the whole time. I won't give you any trouble." She could feel the whine in her voice and she hated it, "Please Joseph, I have to look at something else besides these four walls." She wondered. Would he deny her just for spite? His hesitation to answer was making her heart beat erratically with anticipation.

He grinned and jumped up from the chair, "alright then. Guess it could be a kind of celebration, you know, for finally cleaning yourself up." He looked at her fresh washed hair and clean, totally natural face and an idea came to him. Shannon froze at the calculating look in his eyes, *Dammit, I knew I shouldn't have trusted him.* She regarded him coolly.

"But I do have one condition." He held his index finger up.

'*Oh God, here it comes.*' Her eyes were riveted to that finger, that one solitary finger that would hold the key to her freedom….and her sanity. For Shannon knew in an instant that if she had to stay in that dank dark room much longer, it was very likely she would go insane.

"What?" She asked bluntly.

"You can come out once a day, but only if you will use that time to take your meals with me."

"Wait, what are you saying? That in order to leave this room, I have to agree to eat with you?" This was certainly not going as she had planned.

"Not all your meals. Heck, I'm feeling generous. You get to pick which meal and we will eat it wherever you like, but you have to stay shackled, can't take any chances. You might be one of those crazy marathon runners or something." He eyed her knowingly, "Don't forget, I was there when you were talking about doing all those "extreme sports". I'm pretty sure that once you get your strength back, you're totally able to climb mountains and trek through forests." He wiggled his eyebrows at her, "But what you don't know is that the winter snow has fallen". With his next statement, he hammered the last nail into her coffin, "The trails are impassable. There is no way out of here until the spring thaw."

He grinned at Shannon's sudden intake of breath, "When will that be?" her voice shaky, all the fight drained out of her as her face turned pale. The only thought when Joseph said, "four months" was, *Seth.*

Though she had grudgingly agreed on Joseph's "condition", Shannon could hardly contain her excitement at the prospect of finally seeing something more than her tiny room. As an artist she had been visually starved. As a prisoner, she was anxious to make her escape.

Walking out of the bathroom after her shower, Shannon found another little surprise waiting for her. Lying across the bed was a full evening ensemble, complete with accessories. She picked up the royal blue, full length, velour evening gown and ran the ultra soft material down her cheek, reveling in the feel. It was amazing. The equally decadent looking hand-beaded floral wrap was even more beautiful than the dress. Even with all the multi colored beading, it was deceptively light. She held up the super soft beaded ballet shoes, the jewels sparkling in the low lamp light. The single blue crystal drop earrings set in marcasite and matching single drop necklace was understated elegance.

She had to hand it to him, the man had exquisite taste. There was a small note card on the pillow along with a single white rose. The significance of them on her pillow was disconcerting to Shannon. Opening the card, the small key to her chains slipped out. She was shocked that Joseph had changed his mind about letting her walk freely around the house.

"Wow, you look ravishing!" Joseph whistled as he took in Shannon's attire. The royal blue material set off her hair and eyes perfectly and the matching jewelry was the perfect finish. He laughed, holding up his hands in supplication when she just cocked her eye at him suspiciously. "Relax, I'm just trying to be the perfect gentleman, which is exactly what I plan on being tonight." He extended his arm to her. Instead of linking arms, Shannon rested her hand lightly on his forearm. As they exited the tiny room, she lifted her chin haughtily, putting on an air of aloofness, but her heart raced.

Joseph was the perfect host, pointing out pieces of art and antiques that were almost crammed into every available space. *How could he afford all this? Surely, his law firm wasn't doing all that well.* She pretended to show interest but was actually committing the layout to memory, just in case....

She was on her guard as he turned her toward the back of the house. "I decided to save the best for last." He waved his hand expansively and Shannon's mouth dropped open. The entire rear wall was made of glass. Guiding her closer until she was scant inches away, Joseph waved at the wide expanse of mountain range. "I bought the place as soon as I looked out this window." His statement caused Shannon to cock her head at him, *That's strange. He may be a lunatic but.......* "Yeah, up this high, looking down on the world, I feel like God!" He hit his chest with his fists. *Ah, there he was. The old Joseph she had come to know and loathe.* She turned her attention back to the magnificent view. The entire landscape was covered in a blanket of white. The rays of the setting sun bathed the slopes in oranges and reds. It was truly breathtaking.

'God, she's so beautiful with the light dancing off her hair like wild fire. I just have to play my cards right. I know that eventually she'll come around. By the spring thaw, she will be mine.* "What say we have that dinner now?" He guided her over to a lavishly decorated and very large dining table. Another one of Joseph's acquired antiques, it was clearly from the seventeenth century, but what was more impressive was what graced the table top. There, before her eyes, was a meal fit for a king. The Wedgewood china gleamed under the candle light.

"It's lovely," Shannon said graciously, though inside her heart beat like a scared rabbit. *Oh God, this looks too much like a seduction.* She was going to have to really be on her guard. The smallest bit of encouragement could have disastrous consequences.

Dinner conversation was stilted at best. Shannon was almost noncommittal, answering questions with one or two words. She was so afraid that something would set him off, that she was almost paralyzed. Keeping her head down, she concentrated on the meal, but her fear turned the succulent feast to cardboard in her mouth. Joseph didn't seem to notice, or if he did, kept his emotions unreadable. He continued with his banter while he stepped to the kitchen to retrieve a couple of crystal glasses from the refrigerator. Setting the dish in front of her, he leaned in to smell her hair. It took great restraint not to bury his face in her reddish curls. "I hope you like chocolate mousse."

"Did you cook all this food yourself?" Shannon didn't really care if he did, she was just wondering if he had it flown in or maybe he had a cook. Could he actually have other people in his employ? She'd noticed how neat and spotless everything was, but Joseph crushed her hopes as he puffed up like a proud peacock, "yes, I believe in the old adage, "If you want something done right, do it yourself." He looked at her from across the table, "Thank you for noticing. I did all this for you, you know." Then he did something so bizarre, Shannon thought her mind slipped into an alternate reality. He giggled. Her eyes grew big as saucers. Before she knew what had happened, he rose and came to stand next to her. Bowing low, he offered his hand, "Ms.

Mallory, may I have this dance?" The notion was so ridiculous, that she laughed, immediately slapping her hand over her mouth. Too late, the humor in his eyes was gone in a split second. He glowered at her, "If you won't dance with me, it will ruin the evening, and I will have to reevaluate our agreement".

Cornered, Shannon conceded. "I'm sorry, you caught me by surprise. I didn't mean to laugh." She squared her shoulders and turned in her chair, "I would like to dance, very much", as she let him lead her into the middle of the room. There was some kind of old fashioned waltz flowing from the hidden speakers. *Great, a slow song. That involves touching. Lord, give me strength!* She had to bite her tongue hard to keep her expression serious. He was loony, bowing gallantly like they were in some sort of period movie. He placed his hand on her waist and twirled her around the room.

Shannon's technique was flawless as she went through the motions, keeping her form rigid, fully aware that should she relax just a little, Joseph would take full advantage. He pulled out all the stops, dipping and turning, doing everything to impress the marble statue in his arms. "You could at least try to relax and enjoy yourself." He leaned his head closer. Shannon turned her head to the side as he whispered into her ear, "You have nothing to fear from me Shannon. I promise I won't bite....unless you want me to that is." He laughed when she glared at him. *Keep your cool. You don't want to anger him.* She decided the best thing would be to keep her mouth shut. They continued around the floor until the song finally, blessedly, ended.

Joseph was about to start up again. "I'm sorry. I don't seem to be feeling very well. Do you mind if we sit down?" She kept her voice low and void of the irritation she was feeling. He really was incorrigible.

"Sure, I forget that you aren't used to physical activity, being cooped up in that tiny room for so long." Though he sounded sympathetic, Shannon knew he wouldn't hesitate to throw her right back in there when the night was over. He offered his arm and guided her to a sitting area that looked out the back. Shivers ran down her spine as she looked out the wall of pane glass. With no light behind it, it reminded her of a black hole. She could almost feel herself being drawn into its dark maw. She wished he had on the outside lights. Feeling disconcerted, she instead looked down at her fists, which were in her lap.

She had not even noticed Joseph had moved until he stood in front of her, extending a champagne glass. She looked at it absently and took it, downing the sparkling beverage in two gulps then handed it back to him.

He cocked his eyebrow, a half smile on his face. He had proposed to get her drunk but thought it would be much harder. Filling the glass, he again offered it to her. She drained it again. He filled it for the third time. This time however, she took a sip and set it on the table in front of her.

Shannon needed the alcohol. She was very frightened. This was looking more and more like an intimate date. Not a first date, but more like a "pull out all the stops to propose marriage" kind of date and she knew in her heart that should he be arrogant enough to think that all he had done tonight was going to persuade her to say yes, well then, he was in for a shock and she would just have to live with the consequences. There was no way in hell she was going to say yes to anything he proposed, least of all marriage!

Joseph settled down next to her, his leg touching hers intimately. Jumping up, Shannon walked over to stand in front of the window, looking out at nothing. Anything was better than being next to that monster. She could feel her stomach clench and her body turn to stone as he walked up behind her and placed his hands on her waist. The gesture was tender and intimate, way too familiar. *Oh God, please help me through this night* She wished with all her heart that she could see the mountains. She had a feeling it was going to be the first and the last time she would be allowed out of her room.

I have to get this over with, make it quick, like pulling off a band aid. Taking a deep breath she turned to face him. "Listen Joseph, I don't know what you expected (of course she did) but...." She didn't get a chance to finish as his lips crushed hers, catching her off guard. Recovering quickly, she squirmed in his arms, trying to get away. As she twisted and turned in his arms, Joseph felt his desire spring forth. Deepening the kiss, he pulled her body roughly against him. Shannon's eyes already open, widened as his free hand pulled up the hem of her evening gown. She had misjudged his strength. It was like she was ensnared in a steel trap. Trying to escape, she only succeeded in backing into the plate glass, unintentionally giving Joseph the advantage. His hand traveled up her thigh until his fingers touched the lace on her panties. He ducked his head to her neck and sucked the tender skin painfully.

Shannon cried in horror, tears streaming down her face. Fighting only seemed to excite him more. Suddenly, she knew what to do.

Joseph was in heaven. The writhing of Shannon's supple body was driving him insane. God, she was exquisite. The taste of her lips was so sweet, and the way she melted into him, the effect was intoxicating. He had to taste her skin, as he nipped and sucked on her neck. He was getting ready to take her. She seemed ready for him, but just as he was about to rip off the flimsy piece of lace, the only barrier left between them, she suddenly became still in his arms.

Lifting his head from her neck, he saw the blank look in her eyes. She had become as unyielding as a statue. He tried to get her to look at him but she continued to stare into space, her eyes gone completely blank. Growling, he crushed her lips again, willing her to respond. He might as well have been kissing a corpse. Gripping her shoulders, he shook her until her teeth rattled but she remained rigid, unresponsive.

Bellowing with rage, he slung her away from him. Shannon made no move to cushion her fall as she fell sideways onto the expensive Oriental rug. She lay there, unmoving as he stood over her, fists clutched at his side. Bending down, he raised his hand and slapped her soundly across the face. She was still unresponsive. Grabbing her roughly by the hair, he pulled her upright, staring into her unseeing eyes. "Shannon! Snap out of it!" His hand came down on the other cheek, harder this time.

"Bitch!" He spat at her. "Well, if that's the way it's going to be, I think you need to learn a lesson." Tightening his grip on her hair, he dragged her across the room and through a hidden doorway.

CHAPTER 49

Seth awoke with a start. Something was different. Jumping up, he ran to the mouth of the cave and looked out at a cloudless blue sky. His heart hammered in his chest. 'It stopped snowing.' Overjoyed, he spun around shouting, "It stopped snowing!" over and over again. Grabbing the surprised pony, he kissed her on her velvety nose, "Well, girl, looks like we can be on our way". He had the supplies packed in record time. Gripping the reins, he guided the pony down the side of the mountain. "I'm coming Shannon my love. Don't give up on me."

Several hours later, he had made little progress. The snow had hardened, making the trail treacherous. Caution kept him from barreling through the knee high drifts. He couldn't afford to slip and break a leg. It would mean certain death. He didn't care so much about his safety but he couldn't let Shannon down.

Shannon awoke as from a dream. Shaking her head, she tried to clear the cobwebs from her mind. Her nose itched. When she attempted to scratch it, she realized her hands were bound. Confused, she struggled to lift her head. It seemed too heavy on her neck, her tongue felt like something fuzzy was growing on it. *Drugged, I've been drugged.'* When she tried to move her hands again, she heard a familiar tinkling sound. She was chained, but this time she was standing up, the cold seeping into her bones. Goose bumps broke out all over her body. *Why am I so cold?* Looking down, she got her answer. She was wearing nothing but the royal blue lacy bra and panties she had worn last night. *Oh God, this is bad. This is very bad!* She knew she had made Joseph furious last night. She had learned years ago how to detach herself from unpleasant situations and could almost do it at will. She had vaguely been aware as he threw her on the floor and slapped her, but everything else had been a blank.

Suddenly the door opened and Joseph entered with a tray. She squinted, trying to see his face in the dim light. He flipped a switch and the light from three hanging bare bulbs made her squeeze them shut. She thought her head would explode from the brightness. She had definitely been drugged.

Her eyes flew open when he grabbed her hair and snatched painfully. "Wake up. It's time for breakfast." She peered at him from beneath her lashes, "Where am I?" she croaked past the dryness in her throat. He perused her body and reaching out, pinched her nipple through the lace. Shannon's eyes flew open. She shrank away from him, "Don't touch me". She wished she sounded brave but her voice came out weak. He replied by pinching the other one, a wicked gleam in his eye. She shrank away, but not wanting to provoke him again, kept her mouth shut. "That's better." He picked up a bowl that was on the tray and walking over, shoved the spoon in her mouth. It tasted like cardboard. She tried to talk to him about what happened the night before, but every time she opened her mouth to speak, he shoved another spoonful of the tasteless concoction into it. Fine she would eat it all and then she would try to apologize. When the spoon scraped the last of the gruel from the bowl, she saw her chance, but before she could utter a word, he turned and left the room, leaving her to dangle like a fish on a hook.

She didn't know how long she hung there but she heard the door swing open and instinctively cringed against the wall. The mask had been removed. When she looked into his eyes, she saw…nothing, just a black hole where his soul should be. She remembered looking out of the back window pane last night. His eyes were opaque, cold behind the dark fringe of eyelashes. She decided to try and reason with him. Praying her voice wouldn't crack, she lifted her head, "Joseph, you can't possibly plan on leaving me strung up like some prize fish." He walked over to stand in front of her, "open your mouth". There was no emotion in his voice but it was clearly an order.

"Joseph, why won't you talk to me? If it's about last night…." He shoved the bottle of water into her mouth and she choked as the liquid was sucked down her wind pipe. Taking the bottle from her mouth, he kissed her roughly as she sputtered, trying to catch her breath. His hand reached down and grabbed the front of her panties, squeezing until her knees buckled and she moaned from the pain. She was shocked and terrified at his behavior. *He's treating me like a piece of meat!* She was also scared that perhaps he had stopped looking at her as a person. The fact that he wouldn't engage in conversation with her, left a ball of dread in the pit of her stomach. *He's detaching himself.* She had read that when a psychopath treated his victims as less than human, the victim usually ended up dead. *Oh God, no! I can't let that happen. I have to stay alive!* Determined to make him see her as a human being, she smiled at him. "Joseph, I really need to go to the bathroom."

He looked at her with disinterest but inside he was seething. She had ruined everything! He had worked so hard to make last night special and she had practically spat in his face. She was spoiled and ungrateful and he would teach her a lesson she wouldn't soon forget.

He reached in his pocket and pulled out a key. Shannon sighed with relief. *Thank God, he hasn't fallen off the deep end yet.* She felt the manacles open, and freed, she rubbed her smarting wrists. He grabbed her arm roughly and pushed her to the back of the room. "Be my guest", he motioned to the corner where a small pot and a roll of toilet paper were propped against the wall. She jerked her arm but it was no use. His grip was viselike.

"You can't be serious. Can't I just go back to my room? I'm cold and dirty and I need a bath!" She hated herself for crying in front of him but the drugs combined with the condition of the dungeon like room made it difficult to put on a brave front.

His answer was to shove her toward the corner. Shannon crossed her arms around herself protectively, her eyes bulging as she stared at the impassive expression on his face. "Please Joseph, don't do this!"

He pointed to the pot then crossed his arms over his chest, waiting to see what she would do. *The little bitch, serves her right for humiliating me last night. She has only herself to blame for where she is now.*

Composing herself as best she could, Shannon straightened to her full height and addressed him regally, "This will do." Staring him down, she tilted her head back and looked down her nose, "As I am

sure you are a gentleman and will conduct yourself accordingly......
please, allow me some privacy....?"

The little vixen had him. As much as he wanted to humiliate her
as she had him, he always considered himself a gentleman. Standing
at attention, he turned on his heel and presented his back to her.

Relieved that she wouldn't be subjected to the humiliation of
having to "go" in front of him, Shannon wasted no time. "I'm...."
before she could say "done", he turned back around. Did he hope to
"accidentally" catch her pulling up her panties?

He walked over and stood in front of her. "Hold out your
hands."

"Don't chain me up again. Look, my wrists are chaffing." She
held out her hands to show him, hoping against hope that he would
take pity on her. He grabbed her wrists and pulled her over until
she was standing directly under the manacles. Lifting her hands over
her head he pressed her against the wall, pinning her with his body.
Shannon jerked her head to one side as his mouth tried to capture
hers, leaving her bruised neck vulnerable. His mouth clamped
down on the sensitive skin and she cried out. Moaning, he ground
his pelvis against her stomach. She felt the hardness of him as his
tongue snaked out, licking her from the base of her throat to her
ear lobe. Sensing she was about to go rigid again, Joseph abruptly
stepped away, pulling her towards him. Losing her footing, Shannon
stumbled into him. He set her upright and clamped the chains into
place, leaving her dangling as before.

Determined not to give him the satisfaction of seeing her cry, she
bit down hard on her lower lip. Joseph bowed low, turned on his heel
and left. Just as the door closed, Shannon gave in to her misery. The
sobs wracked her body until she slumped from the exhaustion. How
much more could she possibly bear?

CHAPTER 50

Shannon lost all track of time. Her body ached from being in the same position. She would stand for what seemed like hours until exhaustion won out and hang by her wrists which were scratched and bleeding.

Now and again Joseph would come and feed her some gruel or give her some water or let her go to the bathroom but he never spoke anything but commands. Shannon, cold, hungry, and frightened, gave up trying to talk sense into him. How do you talk to a madman?

The only relief she had was dreaming of Seth when she managed to doze off. The dreams were of sweet reunions, hugs, kisses, oh the kisses they would share. She would run her hands through his long raven hair, feel the silkiness as it glided through her fingers. His eyes, those beautifully impossible eyes, would look down at her with nothing but love and passion.

Shannon heard the familiar squeak of the large metal door but didn't even look up. She didn't want Joseph to read any weakness in her eyes. He walked over and cupped her chin, bringing her head up. She concentrated on his boots as he tried to get her to look at him. "Shannon sweetie, I think the lesson is over. I've come to take you back to your room." His voice was soft. Shannon's eyes flew up to his face. The mask was back in place and he was smiling at her! She wanted to spit in his eye but thought better of it. All she wanted was to get out of this room.

Joseph saw the suspicion on her face as her incredible eyes searched his. He veiled his expression, keeping his voice light, "Do you want to go back to your room now?" As if she could've gone anytime she wanted. Shannon nodded once. He pulled out the key.

Stepping closer until their bodies were touching, he lifted his arms above her head. Shannon was well aware that the action pressed his chest against hers but she was trapped between him and the wall. Gritting her teeth, she endured his touch, feeling her skin crawl, inadvertently causing her nipples to harden.

Joseph felt her nipples harden as his chest rubbed against hers and couldn't hide his triumphant smile. *I excite her. Why doesn't she just admit it?* "Uh, Shannon. There is one thing I need from you before I unlock these chains." She looked up at him as he towered over her. Why did she have to feel so small and helpless?

"What is it you want Joseph?" her voice sounded tired, defeated and he secretly rejoiced.

"A kiss....out of gratitude. That's not too much to ask for is it?" he cajoled.

Shannon's eyebrows cocked as she looked at the man's hated face, 'A kiss....gratitude?' She could feel her anger rising and somewhere, deep within, she found the courage she thought she'd lost. "If you want a kiss from me....then you'll have to take it. I will never...never feel anything for you......but revulsion!" she hissed. "If that means that I hang here until my bones turn to dust..."

She felt the pain, her head snapping to one side, as he backhanded her across the face. Shannon saw stars as she struggled to stay conscious. Her tongue licked the blood from her bottom lip. She threw her head back and glared defiantly, "You can beat me, torture me and starve me......but you will have to kill me before I willingly allow you to touch me". Her voice shook with emotion, "When Seth comes for me..."

Laughing in her face, he grabbed her chin and squeezed hard, unbidden tears sprang into her eyes. "When Seth comes for you? Honey, there's no way in hell he could ever find you out here. We might as well be on Mars. The snow has frozen the trails and the mountains are treacherous. If he were stupid enough to come after you, he's probably dead by now."

The shock on her face made him smile. Shannon wanted to tear that smile from his face. It can't be. Seth would find her....wouldn't he? She shivered to think he might have had a terrible accident and perished in the mountains. No, she wouldn't even entertain the thought. She had to have faith. It was all she had left. "He will come for me…and when he does, I hope he rips your heart out and feeds it to you." She spat the words in his face.

He looked at her, amused by her renewed spirit. She was special. He had never met anyone as strong as her. All his life, he had taken perverse satisfaction in breaking the spirit of women, mostly prostitutes who would do just about anything for money. They weren't very challenging, having been partly broken to begin with. He started picking up hitchhikers, using them, abusing them, and then discarding them like yesterday's trash. He made sure that he drugged them and drove hundreds of miles away, dropping them off on the side of the road. Even if they gave a description to the police, he had a clean record so his face wouldn't show up on any data base. Sometimes he would travel hundred of miles, picking up random victims from dive bars. He had video taped them all, keeping mementos of his "conquests" in a room under lock and key.

But no one had lasted as long as Shannon. Even now, dirty, bloody and about to collapse, she had refused him. She told him he would have to take what he wanted. Well, that's exactly what he would do.

He looked deep into her turquoise eyes, "As you wish"; his hand grabbed the back of her head, holding her still. He leaned close, his eyes leaving hers to stare at her small but full lips.

Shannon knew he was going to kiss her. He was about to do the one thing she told him he had to do, take what he wanted. She waited until she felt his breath on her lips then, taking a deep breath, she spat in his face.

She didn't know what to expect, maybe another slap across the face, or perhaps a fist this time. She watched as he stopped, clearly surprised. Her skin crawled as he smirked, wiping the saliva from his cheek, and licking it off his fingers, "mmm, sweet", he purred. Encircling her waist, he crushed her against him. "I think I'll taste a little more of you." His other hand snaked up her back and Shannon gasped as she felt her bra strap snap open. Her breasts shifted as the support fell away, causing them to brush against his chest. He reached down and slid the material up, revealing her pale mounds. His breath became ragged as he ran his hands over them. "You have the most beautiful breasts I have ever seen. They're so pale and creamy." He rubbed them harder, turning the sensitive skin pink. "Your nipples are like little rose buds, so pink." He pinched them, watching as Shannon squeezed her eyes shut and chewed on her bottom lip. She knew what was coming and bracing herself, became rigid.

Joseph pinched her nipples hard. "Shannon, open your eyes." He increased the pressure. Shannon's eyes flew open, staring wide eyed into his smug face. "If you try that little catatonic act again, I will not stop this time. It won't be as fun, I like my women to be a little more...lively, but I have waited long enough. I will have you, one way, or the other."

Looking into his eyes, she knew he meant it. Her mind was scrambling, trying to think of a way out of this situation. Bar a miracle, this was definitely happening. Resigning herself to the reality, Shannon decided to get the upper hand. If she couldn't stop it, she could make sure it was on her own terms. Besides, there was still that small glimmer of hope.

Joseph saw the shift in her eyes. She had decided something. He looked at her questionably. What had she decided?

"I......Joseph, wait." Her voice softened, "I can't fight you anymore. I don't want to."

He stared deep into her eyes, looking for deception but only seeing surrender. Ah, sweet surrender. His desire grew as he felt he'd finally won, at last. He kissed her hard. His eyes flew open in surprise when she kissed him back. His breath caught in his throat as her tongue snaked out and licked his bottom lip, sucking it into her mouth. She gave a little moan and he thought he would catch fire from the heat building inside him. He wanted her. God, he wanted her more than he'd ever wanted any other woman. She was finally going to be his. He reluctantly broke the kiss so he could unlock her chains. He wanted to feel her arms cling around his neck.

Shannon's eyes were closed as she kissed Joseph. In her mind, it was Seth she was kissing. As long as she kept her eyes closed and he didn't speak, she could pretend.

She felt the chains loosen and then she was being swept up as Joseph carried her out of the room and into the large living area. This was it. He was going to set her down on the floor, or couch or perhaps he'd take her to his bedroom, either way, he was going to have her. Her heart broke as she accepted her fate. Even if she survived, she knew she could never be with Seth again. She couldn't take the disappointment she would see in his eyes every time he would look at her, knowing Joseph had raped her.

Unable to wait any longer, Joseph laid her on the fur rug in front of the fireplace. Shannon opened her eyes and looked around. It was dark. Light from the fire bathed the room in softness. She felt the tears slide from her eyes as she thought of another fur skin rug and another fireplace. She blinked several times as the last of her will slowly started to slip away.

No! Her heart screamed as she felt his mouth on her neck. She was not going to make this easy for him. She may be damaged but she wasn't broken, not yet. She brought her arms up and boxed him on the side of his head. At the sound of his startled cry, her strength came surging back. She fought him with everything she had, biting, scratching, and kicking, like a crazy person, screaming to the top of her lungs, "No!" over and over again. He pushed his hand onto her mouth while his other struggled to get a grip on the lacy panties.

Suddenly, she felt the weight lifted as she continued to rain his body with blows. It took her a split second to realize he was no longer on top of her. She looked up to see him suspended above her, a shocked look on his face, then he was gone and she was looking into the bluest eyes she'd ever seen. She blinked several times. Was she dreaming? Had the torture been too much for her mind and she'd snapped? When he reached down to pick her up, she flinched. It has to be some kind of trick.

"Shannon, my love, it's me." That blessed voice. "Seth!" she cried out his name, throwing herself into his arms. He hugged her close, squeezing the air from her lungs. She opened her eyes just as Joseph loomed into her view. His lip was bleeding and he had murder in his eyes. Seeing the kitchen knife in his hand, she screamed, "Seth, behind you!"

He spun around just in time to avoid being stabbed in the back. Deflecting the blow, he skirted out of the way. Shannon watched with unbelieving eyes as he crouched in front of Joseph. He looked like a wild Indian. His body was covered in animal skins and he was wearing authentic looking moccasins. He was a picture of savage perfection.

"Well well, looks like I underestimated you my friend. I didn't think you'd ever find this place." He circled and Seth matched his movement.

"I don't know why you're so surprised, Joseph. I am, after all, part Indian and that part has generations of trackers." His tone was conversational. Shannon stared, gaping at the scene in front of her. Seth had come after all. He was here to save her! She felt her heart swell with love. She started looking around for her own weapon.

"You know, your timing couldn't be worse. Shannon and I were just about to...... share an intimate moment." His eyes flicked over Shannon's half nude body and she wanted to jump into the middle of the fight and scratch Joseph's perverted eyes out.

Seth growled like an animal, "You son of a bitch! You kidnap my woman, hold her in some tiny little bedroom with a closet bathroom with only one lamp for light and somewhere in that scrambled brain of yours, you think you are seducing her?"

Shannon gasped in shock. How did he know what her prison had looked like? Joseph must've been thinking the same thing, "How did you know...?"

Seth's lip curled up, "I learned a few tricks from an old medicine man, one being how to send my spirit places my body can't go." At Joseph's shocked expression, Seth made to grab the knife but Joseph realized what was happening and swung it, arching up.

Shannon screamed as red blossomed on Seth's right forearm.

Joseph cried in triumph at drawing first blood but his victory was short-lived as Seth swung his other arm and knocked Joseph's knife hand away, allowing him to step closer, grabbing the knife while punching him in the face with the other. Joseph went down hard and Seth wrenched the knife from Joseph's hand, straddling his chest. Joseph's now empty knife hand came up with an upper cut, hitting Seth on the chin, making his teeth clack. But Seth was stronger than Joseph gave him credit. Countering with a left jab to Joseph's cheek, he smiled satisfactorily when he felt the bone crack. Yelping with pain, Joseph bucked and kicked, catching Seth off guard. He managed to throw Seth off balance, springing up as they faced each other again. This time, Seth had the knife. He lunged but Joseph was tricky and side stepped his attack, causing Seth to come within striking distance. Instead of attacking, Joseph bent and grabbed the expensive rug in both hands. Shrieking, he pulled with all his might. Shannon realized a second too late what he planned to do but she screamed anyway, distracting Seth for a fraction of a second. It was all Joseph needed.

Seth felt the floor shift under him as he fought to keep his balance but he over compensated and loosing his footing, dropped to his knees. Shannon screamed again as Joseph launched himself toward Seth. The two men rolled around on the floor, the blade of the knife reflecting blood red in the firelight.

Shannon sat frozen, the fur rug pulled up tight against her throat as she watched the deadly dance in front of her. She breathed a sigh of relief when Seth finally had Joseph pinned beneath him. Seeing the look in Seth's eyes, Shannon's breath caught in her throat. He meant to kill Joseph. She couldn't let him do it. Not because she harbored any feelings for Joseph. He could walk off a cliff for all she cared but she couldn't let Seth do something he was going to regret for the rest of his life. Crazy as Joseph was, he and Seth had grown up together.

Jumping up, she ran over and placed her hand over his as he held the blade inches from Joseph's trembling form. "Don't do it Seth. You don't want to ruin everything we've shared together." He looked at her puzzled. "I don't understand. You want me to let him live?"

"Yes, but I want him to rot in a small cell for the rest of his life." She looked at Joseph with malice. "Death is too good for him, don't you think?" She gently started prying Seth's fingers away from the knife.

"But Shannon, you don't understand. Joseph killed Naome' and my son." His words tore through her heart.

"And when I get the chance, I will enjoy killing you, but not before I make you watch as I take your woman," Joseph spat. Shannon and Seth looked at him and together, "shut up!" They looked back at each other, shocked and pleased. Seemed they still had that connection between them.

"Well, if I can't kill him, what do you suggest we do with him?" Shannon smiled.

CHAPTER 51

Shannon came out of the large master bathroom, a towel wrapped around her luscious body, and one wrapped turban style around her just washed hair. Seth lounged on the large king sized bed, watching her every movement, his gaze smoldering. Shannon blushed attractively as she smiled shyly. "Do you like what you see?" she asked, her voice shaky.

"Mmm, I do." He got up and covered the short distance between them. "I do like what I see", his hands reached out and gripped the edge of the towel, pulling it loose. "But I would love to see more." He pulled again and the towel fell to the floor, leaving her exposed. She didn't try to hide her nakedness from him but lowered her chin and gazed up at him from beneath her lashes. "I'm glad I please you," she whispered.

Seth's heart skipped a beat. Was it his deprived imagination, or did she look even more beautiful? There was a radiance about her, a glow. The effect was arresting. He couldn't take his eyes off her. He took his time, letting his gaze leisurely trail over her body. His eye was drawn to her exposed neck. He frowned at the reddish brown bruises. His gaze moved to her cheek where the skin was discolored. Suddenly he looked past her curves and discovered several bruises on her arms, legs and even her breasts. His jaw muscle twitched and he flexed his fists. *That bastard had caused her physical as well as emotional pain. At least he's not feeling too good right now, chained to the same bed as Shannon and sporting one hell of a shiner.*

Everywhere his eyes traveled, she felt her skin burn. She was obviously thinner than before but her breasts seemed fuller, riper. He was like a homeless person peering through the front glass at a king's buffet. Night after night he had lain in front of the fire, thinking of Shannon, imagining her in his arms…now here she was, unabashedly naked allowing his eyes to feast upon her beauty. He felt a lump in his throat. As he watched, she raised her arms over her head…he noticed the angry marks on her wrists…. and slowly removed the towel from her hair, letting the golden red curls fall around her shoulders.

Seth sucked in air, making a backward hissing sound. His desire, which was already aroused, became painful as he met her eyes. He saw the yearning in their blue green depths. His mouth touched hers gently, brushing from side to side while he huskily whispered her name over and over, "Shannon". He felt moisture on his lip and pulled back to see that she was crying. "What is it my love? Are you alright? Do we need to stop?" He didn't want to hurt her. They had not discussed Shannon's captivity. Partly because he didn't want to dredge up unpleasant memories but also because he was afraid to find out. Knowing that Joseph was just down the hall, he thought he might just have to kill the son of a bitch if he discovered Shannon had been molested. She would tell him in her own good time. Until then, he would go as slow as she wanted, though he wanted nothing more than to ravish her right where she stood.

Shannon looked into his worried face. What did he think had happened? She wanted to reassure him but something inside her had to make sure that he still wanted her no matter what and not because she hadn't been raped. "No, I'm fine. I'm just so happy. I can't believe it's really you. I keep thinking I must be dreaming and I'm just waiting to wake up." She slipped her arms around his neck, "If I am dreaming, don't wake me, okay?" She rose up on her toes and captured his lips.

His response was immediate. He wrapped his arms around her soft waist and pulled her into his embrace. They kissed as two people who'd been without sustenance for weeks. Clinging to each other, moaning, frustrated they couldn't seem to get close enough. She slipped her hands down his bare back and cupped his taut behind. Seth growled into her mouth.

He could feel himself coming unglued. He had to have her…had to have her like he had to have air. "Shannon, I want you," he said against her ear. "I need you". He cupped her bare behind, sliding his fingers into the space between her legs.

The shock wave that rocked her caused Shannon's knees to buckle, too weak to support her weight. He caught her up and carried her to the bed. As he placed her on the top of the satin comforter, she moved her arms up and down, reveling in the softness of the fabric, all the while, never taking her eyes from his.

Seth bent down and shed the doe skin pants, and crawled onto the bed. He loomed over her, taking in the glorious sight.

"I'm not a goddess. Stop worshiping me. I'm a flesh and blood woman. Make love to me." Her voice was soft but demanding, shredding the last of Seth's resistance. His mouth crushed hers possessively. He branded her with his burning kiss. She was his, his beautiful flesh and blood goddess. He couldn't help but smile.

He worshiped her but not as a goddess. He worshiped her body with his hands, his mouth, and his heart. When they came together as one, they cried out their pleasure as one.

Shannon snuggled into Seth's arms as they lay awake, satisfied, and happy. When the silence was broken, it was Shannon who spoke, "How did you find me?" Seth sighed and pulled her closer, kissing her forehead. She traced little circles around his nipples as she listened to his story, stopping once in a while when he would say something especially interesting.

"and then I found Joseph about to…." His voice trailed off. He felt her stiffen at the memory of what almost happened. What if he hadn't gotten here sooner? Would he have been too late? He had a sneaky suspicion he would have.

"What about you?" He held his breath as he waited for her to respond. As the silence drew long, he realized that maybe the pain of recalling her ordeal was too much for her. He rushed to reassure her, "I'll understand if you don't want to talk about it. I don't want to push you or anything. Besides, it doesn't matter to me. I just thought you might like to tell someone." An idea came to him, "You could talk to a therapist. If you want, I'll make sure you get the best.

Shannon's finger paused over his right nipple. Seth kicked himself for bringing it up. "I don't want to talk to a therapist." She answered. She didn't sound angry or upset so Seth relaxed. "I don't want to talk to anyone about what happened here... (Seth felt his heart sink) ......but you." He squeezed her shoulder reassuringly.

"I will tell you everything, but not here. I want to make sure that when I tell you, Joseph is far away." She felt his body stiffen at Joseph's name. "And before you get the wrong idea, it's not Joseph I'm worried about, it's you. Could you truly live with yourself with his blood on your hands? Besides, I want him to live. Don't go thinking I'm some kinda saint either. I want him to rot in jail. I want him to live in a ten by ten room, a prisoner, just like I was. I just want to see him treated the same way he treated me. If he gets the same treatment I did then I will be happy. I do have one question though." Seth shifted to his side until he could face her. They looked into each other's eyes, "What are we going to do with him until spring?"

Seth reached up and touched the tip of her nose with his finger. "Well, we are kinda stuck until the thaw, unless you want to try and make it through the mountains?" He smiled mischievously and kissed her lightly.

"No, I don't think that would be a good idea."

"Well then, I guess we'll just have to stick it out here then." He gave her a wicked grin as his eyes raked over her body. "What will we do with all that time on our hands?"

She slapped him playfully on the arm, "You're incorrigible!" Grinning at him, she ran her hand through his hair. "I wonder if he has a short wave radio for emergencies." She made to get up and Seth pulled her down on his chest.

"We've got all winter to look. Stay with me". He cupped her cheek, pulling her face down to kiss her deeply and thoroughly, leaving her breathless.

"Always", she breathed.

CHAPTER 52

The weeks flew by for Seth and Shannon as they settled into a routine. They had indeed located a short wave radio. Seth called and got in touch with his senator friend who was involved with the search, asking that he let everyone involved know he and Shannon were fine and would see them in a few months. It was as though they were on their honeymoon, except for one small detail…Joseph. Though he had treated Shannon horribly, it just wasn't in her nature to torture him. They made sure he got plenty of food and Seth took him outside to walk the grounds, manacled of course, to get some exercise. It was the only time each day that Shannon felt anxious. She worried that Joseph would somehow manage to provoke Seth into a fight, giving him an opportunity to overtake Seth. He would have no choice but to defend himself, possibly killing Joseph in the process.

Seth strictly forbade Shannon from having any contact with Joseph. "He will never look at you that way again or I will kill him." She had agreed willingly. She didn't want to look at him either. Seth was the only man she wanted to look at her and she took every opportunity to get him to do just that. She found a closet full of clothes that Joseph had purchased in hopes of seducing her and put them to good use.

One day Seth came in after caring for the pony and his mouth dropped to the floor when he spotted her doing dishes in a pale green baby doll nightie. The table was set for two, a simple candelabra being the only centerpiece. He gave her a wolf whistle and she turned and looked at him coquettishly. He walked over and pressed his pelvis against her. He started to wrap his arms around her but realizing he probably smelled like horse, quickly withdrew.

"Hey, where are you going?" She whined as the sudden absence of his body left her feeling bereft.

"I'm just going to jump in the shower. Give me about fifteen minutes."

She looked back at him, her eyes raking over his gorgeous body. "Well, don't keep me waiting long or I might have to come in there and get you."

He saw the heat in her eyes. Giving her a rakish grin, he began to undress while she watched. Unbuttoning his shirt, he slowly peeled it off his broad shoulders. She stared as his muscles bunched under his tan skin. Shannon licked her bottom lip, suddenly finding it hard to breathe. He was a bronze Adonis. She placed her hand on her neck, as he ran his hands down his chest to his belt buckle. Her mouth parted as he unbuckled the belt and worked the buttons on his jeans. He knew what he was doing to her and his heart swelled at the power. As he started to lower his pants, she took an involuntary step toward him. Smirking, he suddenly turned on his heel and walked out of the room, leaving her to gape after him. She realized he had dazzled her with his striptease. *Oh, you're going to pay for that Seth Proudfoot.*

Seth found it hard to concentrate on the gourmet meal Shannon had prepared. His eyes kept drifting down to the baby doll negligee. He had only seen the back before and that was enough to get his blood boiling with the sheer netting and the fuzzy trim that barely covered the matching lacey boy shorts. But the front was distracting in the extreme. The lace bust was cut extremely low, leaving very little to the imagination. He could just make out her rosy nipples in the candle light. The material of his sweat pants was tented over his erection. If the nightie wasn't enough to drive him mad, her table manners made him groan. She was eating with her fingers but instead of it coming off as bad manners, it was amazingly erotic. She would pull the meat off the bone, letting the juices run down her fingers. Looking at him from beneath her lashes, she put the bone in her mouth sucking and licking the juices. He growled for satisfaction. "Dammit Shannon, stop doing that! You're making me crazy!"

She laughed, her voice husky, "You know what they say.... turnabout is fair play."

He realized she'd been playing with him, getting him back for earlier. Jumping up, he quickly rounded the table, his eyes smoldering with unspent passion. Shannon gave a little shriek as he lifted her out of the chair and plopped her on the table. Reaching over her head, he cleared the table with a swipe of his arm. Shannon's breath caught in her throat but her eyes twinkled as he glowered down at her. "I will show you what happens when little girls play with fire." Grabbing her shoulders, he pulled her down until her thighs were straddling his waist. He ground his hips, making her gasp. He felt incredibly hard through his cotton sweats. Raising her up into a sitting position, he crushed her mouth with his, thrusting his tongue inside her mouth. She sucked on his tongue as her hands ran up the inside of his tee shirt. Raking her nails down his chest, she stopped just short of his waistband. Hearing him moan, she felt extremely powerful. His tongue ran down her neck and she leaned back, presenting her breasts to his mouth. "You make me want more than I ever thought I could. You're body is intoxicating and I'm drunk from the taste of you. I can't seem to get my fill. The more I drink, the more I want." He licked her nipple through the lace, feeling it pucker under the material. His other hand untied the halter, pulling it down to her waist, reveling in the sight of her breasts bathed in candle light. Once the top was undone, he went to work on the bottoms. His hand ran down her side to her outer thigh. Grabbing her leg, he hiked it up against his hip then slid his hand to her inner thigh.

Lifting her butt off the table, he quickly pulled the boy shorts down her legs, discarding them on the floor. He touched her soft reddish curls and she sucked in her breath sharply. "You're so soft and warm, but I wonder, are you wet for me?" His fingers separated her folds and she moaned with pleasure. He smiled, "I believe you are". His fingers continued to massage her as he spoke, "You know, I've only ever been with one other woman, but I've seen my share of men's magazines and I can tell you, none of those women even compare to you. Your pussy is beautiful…and it tastes like honey.

"Shannon felt her head buzz as he praised her womanhood in such a sexually blatant manner. It was such a turn on. She wanted him to kiss her but she wanted to hear more. She wiggled against him, making little mewing noises. He continued kissing her breasts and stomach, running his tongue around her navel then plunging inside. Her body bucked instinctively. "Are you hot for me Shannon?" He continued to rub her core. All the sensations combined were too much for her, the sexy words, his fingers, his lips, his tongue, the huskiness of his voice, not to mention his pelvis grinding into her. Her body shook violently as she came. "Oh God!" she screamed as her thighs clutched impulsively. Seth quickly stripped and entered her as she convulsed inside, squeezing his shaft as he pumped his hips, coming just as she was floating back to earth. He pulled her tight against his chest, rocking her, "I love you, from the very depths of my soul. You make me so happy." He buried his face in her hair. "Your scent makes me rut like a bull and makes me weak in the knees at the same time." He gazed into her liquid turquoise eyes, "I could lose myself in your eyes". Feeling him grow inside her again, Shannon's eyes widened. "Again?" she asked, a little shyly. "Oh yes, definitely." He scooped her up and carried her to the master bedroom where he could worship her again.

CHAPTER 53

Shannon was pissed. She grunted and strained and even lay down on the bed, but she couldn't button her jeans. Seth walked in and gawked at the spectacle she made, hair fanned out behind her, face scrunched up from the effort. "Shannon, what's the matter?" She sat up, unshed tears in her eyes. "Oh Seth, I'm getting fat!" He raked his eyes over her appreciatively, "Oh honey, I don't think so."

"But my jeans don't fit anymore and look at my bra." She pulled her top up so he could see. Seth gulped at the sight of her full breasts spilling over the top. "I'm not complaining," he said as he licked his lips.

"Would you be serious for a minute?" She jumped off the bed and pulled off the offensive jeans. Standing in front of the full length mirror, she turned from side to side. Seth lounged on the bed enjoying the view.

"Look at my stomach. It's getting bigger." She pulled her top and bra off. Seth could've sworn the room got hotter. "Look, my boobs are huge! I know I've gone up at least a cup size." She lifted them up with her hands. "They're so heavy!"

It was definitely getting warmer and his pants were beginning to feel a bit uncomfortable. 'So what if she gained a little weight. It looks great on her. Why, she's practically glowing!' He sputtered as the realization hit home.

Shannon turned toward him at the sound. He looked at her, really looked at her. There was a curve to her stomach and her breasts were bigger but the rest of her looked the same. Her arms weren't bigger and her legs were still long and shapely, her hips slim and her butt round and firm. "Uh, Shannon? I need to ask you something."

She frowned at him. He sounded flustered, embarrassed even. He grabbed one of his shirts from the back of a chair and handed it to her. "Get dressed before you distract me and we have to have this conversation at a later date."

Shannon shrugged the shirt on but didn't bother to button it. For some reason she looked sexier than she did half naked. He patted the place beside him and she sat down. He took her hand and gazed into her eyes. He looked way too serious. What could this be about? Her hand trembled. He took it and kissed the palm, sending shivers up her arm.

"When was the last time you had your menstrual cycle?"

"What? Why would you ask such a thing?"

"Please, honey, I need you to think hard. When?"

"I don't think I've had one since before I got sick. How long would that be?"

"Well, you've been here close to three months and you were sick about a month, so I guess maybe four to five months? Does that sound right?"

"Yeah I guess so. Seth, what does that have to do with anything?" She looked at him, unable to keep the agitation from her voice.

"I think you might be pregnant."

She laughed and waved her hand dismissively, "No, that's silly. I can't have children."

Seth slipped his arm around her shoulder, "That's not exactly true. You couldn't have children with Richmond. Did you ever see a doctor to see if you were infertile?

Shannon looked expectantly into Seth's eyes, "No. I only went to the hospital when he got....too rough, but the doctors never did any fertility tests."

"He probably didn't want them to test you because if it turned out there was nothing wrong with you..."

"Then he would be the one who was sterile, and that would destroy his perfect little world!" Her eyes lit up, "Is there anyway for me to be sure?"

"Well, let's see. Have you been nauseas lately?"

She thought of all the times she had vomited in the tiny bathroom after eating and upon rising. "Yes, I got sick a lot when I was being held prisoner. I thought he was drugging me and it was making me sick. Oh Seth, do you really think I'm pregnant?"

He looked at her. She was definitely glowing. She had all the signs. He wished he had his medical bag with him.

Shannon's smile faded at the look on Seth's face. She was excited at the prospect of having a child but how did Seth feel about it? Would having another be a constant reminder of the one he'd lost just a short time ago? She bit her lower lip as she searched his face.

Seth was busy trying to figure out exactly when she had conceived. Hadn't they done a pregnancy test on her at the hospital and it was negative? One test could've shown a false positive. It does happen. He felt a tug on his shirt. Looking down he saw the unspoken question in her eyes. Damn he was a callus bastard. He hadn't reacted as a father to be but as a clinical doctor.

Smiling down at her, he touched her belly. Was that movement? It was light, just a flutter but he was sure it was the baby stirring. "Wow, I must be hungry. My stomach is growling up a storm." He laughed softly and laid his head on her stomach, listening, waiting. Shannon started to speak but he held up his hand to shush her. *What is he doing?* He moved his hand first one place and then another. Suddenly, she felt a flutter and jumped. He looked up at her shocked face. I believe our child is saying hello.

"Oh God Seth, I'm pregnant, really?" She broke down in tears.

Seth was taken aback by her reaction. "What's the matter love, aren't you happy?"

"Oh Seth, I don't know anything about babies. I was taken from my home when I was sixteen, sold into a marriage and was never allowed a moment of privacy. I absolutely know nothing!" She lapsed into tears again.

He took her in his arms and rocked her. "Shannon love, I am a doctor and I can help you with everything. I can even deliver the baby when it comes. Just trust me, everything will be alright." She stopped crying and rested her head on his chest, listening to his heartbeat. Part of that wonderful heart was beating inside her. She smiled.

He chuckled softly, "Well, I guess you can mark two more items off your list."

CHAPTER 54

The next couple of months were heaven. Shannon settled into her role as the woman of the house. She and Seth spent many hours walking around the grounds, talking, making plans, and just enjoying each other's company.

"You know, it's just so lovely here. Wouldn't it be wonderful to have a place like this to get away from it all?" Shannon mused as they walked arm in arm to the make-shift stable in the garage.

"Yes, it would." Seth looked down into her lovely eyes, "but it wouldn't bother you that you had spent the first couple of months as a prisoner?"

Shannon's eyes widened at his question, "Oh, I didn't necessarily mean *this* place...although", she looked around and then back at him, "No, it wouldn't bother me. We have made such wonderful memories here that the others now seem like a bad dream."

He nodded his head. He was glad the nightmare Shannon had experienced was drowned out by the happy times they shared. He wished he could completely obliterate it from her memory.

"The snow is starting to melt. We should be able to leave in another week or so. I've been on the radio with the state police and they are going to try to navigate the roads next week." He pulled her tighter against him. He was excited to get back so they could formally start their lives but a part of him couldn't help but be a little sad. He would be just as happy to stay here with Shannon forever, just the two of them, well, the three of them. He laid his hand on her growing belly and smiled. *I wonder if it'll be a boy or a girl.* He secretly wished for a girl, though he would never say so.

"Maybe you should get back on the radio and tell them not to risk lives to come for us. We can wait a while longer. There's no danger and we have plenty of food." Her voice was full of concern. "I would feel horrible if something happened to one of the rescuers."

He looked down at her, his eyebrows raised, "I find your concern for the safety of the men commendable, but, are you sure that's the only reason you're agreeable to extending our time here?" They were coming around the garage when Seth backed her against the outside wall. Taking her chin in his hand, he tilted it up to gaze into her eyes. He smiled as he saw them twinkle.

"Okay, you caught me." Her hands snaked up his back as she drug her nails downward to the top of his waistband. "I would love to spend a lot more time out here. It would be wonderful to see the mountainside in full bloom." She teased him with her casual words. Determined to get her to admit the real reason she didn't want to leave, he pressed his body to hers, his hands reached up under her coat, cupping her breasts through her camel colored sweater.

His eyes flew to hers in shock. "You're not wearing a bra?" Her hands moved around behind his back until she had worked his shirt loose from his pants. He sucked in his breath as he felt her chilly fingers roam over his back. He moaned as his desire swelled.

Bending down, he kissed her open mouth, "No." He jerked his head back in confusion. She was touching him, arousing his desire, but she didn't want him to kiss her?

She smiled sweetly as she arched her back, pushing her breasts into his hands. "Don't kiss me, not yet. Just look into my eyes. I want to watch them darken with passion….and I want you to watch mine." Her hands moved to his chest, her fingernails scraping across his nipples. He wanted so badly to kiss her and found that because he had been forbidden, it was making the touching excruciatingly pleasurable. "Oh, you are a wicked, wicked woman, Shannon Mallory."

He gazed into her eyes as they became heavy lidded, desire burning in them. His desire was becoming painful as he tweaked her nipples and she moaned, her mouth forming an "o". Her tongue snaked out and licked her parched lips, wanting to feel his mouth on hers but she was determined to make this game as pleasurable as possible. She reached down and cupped his erection through his pants.

"God woman, I want you right here, right now!" His hands reached down as hers had done, rubbing her throbbing womanhood through her jeans, igniting a fire low in her belly. She could see his eyes darken as his passion grew stronger. Satisfied, she lifted her arms and ran her hands through his hair, pulling his mouth down on hers.

He ravished her lips, bruising them, as he pressed her against the wall, grinding his hips into her. He couldn't take her against the wall for fear of hurting the baby so, looking around, he spotted the blanket they had taken from the house and used for a horse blanket. Grabbing it, he laid it out on the hard cement floor.

Shannon looked at him questionably. He pulled her back into his arms and proceeded to take off her pants. Shannon shuddered as the cold air kissed her naked backside. Wasting no time, Seth undid his pants, pulling them down to his knees. Gripping her hand, he pulled her down on top of him on the wool blanket. She was extremely aroused at his urgency, like he couldn't wait to be inside her. She smiled and straddled his waist, impaling herself on his engorged shaft. They both sucked in their breath as the heat between them became a roaring fire in their loins.

The pony whinnied nervously at the strange moaning sounds coming from the couple on the floor. Though the air was chilly, beads of perspiration stood out on Shannon's skin as she rode him with abandon. Seth marveled at her face, strained in the throes of ecstasy. Her release was explosive. She screamed as she took from him, her muscles clinching around him, driving him home.

CHAPTER 55

A few days later, Seth was preparing breakfast for their "guest" while Shannon was in the "stable" feeding the painted pony. "You know, we really should see about giving you a name. You are a very special little pony," she cooed as she fed the pony sugar cubes. "You brought Seth here to save me." She rubbed her velvety nose. "I bet he talked to you a lot while he was searching for me." She wondered what he had said to the animal. Suddenly, the pony whinnied, rearing up...

Seth was bending over, taking out the home made biscuits. As he pulled them out of the oven, he was unaware of the person sneaking up behind him. Breathing in the delicious aroma, he turned to deposit them on the counter when suddenly he was hit on the back of the head with a hard object. Going down hard, he fought to remain conscious. Squinting, he looked up into the face of his worse nightmare.

"Come on you son of a bitch, crank!" Joseph repeatedly pumped the gas of the Cadillac but it refused to turn over. "Shit!" He didn't want to wait any longer for fear Seth would wake and stop him from escaping. He had found a shower curtain hook behind the toilet and picked the lock. It took several days and hours upon hours before the lock finally popped open. Waiting for the perfect moment, he bided his time. Knowing the roads were sure to be open, he knew he could escape with Shannon, leaving Seth with no way to follow.

Slamming his hand on the steering wheel, he had no choice but to abandon the car. But how was he supposed to get away? Spying the pony, he grabbed the saddle and quickly secured it. Next, he draped Shannon's unconscious body over the saddle. Swinging up and placing her across his lap, he made his way through the mountain trail and away from the cabin.

Seth came to with one hell of a headache. Biscuits were strewn across the floor as he gingerly touched the back of his head. Feeling something wet and sticky he brought his hand in front of his face, blood. He had taken a big hit. "Owe!" He struggled to sit up, holding his head between his hands. It felt like it was going to fall off his shoulders. *What the hell happened? I was making breakfast and then....* "Oh my God, Joseph!" He slowly got to his feet, clutching one of the dining room chairs for support. Why was it so dark? Was there a storm outside? "Shannon!" he called, his head throbbing with every breath. He stumbled to the glass wall. It was black. He had been out for quite awhile. Stumbling through the house, switching on the lights, he searched every room. There was no sign of her. He made his way around to the garage, using the outside wall for balance. *The pony is gone!* Could it be that Joseph had taken Shannon and fled on the small animal? He looked at his watch, trying to focus his vision on the hands. 9:42. It had been early morning when he'd been in the kitchen preparing the meal. "That would give them a good half a day's head start. He had no time to waste.

Shannon's head was killing her and she felt like something had crawled into her mouth and died. What was that jostling? Why did she smell saddle soap and horse hair? Willing her eyes to open, she gasped as she realized she was being hauled potato sack style on the back of a horse. Thinking back, she only remembered feeding the pony and having a nice conversation with her when everything suddenly went black. Had she fainted? Oh no! What if it's something to do with the baby? Had something happened and Seth was trying to get her to the hospital the only way he could? "Seth? My back is killing me! I think I can…" she recognized the cowboy boots and terror gripped her. Joseph must've drugged her and then escaped with her on the pony! "Please, Joseph, I need to turn over. This position isn't good for……" She stopped before she said too much, but Joseph laughed bitterly, "The baby? I think it's a little too late to try to hide that bulging belly of yours. How far along are you anyway, four, five months? You slut! You must've jumped into bed with Seth the very first day you came to Sanctuary." His tone was bitter and cold.

"Please, I need to sit up? Can I at least sit behind you, or in front, just not like....like this!" She was frightened the jostling would injure her unborn child and even though the thought of putting her arms around his waist or worse, having him put his arms around hers was revolting, she had to do what was best for the health and welfare of her baby.

"I have a better idea." He dismounted and lowered her to the ground, keeping his arms tightly around her waist, pinning her arms at her side. He leaned in close to her ear, "Don't get any ideas. We have been traveling for over ten hours. You would just get lost if you ran away. These woods are teaming with wild animals. I am going to let you down now. Don't be foolish." He loosened his hold and Shannon stumbled backward until the back of her knees hit a fallen tree. She sat down, the strength drained from her body.

"That's a good girl. Now, I am going to get a fire started so I will be right back with some fire wood." He started to walk into the trees but turned and wagged a finger at her, "Don't you go anywhere now, you hear?" He giggled and disappeared into the night.

Shannon couldn't believe what had happened. 'Oh no! Where is Seth? What did he do with him, to him?' "Oh God, please be okay," her voice was desperate as she prayed for his safety. Wrapping her arms around her belly, she rocked back and forth, sobbing.

"Hey now, we'll have none of that!" Joseph appeared, his arms loaded with sticks of various sizes. Walking several feet in front of her, he dropped them in a pile and lit them with his lighter and some dry straw. Before long, a small fire was lighting the area around them. Shannon continued to stay where she was as Joseph knelt close to the flames, warming his hands.

She knew she probably wouldn't get a straight answer, but was compelled to ask anyway, "What......what did you do to Seth?" She held her breath as her eyes met his through the firelight.

"I bashed his head in with a pewter figurine. It's a shame too. I paid a lot of money for it." His voice was conversational. Shannon felt as though someone had punched her in the stomach. She couldn't catch her breath. *Dead? He couldn't be dead?*

"Yeah, they'll probably find his body in about five or six days. Ewww should be pretty rank by then." Shannon felt like she was going to be sick. The blood drained from her face. He chuckled at his own sick joke. "Well, I guess we better get some shut eye. We've got a lot of ground to cover tomorrow." He approached Shannon and her eyes grew wide. *What's he going to do?* If it weren't for the baby, she wouldn't even care, but she had to be strong and more than anything else, she needed to stay alive. Holding her breath, she waited.

Joseph walked over and pulled out a pair of very familiar looking handcuffs. She cringed as she heard the "click", locking them in tightly onto her wrists. She couldn't believe after everything she'd been through, she was right back where she started.

CHAPTER 56

Clad in the doe skin pants he'd worn during his original search, Seth followed the clues as he tracked Joseph's trail. It was true that they had gotten a pretty big head start, but he was determined to catch up. It was almost impossible to track at night but he trudged on, refusing to rest. He only hoped that they had.

Shannon gritted her teeth as she sat in front of Joseph. He had one hand on the reins and one just under her breasts. She tried to tell him she could hold onto the saddle horn for support but he argued that it wasn't safe enough and that she had to think about the baby. *She* had to think about the baby? He could give a rat's ass about her unborn child. Shannon wanted to knock his sorry ass to the ground but what would she do then? She had no knowledge of these mountains and would probably just end up going around in circles.

She was uncomfortably aware of his crotch bumping up against her behind as the pony maneuvered over the rough terrain. How many nights would she have to spend with him out here in the wilderness? She hadn't slept at all last night, waiting for him to pick up where he left off over a month ago. He had fallen asleep shortly after handcuffing her to the thickest branch of the fallen tree.

The morning was cold, a blanket of heavy fog as thick as pea soup hung low over the mountains. Something familiar about the scene tugged on Shannon's memory. She stiffened. The *dream!* It looked like the picture from her dream. She half expected to look into the depths of the forest and see the giant wolf eyes identical to Seth's. She actually squinted into the fog. *Yeah, you're just acting crazy now.*

They slowly started to ascend up the mountain side, riding straight into the thickest part of the fog. Shannon thought it was thick before but it got harder and harder to see. She put her hand out in front of her. It looked funny, like it didn't belong to her. Suddenly Joseph let out a string of oaths, pulling the pony up short.

"I thought I was on the trail but dammit, I can't see two feet in front in me with this blasted fog!" Shannon strained to see what had caused his tirade and gasped, "Oh God, lookout!" She peered uneasily over the pony's head, looking over the cliff, unable to make out the bottom.

"I guess we'll just have to retrace our steps and try again." He turned and backed the pony up a few feet and then pulled the reins to the left.

Shannon was just breathing a sigh of relief when…

She saw him. She wondered if she was awake. The scene felt eerily unreal. "Seth! You're alive!" She made to dismount but Joseph grabbed her arm painfully.

"Ah, I see you are like a cat. You must have nine lives. I thought for sure that bash in the head would've been the end of you. No matter. I'll just have to make sure I finish the job now." With that, he quickly deposited Shannon on the ground and dismounted after her. Having no means to restrain her and fight Seth at the same time, he let go of her arm. She immediately ran to Seth. They fell to their knees as they covered each other's faces with kisses. "Oh God Seth, I thought you were dead! Joseph told me that he killed you…" reaching up she felt the giant goose egg where the statue had connected with his head. Uttering a cry she flung her arms around him, hugging him tight, but he hugged her tighter. "Shannon, my Shannon, I had to find you! I could never live without you! You're a part of me." He reached down and placed his hand on her swollen belly. He smiled peacefully.

Standing up, he moved in front of her, shielding her from Joseph who had pulled out a hunting knife and was slowly advancing on them. "Stay behind me, no matter what happens!" He turned to face his enemy.

Joseph was tossing the knife from one hand to the other, his back to the cliff. With a savage yell, he ran at Seth. Suddenly, out of the fog, there appeared a giant white wolf. He landed between Seth and

Joseph. As Shannon screamed, he turned toward them, locking eyes with Seth. Shannon's scream froze in her throat. It was the blue eyed wolf from her dreams. The wolf and the half breed stared unmoving for several seconds. They seemed to regard eachother, understanding passing between them.

Finally, the wolf turned and walked slowly toward Joseph, hackles raised, teeth bared. Joseph began to slowly back away, inching closer to the edge of the precipice. Suddenly, the wolf attacked, Shannon gripped Seth's arm, digging her nails in as wolf and man tumbled over the edge and disappeared into the milky fog.

Almost instantly, the mysterious fog began to lift. Seth and Shannon ran to the edge and looked down. There, lying broken on the jagged rocks was Joseph's body, but there was no sign of the wolf anywhere.

They looked at eachother, the unspoken question mirrored in their eyes. What happened to the wolf? Seth pulled her into his arms and cradled her against him. "It's over. It's finally over." He scooped her up and placed her on the saddle. Pulling himself up behind her, he turned the pony around and headed back toward the cabin.

Epilogue

Shannon laughed as she watched the children playing on the new playground. It had been a very busy but happy year. She looked down into her baby daughter's turquoise eyes and smiled, thinking back on all they had accomplished since coming back to the reservation and Sanctuary.

Seth had been welcomed back with open arms and had resumed his position at the hospital. He of course, delivered little Miya and beamed with pride that she had his raven hair and Shannon's eyes.

She had hired Manna to run the "Second Chance" diner. She had changed the name for obvious reasons, and it looked as if the Indians and the whites had finally started getting along.

Her wedding was a huge event. Millie had pulled out all the stops and everyone was invited. Millie looked surprisingly conservative on the arm of her fiancé, the Senator that had helped during Shannon's ordeal. They looked at each other like a couple of love sick teenagers.

Shannon thought about how handsome Seth had looked in his tuxedo. She wore a loose fitting multi-tiered pale blue empire waist gown that tried unsuccessfully to camouflage her huge belly. Seth thought she was the most beautiful thing he'd ever seen and said so every chance he got. Paddy gave her away while Irene beamed with pride, tears streaming down her face.

He'd presented to her after the wedding, a pair of first class tickets to Paris. "I guess that completes your list, huh?" He whispered into her hair as he swept her across the dance floor. "So I take it you'll be starting a new one now?"

"I don't need anymore lists." She smiled up at him sweetly.

He looked into her beautiful eyes and the depth of emotion he saw in them almost drove him to his knees. "And why is that?" his voice hoarse with emotion.

"Because, you beautiful wonderful man, I have everything I could ever want."

She remembered the day she was training Manna at the diner, when someone came running in yelling that there was smoke coming from the direction of Seth's home. Everyone dropped what they were doing and went to help. When they got there, Seth was in the middle of the yard watching as his cabin went up in flames. She had run to him, wondering why he wasn't trying to put it out. He turned toward the crowd of onlookers, "It's okay folks, I set the fire." He slipped his arm around her waist, "I just thought I would build you a new one. You know, make a fresh start, and leave the past in the past."

By the time little Miya arrived, he had done just that.

"You have done a great thing for my people." Shannon was startled by the sudden appearance of the ancient looking Indian. This must be the medicine man Seth had told her about. The sun was directly overhead and she had to squint as she looked up into his dark brown, almost black eyes. He smiled down at her and waved his hand toward the new playground and the area roped off for the new hospital. "My people have found a new purpose because of your generosity. I can go to my ancestors with a peaceful spirit. Thank you."

Her hand came up to shield her eyes as she strained to get a better look at him. He took a step closer, blocking out the sun and Shannon gasped. Was it her imagination or did his eyes just for a second or two, turn blue? Her mind turned back to that day on the cliff when the white wolf had locked eyes with Seth. He reached down and touched the baby on the head, "She will be a great healer one day. She will find cures for ravaging diseases. She will live a long and happy life, full of love and family. I will watch over her and keep her safe." He stepped away, back into the glare of the sun, blinding her for just a moment. Shannon squinted back up but he was gone. She looked around. The trees they had planted weren't big enough yet to hide behind. Had she really seen his eyes change from brown to blue?

Suddenly, one of the young men came running through the streets. Shannon got up and stopped him. "What's wrong? What's happened?" "The old medicine man, he's dead! I just went up there with some bread my mom made and he was dead!"

Shannon knew then that the old man's spirit had appeared to her. Hugging her baby close, she cried both tears of sorrow and joy, for he had given her a most precious gift, the reassurance that her daughter would always have someone watching over her, keeping her safe. It was all a mother could ever ask for and she felt truly blessed.

"Come on little Miya, lets go see your daddy."

THE END